CARE

WHITE HOUSE MEN 5

NORA PHOENIX

Care (White House Men Series 5) by Nora Phoenix

Copyright ©2021 Nora Phoenix

Cover design: Vicki Brostenianc www.vickibrostenianc.com

Model: Josh T

Photographer: Eric McKinney

Editing and proofreading: Tanja Ongkiehong

All rights reserved. No part of this story may be used, reproduced, or transmitted in any form by any means without the written permission of the copyright holder, except in case of brief quotations and embodied within critical reviews and articles.

This is a work of fiction. Names, characters, places, and incidents either are the products of the author's imagination or are used fictitiously. Any resemblance to actual persons, living or dead, businesses, companies, events, or locales is entirely coincidental. The use of any real company and/or product names is for literary effect only. All other trademarks and copyrights are the property of their respective owners.

This book contains sexually explicit material which is suitable only for mature readers.

www.noraphoenix.com

To Richard Schiff

Toby was such a complex, multifaceted character, and you portrayed him brilliantly, showing humor, pain, and a deep humanity behind his gruff exterior. I'm still upset over the stupid storyline with Toby and the military space shuttle. He would've never betrayed the president like that, and he deserved a better storyline.

CONNECT WITH NORA

Connect with me on social media:
Hang out in my FB group Nora's Nook
Follow me on Instagram
Follow me on Twitter
Follow me on Bookbub
Sign up for my newsletter
Become my patron on Patreon

Check out more of Nora's books:
No Shame series
Perfect Hands series
Irresistible Omegas series
White House Men series
Ignite series
Ballsy Boys series
Kinky Boys series
And for an overview of all my books and audio books, head over to my website!

PUBLISHER'S NOTE

This is a fictional series, set in the White House as it exists in reality, though obviously with a fictional president and staff. Any resemblance to real people, living or dead, is a pure coincidence.

I've tried to be as accurate as possible in portraying the inner workings of the White House as well as the several federal agencies, but for the sake of clarity and suspense, I've taken some liberties. These mostly include condensing multiple functions/jobs into one and omitting procedural details. I've included a list of all characters and all the terms used in the front of the book.

OVERVIEW OF CHARACTERS

Some names might be a slight spoiler, so only refer to this list of you've forgotten who someone is! This list only contains important names from this book, not characters you'll only encounter once or from the other books.

Agent Sheehan: FBI Special Agent in Charge on the assassination investigation
Amzi: domestic affairs advisor to President Shafer
Annabeth Markinson: widow to President Markinson
Asher Wylie: Secret Service agent, Milan and Denali's boyfriend
Barry: FBI Assistant Special Agent in Charge on the assassination investigation
Basil King: Mrs. Markinson's step-nephew, co-owner of Kingmakers
Branson: CIA analyst, point person for the investigation (aka "Spookybigdick")
Calix Musgrove: chief of staff to President Shafer, Rhett's boyfriend

Christopher Hales: one of the "fossils" President Markinson appointed to key Secret Service positions
Coulson Padman: FBI Assistant Special Agent in Charge on the assassination investigation, Seth's boyfriend
Delano (Del) Shafer: president
Denali Weiss: server in the residence, Milan and Asher's boyfriend
Diane: Secret Service agent, head of Mrs. Markinson's detail
Donnie Smith: security guard at Baltimore Convention Center (killed)
Dr. Brophy (Navy Commander Brophy): White House physician
Ella Yung: National Security Advisor
Francis Wedmore: Head Butler
Frank: Secret Service agent in charge of President's Shafer's protective detail
Governor Winkelmann (R-NC): Markinson's opponent in first presidential campaign
Gulat Babur: suicide bomber who killed the president
Hamza Bashir: leader of Al Saalihin
Henley Platt: reporter, Levar's boyfriend
(Senator) Joyce Riggs (D-NY): vice presidential candidate
Jon Brooks: owner of Brooks Construction and Demolition, former boss of Wesley Quirk
Kennedy (Kenn) Shafer: President's Shafer's son
Larry: anonymous source to Henley
Levar Cousins: White House press secretary, Henley's boyfriend
Lisandra James: Secret Service Director
Manuel: White House sous-chef
Matthew: Calix's deceased husband
Max: President Shafer's secretary

Milan Bradbury: the first lady's brother, Asher and Denali's boyfriend
Mr. Funnell: Head Usher, the manager of the residence
Mrs. Dunham (Professor Dunham): Mrs. Markinson's sister
Mrs. Morelli: runs the informal kitchen in the residence
Muhammad Bhat: thwarted bomber
Naomi Beckingham: woman who applied for a job with Christopher Hales and hacked his laptop
Officer Abramson: young cop from the Baltimore PD impound lot
Regina King: President Markinson's ex-lover, Mrs. Markinson' step-niece, sister of Basil King
Rhett Foles: White House photographer, Calix's boyfriend, and Levar's roommate/best friend
Rogue: the First Dog
Samantha (Sam): Secret Service agent
Sarah Bradbury Shafer : First Lady
Seth Rodecker: Secret Service agent, Coulson's boyfriend
Warrick Duvall: law professor and Kenn Shafer's tutor
Wesley Quirk: Baltimore PD cop who's suspected of involvement in the assassination
William (Bill) Markinson: former president (assassinated)

LIST OF TERMS USED

Air Force One: the president's plane, a special Boeing 747
ATF - Bureau for Alcohol Tobacco and Firearms
ASAC - Assistant Special Agent in Charge
Camp David: the secondary residence of the president, situated in a remote area in Maryland
CAT - Counter Assault Team, part of the Secret Service
Chief of Staff - the right hand of the President, basically the CEO of the West Wing. Other high government officials often have a chief of staff as well, including the vice president and the First Lady.
CIA - Central Intelligence Agency
DoD - Department of Defense
DoJ - Department of Justice
East Wing - a building adjacent to the White House where offices are located, including that of the First Lady and her staff
EEOB - Eisenhower Executive Office Building, where the offices of the vice president and his staff are located. The vice president himself also has an office in the West Wing.
FBI - Federal Bureau of Investigations

HUMINT - Human Intelligence (intelligence learned through direct human contact)
JTTF - Joint Terrorism Task Force
Marine One: the president's helicopter
NCTC - National Counter Terrorism Center
NSA - National Security Agency
NYPD - New York Police Department
OEOB - Old Executive Office Building
PIAD - Protective Intelligence and Assessment Division, part of the Secret Service
Residence - the part of the White House where the first family lives
SAC - Special Agent in Charge
Secret Service - the agency that protects the President of the United States, as well as the First Lady, the vice president and multiple other dignitaries
SIGINT - Signals Intelligence (intelligence learned through picking up digital signals, eg phone calls, emails, etc.)
West Wing - the building where the president and his staff work, which includes the Oval Office. Technically, this is not part of the White House, but is an adjacent building
White House - technically, the White House includes several public meeting rooms like the State Room and the East Room, as well as the personal living quarters of the president and his/her family
WHMU: White House Medical Unit

1

Two Months Earlier

ONE DAY, Kennedy Delano Shafer—who much preferred to be called Kenn—would be able to meet new people without being nervous to the point of throwing up. Today, however, wasn't that day. Rationally, he knew he had nothing to worry about. His parents—mostly his dad—had carefully selected his new tutor from among many applicants. Yes, the president had actually put out an ad to find a private tutor for his son.

Not that it had been mentioned in the listing that the tutor was for the First Kid—and how Kenn hated that term. He wasn't a child, even if he often still felt like one at twenty-two. Also, the term "first" implied there was a second kid and maybe even a third and a fourth, and that wasn't the case. He was it, the President and First Lady's only son. But that was beside the point.

No, an agency had made the initial selection of candidates, narrowing it down to a shortlist his father had then gone through. After meeting with several candidates, he'd picked Professor Warrick Duvall, thirty-six years old, who had pursued a career in law after an honorable discharge from the Army due to getting wounded in combat. Since Kenn's ambition was to attend law school after graduating from college, Professor Duvall had seemed the perfect candidate to get him ready, his father had told him.

Finishing his undergraduate degree at Amherst was sadly not an option at the moment, not after the assassination of President Markinson and a thwarted attempt to kill Kenn's father, who had been the vice president at the time. Kenn understood, and he'd agreed he was safer in the White House, but that didn't mean he had to *like* it. The tightened security sucked for all of them, but he'd lost all his freedom...and his chance of having sex. Although truth be told, he hadn't managed to score in the three years he'd been at Amherst. Maybe the idea that one more year would've given him the courage to finally get laid was a classic case of self-deception.

Get laid. Score. He scrunched his nose. Such crude expressions. Not that *having sex* was much better. Or *getting fucked*. The latter immediately stated his preference, and he wasn't ready to announce that yet. Just like he wasn't ready to be honest about his...other needs. How would his father react? And Uncle Milan?

Kenn wasn't worried about the gay part of his coming out. That, they'd fully embrace. But how would they feel if he confessed to what he wanted in a relationship, who he was deep inside? Could two such powerful, dominant alpha men ever understand it? He didn't think so.

The bottom line was that he wouldn't have sex anytime

soon, and while that was a relief in some ways—if meeting new people already had him anxious, sex would be an absolute nightmare—it also worried him. How would he ever grow up, become a full adult, if he didn't scale that particular mountain? A virgin at twenty-two...how pathetic.

Almost as pathetic as the crazy flutters in his stomach and the sweaty hands he was experiencing as the time inched closer to Professor Duvall's arrival. Kenn slowly made his way from his bedroom on the second floor of the White House into the central hallway, where Seth had taken up his usual spot against the wall. He had an overview of the entire hallway and the staircase, he'd explained to Kenn.

"Hey, Seth."

Protocol stated that Secret Service agents couldn't strike up a conversation with their protectees, but things were different between him and Seth. With his father's permission, Seth had become somewhat of a friend to Kenn, and he loved that he had someone to talk to. Someone who was gay and as alpha male as possible. Kenn hadn't found the courage yet to ask Seth about certain things—that would be the gay part—but one day he would. Over time, addressing the crazy sexy Secret Service agent had become easier, probably because Seth was genuinely nice and made an effort to help Kenn get over his nerves and shyness.

"Hey, Kenn. How's life?"

"I loved that British TV series you recommended."

"Hustle?"

Kenn nodded.

"I know, right? I keep telling people about it, but it's not that well known here. But it's so good."

"It's got that dry British humor I love, plus action and smart plots."

"I couldn't agree more. Heist movies are my jam, and this whole series centers around heists and smart cons."

Kenn had binge-watched the entire first season of Hustle and was well on his way in the second one. Not much else to do for him but read and watch TV now that he was home all day, but hopefully, that would change soon.

"Your tutor has arrived," Seth said after listening to his earpiece.

A fresh wave of nerves rolled over Kenn, and he bit his lip. "What if he doesn't like me?"

Seth gently squeezed his shoulder. "I wouldn't worry about that if I were you."

"Have you met him?"

"No, but I know he's a good guy. Otherwise, your father would never have hired him. He spent more time selecting the right tutor for you than he did on picking people for staff and cabinet posts."

Kenn couldn't help but smile. Seth had such a way of helping him relax, and in this case, he was probably right. His father had spent an inordinate amount of time and energy on selecting the perfect tutor for Kenn to the point where even his mom, with her endless patience, had given up.

The elevator opened, and a man stepped out. He was shorter than Kenn had expected—maybe an inch taller than Kenn. He didn't have the perfectly toned body Seth had but a much rounder and softer one. It made him look friendly, even in his crisp dark blue suit and a white dress shirt with a blue-and-white-striped tie. He had his finger between his collar and his neck but dropped it quickly when he spotted them.

"Hi," Professor Duvall said, frowning slightly. He took

two steps toward Kenn and extended his hand. "It's nice to meet you, Mr. Shafer."

"Kenn. You can call me Kenn." His voice was way too soft, and he was irritated with himself already that he couldn't project more confidence, but his body wasn't cooperating.

Duvall looked at Seth, but the Secret Service agent stayed silent. "Right. Kenn. I'm Warrick Duvall. Professor Duvall. Which you probably figured out by now."

He was stammering. Wait, was he nervous too? Somehow that thought took some of Kenn's trepidation away. "It's a pleasure to meet you, Professor."

Duvall checked in with Seth again, then turned his attention back to Kenn. "You'll have to forgive me, but I'm not familiar with the protocol here. Do I...?" He gestured at Seth.

Oh my god, he totally was nervous. How about that? "That's Seth. He's one of the agents on my Secret Service detail. Technically, the agents aren't supposed to start a conversation with their protectees, but it's different for Seth. He and I are..."

Shit. Had he said too much? Secret Service agents weren't allowed to be close with their protectees, so had he gotten Seth into trouble? What if Seth's boss wasn't okay with it, even though Kenn's dad was?

"We're friends," Seth said smoothly. "As much as my job allows it. With his father's permission."

Duvall cleared his throat. "Okay. That's good to know."

"Generally speaking, you can ignore the agents. Just pretend we're not there."

"That'll take some adapting, I'm afraid. Ignoring people isn't a habit of mine."

Seth's mouth curled up in a smile that communicated approval. The man appreciated it when people treated him with respect, and Kenn could understand why. Being a Secret Service agent wasn't easy, and Seth had shared some horror stories he'd heard from other agents with Kenn—without revealing the identities of the protectees involved. Seth would never break confidentiality.

"You'll get used to it after a few days," Seth said, then stepped back again, positioning himself in his usual spot.

"Right. President Shafer...your father, I mean...told me you're considering law school. Can you tell me what draws you to studying the law?" Professor Duvall asked.

What did he do now? Were they supposed to stand here awkwardly in the hallway? Seth subtly nudged his head toward the sitting area. Of course. The professor wouldn't take the initiative here. That was all on Kenn. He took a deep breath. "Why don't we sit down for this conversation?" He gestured at the sitting area in the hall. "I'm sure you have more questions for me. Can I offer you something to drink?"

It had come out as smoothly as he'd hoped, and he couldn't hold back a smile. Maybe he was finally getting the hang of this whole being social thing.

"I'd appreciate that. A cup of tea, maybe?"

The professor walked in front of him, his gait somewhat stiff, like he was favoring one leg. Kenn's dad had told him Professor Duvall had gotten injured in combat, so maybe that was the cause of his uneven walk?

As soon as they sat, Denali came hurrying toward them, flashing Kenn one of his sweet smiles. The White House server was pure sunshine, and Kenn was happy they were becoming friends. Denali was one of the few people he didn't feel awkward around, probably because they were close in age.

"Can we have tea, please?" Kenn asked him. "And maybe some of Mrs. Morelli's cookies?"

Denali's smile widened. "She baked fresh chocolate chip cookies for you this morning."

Kenn laughed. "I'd better eat them, then, before my dad smells them. He'll devour them all if he gets the chance."

"The Secret Service agents were complaining that *someone* told the president where Mrs. Morelli hides their stash of cookies. Apparently, he ate quite a few of them." Denali hooked his thumb over his shoulder at Seth, and Kenn giggled.

Seth coughed loudly from his spot against the wall. "I'm pleading the fifth."

"I'll be right back with tea and cookies," Denali said, looking amused, then rushed off.

"Can he do that, pleading the fifth?" Professor Duvall asked.

Kenn turned his attention back to him. "Excuse me?"

"Can a Secret Service agent refuse to answer a question like that?"

"Erm, I don't know. I guess it depends on who's asking the question?"

Professor Duvall leaned forward. "Let's say his supervisor asked him or the director of the Secret Service. Could he refuse to answer?"

Kenn thought quickly. The Fifth Amendment protected people from incriminating themselves, didn't it? "If he was the one who told my father about the cookies, then yes, because answering would mean incriminating himself."

"But does that apply to an employer-employee relationship? Isn't the Fifth Amendment only applicable in a legal situation, say, a police interrogation or a court case?"

"I wouldn't think so because if he confessed to someone, including his supervisor, they could then be called as a witness and testify to what he'd told them. So I'd think in no situation can you be forced to answer questions that would incriminate yourself."

"What if your father asked the question? What if the president of the United States demanded that Seth tell the truth? He'd have to answer then, wouldn't he? The president is the highest authority in the country, superseding even the Supreme Court."

"He's not." This, Kenn was certain of. "The president isn't above the law. That's why we have checks and balances so that the Judiciary Branch can check the Executive Branch. If Seth refused to answer, the government could sue him, I think, but that case could take its course through the system, maybe even ending up at the Supreme Court, which would rule in his favor because of the Fifth Amendment."

Professor Duvall sent him a broad smile. "Well argued. In this case, there are a few things that make it more complicated, since Seth is a federal employee and thus bound by what's called a Kalkines warning that could make it mandatory for him to tell the truth, but we'll get into more detail about that later on. For now, let's talk about what draws to you studying the law."

He'd prepared for this question. "I want to make positive changes in our society through the law. My father does it through politics, but I think people underestimate how important laws are at every level. I want to make a difference by using the legal process."

Denali showed up with their tea and cookies, and Professor Duvall nodded at him, waiting with his answer until Denali had walked off again. "That's a lofty goal. In which areas would you like to make a difference?"

"Social justice, first and foremost, which I don't know much about yet, but I've been trying to learn more about how laws favor white people. I still have a lot to learn and understand, but I know that inequality is built into our legal system and that the system helps perpetuate it."

Professor Duvall's eyes lit up. "I can see why your father thought me a good match. I'm passionate about social justice, and I'd love to teach you more about this if you feel we'd be a good fit."

A good fit? What did he mean? "I'm not sure I understand. My father already hired you."

"He did, but if you were to tell me you're not comfortable working with me for any reason, I'd walk away all the same."

Not comfortable? Kenn had no idea what the man was referring to. What an odd phrase. Maybe he'd meant it in more general terms, as in that Kenn wouldn't like him? "No objections on my end, Professor. I'm excited to learn from you."

A flash of relief passed over the professor's face. "I'm glad to hear it. Let's get started, then. I made a first schedule of topics. Why don't we have a look at that? And you can tell me if anything is missing or if I've listed things you already know about."

2

Warrick suppressed a groan as he slid behind the wheel of his Jeep. Pain in his lower back and right thigh had kept him awake for hours the night before, and he was tired. Still, canceling his first official lesson with Kenn Shafer wasn't an option. He'd see it through. Mind over matter, he knew no other way. After ten years, he'd learned to live with the pain.

As soon as he started the engine, he turned on the seat heating. Funny how that feature had once seemed a frivolous luxury but now had become so important to him. He used it even in the summer, the heat helping him relax his muscles and soothe the constant ache.

Thirty-six, going on seventy—the story of his life. One moment of not paying attention had changed everything. Twice. First with the IED he'd missed, and that had blown up the vehicle he'd been in. It had hit the driver's side hardest, killing both the driver and the other passenger. Warrick had walked away with burn marks and a piece of metal embedded in his back. The survivor's guilt had been real the first years afterward.

And then at St. Edwards, where one moment of carelessness had cost him his job. Oh, the dean of the small, private university had denied Warrick had been fired for being gay, but Warrick wasn't stupid. He'd never told the Catholic institute he was gay...because they'd never asked. "Don't ask, don't tell" had still been firmly embedded in his system.

But when someone had spotted him in a gay bar and reported him to the dean, he'd been forced to come out. Weeks later—they had been smart enough to leave enough time in between so it wasn't too obvious—he'd been told his contract wouldn't be renewed.

At least he wouldn't have that worry with his new position as Kenn Shafer's tutor. With an openly bisexual father who had hired him—and that had been the toughest job interview Warrick had ever experienced in his life—Kenn wasn't likely to object to Warrick's sexuality. In fact, he'd mentioned his sexual orientation, for once certain it wouldn't affect his chances negatively. If he had to take a guess, it had even made him a stronger candidate. After all, President Shafer was committed to diversity in hiring at every level.

By the time he reported in the visitors' foyer in the White House, the heat had eased his back pain, and he could at least walk relatively normally. Long car rides were detrimental to his flexibility, since they tended to make his muscles cramp, but the thirty-minute ride from his townhouse in Virginia to downtown DC was still doable.

"Warrick Duvall," he told the Secret Service agent at the entrance. "I was told to arrange for my picture to be taken for my keycard? Or credentials, not sure what you call it."

"Professor Duvall, yes. One moment, please." The agent gestured at Warrick to step aside, then made a quick phone call. Only a minute or two later, another agent showed up.

"I'm Special Agent Laury. You can follow me, please, Professor."

He followed her into a hallway, where she opened a door to her right, leading him into a library that had him drooling instantly. Holy moly, that was an impressive collection of books, and he loved the floor-to-ceiling bookcases and the comfortable-looking, classic reading chairs. It took him a second to spot a slender man standing there, a camera around his neck.

"This is Rhett Foles, the White House photographer. He'll take your picture."

Should he introduce himself? God, he wished he had an idea of the etiquette here, but no book covered situations like this. "Pleasure to meet you," he settled on.

"Likewise. You can stand right in front of the bookcase. It's actually the section with books about the law. I figured that would make a fitting background."

Surprised, Warrick checked the bookcase behind him and discovered Rhett was right. He knew who Warrick was, then, and somehow that took away his nerves. He smiled at him. "I love that, thank you."

Rhett smiled shyly back and switched on two big lights, shielded by white photography umbrellas that softened the light and spread it evenly. Within minutes, Rhett indicated he'd taken a good picture, which he showed to Warrick on the small screen of his camera. "That looks perfect, thank you," Warrick said.

"You're welcome."

Special Agent Laury, who had silently waited for them to be done, took a step forward. "Follow me, Professor Duvall."

He waved awkwardly at Rhett and followed her back to the lobby, where she disappeared into an office for a moment, then came back with his keycard. "Please wear this at all times when inside the White House. You'll receive additional security training from Special Agent Rodecker later today. He'll familiarize you with all safety and security procedures surrounding Kennedy Shafer."

She set off again. After only a few steps, she seemed to pick up on Warrick's slower gait and decreased her speed. He appreciated that small gesture, which showed she was paying attention. Not surprising for a Secret Service agent. He imagined they were trained to notice even the littlest details.

"Since you'll be spending considerable time in the Residence, we've assigned you a Secret Service code name. Law," she said.

He couldn't help smiling. How perfectly fitting. And seriously, how cool. It might be a little childish and even unprofessional, but the idea that he had a code name sent a thrill through him. "Thank you. Can I ask what Kenn's code name is?"

"He's Honor. The president is Hero, the First Lady is Heart, and Mr. Bradbury is Hazel. These names aren't classified. They're used to shorten real names and avoid misunderstandings, but Special Agent Rodecker will explain that all to you in more detail."

They'd reached the elevator, where an older black man in a neat uniform stood waiting, immediately opening the door. "Special Agent Rodecker is waiting for you upstairs," Special Agent Laury said.

"Thank you."

He stepped into the elevator, and so did the uniformed attendant. "How are you today, sir?" the man asked as the doors closed.

"I'm good. How are you?"

"I'm fine, sir, thank you."

Warrick's eyes fell on the name tag the man was wearing: Jim. Underneath his name was the number fifty-one printed in smaller letters. "You've worked here for fifty-one years?" he asked, astonished.

Jim sent him a beaming smile. "Yes, sir. I started when I was twenty years old and President Nixon was in office. My father worked here as well, serving from President Roosevelt until he retired under President H.W. Bush. And now both my son and my grandson work in the White House. It's our family pride."

"That's amazing. You must've met some dignitaries throughout the years."

The elevator came to a stop. "Everyone from Her Majesty Queen Elizabeth to the emperor of Japan. If I were so inclined, I could tell a thousand stories...but we don't talk. Ever."

"And that's why you made it fifty-one years and why your family serves here with honor."

Jim stood just a little straighter. "Yes, sir."

"Pleasure to meet you, Jim."

The elevator doors opened. "Likewise. Have a wonderful day, sir."

Fifty-one years. Wow. Warrick couldn't even imagine. When he stepped out, it wasn't Special Agent Rodecker waiting for him, but Kenn. He was dressed smartly in khakis and a button-down shirt and yet managed to look adorably cute and younger than his age. He radiated a vulnerability that Warrick found appealing, much more than the snotty attitudes of many students whose sense of privilege and entitlement had spoiled them beyond redemption.

"Mr. Shafer."

"Kenn. Please call me Kenn, Professor Duvall."

Crap, yes. He'd messed up. But if he called him Kenn,

having Kenn use his title felt wrong. He didn't want this cold formality if they were to spend so much time together. But would it be too informal in this environment? He was in the White House...with the president's son. And yet something in Kenn's eyes seemed to beg Warrick to please like him, and he couldn't resist. "My apologies. I promise I'll remember. In return, why don't you call me Warrick? That'll make things easier."

"But...but you're a professor!" Kenn protested.

"And you're the president's son, yet you ask me to call you by your first name."

A blush reddened Kenn's cheeks. "That's because of what my father is. I don't deserve any accolades based on my own merits, but you..."

"Even if I asked you to because I'd prefer it?"

"You would?"

"Yes, it would feel awfully formal otherwise. Besides, technically, I'm not a professor at the moment."

"O-okay. If you insist."

He peeked at Warrick from between his lashes, and softness permeated Warrick's heart, making his chest expand, feel bigger. Kenn was not only shy but also insecure. Vulnerable and maybe even lonely. "I do. I look forward to teaching you, Kenn. You already showed last time that you have a sharp mind and are eager to learn."

Kenn's face lit up. "I'm excited as well. My mom suggested we use the West Sitting Room. Would that be okay with you...Warrick?"

Warrick grinned. At least he'd gotten Kenn to use his name. Progress. "I have no idea what or where that is, but I can't imagine I'd object to any room in this building. It's all quite grand and intimidating, isn't it?"

"True. I like that room, though. It's the one with the half-moon window."

Kenn took them through the hallway, past Seth, who nodded at Warrick, through a door at the end that led into a room featuring pale yellow drapes, cream-colored paneling, and furniture in pastel colors. A rectangular mahogany table—a notebook and pen lying on the polished surface—stood to the side, with two chairs already set up side by side. Warrick couldn't recall ever having been in a room that formal. "It's not the Oval Office, but we'll make do." He winked at Kenn, and that earned him a shy giggle.

They took a seat, and Kenn opened his notebook. Warrick smiled at his eagerness. "Did you read the article I sent you on the US constitution?"

"Of course, sir. I mean, Warrick. I did."

"Can you tell me the difference between originalists and those who see the constitution as a living document?"

"Originalists say that the meaning of the constitutional text is fixed and unchangeable. Living constitutionalists feel that constitutional law should evolve over time because the circumstances and context change."

"Exactly. So, which do you agree with?"

Kenn blinked a few times as if he hadn't expected to be asked for his opinion. Then a shy smile blossomed on his lips. "If I say the second, I suppose you'll ask me to support that with arguments, right?"

"Count on it." Warrick rubbed his hands. "So hit me with it."

He'd hoped he'd get this position, but he'd never thought he'd connect this well with Kenn Shafer. He genuinely looked forward to teaching him. Maybe things were finally improving for him.

3

As much as Kenn had appreciated attending Amherst, it had been nothing compared to the joy he experienced in learning from Professor Duvall over the last month. He still struggled with calling him by his first name and usually tried to avoid it, much to the professor's amusement. On more than one occasion, the man's eyes had danced with mirth.

He was such a great teacher, and the way he could connect history and the law was endlessly fascinating. Every day, Kenn looked forward to spending time with him and learning something new. Warrick never went easy on him, constantly challenging him to form an opinion and defend it with factual arguments. He was training Kenn in reasoning, a systematic approach to facts and truths, and Kenn found himself becoming sharper and more skilled in debating. He loved it.

"Section one of the Twenty-fifth Amendment simply states that when the president dies or resigns, the vice president shall become president," Warrick said, his expression kind. "That's how your father became president."

"I was there when he took the oath of office," Kenn said softly.

"How was that? You must've been so scared after what had happened."

How typical of Warrick to think of Kenn's feelings first and not the historical significance of that moment. "I was terrified. The Secret Service stormed in and took us to... Took us somewhere safe, and when they informed us what had happened, all I could do was cry. My mom cried too."

"I can imagine. It must've been such a shock for you."

And Warrick didn't even know about the second assassination that had been planned, but Kenn did. If the Naval Academy in Annapolis hadn't canceled the event and that cop hadn't pulled over the car with the terrorist, his father, too, might be dead. But he couldn't tell Warrick that. It was classified. No one knew outside of those who needed to know, and that sure as hell didn't include Kenn, but he'd overheard a conversation between Uncle Milan and his dad.

"Standing in the Oval Office, watching my dad take the oath of office was the most surreal moment of my life. I'm glad Rhett took pictures and that news crews taped it because I barely remember it."

"You observed a significant moment in history for sure. The Twenty-fifth Amendment does more than state who's next in the line of succession. It also makes it clear what needs to happen when there's no vice president."

"It says the president should appoint one."

"So why is there still no vice president? It's been six months."

"It needs to be ratified by a majority in the House of Representatives and the Senate, and the Republicans won the midterm elections in November. They're not in a hurry to appoint a new vice president, since they're next in the line of succession with the Speaker of the House. Plus, they don't like the vice presidential candidate my father has nominated, Senator Riggs from New York. She's too liberal in their opinion, even though Democrats consider her a moderate."

He was glad he'd been paying attention when his dad had talked to others about issues like this. He didn't always understand everything, but he'd picked up a lot over the last few months.

"Mmm, can they do that?"

Kenn hesitated. "I mean, they are doing it, so I guess so? My dad can't do much, even though he's the president. But he only needs four Republicans to vote with the Democrats, so the question is how long the Republicans can keep up this deadlock. At some point, someone will have to give in."

Warrick grinned. "I take it your money is on your dad?"

"That man is stubborn. He never backs down from a fight. I wish..." He cast his eyes down. "I wish I was more like him."

"You take after your mom, then?"

"Yes."

"Well, she's a highly respected First Lady, so maybe you're not giving yourself enough credit here."

Kenn kept his gaze on his hands in his lap, but his insides grew warm.

"What else does the Twenty-fifth Amendment state?"

"It provides for a solution when, for whatever reason, the president is unable to govern."

"Such as..."

"Such as when the president would need surgery?"

"Exactly. The first president to make use of that section, section three, was President George W. Bush in 2002. He needed anesthesia for a colonoscopy and formally signed a letter to hand over power temporarily to his vice president, Dick Cheney."

Warrick stopped talking when Kenn's mom stepped into the room, Rogue on her heels as always. As much as that dog loved Kenn and his dad, his first love was Kenn's mom, and he followed her wherever she went with his uneven gait, caused by him only having three legs. He'd lost his right hind leg in a car accident before they had adopted him from the shelter.

"Hey, honey." She walked over to Kenn and kissed the top of his head. "What are you guys talking about today?"

She'd popped in earlier to check in on them like she usually did, but she'd had to take a call and left them alone. "The Twenty-fifth Amendment and how Dad could sign a letter to hand over power to someone else."

She laughed, but it didn't reach her eyes. "I'd love for your father to use that so he can retire. A beach house on Cape Cod sounds pretty good."

Kenn frowned. His mother was looking pale. Was she coming down with something? She hadn't been well for weeks now, having been diagnosed with arrhythmia. But Kenn didn't want to ask in front of Warrick. His mom was fiercely private, always protesting the public knew far more about her already than she was comfortable with.

"He'd have to get a vice president approved first," Kenn said, keeping his tone light.

"Let's talk about section four," Warrick said, his face tight. Was he picking up on something being off about Kenn's mom? Maybe he should say something to her or call the White House physician.

His mom kissed his head again. "Love you, kiddo."

"Love you too, Mom."

She walked away, and Kenn was about to say something when a strange sound behind him had him turning around.

What was that? It sounded like...

He was out of his chair in a flash, just as his mom collapsed to the floor. "Mom! MOM!"

Rogue whined, then barked sharply. Panic clawed at Kenn's insides. She was too pale...and why had she thrown up? And her body was convulsing. Oh god, was she having a heart attack? "Help! SETH!"

Warrick was already on his knees by her side, pressing his fingers against her neck. The door banged open, and Seth and Asher stormed into the room. Rogue made another sound of distress, and Kenn grabbed him by his collar and pulled him aside so he'd be out of the way.

"She's got no pulse," Warrick said, trembling slightly. "Starting compressions."

"Get the defibrillator," Seth snapped, and Asher sprinted away.

"Medical emergency for Heart. Crash team to the Residence, second-floor living room," he shouted into his com.

Seth kneeled next to Kenn's mom, starting chest compressions, while Warrick checked again for a pulse, then leaned in, tilted her head back, and breathed into her mouth while pinching her nose closed.

Kenn sank to his knees, holding on to Rogue with all his might as tears streamed down his face. No, no, no. This couldn't be happening. Not his mom. She had to be okay; she *had* to.

Asher hurried back in, carrying the defibrillator. After that, everything became a blur. They shocked her, then again. She wasn't responding. Seth was communicating with someone else. Then the medical team stormed into the room, taking over. She was so still, so pale...and Kenn *knew*.

"Mom…" Kenn's voice broke as he got up.

Warrick pulled on Kenn's arm, and he let him, stepping into the man's solid embrace, burying his head against his chest. He couldn't watch anymore. He stayed there, even as Seth asked questions, and Warrick explained what had happened. The medical team kept working on his mother. "Another shock. Injecting epi."

"We have a rhythm again. Bring her to the WHMU," Dr. Brophy said. "We'll need to get her stable enough for transport."

Kenn lifted his tear-stained face from Warrick's chest. "A-asher, i-is she g-gonna make it?"

He wasn't even sure he wanted an answer. Maybe he shouldn't have asked.

Running footsteps thumped through the hallway, and then his dad rushed in, his Secret Service detail on his heels. "Sarah! Oh god, Sarah…"

Kenn had never seen his father like that, so distressed and almost panicked. It only reaffirmed what he already knew.

"We need to bring her downstairs, Mr. President," Dr. Brophy said in an urgent tone. "Now."

"Go. Do whatever you need to do. Please…"

Kenn trembled as his mom was loaded onto a stretcher and carried out of the room. For a moment, his father looked dazed, as if he didn't know what to do, but then his eyes met Kenn's. Kenn let go of Warrick and raced over to him. "Dad…"

His father held him tight, so wonderfully tight, with those strong arms around him. "Oh, kiddo, I'm so sorry you had to see that… So sorry." The president kissed the top of Kenn's head, like his mom had done only minutes before. Would she ever be able to do it again?

"Will she be okay?" he whispered, his throat so painful he could barely get the words out.

"I don't know, kiddo. I don't know. But whatever happens, I'm here. I love you, Kennedy Shafer, you hear me? I love you so much. We'll get through this. Come on, let's go down to the medical unit, okay?"

With his father's arm around him, Kenn managed to make his body move, and they ran down the stairs to the ground floor, to the WHMU. In the distance, the unmistakable chuff-chuff-chuff indicated Marine One was ready for take-off. "Can we accompany her?" Kenn asked.

His father shook his head. "No. There won't be enough space with the medical team on the flight. But Marine Two has been summoned and will be here soon, so we'll go to the hospital as soon as we can."

His father held him close as they watched his mom being hurried outside, then loaded into Marine One, which took off immediately. "My last words to her were that I loved her..." Kenn said, his voice breaking.

His father pulled him into his arms again. "She loves you more than anything, Kenn. You know that...and she knows how much you love her."

"Dad, what if...?" He couldn't finish the sentence.

"I don't know, kiddo. I don't know. I've never..." This time, it was his father's voice that broke. "Let's just pray. Pray and hope with all our might."

4

Warrick's throat burned as he watched the president and Kenn leave the room, their arms around each other. That poor, poor kid, having to see his mother like that. Warrick had little medical training aside from knowing first aid from serving in the military, but Mrs. Shafer hadn't looked good, and her chances of making it seemed to be slim. His heart ached for Kenn and the president. How could this have happened? What was wrong with her? She was way too young for a heart attack.

Then he remembered Asher ordering the Residence on lockdown; no one was allowed to leave. Were they…? Ice stabbed through his heart. Were they suspecting foul play?

"I'm calling Coulson," Seth said to Asher. "In the meantime, keep all the staff where they are. No one touches anything. And someone needs to take care of Rogue."

"I'll take him for now," Warrick offered. If nothing else, it would give him something to do, and the dog looked lost and sad as he lay on the floor, focused on the spot where the medical team had worked on Mrs. Shafer.

"Thank you," Seth said. "I'm gonna need you to leave the room, but you can't leave the Residence yet. We'll need a more detailed statement from you once Coulson gets here."

"Coulson?" Warrick frowned. The name sounded familiar, but he couldn't place it.

"FBI Special Agent Coulson Padman." Seth shared a look with Asher.

Why would Seth call in the FBI? Wouldn't the Secret Service be in charge? Unless...

The name clicked. Coulson Padman was one of the lead agents on the investigation into the assassination of President Markinson, and before that, he'd worked in New York City on the Pride Bombing. If they called him in, that had to mean they suspected a link between those two events and Mrs. Shafer's collapse.

Warrick held up his hands. "I won't ask any more questions. Do your job. Tell me where to go, and I'll be available for whatever you need me for."

"Thank you," Seth said. He looked at Asher again. "We have to keep everyone separate as much as possible, but the professor needs a room where he can actually sit comfortably."

Warrick was touched that even under these circumstances, Seth took his physical limitations into consideration.

Asher nodded. "I'll order everyone to split up and use all rooms available."

"Put the professor in Kenn's bedroom. He's got a comfortable chair there and a desk. Plus, a whole lot of books, so he won't get bored." Seth turned to Warrick. "You can take anything from his minifridge. And Kenn keeps some snacks and a water bowl for Rogue in his room as well."

"That works for me. Thanks."

Asher led him into the hallway, and after a short command, Rogue followed them. Kenn's room, next to the staircase, was decorated in various shades of blue. The dark blue curtains and lighter blue chairs were warm and welcoming. One wall had floor-to-ceiling bookcases, and Seth had been right. Warrick would have enough books to last him a long time.

"Please make yourself comfortable," Asher said. "We apologize for the—"

"Don't," Warrick interrupted him. "Please do your job. I'll wait as long as necessary."

"Thank you." Asher hurried out, closing the door behind him.

Rogue let out a soft whine. "I know, buddy. You must be so upset. How about I find something to drink for both of us, and we can sit down and recover from all this as best we can?"

He found a can of Coke in the minifridge, thanking his lucky stars, and in the bathroom, Warrick filled Rogue's bowl with fresh water. He opened some random drawers, mentally apologizing to Kenn for the gross invasion of his privacy, and struck gold on the third one. He took out a few dog biscuits and a Snickers bar for himself.

He grabbed the first book that caught his eye, and as soon as he'd lowered himself into a reading chair, Rogue trotted over and put his head on Warrick's leg. He set the book aside and petted Rogue, taking the time to scratch between his ears. "Such a good boy... You must've been scared to see her like that, huh?"

He fed him a biscuit, which was gone in seconds. The second one disappeared just as quickly, and Warrick smiled. "I know. I'm hungry too. It's a reaction to stress, you know.

The body's processing the adrenaline rush, and that can cause hunger. I always ate like crazy a couple of hours after a mission."

He unwrapped the Snickers and wolfed it down as Rogue made quick work of the rest of the biscuits. "Okay, buddy... Now we wait."

He settled in the chair, the Coke within reach, and picked up the book, which turned out to be a memoir of a former NSA director. That would keep him entertained. He forced all thoughts of what had happened to the background, one of the many useful skills he'd learned in the Army, and focused on reading.

Within minutes, Rogue had found a spot at his feet, slumbering, and Warrick allowed himself to be engrossed in the book. In the background, footsteps thudded, chopper blades whirred, voices rumbled and murmured, but he ignored them. All he could do was wait, and so he would.

After two hours, a knock on the door startled him out of his reading, and Warrick put his book down as he called out, "Come in."

Weird. It wasn't even his room.

The man who stepped inside, Seth on his heels, was seriously off-the-charts hot, and Warrick forced himself to concentrate on other things than the man's fit body. "Professor Duvall? I'm Special Agent Coulson Padman."

The FBI agent held out his credentials, and Warrick checked them, more out of reflex than anything else. He was in the White House, so it wasn't like he'd encounter an imposter here. "Please call me Warrick."

"We'd like to ask you some questions."

Warrick gestured at the other chairs. "Of course. Whatever you need. Can I ask if you have an update on Mrs. Shafer's condition?"

Special Agent Padman's face tightened. "I'm sorry to tell you she passed away."

Oh god. Warrick's heart sat heavy in his chest. Poor, poor Kenn. He'd watched his mother die. How would he ever get over that trauma? "I'm so sorry to hear that. She was a lovely person and a wonderful mother."

"She was. The best." Seth sounded distraught, and Warrick couldn't blame him.

"I'm gonna walk through everything that happened, starting from the moment you arrived here this morning." Special Agent Padman flipped open a notepad. "Did you notice anything unusual when you entered the Residence?"

It took half an hour for the FBI agent to go over every little detail, and Warrick calmly answered all his questions. It became increasingly clear that they did suspect foul play, and it probably had something to do with what she'd eaten. Special Agent Padman kept homing in on that, and Warrick patiently answered, even when the FBI agent asked the same things in three different ways.

Finally, Special Agent Padman looked at Seth. "Do you have any more questions?"

Seth shook his head. "I think we have it all."

Special Agent Padman rose. "You're free to go home, Warrick. We'll contact you if we need anything else."

"What about Rogue?" Warrick asked.

Seth frowned. "The president and Kenn are at an undisclosed location. I assume we can take Rogue there as well, but I'll have to check."

"I'm happy to stay here as long as you need me to," Warrick offered, and relief showed on Seth's face.

"Thank you. We have a lot to take care of right now. It's been…"

His jaw tightened, and for a moment, Special Agent Padman put his hand on Seth's shoulder. That short contact was enough to make Warrick's eyes widen. Those two were together. One hundred percent, no doubt about it. The way the FBI agent was tuned into Seth, the look Seth shot him back...

When Seth met Warrick's gaze, he gave him a small smile.

"He's my boyfriend," he said softly.

"I figured as much."

"Usually, we're better at keeping things separate, but it's been a rough day for me."

"I can't even imagine. No need to explain or apologize at all. It's not like I object in any way."

"Given your background, I didn't think you would, but thank you. And thank you for your flexibility. I'll get the situation with Rogue sorted out as soon as I can."

Warrick waved him off. "Take your time. I'm comfortable here."

They left, and Warrick settled down again. An FBI agent and a Secret Service agent. That in itself had to be a challenge, with two such unpredictable jobs. But when one was the lead agent on a presidential assassination and the other worked for the very agency that was supposed to have protected that president, things would get even more complicated. Still, the way Special Agent Padman had offered Seth that brief comfort had been encouraging.

An hour later, Warrick walked back to his car, his chest tight as he thought of Kenn. With President Shafer still functioning without a vice president, how would he ever have the time to be there for his son and help him get through this unimaginable loss? His administration had been in crisis mode ever since he took office, and this latest tragedy would only make that worse. Who would be there to support Kenn?

He got into his car and dragged his phone out of his pocket. He stared at it for a moment. He had Kenn's phone number—to make communicating with him about their lessons easier—but Seth had made the consequences of sharing it with anyone crystal clear. Could he use it in this case? He saw no reason why he shouldn't. They'd kept their messages practical so far, chatting about their schedule, assignments, and book recommendations, but that didn't mean Warrick couldn't reach out to him after this. Surely these extraordinary circumstances warranted personal use.

Warrick opened the message app. What could he possibly offer that would help Kenn? Nothing would make him feel better, that much Warrick was certain of. But he could at least acknowledge his pain and loss. If nothing else, it would make Kenn feel seen.

Warrick: I'm so, so sorry about your mom. She was a wonderful person and mother. I can't imagine how much you must be hurting right now.

Much to his surprise, it showed up as *read* almost immediately, and he watched the dancing dots for a minute until Kenn's reply popped up.

Kenn: Thank you. I don't know what to say. Or what to do. I'm so empty inside.

Warrick: You don't need to say anything. Just grieve. This will take time to process.

Kenn: Thank you for taking care of Rogue. Seth said you stayed with him until someone could bring him here. Sorry, I'm not allowed to tell you where I am.

Warrick: You're so welcome. He's such a good boy. I hope he can bring you some comfort. And no worries. I understand you can't say anything.

Kenn: He hasn't left my side. I think he knows something's wrong.

Warrick: Of course he does. Dogs are super smart.

Kenn: Thank you for reaching out. It means a lot.

God, that one sentence totally broke Warrick's heart. Please let there be someone Kenn could lean on, someone who was making sure he was okay.

Warrick: I'm here for you if you need anything. Text, call, whatever you need.

If no one else looked after Kenn, he'd have to do it himself.

5

Kenn had loved Camp David when he'd spent time there over the summer and in the fall, but without his mom, the place was bleak and cold. Empty, just like his insides. Numbness battled with pain so fierce and jagged he couldn't stop crying. He preferred feeling nothing, but that never lasted long. His eyes were swollen, stinging from all the salty tears, and his throat was so raw every swallow hurt.

It had been three days since his mom had died. Three days of the deepest hell he could ever have imagined. Three days of feeling so lonely that more than once, he'd wished he were dead himself. His dad had spent time with him as much as he could...but that hadn't been a lot. And with them being at Camp David and having so few people there and in the know, Kenn didn't have much of a support system.

Except Warrick, who faithfully texted him every so many hours. Checking in. Reminding him to eat. Telling him to take his time grieving. Assuring him that over time, the pain and sadness would subside.

His phone dinged again, and he picked it up.

WARRICK: Have you had dinner yet? Make sure to eat. I know you're not hungry, but you need the calories.

ON IMPULSE, he hit the Call button. Warrick picked up almost immediately. "Hey," he said, his voice warm.

"Hey." He didn't know what else to say, except that he needed to talk to someone…or maybe hear someone's voice. "I'll grab something to eat in a few minutes."

"Good. I know it's hard to prioritize self-care in a situation like this, but it's important."

"H-how do you know?" Maybe it was rude to ask, but Kenn couldn't muster the energy to care.

"I lost friends in battle. Men I was close to. It never gets easier, no matter what people say."

"I'm sorry. I shouldn't have asked."

"It's okay. Trust me, if I hadn't wanted to answer, I wouldn't have."

Kenn let out a long sigh and settled on his bed, Rogue immediately snuggling close. The dog hadn't left his side since arriving here. "Is that how you got hurt?"

"The Army truck I was driving hit an IED. The two men who were in the truck with me died, but I survived, though with injuries on my back and legs. Unfortunately, that was the end of my Army career."

"I have a hard time imagining you as a soldier. You seem too smart for it, but I know that sounds wrong. Too scholarly, maybe?"

Warrick chuckled. "I graduated from West Point, Kenn. The scholarly side was always there, except I'd hoped for a longer career as an Army officer. Instead, I never made it past first lieutenant. But during my recovery, when it became clear I'd never return to active duty, I decided to start law school to distract myself from the many hours of physical therapy. I needed to focus on something else, and it worked."

How silly that a conversation like this helped Kenn feel better. Thinking about something else, anything else, for a few minutes helped take his mind off his mom, off his pain and sadness. "Are you still upset that your whole life plan changed?"

Warrick was quiet for a few moments. "It's hard not to be bitter when you work so hard toward a goal and then see it all go up in smoke, but I've made my peace with it now. Not being in the military does offer more freedom in certain aspects."

Kenn frowned. Freedom in certain aspects? What was Warrick referring to? "You mean like no tours abroad?"

"For example. But relationships are pretty hard as well, even more so when you're..."

When you're what? Kenn was about to ask when it hit him. Was Warrick gay? The question was on the tip of his tongue, but no, he wouldn't ask. It was rude, and Denali had taught Kenn the importance of allowing people to come out at their own pace. "I understand," he said quickly. Had he waited so long Warrick would interpret his silence as something else?

"I wasn't sure if you knew. Your father does, and it's not like I'm hiding it. I've been out ever since I left the Army, but..."

He was indeed gay, then. Or bi. "It's not easy being in the military when you're not straight."

Warrick chuckled softly, and the sound settled in Kenn's

belly. "Someone taught you well. Kudos to you for not assuming anything and mislabeling me. I'm gay. Like I said, it's not a secret, though at my last job, I..." He let out a long sigh. "I should never have taken that position."

"What happened?" Kenn vaguely remembered something about Warrick getting fired, but he wasn't sure of the details. Inside him, joy bloomed over the compliment Warrick had paid him. He'd gotten it right, and that felt good.

"I shouldn't burden you with this. I apologize."

"You're not burdening me. It's good to think of something else for a while. It's a distraction, and I need that."

"Hmm, okay. I can see that. I won't bore you with all the details, but I hadn't told the school I was gay. It was a private, Catholic college, so I didn't think it wise to mention it. But someone reported seeing me at a gay bar, and when the school found out, they found a reason to fire me."

Kenn gasped. "Isn't that illegal?"

"It recently became illegal, but they gave a different reason, of course. They often do, and they're counting on people not suing because who has the time and money for that? I don't. So I chose to walk away."

"I'm sorry. That's so unfair."

"I have hope your father will manage to change this. He's proposed federal law to protect people from being discriminated against based on their gender identity or sexual orientation. He's such a trailblazer. I got all emotional when he became vice president."

"I'm gay too," Kenn blurted out, his heart suddenly racing. He wasn't even sure why he'd told Warrick, except that he needed to tell someone other than Denali.

Warrick didn't miss a beat. "Thank you for sharing that. I'm honored you'd trust me with this."

He didn't ask more, and Kenn respected him for that. "My dad doesn't know. No one does except for Denali."

"Ah, yes, I can see why he'd be a good friend to talk to about this."

Of course Warrick had pegged Denali as gay. He would, as a gay man himself. But had he "made" Kenn as well? "D-did you think I was gay? Like, suspect it?" he dared to ask.

Warrick was quiet for a bit. "You know, I try not to speculate about people's sexuality. Even when people say they're straight, there could be lots of reasons why they choose not to be open about who they are…"

And still he didn't ask why Kenn hadn't come out, and Kenn let out a long breath. "I'm not ready yet."

"Then you wait until you are. Take your time."

Kenn stroked Rogue's soft fur. "If I can get permission, would you be willing to travel here to keep teaching me? I need to do something, have some kind of distraction."

"Oh, I don't know, Kenn. I doubt the Secret Service would be okay with that."

"I'll ask my dad for approval. I'm going crazy here. I need something else to focus on, to keep my brain occupied."

"I understand, I really do, but under the circumstances, I'm not sure if it's smart. You're not even allowed to tell me where you are, so how would they be okay with me coming over? Besides, I don't know how far of a drive it is, but that's a consideration as well. I can't do long drives. The muscles in my leg cramp when I sit in the same position for too long."

He didn't want to come. Kenn wasn't sure why it hurt so much, but it did. Somehow, he'd counted on Warrick saying yes, and now that he hadn't, he felt crushed. "I-I understand. I'm sorry I asked."

"No, don't be sorry. I'm flattered and honored you value my lessons so much, but it doesn't seem the right timing."

"I understand. I-I have to go now. Bye."

Kenn ended the call before Warrick could say anything else, and then he sat for a long time, holding on to Rogue. He'd been foolish to think that Warrick would still want to teach him under these circumstances. No one would. Being around him was depressing and maybe even dangerous, and who would willingly sign up for that?

His phone buzzed, and his heart skipped a beat. Had Warrick changed his mind? Nope, it was his dad.

Dad: Wanna have dinner with me?

Kenn: Yeah. Where? And what are we having?

Dad: Our lodge. Just you and me. I asked for pepperoni pizza, your favorite.

Kenn: On my way.

His dad was trying, and warmth spread through Kenn. He found his dad on the phone, but he hung up as soon as Kenn entered the living room. "Hey, kiddo."

He hugged Kenn tightly, and for a minute, Kenn clung to his dad. Maybe he could soak up some of his strength.

"How have you been? You hanging in there?"

What could he say? His dad was trying so hard, but he had too much on his plate to take care of Kenn as well. The country needed him. "I'm trying."

"Good, good."

They sat down and chatted until Denali brought pizza and drinks. "Enjoy," he said, sending them a warm smile.

"Thank you, Denali," his father said, attentive as ever.

Kenn waited until Denali had left again and it was just the two of them. "Dad, do you think Professor Duvall could maybe come visit here and keep teaching me?"

His dad frowned as he chewed. "It's okay to give yourself a break. I don't care about your studies right now."

"I need the distraction. I have nothing to do here, and all I can think of is...is Mom."

His dad sighed. "I can see that. Let me talk to the Secret Service and see what they say. They've been clear that they want to limit the number of visitors here for security purposes."

And Kenn finally found the courage to ask the question that had been on his mind for days. "Dad, was Mom's death of natural causes?"

With a slow motion, his father put down the slice of pizza he'd been eating. He carefully wiped his hands on a napkin, then raised his eyes and met Kenn's. "It looks like it wasn't."

Kenn swallowed. "She w-was m-murdered?"

"We suspect so. Poisoned."

"How?" As soon as he asked, he knew the answer. It had been bothering him the whole time. "The banana."

"Yeah."

"She never ate bananas."

"No, she didn't."

"But you do. Does that mean...?"

"We don't know. It seems likely, but we don't know for sure. I'm so, so sorry. I failed to keep your mom safe."

His father's voice broke, and Kenn slid off his chair and hurried over. He sat down next to his dad, and his dad wrapped his arm around him and pulled him close like he was a little boy again. Kenn hung on to him as they both cried, the pizza growing cold.

"I'm sorry I can't be there for you more," his father whispered, his voice hoarse. "I wish I could, but..."

"You have a country to run. I get it."

"It shouldn't be like this. My job shouldn't be more important now, not under these circumstances."

"But it is, Dad, and I understand."

"I'm still sorry."

"I love you, Dad."

His father tightened his arms around him. "I love you so much. Please tell me if it gets to be too much for you, if the darkness threatens to swallow you. I swear I'll be there if you need me."

Kenn closed his eyes and leaned on his dad's shoulder. "I promise, Dad."

6

He'd fucked up with Kenn. Warrick had known as soon as Kenn had ended the call. He'd cried out for help, and Warrick had turned him down. In hindsight, he could see it so clearly, but at the time, he'd been too concerned about the practical aspects. The security, the commute. The tiny little fact that Mrs. Shafer might have been murdered.

Warrick wasn't stupid. Seth and Asher hadn't outright said anything, but he'd clued into their line of questioning, and he'd understood what they were after. After everything that had happened, being around the First Family was not the best idea.

But Kenn had needed him...and Warrick had failed him. Oh, he'd debated calling him back. He'd picked his phone up countless times, but every single time, he'd put it back down. Even if Kenn wanted him there, that didn't mean it was smart or that he should accept that invite.

Then Seth had called him the night before. Would he be willing to travel to an undisclosed location to tutor Kenn? He'd said yes instantly. Seth had told him the Secret

Service would set everything up and that they would contact him.

Warrick was working through the never-ending, soul-crushing task of keeping up with his email when his doorbell rang. He opened the door and found two men in suits on his doorstep. Ah, the Secret Service had shown up without calling first. He should've known.

"Professor Duvall, I'm Special Agent Cory Inglis, Secret Service, and this is Special Agent Randy Sloan." The older of the two held out his credentials, and Warrick checked them. "Can we come in?"

Warrick stepped aside. "Of course."

"Can I offer you something to drink?"

"No, thank you. We just need a few minutes of your time."

"Okay. We can sit in the living room." He gestured them to walk into the house, and they sat down across from him on the couch. "What can I do for you?"

Special Agent Inglis cleared his throat. "Professor Duvall, the president has requested us to facilitate your presence to tutor Kenn Shafer."

"I talked to Special Agent Rodecker about it."

"Good. When you started as Mr. Shafer's tutor, you signed a strict confidentiality clause. Because of current circumstances and the location of the stay, you'll have security clearance for secret information. The FBI has already started a second background check. But, Professor, we cannot stress enough how crucially important it is that you don't disclose your location to anyone, including family, friends, loved ones...even your partner."

"I don't have a partner," Warrick said automatically. Wait, had they asked him that as some kind of check? The agents showed no reaction, but they were trained professionals, so that didn't mean anything. "But I'm familiar with both the security clearance process and the need for operational security and secrecy from my time in the military."

"The location is set up as a sensitive compartmented information facility, a SCIF, which means you won't have access to certain parts. Other areas will be accessible to you, but you won't be allowed to bring any electronic equipment, including your cell phone. We'll also have to search everything you bring into the facility."

"Not an issue. I'll comply with all security measures necessary to protect the first family."

"We're glad to hear it. Do you consent to us searching your house right now?"

It should've felt like an invasion of his privacy, maybe, but instead, it left Warrick with a warm feeling they were doing whatever they could to keep Kenn and the president safe. "No problem at all."

The two agents went through his house, opening every drawer, looking into every closet, checking every single item in his fridge, even rifling through his books and papers. Finally, they were done, and Warrick was relieved to see they put everything back in order.

"Thank you, Professor. We're ready to take you as soon as you've gathered your things, which shouldn't take more than a few minutes, I assume."

Warrick frowned. "Why would you think I'd be ready to go in such a short time?"

The corners of Inglis's mouth pulled up. "Your house is in immaculate state, even though you didn't know we were coming. No dishes on the counter, every item in its proper place, and your bed was made with military precision. You could pack for a two-week stay in ten minutes and not forget a single thing, Professor."

Damn, these guys were good. He couldn't help but smile back. "Good point."

Special Agent Inglis had been right; it did take him only three minutes to put the things he wanted to bring into his briefcase and grab the Redweld with the documents he'd assembled for his book, as well as some files for Kenn.

The back seat in the black Suburban was large enough for him to stretch his legs and move around a bit, preventing his muscles from locking and spasming. He hadn't asked where they were going, but when they drove deeper into Maryland, he had a good idea, which was confirmed when they passed the gates. Camp David. As if the White House wasn't surreal enough.

The car stopped in front of a gorgeous lodge, but Warrick stayed seated until Special Agent Sloan opened the door. "We're here."

Warrick stretched discreetly as he followed him to the lodge, where multiple agents guarded the door. He nodded at them, and they acknowledged him back, their faces tight and serious. His briefcase was searched, and he had to leave his phone with the agent near the front door. The lodge was smaller and far less luxurious than he'd expected. As opulent as the White House felt, this had a far more homey feel, rustic and outdoorsy.

The agent knocked on a door, then opened it. "Professor Duvall is here," he said, then stepped aside to let Warrick walk past him. Rogue hobbled over, greeting him with a happy bark, and Warrick gave him a good rub between his ears. That dog never seemed fazed by missing a leg.

Kenn was sitting at a small table, his notepad in front of him. Warrick clapped his hand over his mouth to cover a gasp. The kid looked like he hadn't slept in the five days since his mom's passing. His skin was pale and dull, and he looked shaggy, unkempt. Warrick's whole being ached to hug him, make him take a shower, brush his hair, feed him. But above all hug him.

"Thanks for driving him, Randy."

The agent nodded at him, then closed the door behind Warrick.

"Thank you for coming, Professor." Kenn was avoiding Warrick's eyes, instead stroking Rogue, who'd plopped down on the carpet right next to them.

Dammit, he'd gone back to calling him professor? He'd fucked up badly. He sat down across from him and waited until Kenn finally looked up. "I'm sorry I said no initially when you asked me to come. It was selfish of me, and I apologize."

Kenn averted his eyes again. "It's okay. I understand. I'm not your responsibility."

No, he wasn't, but Warrick was rattled by the need to ensure Kenn was okay. "Maybe, but that's not the point. I should've considered it from your perspective."

"It's okay," Kenn said again, but he still wouldn't look up.

"Kenn..." He had the strong urge to add a term of endearment, but he swallowed it back. Kenn was evoking tender, protective feelings in him he'd never felt before. "Are you okay? You don't look so good."

Finally, Kenn dared to meet Warrick's eyes. "You should've seen me yesterday. I got an earful from Denali... right before he forced me to take a shower while he tidied and cleaned my room."

"I'm glad he's such a good friend to you."

"He doesn't have much time for me, though. Not with his job and..." He hesitated for a moment. "He's involved with someone. Two people, in fact, but please don't tell anyone. Maybe I shouldn't have said anything, but he told me, and I literally have no one I can talk to about it, and it's such a big thing that it's hard not to."

Denali was seeing two men? Warrick wasn't even surprised. The boy wasn't his type, but he'd be fun in bed for sure. "Good for him."

"You don't think it's weird?"

"Do you?"

Kenn frowned. "Not weird. That sounds judgmental. But...uncommon? I don't know. I don't think I could ever do it, but that doesn't matter, of course. I hope it'll bring him happiness."

They'd ventured into private, sensitive topics, and yet Warrick couldn't make himself change the subject. "You're not jealous?"

Kenn shook his head. "No. I don't want what he has."

He shouldn't ask. He really shouldn't. "What would you want, then?"

Kenn's eyes widened for a moment as if he couldn't believe Warrick had asked. That made two of them. "I-I don't know. Hadn't thought of it."

"Not ready for a relationship yet?" Fuck, he needed to stop prying.

"I'd better come out to my parents first, no?" Kenn froze, and he swallowed. "To my dad, I mean..."

The utter devastation on his face broke Warrick's heart. "Do you want a hug?" he asked before he could warn himself that was an even stupider idea than discussing personal issues with his student.

"Yes..." Kenn's voice was light as a breeze, but it wrapped around Warrick's heart. He got up, and before he'd even taken two steps, Kenn had run into his arms and clung to him with all his might. Rogue let out a confused whine as he jumped up, circling them a few times unevenly, then lay down again.

Warrick held Kenn, prepared to let go as soon as Kenn would give even a hint that he'd had enough, but he didn't. Oh god, the poor kid. Was there no one to hug him and comfort him and tell him everything would be okay?

They stood for maybe a minute, Kenn practically melting against Warrick's chest. A whirlwind of emotions swirled through Warrick, ranging from worry and concern to tenderness and this worrisome need to hold on to Kenn.

"I'm so sorry," he whispered, his cheek resting against Kenn's head. He liked that Kenn fit so perfectly in his arms, though why wasn't a thought he wanted to contemplate.

"Thank you. I'm sorry I'm so clingy and needy."

"You're not, and even if you were, it's fine. I'm happy I can be there for you."

Finally, Kenn let go, and with reluctance, Warrick did the same. "Warrick..." Kenn's blue eyes were big and insecure as he stayed close to Warrick.

"Yeah, b... Kenn?" Damn, that had been a close call. How the fuck had he almost called him *baby*? It had to be because Kenn felt so very young right now, so vulnerable.

"Denali suggested that you could maybe stay here so you wouldn't have the long commute. I know it's a big inconvenience, and there's not a lot to do here in the winter. Plus, the security is really tight, so it's not very relaxing, but... You'd maybe have time to read more and work on your book?"

Warrick latched on to that last part. He needed time to wrap his brain around the enormity of Kenn's request. "How do you know I'm writing a book?"

Kenn's eyebrows drew together. "Was I not supposed to know? I'm sorry."

"No, that's not it." Warrick put a quick hand on his shoulder. Well, the idea had been a quick touch, but when Kenn leaned into it, Warrick kept his hand where it was. "I was surprised you knew because I can't remember telling you."

"You didn't, but whenever you had me working on something, you'd type away on your laptop, and you had Scrivener open, which I looked up, and it's writing software, so... I didn't mean to put you on the spot."

Always so apologetic, as if he felt like he was too much, like an intrusion, an annoyance. "That's a smart deduction on your part. And yes, I'm writing a book. It's in the very first stages, but I love working on it."

"What's it about?"

"Social justice and the armed forces. I hope to narrow it down further once I've done more research."

"I could help you with the research if you wanted?"

So eager to please... It pressed buttons inside Warrick he'd never even known he possessed. "Are you sure it would be okay for me to stay here? Did you talk to your father about it? The Secret Service?"

"Seth said it would be okay after the funeral, so in a couple of days. Does that mean that you'd consider it?"

Warrick could think of a hundred reasons not to do it, most of them of a practical nature with some big boundary issues mixed in, and yet the answer came easy. "If the Secret Service approves it, I'll come stay here."

"You'll do it?" Kenn's eyes grew watery. "Thank you. That means a lot to me. Thank you so much."

Before Warrick knew what was happening, he had a clingy boy in his arms once again, and this time, Kenn broke down. He hid his face against Warrick's shoulder, his arms wrapped tightly around Warrick's waist. Loud sobs racked his body as Warrick cradled him in his arms, and his button-down shirt got rapidly soaked with tears.

"Sshh, it's okay… Let it all out," he whispered. "I know you're hurting. Release the pain, sweetheart… Don't hang on to it. I'm here for you."

He kept murmuring to him, not even sure what he was saying anymore, and Kenn didn't stop crying for a long, long time. When he finally did, he sagged against Warrick, still not letting go. "I'm sorry…"

It came out muffled against Warrick's shirt, and that weird tenderness invaded Warrick again. He kissed the top of Kenn's head. "Don't be. I'm here for you with whatever you need, including a literal shoulder to cry on."

He embraced him until Kenn finally let go, his face all blotchy and red, and all that time, one thought kept repeating in Warrick's head: who the fuck was taking care of Kenn Shafer?

7

It should've rained. Or snowed, maybe. The cloudless skies felt cruel to Kenn as he boarded Air Force One to fly to Boston for his mother's funeral. It didn't make sense for the sun to shine this brightly, for the skies to be this blue and perfect when his mom was gone forever and his heart was so empty and dark. Would he ever feel truly happy again?

At least it was cold. That counted for something, if only because his mom had loved winter. She'd never been a summer person, and she'd been the happiest when surrounded by snow. Boston had, in that sense, suited her to a T. She'd been giddy with every Nor'easter, much to his father's amusement. More than once, they'd gone outside in a snowstorm at his mom's urging to build a snowman.

"Come sit with me, kiddo," Uncle Milan said, and Kenn didn't even hesitate and followed him to a private corner of the plane, where they found seats next to each other.

"Where are Asher and Denali?" Kenn asked, then immediately blushed. Oops. Was he supposed to know about that?

Uncle Milan quirked an eyebrow. "Heard about that, did you?"

"It's the White House. Not a whole lot stays secret there."

Uncle Milan let out a long sigh, rubbing his temples. "Yeah, so I discovered. Don't understand how your dad does it, living in a glass house like this. It would drive me insane."

"Technically, you live there as well."

Uncle Milan snorted. "Thanks for pointing that out. Very comforting. But to answer your question, Asher is working, and Denali..."

"...couldn't come," Kenn finished his sentence. "'Cause why would a junior White House staff member attend the funeral?"

Uncle Milan nodded. "That damn glass house again."

Kenn shivered.

"Cold?"

"I'll warm up once we get in the air."

"Listen to you, all experienced in flying on Air Force One. You're getting spoiled, kid."

"This is only my third flight. And I wouldn't call losing my mom getting spoiled."

Uncle Milan laid his hand on Kenn's thigh. "I didn't mean... Fuck. Sorry. Yeah, that came out all wrong."

He looked distraught, filling Kenn with guilt. "I know you didn't mean it in a bad way, Uncle Milan. I'm just... I'm tired and snappy."

The pilot made the pre-take-off announcement, and Kenn double-checked his seat belt.

"What would you like to drink once we're in the air?" a flight attendant asked. Kenn had learned all flight attendants on board Air Force One were airmen who had applied for that position after first serving somewhere else in the Air

Force. One of them, a staff sergeant, had told Kenn competition was fierce, and he had no trouble imagining why.

"Vodka. Cold, straight up," Uncle Milan said.

He was ordering alcohol? It wasn't even noon yet. "A Coke, please," Kenn requested.

"We're also serving light snacks, so I'll come by with a selection later."

"Coke?" Uncle Milan asked once the server was gone. "I thought you didn't drink caffeine?"

"I don't drink coffee. I like Coke."

"That much caffeine and sugar isn't good for you."

"Says the man who ordered a vodka at eleven in the morning. No offense, Uncle Milan, but you're about the last person to lecture me about anything."

Uncle Milan blinked a few times, then smiled. "Good point. I was trying to..." He waved his hand. "Never mind."

"You were trying to...what, exactly?"

"You're being awfully assertive this morning. I'm strangely proud of you."

See? That reinforced what Kenn already knew, what he'd always known. Both his father and Uncle Milan responded much better to dominance and strength than they did to insecurity and a lack of confidence. With them, he had to be an alpha man if he wanted to make an impression, no matter how unnatural it felt to him. If he wanted them to take him seriously, he'd have to pretend.

"Thank you, but that still doesn't answer my question."

Uncle Milan shifted in his seat, looking vulnerable all of a sudden. "Your mom was like that, making sure you ate healthy and didn't eat or drink too much junk. I just wanted... I don't know. I thought maybe someone should look out for you."

How sad that that pathetic attempt made Kenn's heart beat a little faster and warmth spread inside him. "Thank you, Uncle Milan. That's nice of you."

"Nice..." Uncle Milan harrumphed. "I don't do nice on a good day, let alone a day like this."

How different Uncle Milan was from his sister, Kenn's mom. As soft and kind as she had been, as hard and unyielding Uncle Milan was. And yet underneath, Kenn had always sensed a heart much bigger than Uncle Milan let on. Plus, his brutal honesty was nothing if not amusing.

"H-how are you doing?" Kenn dared to ask.

The plane was taking off, and they were pushed back in their seats for a moment, the engines roaring as the massive Boeing lifted off.

"I don't know how to answer that question, to be honest. I don't have words for how I feel. Numb, empty, black...."

Yeah, that sounded familiar. "And grandma and grandpa?"

His grandparents had arrived in DC two days earlier, and they'd been grieving deeply. They hadn't known about her heart issues, and their daughter's death had come out of nowhere.

Uncle Milan's face softened. "My mom is heartbroken. I don't know if she'll ever get over this. I don't have kids, so I don't know how it feels, but I've been told there's nothing worse than losing a child. It's unnatural, you know? Parents are supposed to go first. That's the natural order of things."

"There's nothing natural about Mom's death," Kenn mumbled.

Uncle Milan took a sharp intake of breath as if he wanted to ask something, but then he blew the air out again, shaking his head at himself. "I'm sorry, kiddo. I keep saying the wrong things. I clearly suck at the whole emotional support thing, so that's the best I've got. If you want more than that, you'll have to go to..."

His uncle winced. Kenn's mom had always been his anchor, even more so since his dad had become vice president and then president. But now she was gone, who could Kenn turn to?

Uncle Milan grunted. "Goddammit. I fucked that up badly."

Kenn wanted to shout, *There's no one else for me. Dad has no time, I don't have friends, and Mom's dead.*

Denali, the one friend he'd made, was more focused on Uncle Milan now, so Kenn had lost his support as well. But he didn't say any of it. Uncle Milan needed people to be there for him as well. He'd lost his sister. Kenn wouldn't make him feel guilty on top of everything else.

But oh, how he wished he had someone who took care of him now. Someone who checked in on him, who made sure he ate his veggies and didn't drink too much soda, who told him to go to bed on time, brush his teeth, and clean his room. At twenty-two, he shouldn't need someone to tell him all that, but he did. Without it, he felt like he was floating aimlessly, drifting without a tether.

When he got off the plane, frigid cold air slapped him in the face, and he shivered. His dad slung his arm over his shoulder, even as the press aimed their photo and video lenses at them to capture every moment. "We'll get through this," his dad said softly.

How? How did he learn to live without his mom? Again, not a question he verbalized.

His father didn't leave his side as they drove to the cemetery, then walked in a solemn procession to where his mom would be laid to rest. In the church—though that seemed too plain a name for the grandeur of National Cathedral—he'd managed to keep his emotions in check, but as his mom's coffin was lowered into the ground, he fought against the tears.

How the hell had this happened? And why? Why would anyone want to kill his wonderful, sweet mom, a woman who had never hurt anyone in her life? It was so unfair, so cruel.

Now he'd have to grow up without his mom. She'd never watch him get his college degree. He'd never be able to tell her he was gay. If and when he found a boyfriend, he'd never be able to introduce him to her...and she'd never be there for his wedding, see the kids he might have, the family he'd build. All that had been taken from her...and from him.

Pain ripped through him, clenching his lungs, clawing at his chest, his throat raw from holding back the tears. And then they spilled over. Once the damn burst, he couldn't hold back the sobs. He stopped caring because his mom was dead, and he should be able to grieve her. His father held him, crying himself, and somehow, that made Kenn feel better. If the president of the United States was allowed to grieve and mourn, surely his son would be as well.

When the priest had said his last prayer and everyone left, he and his father stayed behind. The Secret Service had pulled back to allow them some privacy, and Rhett had stopped taking pictures.

"This is it, kiddo," his father said, his voice breaking. "It's time to say your final good-bye."

Kenn swallowed, staring at the coffin, which was covered by the handfuls of dirt the attendees had thrown as they'd walked by. It was so cold, and now her body would be in that frozen ground forever. Dust to dust, ashes to ashes. What did that even mean?

He put his head on his dad's shoulder. "I know you and Mom were close," his dad said hoarsely. "And I won't even pretend I'll ever be able to fill the role she had in your life. But I swear I'll try to be there for you as much as I can."

"I know, Dad. But you have a responsibility to the country as well."

"You have no idea how much I wish I didn't. I've never hated this job more than I do now, and the temptation to walk away from it all is real."

"You'd do that? For me?"

His father gently released him, then grabbed his cheeks and looked him straight into his eyes. "Kennedy Delano Shafer, nothing and no one is more important to me than you. Nothing. I'd resign in a heartbeat if you needed me to."

His body was freezing, but his insides warmed at those words. "I don't want you to. You can make such a difference in the lives of Americans, especially the LGBTQIA+ community. Warrick said it as well, how much of a trailblazer you are. I don't want you to give that up because god knows what your successor would do. Even more so since we don't have a vice president right now."

"That's the only reason I'm staying, the realization that if I resign now, lives will be lost, and a lot of the progress we've made will be turned back. But remember this, Kenn. If you ever need me to, I will. That's my solemn promise to you."

"Thank you, Dad. That means a lot to me."

"I hope you know how much I love you. No matter what. I always will."

His dad pulled him into another fierce hug, and the tightness in Kenn's throat eased a smidgen. Maybe he'd be okay. Maybe he'd get through this if he took it one day at a time and focused on the good things he still had, like his dad loving him, Uncle Milan being in his life, his lessons with Warrick, and a future where he'd be able to make a difference. Maybe.

8

Warrick had watched the funeral service on TV. He'd barely known the First Lady, and yet he'd found himself close to tears as he listened to the speeches. Kenn hadn't spoken in the church. Warrick had asked him about it a day before the funeral. Kenn had told him his father had given him the choice and that he'd opted not to, too scared he wouldn't be able to keep it together. Plus, he hated public speaking in the first place.

Warrick had been relieved no one had pressured Kenn and that he had instead been allowed to process his pain and grief in his own way rather than having to cater to the wishes of others. Commentators had been mixed in their reactions, some calling it understandable, while others wondered why he wasn't willing to publicly honor his mother.

Fuckers. No one should be forced to mourn in public, let alone someone as sweet and vulnerable as Kenn. The boy had been dealt an unimaginably rough hand, and making him do things he hated while coming to terms with losing his mother would have been cruel. Warrick was glad the president had realized that as well and had supported Kenn's decision not to speak.

He'd just turned off the TV when he received a call that a car would pick him up in an hour to bring him to Camp David. Kenn must've gotten permission from both his father and the Secret Service to have Warrick stay there. Why it made Warrick feel so good that Kenn had gone to such lengths to get Warrick there, he wasn't sure. Was it because Kenn needed him and Warrick hadn't felt this wanted and needed in a long time? Never, perhaps.

And it didn't merely stroke his ego. Of course, knowing that his presence was wanted gave him a thrill, but this feeling settled inside him on a much deeper level, triggering reactions and pressing buttons that were new to him. It felt *right*, somehow. Like he was exactly where he should be, though why he couldn't explain. Maybe he shouldn't try to and just trust his gut.

He was packed in fifteen minutes and waited for the Secret Service car to show up. The weather was gorgeous, the sky a blinding blue. With snow-covered trees dotting the hills, Camp David looked almost like a fairy tale or a movie set, too pretty to be real. Though the heavy presence of Secret Service agents and military personnel made reality sink in fast enough.

The first time he'd arrived at Camp David, he'd been brought directly to Kenn, but this time, he was dropped off and welcomed by a female Secret Service agent who introduced herself as Sam. "I wanted to give you a quick overview of the layout to help you get your bearings."

"Thank you."

She gestured at the building behind her. "This is the Laurel Lodge, which is the main meeting lodge. It has several meeting rooms, and the president and his staff mostly work from here when they're at Camp David. This is also where the meals for the president and his guests are served, since it has the biggest rooms. Half of this building is a secure facility, so you can't bring any electronic equipment in there, including your phone and watch. Since you don't have clearance yet, we kindly ask you not to enter the secure part of the building until you do."

"No problem."

They continued their way on the sprawling grounds while Sam pointed out various buildings and briefed him on the security measures in place. The Aspen Lodge, where the president and Kenn were staying, sat atop a hill and had a perfect view over the surrounding countryside.

"It's beautiful here," Warrick said as he took in the stunning sight.

"It is. That's your cabin, Professor. Your luggage has already been brought in."

His cabin, Witch Hazel, a pale blue building, was the closest to the Aspen Lodge.

"The staff has set up a study for you and Mr. Shafer in the sun-room of the Aspen Lodge. It's a light, sunny room that has a beautiful view."

Light and sunny. He was happy to hear that. It would do Kenn good to be in a positive, light environment.

After double-checking he had all location services turned off on his phone, including *Find my Phone*, Sam made him add some emergency numbers to his phone, then left him on his own to explore his cabin. It held two bedrooms, a living room, a bathroom with a surprisingly roomy and modern shower, and a kitchenette. It was rustic yet lovely, sparse enough to feel like a cabin but still comfortable.

Putting away his clothes in the drawers and his toiletries in the bathroom took all of five minutes. He then walked around the grounds a bit to get his bearings and was about to head inside again—his leg hurt after the long ride—when the whirring of helicopter blades alerted him to the president's arrival. He watched as Marine One landed—a special sight in itself—and the president and Kenn stepped out, followed by Milan Bradbury, Calix Musgrove, and Rhett Foles. Warrick had discovered that the White House photographer was Calix's boyfriend.

Warrick only had eyes for Kenn. His father hugged him tightly, and he got a hand on his shoulder from Calix and a quick ruffle through his hair from Milan, and then they wandered off, leaving him on his own. Warrick's heart went out to the boy, whose shoulders slumped as if they carried the weight of the world.

He walked up to him as fast as his body would allow, ignoring the cramps in his leg. When Warrick was within ten feet of him, Kenn glanced up, his face breaking open in a wide smile that shot straight to Warrick's heart. "You're here!"

Before Warrick knew what was happening, Kenn had jumped in his arms, and he pulled him close, ignoring the widening eyes of the Secret Service agent who was watching them. The boy was in so much pain, so desperate for affection. "Did you get through the day okay?" he asked as Kenn finally let go of him.

"It was so hard..." Kenn whispered. "The service was doable, but the funeral... And if that wasn't bad enough, that horrible news on the way home."

Horrible news? What was he talking about?

"You didn't hear it?" Kenn asked.

"No. The Secret Service told me to turn off my phone. What happened?"

"Someone called into a radio station, claiming that he knew my mom was murdered...and so was Annabeth Markinson."

Warrick's breath hitched. Holy shit. The former First Lady's drowning hadn't been an accident? Had the president known this? "Do they know who the caller is?" As soon as he'd asked the question, he held up his hands. "Never mind. I know you can't tell me."

"Didn't you get security clearance?"

"Not yet. The Secret Service said they're working on it."

"Oh." Kenn looked as if he was warring with himself.

"Don't say anything. It's okay. I don't want you to risk revealing more than you should. Instead, tell me how you're feeling about it."

Kenn's shoulders dropped. "I'm scared... I'm so scared. For my dad, mostly, but also for me. If they could get to my mom and Mrs. Markinson, I'm not safe either."

Neither was anyone around them, including Warrick, but he kept that thought to himself. "That must be a terrifying thought."

Tears shimmered in Kenn's blue eyes. "I don't want to die...and I don't want anything to happen to my dad. I'm already so alone. Without my dad, I'd be..."

Warrick put a hand on his shoulder. "Sshh, try not to think about that. I know it's hard, but it won't help you. Try to concentrate on things that distract you, that still bring you joy."

Kenn leaned into his touch. "I'm so happy you're here."

Those simple words fired Warrick up in a way he'd never experienced before. What did it mean that Kenn would think of him first when he was told to consider things that brought joy? He shouldn't attach too much meaning to it, but his heart was beating faster.

"I'm happy to be here too." He checked his watch. "Have you had something to eat yet? You must be exhausted from everything."

Kenn sent him a watery smile. "I had a few snacks on board Air Force One."

"Right. Of course you did. I bet they were pretty amazing too," Warrick said dryly.

Kenn's smile grew mischievous. "Sometimes they have little boxes of M&Ms with the presidential seal on them."

"Talk about a collector's item. Some day, you'll write your memoirs, and you'll be able to say you had M&Ms on board Air Force One."

"I'd rather write about something I did myself, about an area where I made a difference."

"And you will. I have high hopes for you, Kenn."

"You do?"

Warrick frowned slightly. "Why would you doubt that?"

Kenn lowered his gaze, shuffling his feet. "Most leaders have strong, dominant personalities. They lead others and inspire them. I couldn't even speak at my own mother's funeral service."

The downside of his father being the president: people always compared Kennedy to him. In Kenn's case, that comparison didn't do him any favors as he took much more after his mom, as Warrick had learned. Not that she hadn't been a formidable woman in her own right, but her talents had been more subtle and behind the scenes, as were Kenn's. "That last thing is nonsense, and you know it. You're allowed to grieve your mom in your own way, and not speaking at her funeral doesn't mean you didn't love her or that you're not a leader. You're young, Kenn, and you went through some life-altering events over the last six months, even the few last years. Extend yourself some grace there."

Kenn sighed. "Rationally, I know that, but it's hard not to let all the sharp comments get to me."

Much to Warrick's surprise, he discovered he still had his hand on Kenn's shoulder, so he squeezed it again. "Maybe don't read or listen to those comments, then. Reduce the number of people you allow yourself to be influenced by."

Kenn nodded slowly. "Yeah, I think that'd be smart."

"You know, I'm starving, and I'm sure you can tell me where to get some food. Any good restaurants around here?"

The tension left Kenn's body, and he giggled. "Mrs. Morelli made mac and cheese, my mom's favorite. She said it was fitting. Usually, we eat in the Laurel Lodge, but my dad and the others are all in a meeting because of that radio show leak, so maybe we could eat in the Aspen Lodge?"

"That sounds wonderful. Lead the way."

Kenn's smile stayed as he walked toward the presidential lodge, Warrick on his heels and the Secret Service agent at a respectable distance behind them.

"Where's Rogue?" Warrick asked.

"He couldn't come to the funeral, so he's with Commander Cousineau. She's the camp commander of Camp David, and she's great with him. I'm sure she'll bring him over in a bit now that we're back."

Inside, the Secret Service agent stayed at the entrance. Denali stood waiting for them. He took one look at Kenn, then broke all protocol and hugged him tightly. "I'm so sorry," he whispered. Warmth spread through Warrick seeing someone else express concern for Kenn's well-being.

"Thank you."

Kenn held on a little longer, then let go.

"Can I get you anything to drink and to eat?" Denali asked.

"Could we get mac and cheese?"

"Of course. I already had some, and it's delicious. With a Sprite for you?"

Kenn nodded.

"And for you, Professor?"

"The same but with a seltzer, please. Thank you."

"My pleasure," Denali said, and funnily enough, it sounded like he truly meant it.

Kenn and Warrick sat down in the small dining area of the living room, and mere minutes later, Denali was back with their food and drinks. "Enjoy." Then they were alone again.

The buttery, luscious aroma of the melted cheese wafted into Warrick's nose, his stomach grumbling in response. The first bite had him almost moaning in pleasure as the rounded, rich taste of the mac and cheese exploded in his mouth. No wonder Kenn's mom had loved this. Mrs. Morelli was a goddess in the kitchen.

"How do you like it here?" Warrick wanted to talk about something else than the funeral or any heavy stuff.

"Much better than in the White House. It doesn't feel as much like a museum here. This could be any vacation retreat, you know? Aside from the Secret Service and Marine One and everything else, but it's not as formal and oppressive as the White House."

"Mmm, I can see that. It's much more rustic than I'd imagined. I thought it would be more luxurious."

"Me too, the first time we came here, but it felt wonderfully normal instead."

"How did you feel about your father becoming vice president?"

Kenn let out a sigh, silently chewing his mac and cheese for a moment. "I hated it," he finally said timidly. "I love that he's a trailblazer and has the unique ability to make a change, but I was upset. I loathe being in the spotlight. I detest the attention of the press, all the stories that came out about me... It's been crippling for my self-confidence, and that wasn't too high to begin with."

Warrick could barely refrain from patting Kenn's hand, which lay inches away from his own on the table. "I'm sorry. You didn't choose this, but you still have to deal with the consequences. Was it your choice not to return to Amherst?"

Kenn hesitated. "I think that was a mutual decision. Yes, I wanted to stay there, but at the same time, I didn't feel safe anymore, so when my dad suggested I defer for a year, I took the chance. But I was sad to give up so much of my freedom."

Considering the college campus had been off-limits to the press, Warrick had no trouble understanding how much freer Kenn had felt there. Camp David offered that same sense of distance, since it was closed off to the public and prying eyes of reporters. When did the president intend to return to the White House? That was probably information he shouldn't have, so he didn't ask.

"Let's make the best of the time we get to spend together here," he said warmly, and Kenn's eyes lit up with an inner glow.

"Can we start after dinner? I want something else to focus on."

His eagerness was such a motivator. "Absolutely. Finish your dinner, including the salad, and we can get started."

Frowning, Kenn glanced from the untouched bowl of salad next to his plate to Warrick. "You want me to eat the salad?"

"A sharp mind requires proper nutrition. Junk food doesn't nourish your body, Kenn."

Kenn hesitated for a moment, then picked up his fork. "Okay."

Somehow, Warrick felt like he'd scored a victory. Since when had making Kenn feel better become his goal?

9

"They've scheduled the hearing!"

Calix burst into the president's study in the Laurel Lodge, and Del looked up from his laptop. "When?"

"It starts next Monday. Fucking finally…"

Calix plopped down in the chair next to Del's desk, dragging a tired hand through his hair. What a nightmare this had been. Six months, Del had been president, and all that time, the Republicans had refused to schedule the hearing and subsequent vote on a new vice president.

First, they'd cited that the country needed to recover from the assassination of President Markinson. Then, once the polls had looked favorable to them, they'd waited until after the midterms, and right after those, the holidays had arrived, and Congress had gone into recess. January had come, and still the Speaker of the House and Senator Mackay, the Senate Majority Leader, hadn't been in a hurry to make the hearing happen. Now, a week after Sarah's funeral, they'd finally gotten their ass in gear.

"What did the trick?" Del pushed his laptop back.

Calix winced.

Del let out a soft curse. "You had to drag Sarah into this, didn't you?"

"I had to play hardball and threaten to have Levar make an official statement at a White House press conference that not only were the Republicans dishonoring the memory of President Markinson and Sarah but also endangering the democratic process as outlined in the constitution. I dropped several hints that after three deaths, they might take that line of succession more seriously and not treat it as some kind of joke and power grab. It helped that the press got on their case as well. An op-ed in the Times called it reckless and irresponsible. I don't know which one was the deciding factor, but we're good to go."

"Thank fuck. I desperately need some shit off my plate, and Joanna Riggs is experienced enough to hit the ground running."

Calix nodded. "I called her and let her know. She's already preparing by reading files. Nothing classified yet, though she has clearance for some things from being on the Judicial Committee."

"Good. How do you gauge the vote will go?"

"I wouldn't have pushed so hard if I didn't think they'd approve her. Seriously, they're hard-pressed to find arguments to vote against her. She's a moderate, she's well liked and well respected, and she has a history of bipartisanship."

He wasn't telling Del anything he didn't know already, but it was worth repeating to reassure him.

"Did you take the Democratic leadership's temperature on Lisandra's position?"

The pressure to fire Lisandra James had been strong, but so far, Del had refused. That decision was hard to defend, though, since they couldn't share what they knew about the real problems with the press or even congressional delegates.

"They're on the fence but leaning toward asking you to fire her, if only so you have one less problem you need to devote time and energy to. And they do have a point. You can only fight so many battles at the same time."

The man had too much on his plate, and that while he was still reeling from losing Sarah. Calix couldn't think about Sarah's death too much. If he did, he wouldn't be able to do his job. The only time he allowed himself to feel the depth of that loss was at night, when he crawled into Rhett's arms. He'd cried every single night, but he'd never told Del. His friend didn't need Calix's grief on top of his own...and that of Milan, although Asher and Denali were keeping an eye on him. How typical Milan had ended up in a threesome. The press had better not get wind of it, though. Another reason to be grateful they were secluded here at Camp David.

"How long do you think we can get away with holing up here?" Del asked as if reading Calix's thoughts.

"I don't know, but so far, we're good. Now that the truth about Annabeth Markinson's death has leaked, a speculation storm about Sarah's passing has erupted. The press agrees that, for now, the president should stay safe."

"I like being here. Far less stress."

Calix studied his friend. Fuck, Del looked tired. Years older than two weeks before. How drastically things could change in fourteen days. "And maybe less that reminds you of Sarah?"

Del nodded, his face tight. "Her presence lingers too much in the White House, even though we've only lived there for a few months."

"I can imagine."

"Yeah, you actually can. It's such a cliché phrasing for many people, but you know how this feels."

Calix let out a sigh. "You're part of a club I never wanted you to belong to, Del. How I wish you'd been spared this pain."

"Just..." Del swallowed. "Just tell me it gets better."

"It does, and one day, you'll be able to experience joy again...and love. But it'll take time."

"You didn't think you'd find love again after losing Matthew."

"No, I didn't. I thought that part of my life was over...and then I met Rhett. He brings me such joy, Del, such incredible happiness and love. I never thought I'd feel like this again, to fall in love again, but I did. I love him so much."

Del's eyes were wet. "The kid has hearts in his eyes when he looks at you. He has it bad for you."

Calix slowly shook his head. "It still baffles me. How the hell did that happen? How did someone that sweet and cute fall for a grumpy old man like me?"

Del snorted. "Please don't call yourself old. I'm four months older than you, asshole."

"Sure, but you're much better looking."

"True. Though Milan has us both beat with his two men."

"I don't know how he does it..."

"Oh, I do. Good luck saying no to him when he wants something. Trust me, I've tried..."

"Like when he persuaded you to practice blow jobs on him. Fuck, that was genius on his part."

Del held up his hands. "In my defense, I was single at the time and hadn't met Sarah yet. And second, I really did want to learn so I could blow Fergus McDonald, that Scottish exchange student. Remember him?"

Calix let out a wistful sigh. "Hell, yes. With the stunning ginger hair and the freckles all over his body. And I do mean *all* over."

Del raised an eyebrow. "Do tell, 'cause I never got past first base despite my offer of a blow job."

"Oh, I hit a home run…multiple times. That was one fine *tool* he hid under that kilt. Knew how to use it too. But yeah, he had gorgeous freckles all over his body. In one of my more romantic moments, I promised him I'd count them all, but I don't think that impressed him much. He wanted my ass, not my heart, sadly."

"That explains why he blew me off because I made it clear I was an equal-opportunity player. No one-sided blowing or bottoming for me."

"You should've made an exception for him. I saw stars, my friend. Actual fucking stars."

Del shrugged. "I think I did pretty well…especially when I met Sarah."

Calix grew serious. "She was the best woman I've ever known. You were so lucky to have her love and devotion."

"How long did it take you to start talking about Matthew in the past tense? It's so jarring to hear you speak about Sarah like that. I know she's gone. We laid her to rest a week ago, for fuck's sake, but I can't bring myself to switch to the past tense. It's like once I do that, she'll be really gone, which makes no sense."

Calix leaned forward and put his hand on top of Del's. "You go through this at your own pace."

"I don't know how. Cal, you know me. I always do research. I don't start something unless I know how to do it. But this…there's no manual for this, no how-to. How do I do this? How do I learn to live without Sarah?"

Calix's heart broke for him all over again. He shoved his

chair back. "Come here," he said roughly, then pulled Del into a fierce hug. "There are no guidelines for this. I'm sorry. You'll have to tackle it one day at a time. That's all I have for you. But you will get through this, Del. I promise."

"I miss her so much. It's almost unbearable at night, alone in bed. She's a snuggler, and holding her always makes me feel like home."

The last part came out a sob, and Calix said nothing as he held Del while he cried, his grief tearing through his body. It was about time Del let it out, and as hard as this was for Calix, he wouldn't want it any other way. Del had been there for him when he'd lost Matthew, and now Calix would stand strong for him. He'd be his pillar and hide his own pain from him, just like Del had done at the time, only sharing it with Sarah.

When Del let go, his eyes were red-rimmed. "I don't know if I can do this, if I can be president and a dad and grieve. It's too much."

"We'll take it one step at a time. And if it becomes too much, there are options."

Del swallowed. "You mean resigning."

"Yes."

"No one has ever done that."

"No president has ever had to experience what you have, so there's no precedent for this. You make your own choices, Del. It sounds lofty to put the country first, but at the end of the day, someone else can be president. There's only one of you to be Kenn's dad...and Sarah's widower. Keep that in mind."

Del put a hand on Calix's shoulder. "Thank you for saying that. I told Kenn the same thing after the funeral, but I hadn't brought it up with you or others. I should've known

I'd have your full support. I'm so grateful to have you by my side. You and Milan both."

"If he can stop fucking his men long enough to get something done, yes."

Calix kept his tone light on purpose. Del was teetering on the brink of despair. No need to send him over the edge.

Del raised his chin, determination settling on his face. "Have you seen those men? Dude, if you had to pick between doing something serious and fucking Asher Wylie, I damn well know which one you'd pick. That man is..."

"...a god, is what he is. Then again, so are Seth and Coulson. And let's face it, Levar and Henley aren't bad looking either, and Denali is cute as a button and damn sexy with that bubble butt of his. I mean, not as cute as Rhett, obviously, but don't tell me you haven't noticed that."

"I'm married, not blind. Or at least..."

"You're still married as long as you want. I didn't let go of Matthew until I was ready to, and that was when Rhett and I were getting serious. All that time, I considered myself a married man."

Del nodded, then bent in and kissed Calix on his cheek. "Thank you. For everything."

"Always and anytime. It's an honor to be by your side, Del."

10

A watery sun did its best to heat up the room after the snowfall the day before. Rogue had loved playing in the snow earlier that morning when Kenn had taken him for a walk, and now he was snoring at Kenn's feet as Warrick was teaching him. Warrick had been at Camp David for over two weeks now, and Kenn loved having him.

Warrick's teaching style was so engaging, a mix of telling stories, sharing knowledge, asking hundreds of questions, and constantly challenging Kenn to support his statements with facts and evidence. Kenn could already tell it was training him in building better arguments. He almost automatically checked the validity of his evidence before speaking up.

But aside from learning from him, Kenn also loved hanging out with Warrick. They spent pretty much every day together, including lunch, then joined the others for dinner in the Laurel Lodge. The discussions were usually lively, and Kenn had even participated a few times, feeling more confident after sparring with Warrick every day. When his father had asked him how he felt about Senator Riggs being confirmed as vice president, he'd been able to talk about the Twenty-fifth Amendment in a way that had made his father's eyes light up with pride.

As much as Kenn worried about more attacks and the reason they were at Camp David, he loved the routine Warrick and he had built. And every day confirmed that he delighted in learning about the law. Today, they were discussing the history of the Supreme Court and the role it had played in some of the most groundbreaking changes in the history of the US, like Roe v Wade and Brown v Board of Education.

"What do you think the effect would be if the number of Supreme Court justices would be increased?" Warrick asked, interrupting Kenn in his thoughts.

Kenn chewed on his pencil, frowning. "The weight of the individual votes of the current Supreme Court justices would become less, which may not be good for their ego, but—"

BOOM!

The air was sucked from Kenn's lungs as the whole lodge shook, glass from shattering windows raining down on the ground. Rogue burst out in frantic barking and high-pitched whining. Before Kenn's brain had even processed what was happening, Warrick was out of his chair, yanked Kenn down by his wrist, and pulled him under the dining table they'd been sitting at. Warrick folded himself over his body protectively, and Kenn felt safe despite the explosion that had just rocked through the building.

"Rogue!" Kenn shouted, and the dog bounded toward him, seeking a spot against Kenn's body. He held on to him as Warrick shielded them both.

"What happened?" Kenn's ears were still ringing, so for all he knew, he'd been shouting, but whatever.

"I don't know, but we're staying here," Warrick said, his mouth close to Kenn's ear.

The door banged against the wall, and footsteps hurried into the room. Kenn caught a glimpse of the person from under Warrick's arm, which held him down like a steel bar. Legs in a suit, but with the sensible shoes Secret Service agents wore. Then the man's face appeared as he peeked under the table. Yup, Kenn had been correct. Joe, a Secret Service agent.

"I have Honor and Law," Joe said in his com, relief painted on his face. "Stay there for now," he told them, and Kenn breathed out a slow breath as the ringing in his ears subsided. What had that explosion been? What had happened? A bomb? Another terrorist attack? But how the hell had they gotten into Camp David?

Oh, god. A terrorist attack. He pushed Warrick's arm down. "Is my dad okay?" he called out to Joe. He'd straightened but hadn't moved out of Kenn's line of sight.

"Yeah, we have him and your uncle as well. Everyone is accounted for."

Oh, thank god. The tension in his body eased a little, but then he became aware of Warrick still hovering over him. Because Camp David was such a secure location, his agents weren't with Kenn in the room at all times. When Warrick was tutoring him, they stood outside the room. But Warrick had reacted before anyone else, pulling him to safety and protecting him with his own body. And even now, when the immediate danger seemed to have passed, he was still shielding him.

Warrick's hot breath heated Kenn's neck, and the rise and fall of Warrick's chest pressed against his back. The subtle cologne Warrick wore tickled his nose in a tantalizing way, an olfactory reminder of his masculine presence. But the best feeling was the sanctuary of his arms, which still held him tight, like a cocoon of safety.

Never before had Kenn been this close to the body of a man who wasn't related to him. And Warrick wasn't a boy or someone Kenn's own age. He was a *man*. A man who had graduated from the toughest military institute in the country, who had gone to war and had paid the price. A man who was out as gay and proud of it. Pretty much a hero in Kenn's eyes, and the way he'd reacted to this incident cemented that.

"It's an explosion near the kitchen," Joe said, apparently getting updates through his com. "We're evacuating as soon as we feel it's safe."

"Where's my dad?" Kenn asked. Even though he'd asked before, but he needed to know his dad was truly safe. Even the thought of something happening to him made breathing impossible.

"He's okay, I promise." Joe's voice was kind. "He's in the bunker."

Underneath the Laurel Lodge was a nuclear bunker, which Kenn had once thought a relic from a time when those safety measures had been deemed necessary. Now, he wouldn't object to his dad working from that bunker all day, every day. Everything to keep him safe.

Kenn relaxed again, keenly aware of the male body pressed against his own. He'd always imagined how it would feel to be held by a man, by his…his lover, his boyfriend. Warrick wasn't either of those, and yet his strong presence made his body respond and awoke feelings inside Kenn. Feelings he'd never experienced before. What a strange moment to think about that.

"We've got the all clear." Joe ducked his head under the table. "Come on out, but stay on the right side and mind the glass."

As soon as Warrick released him, Kenn shivered at the sense of loss. Or maybe it was the lack of warmth. He let go of Rogue and gently pushed him toward the side where the floor wasn't littered with glass. Once Rogue was safe, Kenn crawled from under the table and stood. The explosion had blown out two of the windows, the glass covering the floor, chairs, and table on that side.

"For now, we'll escort you to the Laurel Lodge. Your father wants to see you," Joe said to Kenn.

Behind him, Warrick softly groaned, and Kenn spun around. Warrick was still on the floor, his face distorted in pain as he tried to push himself up. Had he hurt himself when he'd thrown them down under the table? Kenn didn't want to embarrass Warrick by asking him in front of Joe.

Instead, Kenn held out his hand, and Warrick accepted it instantly. Carefully Kenn pulled him up, firmly planting his feet and offering enough counterweight to make it smooth.

"Thank you," Warrick said when he stood upright again, his eyes radiating his gratitude.

Joe was clearly in a hurry as he ushered them out of the room, but Kenn didn't let him rush them. Warrick walked with more difficulty than usual, his posture stiff and his gait unsteady. Kenn didn't ask if he was okay. The answer would obviously be a resounding no. Instead, Kenn adapted his pace to Warrick's, Rogue right by their side, and once Joe caught on, he slowed down considerably.

When they entered the Laurel Lodge, Kenn's father waited for them in the hallway and enveloped Kenn in another bear-crushing hug. "Goddammit, that scared the bejesus out of me."

"Me too, Dad. What happened?"

After a last squeeze, his father released him. "A propane tank exploded, but we don't know the cause yet. The Secret Service will investigate it."

Then he turned to Warrick. "My apologies for the shock, Professor. I hope it didn't trigger bad memories."

Bad memories? Oh, the IED. How attentive of his father to think of that. It hadn't even occurred to Kenn, probably because he wasn't familiar with triggers like that. His father would know, having served himself.

"No worries, Mr. President. I'm fine." Warrick's voice was friendly enough, but Kenn still noticed how tight it sounded.

After a moment's hesitation, he stepped close to Warrick. "You should have Dr. Brophy check you out."

He'd kept his voice so soft only Warrick and his dad had heard it, and his dad immediately drew closer. "Did you get hurt?" he asked Warrick, concern lacing his voice.

"He pulled me under the table to shield me, Dad," Kenn said. "But it was quite a sudden move, and he took the brunt of the impact."

"I'm okay," Warrick said, his face tight. "It'll pass."

He wasn't denying he was in pain.

"Please, Professor, allow Dr. Brophy to make sure you're okay. I owe you at least that much." When his father used that tone, no one had ever been able to say no, and Warrick was no exception.

"Thank you, Mr. President. I'd appreciate that. But I can wait until others have been taken care of."

But Kenn's dad signaled Joe, who spoke in his com and informed Dr. Brophy Warrick would be coming to the medical unit. "I'll take you, Professor," Joe said, and after shooting Kenn a look he couldn't decipher, Warrick followed the Secret Service agent out of the room.

"He pulled you under the table?" his dad asked.

Kenn nodded. "Before Joe had even opened the door, Warrick had dragged me under the table we'd been working on and threw his body over mine."

His father looked a tad smug. "I picked the right man for the job."

"I thought his job was to make me smart, not to protect me. Isn't that what the Secret Service is for?" Kenn teased.

"Psh, no one needs to make you smart. You already are. And with the way things are going..." His father's face lost the humorous expression. "I'll take all the help I can get to keep you safe."

"Mr. President," Seth said, and they both turned toward him. "We've confirmed that a propane tank in the kitchen exploded. Manuel, one of the sous-chefs, is being airlifted to the hospital with second-degree burn wounds. Denali had some scrapes and a sprained wrist from getting knocked off his feet by the blast, but that's it."

"What's the structural damage?"

"The outside wall of the kitchen has a big hole in it, and the blast knocked out several windows, including those in the sun-room and one in Kenn's room. Maintenance is fixing them, but they're not standard-size windows, so they'll have to special-order them. For now, they're boarding them up, but, Kenn, you won't be able to sleep in your room tonight."

Kenn frowned. "Where will I sleep, then? And Rogue too because he stays with me."

"You can share my room," his dad said. "Or we can drag your bed into my study."

The Aspen Lodge technically had three bedrooms, but

his father had turned one into a study, since so many people were using the president's study in the Laurel Lodge as their office. But sharing a room with his dad? He wouldn't sleep at all. The man never slept for more than a few hours because of the demands of his job, and when he did, he snored.

"No offense, Dad, but I can't run on three hours of sleep like you."

His father sighed. "Good point. And if the windows have to be ordered, it could take a few days. What about another cabin, Seth?"

"We're full, Mr. President. We already have staff sharing rooms and cabins, and there's nothing free anymore."

An idea popped into Kenn's head. He couldn't ask him, since Warrick was with Dr. Brophy, but surely, he wouldn't mind under these circumstances. Especially after what had happened. Besides, there wasn't another reasonable and practical solution.

"Professor Duvall has a room free in his cabin. I could stay there until my room has been repaired. He's already used to having Rogue around, and both rooms have individual bathrooms."

His father's eyes lit up. "That'll work. What do you think, Seth?"

Kenn didn't like the look in the man's eyes at all.

Seth took a deep breath. "Mr. President, while it seems the explosion was an accident, we'd feel better if all nonessential White House staff went home temporarily to give us the time and opportunity to investigate this."

"I don't understand. All nonessential personnel is already at the White House. We brought only a skeleton crew here," his father said.

"He means Professor Duvall." Kenn struggled to hold back his bitterness.

"Kenn, I know it means a lot to you to have him here, but he's not essential," Seth said in that horribly reasonable tone.

"Not to you, he's not. He is to me."

"If Seth thinks it's better Professor Duvall goes home for a few days until this has all been sorted out, I think that—"

"No. He's not leaving," Kenn interrupted his dad. "I don't care what you say. He's not going home. I need him."

"Kennedy Shafer, I won't tolerate that tone. You'd better watch your—"

"I don't care." Kenn pushed past the lump in his throat, the tremor in his voice. "I don't care if you think I'm rude or disrespectful. I need you to listen to me, Dad. He's the only one who has time for me. While all of you are working all day, every day, doing god knows what, he's here for me. He's here for breakfast and lunch and every hour in between when you're up to your eyeballs in work. I get that you're busy, I do. But you can't take the one person away from me who's actually helping me not think about Mom every second, who's distracting me and being my friend... You can't, and if you do, I'll never forgive you!"

11

Dr. Brophy was kind and courteous as he examined Warrick. "It looks like you aggravated your injuries. Without further scans, it's hard for me to be one hundred percent sure, but I don't think you sustained any new injuries, merely exacerbated your existing ones."

Warrick let out a slow breath of relief. "Thank you. I was hoping that was the case."

"I can prescribe you some painkillers and muscle relaxants."

"No, but thank you. I'm reluctant to take pain meds. Too easy to get used to them."

"Do you have a history of addiction?"

"No, but it would be easy to become dependent on them, considering the chronic pain I'm dealing with."

"I understand, Professor Duvall, but I wouldn't prescribe them for more than, say, three or four days. And what with you staying here, I don't see how you would even have access to more, if you don't mind me being blunt. They would help you recover much quicker from this setback."

Warrick hesitated. He'd taken pain meds, of course, in the first weeks and even months after his injuries. He'd hated how they'd made him feel, so hazy and doped up, like he wasn't in control of himself. But Dr. Brophy did make a valid argument that if Warrick didn't use them, it might take him much longer to recover, and that didn't help anyone either, least of all himself. And Kenn. If the pain kept bothering him, he wouldn't be able to be with Kenn. To teach him.

"For three days, then. Thank you."

"Take the first dose now, another one tonight, and then three times a day for the next three days. That's it. You'll know if you don't need them anymore. If you do, we can reevaluate."

Warrick sighed, then took the meds the doctor offered him. After providing Dr. Brophy with the contact information for his personal physician so he could inform her about the diagnosis and what he'd prescribed for Warrick, Warrick slowly made his way back to the Laurel Lodge. Seth stood waiting for him at the entrance with an expression on his face Warrick couldn't interpret.

"Do you have a moment for me, Professor?" Seth asked.

"Sure, provided we can sit down somewhere. Also, I have to warn you that I took opioids, so I might appear a tad dazed in a few minutes. And please call me Warrick. We've spent enough time with each other now that those formalities feel forced."

Seth smiled at him, shaking his head. "It's not easy doing my job under these circumstances. Secret Service protocol requires me to formally address everyone, but you all keep insisting on me being informal. One of these days, I'm going to mess up in front of the wrong person."

"I can imagine, but these aren't exactly normal circumstances."

Warrick followed Seth into the Laurel Lodge, where the agent led him into a small room, then closed the door behind them. Uh-oh. Was something wrong? Warrick carefully lowered himself in a chair, folded his hands in his lap, and waited.

"As far as we know, the explosion in the kitchen was an accident, but the Secret Service will still do a thorough investigation. Pending that investigation, we feel it's better to temporarily send you home rather than have you stay here."

Warrick's heart skipped a beat. "Why? I hope you don't even consider it a possibility that I was somehow involved with it."

"No, not at all, but the more people we have to keep an eye on here, the harder it is to do our job. We wanted to eliminate as many distractions as possible, so to speak, so we've asked all nonessential personnel to leave for now. I'm sure you understand."

Warrick sat up a little straighter, ignoring the stabbing pain in his back. Those drugs had better work fast. "Actually, I don't. I may not be essential in your eyes, but Kenn needs me. You don't understand how much he's struggling and how much he values the time we spend together. He needs this distraction, and with all due respect, it's not like anyone else has time for him. The president is in an incredibly tough spot, having to choose between running the country and being there for his grieving son, but Kenn needs someone, and if it can't be his father, then someone else will have to do it. Don't take that away from him."

Seth studied him for a long time, his face expressionless. "Interesting," he finally said. "Kenn made almost the exact same argument, though his was a little more emotional."

"He did?" Warmth spread through Warrick. He'd done the right thing, then, advocating for Kenn. It made him feel proud that he'd gauged the importance of their relationship correctly.

"I believe his exact words were that if his dad took away the one person who was actually helping him and being his friend, he'd never forgive him."

Hearing that shouldn't make Warrick feel as good as it did. It sounded almost childish, that threat, even more so when considering it was aimed at the president of the United States. And yet a deep satisfaction settled inside Warrick at the knowledge that Kenn needed him. He stayed quiet, curious where Seth was going with this.

"Can you explain to me why Kenn feels so strongly about your presence?" Seth asked.

His tone held an edge, something Warrick couldn't quite place. "I'm not sure what you're referring to."

"I'm simply asking you why you think Kenn feels so strongly about your presence."

"Let me repeat my earlier statement. Kenn needs a distraction, and I'm the only one who has time for him."

"Are you certain that's the only reason?"

Warrick met Seth's inquisitive blue eyes straight on. "What are you hinting at, Agent Rodecker?"

"I see we're getting formal again?"

"Considering your tone and line of questioning, you leave me with little choice. This doesn't sound like a friendly, neutral conversation but like the beginning of an interrogation, and as you might understand, that makes me a little hesitant to continue in an informal way."

They were dancing around the subject, and Warrick still wasn't sure what Seth was trying to say. What was his problem?

Care 87

"As a Secret Service agent, I'm primarily responsible for keeping my protectee safe. Despite the complicated circumstances, Kenn is still my protectee and thus my first priority."

"Yes, so? I'm still not sure where you're going with this."

"Legally, Kenn is an adult, and if he were to choose to engage in certain...*adult* activities, I wouldn't feel obligated, legally or morally, to report those to anyone, including his father, but I would want to know. I'd still look out for his best interests."

Adult activities? The man made it sound like Kenn was performing in some kind of porn movie. Then it hit. "You're suspecting me of *sleeping* with Kenn?"

Seth crossed his arms. "The thought had come to mind."

"Are you fucking insane? He's my student. What's more, the president of the United States entrusted me with tutoring Kenn. I'd never in a million years dishonor that trust by developing an inappropriate relationship with him, and I honestly don't understand where you could get the idea something like that was going on." A horrifying thought occurred to him. "Please don't tell me you think my university fired me for inappropriate contact with a student."

Seth's eyes softened, and his expression changed. "No. First of all, I'm a better judge of character than that, and second, trust me when I say the FBI did a thorough background investigation into the circumstances of the abrupt ending of your contract. I apologize for the suggestion, but, Warrick, are you aware of how attached he is to you? The way he defended your presence here, the passionate outburst, and even the suggestion of you going home... He cares deeply for you."

Seth's suggestion implied he was aware of Kenn's sexual identity or that at least Kenn not being straight was an option to him. Did that mean the president knew as well? Something Warrick would need to think about more.

"What are you saying, Seth? Please let's cut out all the polite beating around the bush. Give it to me straight."

Seth took a deep breath as he straightened his shoulders. "I'm worried Kenn is developing a crush on you. A serious one. I'm not saying you're encouraging it or that you would be interested in him that way, but I'm not certain you realize how deep his feelings run. I know him, Warrick, and I'm concerned. And so is the president."

Warrick almost choked on his own breath. Kenn was *crushing* on him? The thought was equally shocking and exhilarating, with a solid dose of genuine surprise mixed in. Stupid, because now that Seth had mentioned it, Warrick was seeing some of Kenn's actions and words in a different light. But that wasn't his biggest concern. "The president agrees with you?"

"No, not like that. Kenn is his son, and I'm not sure that despite the president's openness to things like this, he's completely ready to see Kenn as an adult yet. Maybe also because in some ways, Kenn is still quite...innocent. No, the president was shocked by Kenn's outburst and is now concerned for his emotional stability. He's so vulnerable, so fragile. I don't want to see him get hurt."

At least Seth's words made it clear he genuinely cared for Kenn. "Trust me, neither do I. But, Seth, you have to believe me when I say that sending me home will hurt him. I don't know if you're right. All I can say is that the thought hadn't occurred to me, and I certainly never discussed it with Kenn. I'm grateful you told me so I can keep this in mind in my interactions with him, but please don't make me leave. It'll crush him. Whether he has developed feelings for me or not, he does need me. I'm the only one who's there for him, and if you take that away... I don't know how he'll be able to cope with everything."

Seth cocked his head, studying him for a few beats. "I see your point. But please, please... Tread carefully. Don't break his heart."

Warrick slowly made his way to his cabin, Seth's words tumbling through his head. Kenn was crushing on him? The thought was confusing but thrilling at the same time, which was ridiculous. He shouldn't be flattered that a student liked him that way, even more so considering the fourteen-year age gap between them. Fourteen years and a world of experience, what with Kenn being so innocent.

Warrick would bet all his money on the boy being a virgin. A gorgeous, innocent virgin, about to take his first steps to exploring his sexual side. That in itself was a thought Warrick shouldn't ponder too much. He'd tried hard to keep seeing Kenn as his student, as a boy, but the truth was that for all his naïveté, he was an adult. A guy who was past the age where it would be normal for him to have sex, a relationship, hookups, and quick blow jobs in the bathroom of some club, just like Warrick had done when he'd first come out. A cute, adorable guy whose vulnerability made Warrick want to gather him close and protect him from all the vultures that would like to corrupt him.

Was Seth right, though? Had Kenn's undeniable affection for Warrick grown into something more? If so, that couldn't happen. As much as Warrick liked it, he needed to nip it in the bud. His career wouldn't survive a second scandal, and he couldn't afford to get fired because the president caught wind of it. No, he'd have to distance himself from Kenn. He'd be there for him and teach him, but he had to subtly discourage anything more.

But even though he knew this was the right decision, his

chest tightened at the thought of spending less time with Kenn. He slumped down on the couch in his cabin. It appeared he needed that distance as well before he himself got too attached.

12

Leaving Camp David felt strange after spending the last few weeks there. Milan stared out the window as Seth drove them toward the hospital where they would meet with Manuel, the sous-chef who had gotten wounded in the explosion, to ask him a few questions. Seth had asked Milan if he'd be willing to help him with the investigation, and he'd immediately said yes.

Technically, the bigger investigation into the bombing, the assassination, and Sarah's murder should keep him occupied, but he relished the opportunity to focus on something a little more short term and practical. Besides, his sweet baby boy had gotten hurt in the explosion, even if only a little, and he wanted to make sure it had indeed been an accident.

"Is Denali okay?" Seth asked as if he'd been able to read Milan's mind.

"Yeah, he had some scrapes and bruises. I think I was more shaken up than he was."

Seth shot him a sideways glance. "Yeah, I vaguely

remember something about you being worried about him," he teased.

Milan rolled his eyes, even though Seth couldn't see it. "Yeah, whatever. Apparently, I needed that to realize how much he meant to me. He and Asher both."

"So you guys are now together? Like, officially?"

Milan snorted. "Officially? What, like I'm going to take out a half-page ad in the Washington Post to announce the president's brother-in-law is in a gay threesome? I'm sure that would go over well and not get Del into trouble at all."

Seth grunted. "You guys are killing me with the extreme informality. You do remember he's Mr. President to me, right?"

"Good luck with that. The chances of me calling him Mr. President in this kind of company are zero. He's lucky if I even remember it in a more official situation. He sucked my dick, you know? Kinda hard to call him Mr. President after that."

"Oh, for fuck's sake. Did you have to tell me that? I could've lived a happy and fulfilling life without ever knowing that."

Milan grinned. "You're welcome. Admit it. You totally had a visual just now."

"Like I'd be stupid enough to confirm or deny that. My dad didn't raise me a fool, you know? Anyway, back to the topic at hand. All joking aside, I'm happy to see the three of you have found your way to each other. You're a good fit."

"You think so?"

"You still have doubts?"

"Considering this is the first actual relationship I've been in, yeah, I still have a lot of doubts. Not so much about what I feel for them. I've never experienced anything like this, so it's safe to assume that for the first time in my life, I've actually fallen in love. And because I'm me and I've never been able to do anything the normal and easy way, I had to do it with two men at the same time."

"Then what do you have doubts about?"

Funny, Seth had the same casual style of asking questions as Asher did. Without realizing it, Milan revealed much more than he'd intended to. But they asked it so smoothly that he automatically answered. "I'm still not sure whether I'm truly relationship material. I'm not a nice or kind man, as we both know. I'm trying to change, but all I can do is hope that'll be enough."

"Asher has been in love with you since forever, and sweet Denali has those little hearts in his eyes whenever he looks at you. I think you'll be fine..."

He could deny it all he wanted, but hearing those words from Seth, who Milan truly respected for his sharp mind and insight into people, did mean a lot. Not that he'd admit that to him. He was changing, but that didn't mean he was turning into some emotional sap. "What about you and your man? Has he had his fist up your ass yet?"

Seth all but choked on a breath. "You need to work on your segues, dude. At least give a man a warning when he's driving."

Milan shrugged. "You know me. I'm not one for small talk and pleasantries."

"Doesn't mean you can't ease into it like normal people. But to answer your question, Coulson and I are good. I'm beyond grateful he's staying here as well so that we get to spend as much time with each other as possible. He's under an incredible amount of pressure from the FBI director, and I'm glad I can be there for him. And no, we haven't gotten to that stage yet."

Milan studied the Secret Service agent. The dark circles

under his eyes were a sure sign of lack of sleep. Seth might say Coulson was under a lot of stress, but so was he. "I hope you've been honest with him about how much that means to you, how important it is to you."

Seth was quiet for a long time. "I don't know how to bring it up with him. He knows it's something I used to do, something I love, but I'm not sure he understands how big of a stress reliever it is for me. And with everything he has on his plate right now, I don't feel comfortable telling him because he'll feel pressured to do it, even when he's maybe not ready for it."

"I get that, but by not telling him, you're also robbing him of an experience that could make him feel even closer to you. You know how much trust fisting requires and what a special bond you can develop with someone who can give you that experience. It could bring a new level of intimacy."

Seth chuckled. "I guess you're serious about trying to be nicer to people, huh? Good job being understanding and not being a sarcastic asshole."

Milan didn't take offense at all. "I know, right? I'm reaching whole new heights of emotional maturity here."

Seth pulled into the parking lot of the hospital, and they didn't talk until he'd found a spot and they got out of the car. "What role do you want me to take?" Milan asked.

"Why don't you lead the questioning so I can observe? I genuinely don't think anything suspicious happened, but we have to make sure."

They found Manuel in the burn unit, where he was awake and waiting for them. His chest was wrapped in bandages, as were both his arms and the right side of his face. His facial hair had all been seared off, and his dark hair had been shaved. He looked awful and in pain, but he was alive, and considering how close he had been to the tank when it exploded, that was a miracle in itself.

"Thank you for agreeing to speak with us," Milan said after they had inquired about his well-being. They'd found seats next to his bed on the same side so Manuel wouldn't have to turn his head. "We have a few questions to make sure what happened. What can you tell us?"

He loved starting interrogations with broad questions like that. Those who wanted to talk often revealed a lot more than they were aware of, and for those who were suspicious or reluctant, it immediately set the tone so Milan knew what to expect.

"It was my fault, but I swear it was an accident. The president wanted steaks three days ago, so I'd connected the tank to the barbecue outside. Protocol says I have to store it in the maintenance shed when it's not hooked up, but it started snowing, and the grounds were getting slippery. So I brought it with me back into the kitchen, thinking I'd drop it off at the shed the next day. And then I forgot."

By the time he was done, he was panting, and Milan waited patiently to allow him to catch his breath. Manuel had been apologetic, full of guilt and remorse, and as of now, Milan had no reason to suspect he was lying. "That explains why the tank was in the kitchen, but why did it explode?"

Manuel swallowed, looking away for a moment. "I can't believe I forgot. In my hurry to bring it inside before the snow hit, I plain forgot."

"Forgot what?"

"I'd mentioned to Mr. Funnell that the tank needed to be replaced. I noticed it was running out of gas faster than it should, indicating there might be a leak. I thought the hose had a leak, but maybe it was the valve. Or maybe I didn't close it properly after disconnecting it from the barbecue. I-I don't know. I was in a hurry. We're understaffed, and we still want to take care of the president and guests the best way we can. You have no idea how awful I feel. I'm so, so sorry... Please convey my deepest apologies to the president. I feel like I let him and everyone else down."

Seth put his hand briefly on Manuel's hand, which looked like it had escaped any burn damage. "Mistakes happen. Let it be a consolation that you were the only one who got hurt. No one else got injured except for a few minor scrapes."

Seth sent Milan a hard look as if challenging him to bring up Denali's injuries. He wouldn't. Seth was right. Those injuries were minimal. In that sense, they'd gotten lucky. If more people had been in the kitchen, like Mrs. Morelli, things could've ended differently.

Milan asked Manuel a few more questions, but his answers were consistent with his story, and after about fifteen minutes, Manuel's eyes started to droop, and they left. "What are your thoughts?" Milan asked Seth as they got back into the car.

"We'll still have to talk to Mrs. Morelli and probably to Denali, considering how close he was to the explosion, but so far, I haven't heard anything that makes me question whether this was an accident."

"I agree. Manuel had a clear explanation without any contradictions."

"Let me put in a call to Mr. Funnell to double-check what Manuel said about suspecting the tank needed to be replaced." Seth already hit a speed dial button on his phone. "Mr. Funnell, good morning. This is Seth Rodecker. I have a quick question for you. Do you remember a complaint being brought to your attention about a propane gas tank?"

Seth's phone had connected to the car speakers, so Milan could listen in to the call.

"Yes, yes. Manuel told me he suspected a leak, since according to him, the tank ran empty much faster than it should have."

"Did you ever get that fixed?"

"No, I deeply regret to say that I didn't. It wasn't a priority, since we weren't expecting the first family to spend much time at Camp David over the winter, let alone use the barbecue. We haven't had a president who didn't mind the cold weather for a while. And with everything else that happened, it didn't seem urgent. Of course, in hindsight, I should have. But that's water under the bridge now."

"I understand. Thank you for your time, Mr. Funnell." Seth ended the call. "As far as I'm concerned, we have no reason to suspect foul play. We'll still have the scene investigated by our forensics units, assisted by the FBI, but I don't think anything will come of it."

That, at least, was one headache less, but that still left plenty going around.

13

Something was wrong. Kenn couldn't put his finger on it, but something had changed since the explosion. Warrick was different. Not so much when he was teaching, when his passion and enthusiasm shone as brightly as they had before. They were still studying the influence of the Supreme Court throughout history, and Kenn hung on his every word. That wasn't the problem.

Outside of their lessons, that was when Kenn felt a marked difference compared to before. First, his proposal to temporarily share Warrick's cabin had been shut down. Warrick's excuse had been that he needed his rest after exacerbating his injuries. Kenn hadn't been sure how his presence would make that worse or better, but he'd accepted the inevitable and had shared a room with his father for one night. The day after, maintenance had managed to fix the window in his room, and he'd been able to return to his own bedroom that night. Yes, that hadn't been what he'd hoped for but considering everything else only a minor setback.

No, Warrick's attitude was the issue, the way he treated

Kenn, even how he looked at him and talked to him. He wasn't rude or unfriendly, but he'd erected an invisible wall that kept Kenn at a distance. Gone was his warm, friendly demeanor, which had been so comforting to Kenn. He hadn't touched or hugged him since the explosion, and that had been...disappointing. Hurtful.

Maybe Warrick was in pain? That wouldn't explain his changed attitude, though, unless being under the influence of pain killers and muscle relaxants can change one's personality. Maybe it did. What would Kenn know? He'd never taken anything stronger than ibuprofen. If that were the case, things should improve rapidly as this was the last day Warrick would be taking them, as far as Kenn knew.

"We're done for now. Why don't we meet here again at two?" Warrick shoved his chair back.

"You're not coming to lunch with me?" Kenn asked, unable to keep the disappointment out of his voice.

Warrick didn't look at him as he pushed himself up. "No, I've requested lunch to go so I can take a walk. Dr. Brophy said it's important to keep my muscles moving."

"I could come with you." Kenn hated how insecure he sounded, how needy. Almost begging. "I could join you on your walk..."

"That's sweet of you, but I need to clear my head for a bit. I'll see you at two, okay?"

Before Kenn could say anything else, Warrick had walked out, leaving Kenn sitting at the table. Dejected, he got up as well. Rogue blinked a few times, awakening from his slumber, then scrambled up and hobbled over to Kenn.

"At least I have you," Kenn whispered, tears burning in his eyes. Why was he so stupidly emotional over this? Warrick wasn't required to spend his lunchtime with Kenn.

In fact, Kenn wasn't sure for how many hours the man got paid, but he had to have spent quite a few of his personal hours with Kenn. He could hardly complain, then, that Warrick was finally choosing to have some time for himself. And yet...

His feet felt like lead as he made his way to the Laurel Lodge, where he picked up a club sandwich, then trudged back to his room. Where else would he eat? Everybody else was busy. As always. But when he'd almost reached his room, he ran into Denali.

"Hey, Kenn! Are you having lunch in your room? By yourself?"

He wouldn't play the sad card. "It's okay. Professor Duvall went for a walk, and everyone else is always busy around lunchtime."

Denali stared at him for a few beats. "I'll come hang out with you if you want."

"Are you sure you have time?"

"Let me just tell Mr. Funnell I'm taking a break. It shouldn't be an issue, since I already brought lunch over to the Laurel Lodge."

Denali got on his walkie-talkie as Kenn made his way into his bedroom, Rogue on his heels, and within thirty seconds, Denali had arranged to take a lunch break. "I'm happy to share my sandwich with you. It's too big for me anyway," Kenn said.

"Sure, I'll take half."

Kenn was glad he'd made at least a bit of an effort to keep his room tidy after Denali had cleaned it. He'd dropped some clothes on the chair, but not so much he couldn't easily lift them off and offer Denali a place to sit. Kenn settled on his bed, and Rogue lay down next to him, begging him silently with his big brown eyes to share some of the delicious turkey with him. How could he say no to that?

"How have you been?" he asked Denali. "I heard Uncle Milan was worried about you after the explosion."

Denali chuckled, but his eyes shone. "He was. He told Asher and me after that he was in love with us."

Kenn almost choked on the food in his mouth. "He told you he loved you?"

Denali nodded. "He did. We're officially together, though for obvious reasons, we're not going public with it. But your father knows, and now you know, and I guess everybody who matters to us is aware, and that's it."

Wow. Kenn would never have guessed in a million years that his hard-core bachelor uncle would ever capitulate to love. "I'm so happy for you."

"Even if it's not the kind of relationship you'd want?"

Kenn looked away. "I don't know what I want anymore," he mumbled.

"What's wrong?"

Kenn shook his head. "No, it's fine. We were talking about you and how happy you were. I don't want to make this about me or drown your happiness in my sorrow. My apologies because that came out a hell of a lot more dramatic than I'd intended."

"We can have both side by side, happiness and sadness, joy and sorrow. At the risk of sounding equally dramatic, but isn't that what life is like?"

How young Denali was and yet how wise. He was Kenn's age, and yet he seemed so much more mature. Hell, he'd managed to bring two grown men to their knees and made them fall in love with him. "I suppose you're right, but I didn't want you to feel like I was jealous or that you couldn't be happy."

Denali put his sandwich down, looking thoughtful as he chewed. "I genuinely don't feel that way. Like, Milan is grieving for his sister, and I understand that tempers his happiness about his relationship with Asher and me, but that doesn't upset me. I wouldn't be offended if you couldn't muster what others would see as an expected level of happiness about my news. You lost your mom, Kenn. You're allowed to be sad. It would be cruel of me to expect you to forget about that and hide your real feelings from me. That would mean we weren't true friends, and that would make me far sadder. Does that make sense?"

"Thank you for understanding. It's a hot mess in my head with all these warring emotions."

"I can't even imagine. But you're holding up okay?"

"I am. Or at least, I was. I don't know...maybe I'm imagining things, but..."

"Want to tell me about it?"

Should he? He had to talk to someone, and it wasn't like the list of people he could confide in was a long one. Plus, he knew Denali wouldn't tell anyone. He could trust him. "Since the explosion, Warrick has been different. Much more distant. I feel like I did something wrong."

"What could you have possibly done wrong? Did you guys have an argument of some kind? A disagreement?"

"Not that I can think of, and trust me, I've racked my brain. The only thing I could come up with is that... It's stupid, and it's probably why he's upset with me. I should've asked him, but I didn't, and maybe he felt I was overstepping my boundaries."

Denali smiled at him. "It helps if you actually tell me so I know what we're dealing with."

"Right. After the explosion, that window was broken." Kenn pointed to the window in his room that had been replaced. "So I couldn't sleep here for that first night, since maintenance didn't have a spare one and needed to arrange for one. My dad offered to let me sleep in his room, but I thought, since Warrick had a cabin with two bedrooms, I could maybe share his cabin with him. I mean, they both have their own bathroom, so it's not like I would've been in his way. But I didn't ask him before I suggested this to my dad, so maybe that's why Warrick's upset. And then Seth said he'd feel better about Warrick going home until the investigation into the explosion had been wrapped up and they knew for certain it was an accident, and...I guess I kind of lost it."

"Define *lost it*."

Kenn's cheeks heated up. "There may have been some yelling involved...aimed at my dad. I told him that if he sent Warrick home, I'd never forgive him."

Denali's eyes grew big. "You yelled at your dad? How did he respond?"

Kenn let out a long sigh. "I think he was more shocked than upset. Worried about me."

"Considering I've seen Professor Duvall walking around, I assume your dad granted your request."

Kenn snorted. "That wasn't a request. I don't even know why I got that fired up, but I did."

"No? No idea why you wanted him to stay so much?"

Denali's tone was a little too neutral. What was he hinting at? "Our relationship has definitely developed past what would've been normal between a professor and student or a tutor and student, but under the circumstances, I don't think we can be blamed for that. It's just that... No one has time for me. I hate how whiny that makes me sound, especially because I understand the reason behind it. So many things are happening at the same time. My dad has a country to run, you have two hot boyfriends, Uncle Milan has two hot boyfriends, and everyone is busy...but Warrick had the time to focus on me."

Denali's face softened. "I don't think it's weird at all in this situation. Besides, look at how all the professional relationships are getting messed up. Seth and Coulson are working together, but they're also boyfriends. Calix, Milan, and your father are best friends. Asher and Seth know each other from before, and then there's Rhett, who's Calix's boyfriend but also Levar's best friend, and the whole thing is messy and complicated. Anyone who faults you for developing a relationship with Professor Duvall beyond the formal one should take a hard look at himself. Hell, I had a very uncomfortable but mercifully brief conversation with your father about my relationship with Milan."

"Oh my god, really? When was that?"

Denali waved his hand. "Before the explosion, when I was cleaning your room. He mentioned something about him knowing what I was doing with Milan and Asher, and it was one of those conversations I hope to never have again in my life. No offense because I know he's your dad and all, but talking to the president of the United States about your sex life is one thing, but doing it while he's referring to his own brother-in-law is... God, it was so fucked up."

The sheer horror on Denali's face made Kenn laugh. He could picture it easily, and even now, days later, Denali's discomfort was palpable. No wonder. The thought of talking to his dad about his sex life was horrifying, and he was his father first and foremost and only the president second. "I don't know why, but that makes me feel better, so thank you for making me laugh."

"My pleasure," Denali said, and Kenn could sense he meant it. "I know we don't get to hang out that much, and I wish I could, but it's hard with Milan being your uncle. He's not sure you're ready to see him being physically affectionate with Asher and me. And I think Asher is worried you'll see him differently. Less professional, if that makes sense. Another example of how complicated this whole situation is."

"I'm not going to lie and say it wouldn't be an issue," Kenn said slowly. "But let me think about it, okay? Because if I get to see you more by including Asher and Uncle Milan, then I may have to find a way to get over myself or get used to it. I don't want to be alone anymore. And I don't think it's fair to put this much pressure on Warrick. He needs to be able to say no and not have to spend every waking minute of his day with me."

"If it's any consolation, I don't know what has changed since the explosion, but I've never had the impression he minded being with you. He always seemed to be genuinely happy in your company."

"So you think he's upset for me suggesting I stay in his cabin without him asking?"

"It could be, though he doesn't seem like the type to be irate about something like that, but what do I know? My advice? Talk to him." Denali rolled his eyes. "That seems to have become my mantra these days. Talk to each other. I feel like I'm sixty years old at times with my two stubborn alpha men who I have to almost force to sit down and actually communicate with each other."

"Maybe you should spend a little less time having sex and a bit more time talking," Kenn teased.

Denali laughed. "Nah. As much as I appreciate a good

conversation, I've got my priorities straight. Dick first, talk second."

They both giggled at that wonderfully inappropriate comment.

"But seriously, Kenn, talk to the professor. Don't let this ruin your friendship."

14

Warrick felt like the biggest asshole on the planet. He had Kenn's best interests at heart and his own as well, he kept telling himself, but it grew harder to convince himself of that truth every day. Why was keeping his distance from Kenn so painful? Had he grown that attached to him in such a short time? He'd known he'd become fond of him, but he'd never expected to actually miss not being with him. It physically hurt.

It only confirmed that distancing himself was the right choice. Nothing good could come from growing too close to the president's son. It was a recipe for disaster for too many reasons to count, not in the last place because pissing off the man who held the nuclear codes to the entire United States' weapon arsenal wasn't smart. To put it lightly. Not that Warrick suspected the man would sic some special ops team on him, but the fact that he even had that ability was cause for concern.

He needed this job, and maybe even more importantly, he'd need a positive recommendation afterward. If he ever wanted to teach again, he'd better get the president to write a glowing endorsement of his qualities as a teacher, or he'd be teaching at a high school for the rest of his life. In itself a worthy profession, but not what he wanted.

But god, it was damn near impossible to keep his resolve when Kenn gazed at him with those sad eyes. Up until now, Warrick had always associated puppy eyes with brown eyes, but Kenn had proved that having blue eyes didn't mean you couldn't look utterly forlorn and sad and dejected to the point where Warrick wanted to haul him onto his lap and cuddle him until he felt better. *So* not a good idea...

"I'm done," Kenn said softly, and Warrick glanced up from the book he'd been pretending to read while Kenn had worked on a one-page rebuttal to critics of court packing.

Warrick extended his hand. "Let me have a quick look."

Kenn's fingers brushed his as he handed him the paper, and a little shiver danced down Warrick's spine. He gritted his teeth and ignored it. He perused what Kenn had written, once again impressed with the boy's sharp mind. Orally, he wasn't always the most eloquent, often hindered by his shyness. But in writing, his analytical skills and especially his persuasive reasoning shone, and Warrick was proud of him.

"I'll have to read it more thoroughly, but this looks great, Kenn. Well done."

For a moment, Kenn's face lit up like the sun, and it hit Warrick like a ton of bricks that he hadn't seen him smile like that in...days. Five days, to be precise. The day of the explosion. After he'd consciously pulled himself back emotionally, Kenn had stopped smiling. Warrick felt like an asshole all over again.

Before he could stop himself, he laid his hand on Kenn's

arm. "I'm proud of your academic progress. You already show the potential to become a great lawyer."

Kenn was beaming, positively glowing, and Warrick had to force himself to breathe. Why the hell did it feel like the sun had started shining again after months of dreary weather? His whole being responded to it, body, mind, and soul. Alarm bells blared inside him, and he pulled his hand back. No more touching. He couldn't. He had to protect himself. Both of them.

"Let's take a break for lunch," he said, his voice not quite steady. He pushed his chair back. "I'm going for a walk."

He was almost at the door when Kenn called out, "Professor Duvall?"

How he hated that Kenn was calling him that again. And the strained tone with which Kenn had said his name stung even more. He slowly turned around. "I've told you to call me Warrick, Kenn. There's no need for that formality."

"That's not the impression you've given me over the last few days."

Kenn's voice wavered, and his cheeks grew red, but he'd gotten up from his chair. With his hands stuffed in his pockets, he was taking a stand, and Warrick was strangely proud of him for forcing the topic. Not that he would admit that. "What do you mean?"

A flash of frustration passed over Kenn's face. "Playing dumb is beneath you."

Oh, hello, the boy had little claws. Warrick kept silent, not knowing how to respond in a way that wouldn't make him lie or look like an idiot while at the same time wouldn't confess too much.

"You've been treating me differently the last few days, and I want to know why," Kenn finally said.

Warrick hesitated. What reason could he possibly give

him that didn't entail flat out telling the truth—which would embarrass Kenn—but also didn't mean lying? "In what way?"

Kenn's face tightened. "Did I do something wrong? Did I upset you or make you angry?"

Those words stung, burning in Warrick's heart. He'd wounded him, but how could he explain all this? "No, you didn't. You did nothing wrong, Kenn."

"Then why are you suddenly so formal and distant? You don't want to eat lunch with me anymore or spend time with me after our lessons, and I don't know why it changed. What happened?"

The conversation with Seth, that was what had happened, but he couldn't tell Kenn that. The boy would be mortified if he discovered his Secret Service agent suspected him of having a crush on his teacher. "I wanted to be there for you after your mom passed away, but in the long run, it's better if we keep our relationship professional, Kenn. You need to think of me as your teacher, your professor. Not as your friend."

The hurt in Kenn's eyes was so stark it almost brought Warrick to his knees. But then the boy raised his chin, and his expression changed into something tighter. For the first time, Warrick saw his father in him, that same steely resolve the president had shown at times. "Message received. I hope you have a nice walk, Professor."

Kenn stalked off with his head held high, and every fiber in Warrick's body was screaming at him to stop Kenn from walking out, to apologize, to tell him to forget about what he'd said. But he let him go, then stumbled back to the table and sat down with trembling hands.

"Why did you lie to him?"

Warrick spun his head around. Denali was standing in the doorway, his eyes blazing fire. "Excuse me?"

"One of the most important aspects of my job is to pretend I don't hear or see anything, and so far, I've always followed that rule. But I overheard what you said to Kenn, and I can't keep my mouth shut. Why did you say that to him when you know it's a lie?"

Warrick sighed. "You don't know what's going on, Denali."

Denali stepped into the room. "Try me."

"I can't. It's complicated, and you have to believe I'm doing it to protect Kenn."

"Are you? Because from where I'm standing, it looks more like you're protecting yourself."

Warrick shook his head. "I'm doing this for him. I don't want him to get hurt."

"You think he's getting too attached to you."

Denali saw far more than people probably gave him credit for. "It hadn't occurred to me until someone else brought it to my attention. I'm not here to stay, Denali. This is for a year at the most so he can finish college and apply for law school. At some point, I'll have to leave, and he'll be alone again. I can't do that to him. Besides, he's my student. Nothing can ever come from this."

"And you think that by being an asshole to him, you can prevent him from getting his heart broken? Have you seen how he looks now, how much you're hurting him now?"

If his words hadn't stabbed him like ice pricks, Warrick would've probably laughed at the fact that he was getting lectured by what he'd always assumed to be a sweet little twink. The boy had spunk. And balls.

"I never meant for him to get hurt…"

How weak that sounded, even to Warrick's own ears.

"Intentions are all good and well, but the reality is that he's in pain right now. He thought you were his friend, and in case you missed it, he doesn't have a whole lot of those."

Warrick groaned. "How can I be his friend when he's the president's son and I'm his teacher? It's too complicated."

Denali crossed his arms. "I'm a server in the White House, and I share a bed with the president's brother-in-law and a Secret Service agent. Wanna talk to me about complicated?"

"Weren't you scared the president would fire you?"

Denali's expression softened. "In the beginning, I was. But the president is a man in the first place, and a good man at that. He's a friend and a brother-in-law and a father before he's the president."

"Not sure him being a father would help in this case. That's his son I'm..."

That I'm involved with, he'd wanted to say, but that wasn't right. That he was friends with was more like it, but what objection would the president have against that? No, friendship wasn't the issue. It was what could grow from that, what that friendship could evolve into. But how could he explain that when he wasn't even sure if Kenn had come out to Denali? He wouldn't break his trust like that.

"I know Kenn is gay and that he came out to you." It seemed that Denali had followed the same line of reasoning

Warrick breathed out with relief. "He did, but his father doesn't know, which makes it all the more complicated. What if Kenn falls for me? What if I unintentionally break his heart? Still feel the president would be so nice and forgiving, then?"

"Maybe not, but he'll be reasonable at the end of the day. You and I both know that man won't have an issue with Kenn being gay. Hell, I bet he suspects already, so it won't come as a shock. But I still don't think that's the real issue here. You keep saying you're doing it to protect Kenn, but what about you?"

"What do you mean?"

"Are you sure you're not keeping your distance because you're scared you'll get too attached yourself?"

Holy shit, the boy didn't mince words, did he? "I'm... I don't know. Maybe. He's easy to grow attached to, that's for sure."

"He is...so maybe he's also worth the complications and the risk."

"Denali, he's my student. He's fourteen years younger and the president's son."

Denali chuckled. "At this point, I'm not sure why you keep repeating this because it's not like I need a reminder. I'm his age, so I'm well aware of the age difference between you two. And by the way, Milan is forty-seven, so the gap between him and me is a hell of a lot bigger, and Asher is your age, so who are you telling this? Me or yourself?"

Denali nodded as if he'd said enough, then walked out, leaving Warrick behind, his head spinning. Was Denali right? Had he really been protecting himself and his own heart more than Kenn? The thought left him unsettled. He rubbed his chest, where it still ached. How attached had he already grown to Kenn?

15

Seth was beyond tired, but alas, there was no rest for the weary. The conference room in the Laurel Lodge was filled with the inner circle of the president, minus Coulson, who was working in DC that day, and Henley, who was teaching at Georgetown.

"It's time to make our final decision, Del," Calix said, and Seth sat up a little straighter. President Shafer had been going back and forth on whether he should make the State of the Union—his yearly speech to Congress—in person or through a telecast, and today was the deadline.

"I know. Any updates on the security situation, Seth?"

Seth hesitated. "That's not my place to say, Mr. President. I'm not in charge of your detail."

His favored position in the president's inner circle had caused enough friction with his fellow agents already. Many were flat out pissed that, despite not being the head of either the president's or Kenn's security detail, Seth was the one the president turned to.

Calix shot him a frustrated look. "We're well aware, Seth, and yet we're asking you."

Seth didn't need to see the paleness of Calix's face or the dark circles under his eyes to know that the man was running on fumes. He'd been working around the clock over the last few days to finalize the president's speech, which had to be written, regardless of whether the president would give it live from Congress or through telecast from an undisclosed location.

The president held up his hand. "He's doing his job, Cal. If we keep asking him for information that bypasses his superiors and the line of command within the Secret Service, we create bad blood between him and the other agents."

Calix sighed, rubbing his neck, which seemed to be bothering him. "I know, I know. Sorry, Seth. I'm...exhausted. Didn't mean to take it out on you."

"I understand. No worries. I'm reluctant to make statements on information I'm technically not supposed to provide."

"Understandable," the president said. "But I imagine that if anything had changed, Lisandra would've informed me, so for now, let's assume the Secret Service can guarantee my safety. Where does that leave us?"

"We need to look at the bigger issue, the broader decision. Giving a speech is one thing, but how long are we staying here? We've been here for over a month now, but this isn't a solution for the long term," Milan said, surprising Seth by being the voice of reason.

Calix scoffed. "Why not? This is government property, he's well protected, and the last month has proven that he can run the country perfectly from here."

Seth suppressed a smile. A tired Calix was much more likely to let himself be guided by his emotions.

Milan rolled his eyes. "If you keep spouting bullshit like

that, maybe you should take a nap. Come on, Cal, get real. The president belongs in the White House. He can't keep hiding here. In fact, it's already been longer than it should've been."

Aaaaand the Milan Seth knew was back again. God, the man was a riot. No filter and zero fucks to give. It made for a somewhat reckless though entertaining combination.

"I know..." Calix said with a sigh. "Doesn't mean I have to like it."

"Trust me, I don't like it either," Milan said. "In case you weren't paying attention, I appreciate the privacy I have here. We won't get that once we return to the White House."

"The idea of going back scares me." The president's voice was soft, and he looked older all of a sudden. "No offense to the Secret Service, Seth, but...it makes me vulnerable again, and it opens up a lot of bad memories that are now linked to that place."

"None taken, Mr. President, and I completely understand. I wish I had a solution for you, but I don't," Seth said.

Calix leaned forward, his eyes growing sharper. "As much as I hate to admit it, Milan's right. The optics of staying here in the long term aren't good."

Levar nodded. "So far, public opinion has been on our side, with the White House stressing the need for the president and Kenn to grieve in private. But that won't last much longer, especially now that speculation about the fate of both Sarah and Mrs. Markinson is running wild. The press is smelling blood in the water, and Henley feels it won't take much longer for the press to connect some dots."

"I guess the idea of being able to stay here was a pipe dream. An attractive concept but unrealistic nonetheless." The president sounded dejected, but maybe fatigue played a role for him as well. He seemed to be handling the lack of sleep better than Calix, but that didn't mean he was immune to it. And they'd been burning the candle at both ends this week.

"What do you want to do, Del? Technically, we can pack up and leave tomorrow and have you do the State of the Union the day after in person from Congress," Calix said.

The president shook his head. "No, that's too soon. Give us another week. We'll leave a week from now, okay? That'll put less time pressure on the staff to arrange for that transition. Plus, Kenn may need some time to prepare himself emotionally for returning."

"How's he doing?" Calix asked.

That triggered a deep sigh from the president. "I don't know. Not well, I think, but I don't have anything to compare it to. What can you expect from a young man who just lost his mother, whom he was very close to? He's devastated, and it'll take him a while to recover from this."

"Believe me, I know," Calix said. "And yes, it's a cliché, and I hated it when people would tell me that, but unfortunately, it's the truth. Grief is one of those strange emotions that does soften over time until it becomes bearable. But it'll never fully go away. He lost his mom way too young, and that's not something he'll ever get over."

"I wish I could spend more time with him. I feel like the worst father on the planet, abandoning my son when he needs me the most, but I don't know how to be there for him and do the things I have to do at the same time. At least he has Professor Duvall. From what I can tell, they've become friends, and I'm glad Kenn has him as a support."

Seth listened intently, scrutinizing the president's facial expressions and nonverbal communication, but he didn't spot any sign that the president was worried about that relationship. Had he imagined it that there was more than tutor and student? Had he been out of line by bringing it up with Warrick? Maybe he shouldn't have said anything. Surely if the president wasn't worried about it, why would Seth be?

Then again, the president had flat out admitted he hadn't been able to hang out much with Kenn, so how would he even know how things were going? He wouldn't be able to pick up warning signals if he never watched the two of them together like Seth had done. No, bringing it to Warrick's attention had been the right thing to do.

In the week since that conversation, he'd definitely sensed a difference. Warrick was more distant and no longer spent every waking moment with Kenn. At first, Seth had been relieved that his talk with Warrick had had an effect. But as the days had progressed, Kenn had become sadder and sadder, hiding in his shell, and Seth had questioned himself all over again.

He felt caught between a rock and a hard place. If he hadn't said anything, Kenn might've fallen for the professor —if he hadn't already—which could've only led to heartbreak. But since Warrick had distanced himself, Kenn had appeared distraught and downhearted over losing the friendship. No matter what choice Seth had made, Kenn would still end up getting hurt, and Seth hated that he hadn't been able to prevent that.

"... Seth?"

He looked up when Calix mentioned his name, then blinked. "Sorry, my mind had drifted off."

Milan laughed. "We must be getting boring if even the Secret Service falls asleep."

Seth was sorely tempted to stick out his tongue, but such childish behavior was beneath his stature, so he shot him a look that would have made lesser men pee their pants. Milan just laughed harder, clearly unimpressed. Fucker.

"Since Coulson is in DC, we were wondering if you can give us a quick update on where we stand with the investigation," Calix said.

Seth refocused. "Yes, he gave me permission earlier today to catch you all up. Needless to say, things are getting more complicated by the day, with so many avenues to explore and details to investigate. More FBI agents have been added to the case, and both the CIA and the NSA now have a dedicated contact person all information has to run through. Requests have been made to some other agencies to do the same."

"What's the thought behind that step?" Levar asked.

"One of the things that came to the surface after 9/11 was how bad the communication between the various intelligence agencies had been," the president said. "Warnings about the terrorists who ended up flying the planes were sent but not received or not run through the proper channels, and crucial information was never seen on time. The agencies were territorial, competitive, and not focused on working together to get a complete picture. Measures like this are intended to change that and prevent information from getting lost."

Seth nodded. "Exactly. History has shown that the FBI and the CIA especially have trouble playing nice together. In this case, the Secret Service is added to that mix, as is about every other intelligence agency the US has. Because of the ever-widening scope of this investigation, the FBI director has requested all agencies involved to appoint a designated contact person who collects all information and has the overview so crucial intel won't get lost."

"Gotcha." Levar scribbled down on the notepad that

never left his side.

"So far, the agencies are trying to work together. The Secret Service is focusing on six questions that pertain to events that happened on our watch." Seth read from his notes. "How did Basil King get into that party, what happened to Annabeth Markinson's burner phone, how did those scuba divers know how to get into Annabeth Markinson's boathouse, how did the suicide vest make it into the Baltimore Convention Center, where did Babur get a Secret Service pin, and why did President Markinson order extra Secret Service protection for his family. That's everything still unsolved on our end."

"They may seem like small details, but they could potentially expose weaknesses in our processes and offer more clues to the identity of the people behind it all," Asher spoke up for the first time. "Every little detail matters. Coulson has been crystal clear about that."

"The CIA is concentrating on Hamza Bashir, as they've been for the last few years, and they're tracing every step of the three pride bombers and the two men connected to the assassination. They sent more agents into the region to run down leads and dig deeper, hoping to get more clarity on who Hamza Bashir is." Seth checked his notes again to make sure he hadn't forgotten anything. When he was this tired, even his memory failed him at times.

"Now that we suspect Brooks' company was involved in assembling the bombs, the ATF is working on connecting him to the bombs through the make of the explosives that were used. And last but not least, the FBI has the longest list of issues that need more investigation. Their biggest focus is on Kingmakers and the people whose identity we've established so far, including Wesley Quirk, Naomi Beckingham, and Jon Brooks. Their backgrounds are being investigated until, as Coulson put it, they know everything that happened to them between being born and today, even what they had for breakfast yesterday. The FBI is also reopening the investigation into the supposed suicide of the three pride bombers, hoping to find new evidence now that we know better where to look."

He consulted his notes one last time, then looked up, confident that he'd shared everything Coulson had told him to.

The president whistled between his teeth. "That's quite the task list, but it feels to me as if the net is closing."

"Coulson said the same thing, but he also warned to be careful that they don't slip through the net before it's fully closed. The biggest challenge is to make sure none of the suspects know we're on their heels," Seth responded.

"I'll admit that worries me, considering even more agents were added to the case. The more people know, the higher the chances of someone leaking information," Calix said.

"I don't think it's a risk we can avoid," the president said. "We need all hands on deck for this investigation, and we need broad involvement from the entire intelligence community, even from foreign intelligence agencies. We can't keep it in this small circle anymore. If we try to do that, we only risk the chance of more attacks. We have to share information, especially on Hamza Bashir and Al Saalihin."

Seth nodded, glad the president saw the bigger picture. "Coulson pointed something else out. It's important to realize we don't merely need to find out who's behind it, but we also need proof. Irrefutable, hard evidence that will stand up in court. Because if, as we now suspect, the masterminds behind it all are Americans, this will go to trial, and it'll be the highest-profile court case this country has ever seen. We have to do this by the book, step by step, not skipping a single phase until we have overwhelming evidence that no jury can throw out."

16

It had been a month since he'd buried his mother. People had assured him it would hurt less over time, but Kenn hadn't seen much evidence of that. Sure, he wasn't crying all day anymore like in those first few days, but the weight of his loss still pressed like a boulder on his chest. Every morning, she was the first person he thought of when he woke up, and every night, he cried himself to sleep, missing her so much it hurt to breathe.

How did his father do it? And Uncle Milan? How were they able to compartmentalize their grief and give it a place where they could still function and do their jobs? Kenn didn't understand. He didn't blame them for going through life normally, at least to the eye. No, he wanted to be able to do the same. He was envious.

The only time the grief was bearable was when Warrick was tutoring him, when Kenn's mind was focused on knowledge and learning something new. It had been twelve days since the explosion, and Warrick was still keeping his distance. The time when he hadn't seemed like a distant memory, almost a dream. But even then, Kenn still treasured every moment with him, if only because when he was with Warrick, the grief was less.

But today, a mild Sunday morning, Warrick was off. Kenn had slept in, had showered and eaten breakfast, and then he'd headed out with Rogue. The dog loved to explore the many trails surrounding the cabins, and even though Kenn had never considered himself to be much of an outdoors fan, he'd come to appreciate spending time in nature. He'd better enjoy it while it lasted because three days from now, they'd be back in the White House.

They'd found a trail they hadn't walked before, and Rogue happily trotted in front of him, not in the least bothered by his missing leg. He'd adapted his gait and seemed completely used to it, as if he'd never had a fourth leg. He was constantly sniffing the ground. Was it too early in the season for rabbits and squirrels to be out? It was only mid-February, and Kenn had no idea if those animals kept some kind of winter schedule. After a few mild days, most of the snow had melted, transforming the trail into a muddy mess, but Kenn didn't mind. Nothing a pair of good boots couldn't overcome.

Asher was his agent for the day, and for the occasion, he was wearing something more suitable for hiking than a suit and nice shoes, but he was following him at a distance. If Kenn asked him to, Asher would join him, but he didn't feel like talking. What would they even talk about in the first place? Asher's relationship, which included Kenn's best friend plus his uncle? Yeah, Kenn didn't think so. And the whole investigation was off-limits as well. Technically, Kenn had the security clearance for it, but not the need nor the desire to know, so he kept himself out of it. All he'd asked was to be informed of significant developments, but he didn't want to be burdened every day with the snail's pace at which the FBI, aided by the other intelligence agencies, made new discoveries.

The trail meandered up a hill, and Kenn took his time, his lungs protesting whenever he went too fast. He was out of shape, embarrassingly so. Another example of things his mom had always encouraged him in. She'd been the one to make sure he exercised at least three times a week. It wasn't so much that he didn't like exercising—although he certainly wasn't a fan—but he often forgot. When presented with the choice between working out and reading, well, that was a no-brainer. Books won every single time.

He'd always known he was a bit of a mama's boy, content to let his mom take care of him and help him make good choices on a day-to-day basis. Even when he'd gone off to college, he'd talked to her every day, and she'd never failed to text him reminders to get enough sleep, to study for his exams, to eat healthy, practice his yoga, and do his breathing routines.

The thought made his throat close up, those pesky tears burning once again behind his eyes. When would it stop? How long would he walk around feeling like a shell of his former self, like he was empty and dark and dead on the inside? Would it ever go away, or would he spend the rest of his life feeling like a part of him was missing?

He'd reached the top, where he sat down on a big fallen tree to take a breather. Rogue immediately came trotting toward him, his tail wagging so hard he was about to achieve lift-off. Kenn chuckled. "You're such a happy boy." He scratched the German shepherd behind his ears. "Such a perfect, happy boy. I'm so glad I have you."

He swallowed, and this time, the damn broke. He hugged Rogue, burying his face in the soft, damp fur as he let his tears run free. Rogue whimpered, then licked Kenn's face with the undying affection of a canine. "You're the only one who's always there for me," he said between sobs.

The sound of voices startled him. Warrick was talking to Asher, who was holding the professor back with a hand to his chest. "He wants to be alone," Asher said firmly, his voice carrying on the wind. He'd used what Kenn called his Secret Service tone. No wonder Denali loved kneeling for him. Kenn would do the same if the man told him to in that voice. And he appreciated that Asher was looking out for him.

"Let him through," he called out. "It's okay, but thank you, Asher."

Asher pulled back his hand and stepped aside, letting Warrick continue. Kenn quickly wiped off his tears, but he stayed seated. Rogue bounded toward Warrick, barking, tail wagging. Warrick bent down, petting the dog as he whispered some soft words Kenn couldn't hear. But Rogue seemed to understand as he raced back to Kenn and licked his hand, then lay down at his feet. Warrick closed the distance between them until he stood a few feet in front of Kenn.

Kenn raised his chin. "What can I do for you, Professor?"

Warrick winced. "I wanted to make sure you were okay. I was walking and heard you..."

"No, I'm not okay, but you've made it crystal clear you didn't want to make that your problem or responsibility, so I'm not sure what you're expecting me to do here."

He couldn't believe he'd managed those words, and in a firm tone at that. Progress, at last.

"Kenn... That was never what I intended to say. I meant that—"

"You insisted on us having a professional teacher-student relationship and nothing more. Definitely nothing personal. I don't know about you, but this is a personal situation for me. It's outside of class, outside of what we could arguably consider our school, so clearly, this is outside of your responsibilities."

Warrick stumbled back as if Kenn had slapped him, his eyes wide in shock. "That's not... Kenn, this wasn't what I meant to say."

"Then what did you mean? Because I was quoting you verbatim."

Warrick took a deep breath, then pointed at the fallen tree Kenn was still sitting on. "Can I come sit next to you? My leg is bothering me."

"Of course. Maybe not the smartest thing to climb the hill?"

Warrick chuckled dryly as he carefully sat down. "Oh, for sure, but I saw you making your way up, and you looked...sad. Lost. I needed to be sure you were okay."

Warmth spread through Kenn's chest at the idea that Warrick had chosen discomfort because he wanted to check in on Kenn. But what did that mean? After everything he'd said about them being nothing more than a student and a teacher, why would he do this?

"I appreciate that, but I must admit I don't understand it anymore. You, I mean. I don't understand you."

Warrick buried his face in his hands as he rubbed his temples. "Join the club, kid. I'm a man of contradictions. What can I say?"

"You could try to explain what you meant when you said we should keep it professional."

"To be honest, I'm not even sure anymore. We should be professional, but I'm tired of it and frustrated, and I find it damn near impossible to keep away from you."

What did that mean? Now Kenn was even more confused. "I'm sorry, but it still doesn't make sense."

Warrick glanced at him sideways. "Have you ever been in a situation where your heart was telling you one thing and your brain was saying something else? Rationally, I know I should keep a professional distance from you, but when I see you being this heartbroken and hurting, that's hellish. It feels to me as if no one else is taking care of you."

The truth fell right from his lips. "That's because no one is. You were the only one who had time for me. And yes, I'm well aware of how utterly sad and pathetic that is. Clearly, I need to work on my social skills."

"It's not your doing that your father is president, that your best friend has a job and two boyfriends, and that the world around you has gone utterly crazy. How would you even be able to make friends, what with you being so isolated here?"

He couldn't help it. He had to ask, even knowing that the odds of him getting rejected all over again were astronomical. "If you know all that… If you knew all that… Why did you distance yourself from me?"

Warrick looked away from him, his face tight. "I was trying to do the honorable thing, but now I don't know if I made the right choice. I hurt you, and I'm so sorry, but you have to believe me that I thought I was doing what was best."

Kenn lowered his gaze to Rogue, who was snoring softly. "I want to believe you, but it's hard for me to imagine any scenario in which pulling away from someone who needs you is the best option. I don't understand, and I can't help but think it was something I did. All I wanted was for you to be my friend, and I thought you were, but now I feel like I messed that up somehow."

When Warrick didn't answer, Kenn stole a glance sideways and caught Warrick shaking his head, then peering at Asher, who had his back turned toward them, scanning his surroundings.

"Oh, fuck this," Warrick mumbled, then scooted closer to Kenn and slung his arm around Kenn's shoulder. "I'm sorry. I'm so sorry."

The relief was so overwhelming, so intense, that the tears started falling all over again, and no matter how hard Kenn tried to hold them back, he couldn't.

"It's okay," Warrick whispered. "Let it all out. I'm here, I promise. I'm sorry for making the wrong choice."

Kenn still didn't understand what had happened, but he was too tired, too worn down to question it. If Warrick wanted to be his friend again, Kenn would accept him back without protest. Maybe that made him spineless and without any pride, but so be it. He needed Warrick, and right now, that surpassed anything else, including his dignity.

He leaned into Warrick's embrace, putting his head on the man's shoulder as the tears flowed freely. "I miss her so much," he sobbed. "I don't know how to do this. How do I become an adult without her? How will I know what to do? She was always the one to help me."

"I know, b— Kenn. I'm so sorry for you."

What had Warrick wanted to say? Or had he imagined it? Kenn let it go, too drained to spend energy on what must've been a slip of the tongue.

They sat like that for a while, and even though Asher had turned around, watching them intently, Kenn stayed where he was. He needed Warrick's presence, the man's kind words, his touch, and he didn't have the energy to care about what Asher thought of it. Besides, the man had to keep what he saw confidential, so who would he tattle to? And what was there even to report back?

Nothing. Just friendship. That was all. A wonderful, amazing friendship that made Kenn feel warm inside despite his tears.

17

Up until the moment he knocked on the door of the president's study, Warrick hadn't been sure if he'd possess the guts to go through with it. And even as he stood there, awaiting the president's permission to enter, he still debated with himself. Was he about to make a monumental mistake?

"Come in," the president called out, and now it was showtime. Unless Warrick could come up with another reason he wanted to talk to the president.

He opened the door and stepped inside, taking a deep breath. He'd never been in this room before, and though it was cramped and much smaller than he'd expected, it was neat and organized. President Shafer was clearly someone who valued structure and order, and if nothing else, they had that in common.

"Professor Duvall." The president rose from his chair. "Everything okay?"

"Yes, thank you, Mr. President. I just wanted to talk to you about something. About Kenn."

The president's face pulled tight with worry. "Is he okay? Is something wrong?"

No, Kenn wasn't fine. If he was, Warrick wouldn't be here. He couldn't lie, not even a quick lie like this. It was time to find his courage. "I'm worried about him, Mr. President."

Shafer let out a sigh. "So am I." He gestured at a chair across from his desk. "Grab a seat, and please tell me what made you come here."

They both sat down, and to his dismay, Warrick's hands shook a bit. How was it possible that he'd been cool as a cucumber under the toughest conditions in the Army but was shaking in his metaphorical boots facing the president?

"It's my impression that Kenn's struggling," he said carefully.

"Struggling in what sense? Obviously, he's grieving his mother, but you wouldn't be sitting down with me if that was all."

"I can't even imagine the amount of stress you must be under. Having to be president under these circumstances is almost too much to ask. It leaves you little to no time to grieve yourself."

Shafer nodded. "It's far beyond what anyone should bear, but I'm not sure what this has to do with Kenn."

"Kenn's support system is small. He has you, his uncle Milan, and his friend, Denali, and even that last friendship is relatively recent from what I understand."

"If you have a point, Professor, I suggest you get to it. There's no need to beat around the bush to spare my feelings. If I messed up, I much prefer to know."

Shafer's eyes were razor-sharp. How much did the man already know or suspect? After all, he'd been the target of Kenn's outburst when the boy had been told Warrick would have to leave. Surely the president had come to his own conclusions based on that. Though he'd allowed Warrick to stay, so clearly, whatever opinions he'd formed weren't too negative.

"No one's taking care of Kenn, Mr. President. That's my point. That's the bottom line, my reason for being here. Both you and your brother-in-law are too busy with other things, which I completely understand, and maybe you're both too busy grieving. But Denali has a job with long hours and two boyfriends, one of whom is grieving as well, so that leaves Kenn with no one."

He held his breath, hoping that the president's statement that he preferred to be told the truth flat out had been true.

"He has you."

The president's voice was soft but firm, leaving no doubt that Warrick had heard him correctly. "Excuse me?" he said nevertheless.

"He has you, Professor."

Warrick couldn't explain it, but he was suddenly uncomfortable with the formal way the president addressed him. Maybe because of the direction the conversation was going? "Please, Mr. President, call me Warrick. We're long past the stage where there's a need for such formality."

Shafer smiled at him. "I could say the same to you, but I've found that people have a hard time calling me by my first name. Still, the invitation stands. You should know me well enough by now to be aware that I'm not a president who insists on formality and titles."

Warrick chuckled. "I can try, but my experience in the Army has left me with an almost automatic habit of using titles."

"Fair enough. But let's get back to the point... Warrick. My son has you, doesn't he?"

The president's eyes bored into Warrick's, and he resisted the urge to squirm in his seat. "Should he? Should I be the one to be there for him?"

"You said it yourself. There *is* no one else. Not while we're here at Camp David, though I doubt that going back to the White House tomorrow will change that. Young Denali might have a bit more time for Kenn, but Kenn has never been good at making friends quickly. In that sense, he's like Sarah, who took quite a long time to warm up to people. But once she'd given you her friendship, she was loyal till the end."

"But, Mr. President..." No, he couldn't get his first name past his lips. "He barely knows me. I'm sure there are people far more suited and qualified to take care of him emotionally."

The president leaned back in his seat, crossing his arms, but his eyes never lost that sharpness. "I don't know, Warrick. My son seems to have grown attached to you rather quickly, judging by his passionate plea to allow you to stay here at Camp David."

Warrick opened his mouth, then closed it again. What could he say to that? They both knew it to be the truth, but should he explain? Defend himself? Assure the president that he hadn't done it on purpose?

"Do you have a problem with that, sir?" he finally asked.

"Should I?"

God, the man was good. He kept putting the ball in Warrick's court, forcing him to show his hand and come clean. Did he know about Seth's conversation with Warrick? Denali had said he suspected the president knew Kenn was gay, even if the kid hadn't come out to his father.

Still, Warrick was hesitant to reveal more, fearing that even the slightest bit of information might out Kenn against his will.

"I only did it because no one else seemed to have time for him. If you don't want me to, I'll back off."

Shafer shook his head. "That's not what I'm saying. Believe me, I was beyond grateful to see you stepping up. You have no idea how hard it has been for me over the last few weeks. I wanted nothing more than to spend more time with Kenn, to talk to him about his mom, to help him process it all, but I can't. I'm only one man, and I'm already making eighteen-hour workdays. I try to make more time for him, but it's impossible."

"I know how hard you work, Mr. President, and I also see how hard you try with him. It's not a matter of not wanting to be there for him, but there's only so much you can do. That's why I developed a friendship with him, why I tried to be available for him. I hope you don't object to that."

"Not at all. That's not the issue." The president hesitated, then leaned forward, his face softening. "Warrick, I've suspected Kenn to be gay since he was ten years old. He hasn't told me anything, and I'm not asking you to confirm if he talked about this with you. That's between you and him, and he'll come out to me when he's ready. But I'm not blind. My son cares for you deeply, and I'm asking you if that's something I should be worried about."

Warrick straightened his shoulders. "I care for him as well, Mr. President, and I'd never deliberately do anything to hurt him."

"Care to explain to me then why he's been walking around alone the last few days? I've barely seen you at meals, and Kenn has been nothing but sad and dejected."

Oh, he had to tread so carefully here. "I was under the

impression that creating a bit more distance between Kenn and me would be smart."

The president blinked a few times, baffled, until understanding dawned in his eyes. "You fear he's growing too attached to you."

"I'm not the only one, Mr. President. To be honest, it hadn't even occurred to me until someone else pointed it out to me. But yes, that was my fear."

Shafer took a deep breath, letting his head drop to the left, then to the right until a satisfying *crack* sounded. "You know what I hate most about being president? It's that everyone assumes that I'm president first and foremost, but I'm not. I'd like to think I'm a husband first—or at least, I was—and that me being a father outweighs me being president. I'm a friend, a brother-in-law, and a man before I'm president. Watching Kenn grow up has been a joy and a privilege, and I'm beyond proud of my son."

Warrick wasn't sure where the president was going with this, but warmth spread through him at his last statement. Shafer's love for Kenn was crystal clear, and how happy Warrick was to hear that. He wasn't sure why Kenn doubted his father's feelings for him, though not so much his love as his pride, why he doubted he was good enough for his father, considering how different his character was. But the president's tone and expression had left no room for doubt that he genuinely embraced his son the way he was.

"He's twenty-two, Warrick. He's an adult, and he has been one for four years. Part of becoming an adult is experiencing what we've all gone through at one point or another. Our first crush. Our first broken heart. Our first sexual experiences. I'm not expecting my son to share everything with me, but I'd like to think I've been involved enough in his life to know that he's a bit of a late bloomer. Combined with losing his mother, he's vulnerable. All I'm asking is that you're gentle with him."

Warrick's breath caught in his lungs. Be gentle with him? Why was the president talking about crushes and sexual experiences? What the hell was he pointing at? "I'm not sure I'm following, Mr. President."

"As I've said, Warrick, I'm not blind. I see how much my son cares for you, but I've seen your affection for him as well. You weren't hanging out with him because it was your job or you were getting paid for it. You did it because it brought you joy to be with him."

Warrick's cheeks heated instantly. Fuck, was the president suggesting that Warrick felt more for Kenn than mere friendship? Or was he simply describing a relationship that went deeper than that of a teacher and a student? Warrick was completely lost by now. "I do care for him. He's very easy to grow attached to, and I do enjoy spending time with him."

Shafer laughed. "On a scale of one to ten, how uncomfortable is this conversation for you?"

"A twelve," Warrick deadpanned. "And honestly, sir, I'm not sure it would make a difference if I were talking to you as the president or as Kenn's father. Both are equally intimidating."

"I'd fail in my role as a father if I wouldn't at least try to protect my son. But that's where my involvement ends, Warrick."

"I'm sorry, sir, but I'm still not quite sure what your point is."

"Let me put it this way. I'm telling you the same thing I said to Denali when I heard about his involvement with Milan and Asher—your job is not at risk, regardless of what happens with Kenn. I hope you'll be able to be a comfort to him, to offer him the friendship he so desperately needs. But if you decide that's not what you want, you'll still have a job. And if it turns out that my son develops feelings you can't reciprocate, you'll still have a job. All I ask is that you're gentle with him, that you don't break his heart on purpose. I can't ask for more."

Warrick was at a loss for words. Out of all the scenarios that had gone through his mind as he prepared himself for this conversation, he'd never imagined it to take this direction. Unless he was dreaming or severely mistaken, the president had just sort of given him his...blessing? His approval? Warrick wasn't sure what to call it, but the bottom line was that the president had, in the most circumspect way possible, told Warrick that he could develop a friendship with Kenn. And possibly even more. Or had he read too much into it?

The president's words had blown Warrick's mind. This conversation had *so* not been how he'd expected it to go. And yet, as it all slowly sank in, it hit him that it perfectly fit this amazing man who was trying so hard to be everything to everybody, including an entire country. And to be able to do that, he was trusting Warrick to take care of the one person who meant most to him in the whole world —his son.

"Thank you for your trust, Mr. President. You have my word."

18

Home had become such a fluid concept for him, Kenn mused as the presidential limousine, commonly referred to as the Beast, drove him and his dad back to the White House. For the almost six weeks they'd been at Camp David, that place had felt like home to him. Strange how that worked.

Despite all his quirks, he'd always easily felt at home somewhere. Not so much with people but with places. He'd loved the house in Boston he'd grown up in. His father had assured him they still owned it and that it was waiting for them to return to once his father's presidency was finished. But it would never be the same without his mom, and neither would the White House. Would it even feel like home, a safe place, again now that she was gone?

Maybe it had never been in the first place. After all, it was hard to truly feel comfortable in a house where the furniture cost more than most people earned in a lifetime. Hell, there had been dishes that cost more than an average person's yearly salary. Not exactly the environment that made him relax.

His father ended the call he'd been on. "How you doing?"

"A little nervous about going back," Kenn answered honestly. To others, he might attempt to keep a brave face, but not to his dad.

His dad took his hand and held it with his bigger and stronger one, just like he'd done when Kenn had been a little boy. "So am I."

"Yeah?" Strangely enough, it made him feel better he wasn't the only one who was apprehensive about returning to the scene of the crime. Literally, in this case.

"We've only lived here for a short time, but the place still holds memories of your mom, unlike Camp David. It'll be hard to be in a bed by myself without her next to me."

His father's voice broke near the end, and Kenn scooted as close as his seat belt allowed, careful not to kick Rogue, who was at his feet on the floor, then put his head on his father's shoulder. "I know."

For a while, they sat quietly, united in grief that needed no words.

"Was Warrick happy to be able to go back to his own home?" his father asked.

Kenn set up straight again. "You're calling him Warrick now?"

His father let out a soft chuckle. "That's what you call him. I figured I'd follow your example."

"Yeah, but I know him much better than you do."

"Are you telling me that the president of the United States has to call him professor? I can't use his first name?"

"Of course you can. I was just... I was surprised, that's all. You don't mind me using his first name, right? It's not like I don't respect him."

"No worries, kiddo. As long as he's okay with it, it's all fine with me."

Kenn relaxed his shoulders. "I think he was rather sad to go back home, to be honest. He liked Camp David, and I can't blame him."

"Trust me, if I thought I could've gotten away with it, I would've stayed there."

Kenn had wondered why they had to go back and asked his father about it. His father had explained that the optics of the president hiding weren't good, and as much as Kenn hated to admit it, it made sense. Besides, for obvious reasons, the Secret Service had strictly limited the number of visitors to Camp David, and the president needed to be accessible. But knowing that his father was reluctant to go back made him feel better.

"I've been wanting to bring something up with you," his father said slowly. "And I've gone back and forth on how to say this and when to say it, but the timing never seemed right. My guess is that the next ten minutes until we arrive are as much private time as we're going to get, so I figured I'd just come out and say it."

Kenn frowned. What on earth was his father talking about? What did he want to discuss with Kenn? The gravity of his tone and the fact that his father wasn't looking at him suggested it wasn't a fun topic, and his stomach swirled uncomfortably. "What's wrong, Dad?"

"I've had a conversation with the head of your security detail. Now that we're back in the White House, the Secret Service will resume their normal protective detail of you."

"I assumed as much. The condensed protection like they did at Camp David clearly wouldn't work. So what's the problem?"

"No problem. Just... I've made it crystal clear that I don't want the Secret Service to report anything you do to me unless it's something that jeopardizes your safety or my own. And I've said the same thing to Mr. Funnell, who promised me he'd communicate it to the entire White House staff."

What? Kenn still wasn't following. "I'm not sure I understand, Dad. What do you mean?"

Finally, his father turned sideways and faced him. "What I'm saying is that you're twenty-two, and instead of being away at college, where you would've been at liberty to explore and discover who you are, you're back under the same roof as your parents... Your dad, I mean. Me. And not just that, but this particular roof also includes a staff and Secret Service protection. That's not a lot of privacy for you for the foreseeable future. So I tried to give you as much privacy as I can by issuing a direct order that neither the staff nor the Secret Service is to alert me to any...personal activities you might engage in."

Personal activities? It took another second or two, but then it finally registered. Oh god, his father was talking about sex. How the hell had he gotten into this conversation? And even more importantly, how did he end it as soon as possible?

But before he could say anything, his father continued. "I know this conversation makes you uncomfortable, but that kind of comes with the job as your dad. I want you to know this because it matters. I don't want you to feel like anything you do would be reported back to me. It won't. So you're at liberty to, I don't know, go on a date or something. I'm sure Levar would be happy to give you some tips on handling the press, should that become an issue. And you know you can always come to me for any advice or questions you might have, and of course, Uncle Milan is always there for you as well."

Kenn's cheeks were burning so fiercely sweat broke out

on his forehead. What the hell did he say to that? He couldn't think of anything more mortifying than having to talk about sex with his father, even aside from the fact that his father didn't know he was gay. Or did he?

A glance sideways brought him eye to eye with his dad, whose face showed nothing but acceptance, even if he, too, looked uncomfortable. The love in his father's eyes took away his last bit of doubt that the man would accept him exactly the way he was. "Dad, I have to tell you something."

He swallowed. He couldn't go back now, not after those words. And he didn't want to, even though he was trembling from the nerves speeding through his body.

"Nothing you could tell me would ever make me stop loving you. I need you to know that."

The emotion in his father's voice was thick, and Kenn's heart skipped a beat. He knew. His father had known all along, and he'd been waiting patiently for Kenn to be ready.

"I'm gay, Dad."

His father's face broke open in a wide smile, even as his eyes teared up. "Thank you for sharing that. I love you so much. I'm so proud of you."

Kenn wasn't even surprised he couldn't hold back his own tears. God, he'd been crying every day since his mom had died. "Dad, did you and mom know? Did you suspect? Because I never got to tell her, and I hate the idea of her thinking I didn't trust her with this. I just wasn't ready."

His father's strong hand curled around his cheek. "Kiddo, we've known since you were a young teenager. But like you said, you weren't ready yet. This was your journey, not ours, and your mom never blamed you for not coming out."

Sweet relief bloomed in his chest. "She didn't?"

"Not once. Everybody walks their journey at their own pace, and this was yours."

Kenn leaned into his father's hand, closing his eyes for a moment, which caused a flurry of tears to drip down his cheeks. Why had he waited this long to tell him? He should've known his father would react like this. How could he have ever doubted him?

But then the truth hit. He'd told his father only one aspect of his sexual identity, and while it was a big step for him, it hadn't been the one he'd been worried about most. No, deep down, he'd known his father would accept him as gay. But would he also accept Kenn's needs? How he was wired? Especially when it was so different from how his dad was and his uncle Milan.

But he'd fight that battle another day. At least he'd gotten this out, and that was something to be proud of.

"If you'll allow me one more uncomfortable remark..."

Kenn laughed. "Just when I thought this conversation couldn't possibly get more mortifying."

"Because of who I am in my job, you have limited resources available. It's not as easy for you as it is for others to find out what you need to know or procure things you might want or need."

Things he might want or need? God, his father was being cryptic again. "Like..."

"Like condoms or sex toys."

Kenn all but choked on his own breath. "Dad!"

"What? You made me say it. I tried to be all discreet about it, but you forced me to use the actual words. It's not like it's something to be ashamed of. You're twenty-two, Kenn. It's okay to have needs, to want to explore and discover yourself and others. All I'm saying is that it's not as easy for you as it is for others, but don't forget that I have a lot of nonstraight men working for me who would be happy to help you out. And none of them will ever breathe a word to me, I promise you."

Kenn groaned. "Seriously, Dad. I hope you don't expect me to give Seth a shopping list, because that's never going to happen."

His father's booming laugh filled the car, and despite everything, Kenn laughed as well. "Personally, I'd ask Uncle Milan, since it's more his specialty, but I'll leave that to you." His dad grew serious again. "Promise me you'll be good to yourself and that you'll give yourself permission to discover who you are."

19

Warrick had thought he'd be happy to return to his own house, but much to his surprise, he missed Camp David. Maybe it was one of those experiences that, in hindsight, seemed much more perfect than it had been in reality. Or maybe he'd been more starved for human contact and friendship than he'd realized. He'd spent most of his time with Kenn, but during their shared meals, he'd also had ample opportunity to meet the others and connect with them. He missed it. He missed feeling like he was part of a team. A family, even.

And if he were honest, he missed Kenn. Loud alarm bells were going off every time he admitted it to himself, but denying the truth wouldn't help either. Apparently, Denali had been right that it hadn't been just Kenn who had gotten attached so quickly. Warrick had fallen victim to it as well. And now that the president had sanctioned their friendship, Warrick saw no reason to keep his distance from Kenn anymore.

After having seen the boy's hurt and sadness over Warrick pulling away from him, he would've made that decision anyway, regardless of what the president had thought. Kenn needed him, plain and simple, though the reality that Warrick needed him in equal measure was becoming clear as well.

Security around the White House was much tighter than it had been before the First Lady's death, and Warrick's bag was thoroughly searched before he was let in, even though he was wearing his all-access pass. He didn't mind. Anything to keep the president and his family safe.

Jim was working the elevator again. "Morning, Professor. How are you today?"

"I'm well, Jim. It's good to see you again."

Jim closed the elevator doors and pushed on the button for the second floor. "It's an awful tragedy what happened to Mrs. Shafer. I still can't get over it."

"I know. She was such a lovely woman."

"You know, Professor, not many people hold my job in high esteem. I'm used to being ignored or only perfunctory acknowledged. But Mrs. Shafer, she *saw* me. She always talked to me and made sure to make me feel appreciated."

Warrick put a firm hand on Jim's shoulder and squeezed it briefly. "That speaks volumes, doesn't it? Character is what you do when no one else is watching."

Jim nodded. "Yes, sir, it is. And Mrs. Shafer spread nothing but kindness. We'll miss her around here."

Upstairs, Kenn stood waiting for him with Rogue by his side, his face breaking open in a wide smile when Warrick got out of the elevator. For a second, Warrick thought Kenn would hug him, but then the boy stepped back, though his smile remained. "I'm happy you're here, Professor."

"Warrick," Warrick corrected him as he bent down to give Rogue a good rub.

"Warrick," Kenn repeated. "I didn't mean to call you professor. I was just thrilled to start again."

"I wish all students were as eager as you."

"That may also be because I have little else to do."

"True, but you're truly interested in what I'm teaching you, and it makes all the difference."

He followed Kenn to their usual spot in the West Sitting Room, where Rogue settled at Kenn's feet. Warrick frowned as he took in Kenn's frame. Had he lost weight? He seemed thinner than before, which in itself wasn't an issue, but it would be if it hadn't been intentional. His face was pale as well, and the dark circles under his eyes told Warrick he wasn't getting enough sleep.

"How are you feeling?" he asked.

Kenn shrugged. "Sad. Lonely. The same as always."

"You look tired. Are you getting enough sleep?"

Kenn hesitated. "I have trouble falling asleep," he said finally, casting his eyes at the floor.

"Nightmares?"

"No. I can't get my head to stop thinking."

"Is it productive thinking, like thinking about something interesting or making plans?"

"No, all these weird thoughts that I can't let go of. Wondering what would've happened if my father had eaten the banana instead of my mom. Or if I had taken it. If we would've survived and she'd still be alive. If we could've or should've done everything to keep her safe. If she'd gone to the hospital when the doctor had recommended it..."

Warrick's heart went out to him. "I'm so sorry, Kenn. I don't think you need me to tell you those thoughts aren't helpful, but I know what it's like to have them. They're hard to beat."

Kenn tilted his head. "You've had them too?"

"Not about your mom, but about the incident in the Army where I was wounded. I've lain awake so many nights, going over every second in my head, wondering what I missed, what I should've done differently. It took me a long time to get past that. Part of it is what's called survivor's guilt, feeling guilty for being alive when someone else died. Completely irrational, but it's normal to feel that way."

Kenn averted his eyes again. "What about wishing you'd died instead? Is that normal too?"

How Warrick wished he could bear Kenn's burden for him. His grief, his sadness, his despair. Kenn might technically be an adult, but in that moment, he felt so much younger. Like someone he wanted to shield and protect. "It is, but can you tell me why you feel that way?"

Kenn stayed quiet for a long time. "I'm not depressed. I'm smart enough to know that when I make a statement like that, that would be the first thing other people would think of, but that's not the case. My mom was such a wonderful person, and even in the short period that she was First Lady or as the vice president's wife, she was making a difference. I can't help but think that her life was so much more valuable than mine. I'm not like her or like my dad. Both of them have so many talents, and I don't see those in myself."

Those words made it crystal clear for Warrick. No, Kenn wasn't struggling with depression. On top of the grief for his mom, he was suffering from a deeply rooted lack of confidence, self-doubt, and insecurity. In itself not uncommon for someone his age, but it seemed as if it had reached a crippling stage where it was holding him back.

"When your father is the president of the United States, it's hard not to feel like you could never measure up."

Kenn slowly nodded. "He's always been like that,

though. Not perfect, but pretty close. He served in the military, became a senator, then vice president, and now president. How can I ever compete with that?"

"You can't. And you shouldn't want to. You're your own person, Kenn. You can't be your dad...or your mom. You are you, and you're perfect the way you are. There's a saying. 'Comparison is the thief of joy,' and that's so true. You'll never be truly happy if you always compare yourself to others. You're unique, special. There's only one you."

Kenn blew out a long breath. "I never heard that saying before, but yeah, I guess that's true. It's hard not to, though. I feel so insignificant, and my grandfather never ceases to remind me that with my heritage, I'm destined for greatness."

Warrick scoffed. "God save us from men who put pressure on their kids and grandkids to live their dreams rather than their own. You're not destined for anything but to be who you are."

"Thank you. I'm not sure if I can fully believe that yet, but I definitely needed to hear that."

"Kenn, can I ask you something else?"

Kenn met his eyes. "Of course. I have no secrets from you."

Warrick suppressed a smile. The boy could be so wonderfully naïve at times. He loved that he'd managed to hang on to his almost childlike innocence. "Are you taking good care of yourself otherwise? I'm worried about you."

Another deep sigh. "I'm not good at that. My mom always sent me reminders. I know I need to take more responsibility for myself, but it's hard for me."

"Would you like me to help you?"

Kenn's eyes widened in surprise, and then a slow smile spread across his lips. "Would you be willing to do that?"

"Of course. I'm here to help, b—" He swallowed back the term of endearment that had almost popped out. Again. Why did he want to keep calling Kenn *baby*? It had to be because of the protective instincts the boy triggered.

"Let's talk about some rules, then," he quickly said to cover himself. Much to his surprise, Kenn didn't even object to the word rules but quite happily nodded. "You need to eat at least three meals a day. Healthy meals. Fiber, vitamins, all that stuff."

"I can do that."

"You also need eight hours of sleep every night. It seems to me your sleep pattern is completely out of whack, which is understandable, but it's imperative we get that back into a solid rhythm. So I suggest you go to bed at ten, then read for half an hour or so to help your mind calm down, and then you go to sleep. How does that sound?"

"I think that would make me feel better. I'm exhausted during the day."

"Good. So we have food and sleep. What else do you need help with?"

Kenn bit his lip. "Exercise?"

"What options do you have available for you? I don't suppose you can just go to a gym."

Kenn broke out in a giggle. "The Secret Service would have a heart attack... Though I wouldn't mind seeing some of them in shorts and workout shirts."

Warrick snorted. The kid had just made his first gay reference. He was strangely proud of him. "I'm with you on that. So what could you do?"

"One of the perks of living in the White House is that we have a workout room. There's also a pool, but it's an outdoor one, so we can't use that in the winter. It's heated, though, so you can start swimming early in the season."

Warrick whistled between his teeth. "Nice. So how many times a week do you think you should exercise?"

Kenn tapped his mouth with his forefinger. "I always thought twice a week was enough, but my mom insisted on three times, so let's go with that."

"Three times a week it is. Is that something you'd want to do first thing in the morning?"

"Maybe before lunch? After sitting still the whole morning?"

"Sure, that makes sense. I can entertain myself for an hour three times a week."

"Or you could come with me. To work out as well, I mean."

Huh, there was a thought. Warrick hadn't even considered that. "Are you sure that would be okay?"

"If previous presidents could offer high-rolling donors a night in the Lincoln Bedroom, I'm pretty sure it would be okay for me to have you work out with me. It's not like it would cost anybody anything."

He had a point. "True. Monday, Wednesday, and Friday. Which means we'll start tomorrow."

"Yay, I can't wait."

Warrick laughed at the thick sarcasm in Kenn's tone. "It'll be fun."

"No offense, but working out isn't what I'd consider fun. More like a necessary evil."

"Well, I could always ask one of the agents to work out with us, give you some eye candy to distract you."

The joke felt daring to Warrick. He and Kenn had never so openly acknowledged their shared sexual orientation, but after Kenn's previous remark, he wanted to affirm to the boy that it was okay to say things like that. He needed to become more comfortable in his own skin, and casual jokes like that could help.

Kenn giggled again, then grew serious. "I came out to my dad."

"You did? How did it go?"

"He said that he loved me no matter what and that he was proud of me. I don't know why I waited so long. I even asked him if he and my mom knew, and he said they'd suspected it for over ten years. Now I feel silly I didn't tell him sooner, but my dad said this was my journey and that I shouldn't feel bad about it."

Warrick laid his hand on top of Kenn's. "Your father is right about that. Even if you know coming out is safe, that still doesn't mean you're required to do so. You can do all this at your own pace. But I'm so happy for you your father reacted well."

Kenn stared at their hands, then peered up at Warrick, his cheeks reddening. "My dad also said I should explore and experiment."

Warrick coughed as a breath got stuck in his lungs. "He said what now?"

"He told me it was okay for me to explore and experiment. And he meant, like, sexual stuff. He even mentioned condoms and other things, and it was the most embarrassing, mortifying, uncomfortable conversation I've ever had in my life, and I never want to talk to him about that ever again."

Warrick couldn't hold back his laughter. God, that poor kid, having to have that conversation with his father...the president. "I can't even imagine, but on the other hand, be grateful he's so accepting. He's trying to give you the space to be yourself, even under these impossible circumstances."

He was still holding Kenn's hand, and the boy had made

no attempt to pull it back, but it was getting awkward, right? Even though it didn't feel that way but rather seemed like the most natural thing in the world. He liked touching Kenn, and the boy clearly craved physical contact.

"He is, and I do appreciate it, but that still doesn't mean I need a repeat of that conversation. Having him tell me that if I need advice or supplies, I can turn to gay staff members wasn't what I ever wanted to hear out of my father's mouth."

Warrick's heart skipped a beat. Supplies? Advice? The deeper meaning of what Kenn was saying registered with him. Kenn was ready to explore his sexuality, to become sexually active. Warrick had never asked him, obviously, but he'd long suspected Kenn was still a virgin. And now he was ready to take his first baby steps into the world of gay sex or maybe gay dating. Completely normal at his age, so why did unease gnaw at him?

"I hope that by now, you have enough faith in our friendship that you know you can come to me as well. I'd be happy to answer any questions you might have."

20

One week into his new schedule, and Kenn could already tell the difference. He had far more energy, he no longer looked like a corpse, and he'd even gained some weight. Amazing what sticking to those simple rules had accomplished in such a short time.

Why had he no trouble following Warrick's schedule when he'd been unable to do it for himself? What had made the difference? All Kenn knew was that he lived for the moments that Warrick praised him, told him he'd done a good job. Stupid and infantile, maybe, but it did something for him, filling him with joy and happiness in a way that few other things could accomplish.

Like right now, when Warrick was reading an essay Kenn had written, and he was eagerly awaiting his verdict. He knew he'd given his best effort, quoting reputable sources for his arguments, but Warrick excelled at finding the weaknesses in his line of reasoning. He wasn't trying to be difficult or discourage Kenn. No, he wanted to push back hard so Kenn would learn to make his statements ironclad.

Joe stepped forward from his spot against the wall. "Excuse me."

Kenn didn't like the look on his face, and Rogue got up from where he'd been dozing on the floor as well, trotting toward the Secret Service agent, who briefly patted his head. "What's wrong?"

"That snowstorm that was expected for tonight is moving in faster than anticipated. The first bands have reached us, and it looks like it's going to be a big one. I just thought you'd want to know, Professor, considering your commute home."

"Yes, thank you, Joe," Warrick said, pulling up his phone. He groaned, then showed Kenn the radar images that depicted nothing but the darkest blue, predicting upward of a foot of snow.

"I need to leave," Warrick said. "I hate to cut our day short, but I want to make it home before the roads become impassable."

"Stay here." The words were out before Kenn realized it.

"Kenn..."

"No, I mean it. Stay here. We have plenty of room, and you heard what Joe said. It's gonna hit hard. If you get stuck in traffic, you won't make it home before the heavy bands hit. Besides, you know snow shoveling is bad for your back, and you'd have to dig yourself out tomorrow morning...if you even manage that."

Warrick chuckled. "I see you're not above using things I told you against me."

Kenn shrugged, grinning. "Whatever works...and is legal."

Warrick stared at him for a few moments. "I'm tempted to take your suggestion, but are you sure this would be okay with your father? Do you need to check with him?"

Care

"He'll be fine with it. Our house was always open to my or my parents' friends if they needed a place to stay. My mom made it clear I never had to ask."

As always when he mentioned his mom, a wave of sadness rolled over him. His voice caught, and his heart always clenched tightly whenever he thought of her. Six weeks in, the grief was still so real and deep.

He took a moment to compose himself, then met Warrick's eyes again. "Sorry, I didn't mean to put pressure on you by mentioning my mom."

Warrick put his hand on top of Kenn's, sending sparks through his body. "I know. That's way more manipulative than you're capable of. You already had me convinced anyway. Thank you for offering. I feel relieved that I won't have to go out there."

"You're welcome."

Warrick took his hand away, and Kenn blinked at the strange sense of loss. He'd liked the contact. A lot. He cleared his throat. "Let me go tell Mrs. Morelli so she can count on you for dinner, and I'll ask Mr. Funnell to get a room ready."

"Thank you. I'll finish reading through your essay a second time. I have to say, Kenn, it'll be hard to find something to criticize so you can improve. I'm impressed."

A thrill shot through him at those words of praise.

"Rogue, stay," Kenn said. Mrs. Morelli loved Rogue, but she was strict about not allowing him into the kitchen, and Kenn could understand why. Rogue obediently plopped down at Warrick's feet, where he looked completely relaxed and at home. No wonder. By now, the dog was as used to Warrick as he was to Kenn.

Kenn was still smiling as he made his way to the kitchen, where Mrs. Morelli was stirring in a massive pot. He sniffed the air. Oh, god, her homemade tomato soup. "Is that what I think it is?"

She winked at him. "It sure is, honey."

He loved that she always called him honey, regardless of his status as the president's son. "It smells so good."

"I thought that would go well with this weather. I'm serving it with two kinds of Italian bread, herb butter, and four kinds of cheeses."

"I'm sure you'll have enough, but I just wanted to tell you that Professor Duvall will be staying here tonight."

She nodded. "I thought he might. That weather isn't fit for man or beast."

"Would you happen to know where Mr. Funnell is so I can let him know?"

She waved her hand. "I'll take care of that, honey. I'll serve dinner for you two at six. I know the professor is a man of schedules."

He was, and if she hadn't said it herself, Kenn would've suggested it. "Just us two?"

His stomach did a happy twirl at the idea of another dinner with Warrick.

"Mmm, your father is having late meetings and won't be here until eight. And Mr. Bradbury is at Mr. Wylie's house."

"Ah, okay. Thank you. Mrs. Morelli."

"You're welcome, honey. You go spend time with the professor. He's a good man."

Funny how much it meant to him to hear her say that. Technically, it shouldn't matter what others thought of Warrick, especially someone who wasn't his family or a close friend. And yet it did, almost like it affirmed his own opinion of him, like Kenn wasn't crazy for admiring Warrick so much. "Thank you, Mrs. Morelli. Can you ask Mr.

Funnell to prepare the Lincoln Bedroom? I think the professor would get a kick out of sleeping there."

She laughed. "He sure would. Shouldn't be an issue, but I'll let him know. Now, go back to your professor, honey."

She shooed him out of her kitchen. Your professor. What did she mean by that? It sounded almost intimate, as if she was implying Warrick was more to him than his tutor. They were friends, and they'd grown even closer since Camp David. Was that what she meant? But then why had she called him *his* professor? It didn't make sense.

He shrugged it off as he walked back to Warrick, who had taken out his infamous red pen and was scribbling something in the margin. "I see you found something after all?" Kenn teased.

Warrick chuckled. "I had to look hard for it, trust me. This is fantastic work, Kenn."

Fireworks lit up inside him. "Thank you."

Warrick put his pen down, and Kenn sat down again opposite him. Rogue briefly lifted his head to see what Kenn was up, then relaxed again. "I'm so proud of you on your progress, both academically and with getting your life back into a solid rhythm."

"I'm feeling much better, even after a week."

"I can tell."

"Thank you for helping me with that. I know I shouldn't need it, but..."

Warrick's eyes were kind. "Says who? We're all wired differently, and needing help is not something to be embarrassed about. It doesn't make you weak or immature if that's what you think."

Warrick so often seemed to be able to read Kenn's mind, taking away worries and concerns before they'd even fully formed in his head. He'd never been close to someone like him, and the experience exhilarated him. If he imagined himself in a relationship—which, he had to admit, was hard to fathom, considering who he was and where he lived—he pictured it like this.

An older boyfriend, someone wise and mature who would take care of him, who would protect him and guide him, help him find his way. He didn't want someone his own age who'd make fun of him for being naïve and immature. No, he needed a caring, patient Dom who'd fit his submissive character. Someone like...like Warrick, though that was ridiculous, of course.

"Where'd you go?" Warrick asked, smiling softly.

Kenn startled. "Sorry, lost in thoughts."

"No worries." Warrick checked his watch. "Do you happen to know what time dinner is?"

"At six. Mrs. Morelli and I thought you'd like to eat early."

"I do, but not if it's an inconvenience."

"It's not. But it will be the two of us. My dad is working till at least eight, and Uncle Milan is at Asher's. I hope you don't mind."

"I never mind having dinner with you." Warrick's voice sounded a tad hoarse. He cleared his throat. "We always have stimulating conversation, don't we?"

Kenn nodded. "We do. I like that too. Oh, and I requested the Lincoln Bedroom for you. I thought you'd like that."

Warrick's face lit up. "You did? What a special treat, Kenn. Thank you. That's an absolute privilege."

"I gotta warn you, though, that the bed is not the most comfortable."

"You tested it?'

"Duh. I slept there one night, and while it was cool, my own room is much more comfortable."

"Noted. I'll suffer some inconvenience for the treat of spending a night in such a historical room."

They chatted so amicably time flew by until dinner was served, and they seamlessly transitioned into the family dining room, never lost for words or searching for new topics to talk about. Rogue was gnawing on a massive bone in the corner of the room, perfectly content.

"Why did you decide to go to West Point?" Kenn asked when his belly was pleasantly full of the rich tomato soup and all the amazing bread Mrs. Morelli had baked. "It doesn't seem like the most logical choice for a gay man."

Warrick leaned back in his chair. "You'll laugh at this, but when I was a teenager, I happened to come across North and South on TV. Have you ever heard of it?"

Kenn shook his head.

"It's a TV series about the Civil War, made in the eighties with Patrick Swayze in one of the lead roles. Anyway, it's about these two men, one from the North and one from the South, who meet at West Point and become best friends. For some reason, the idea of West Point stuck with me, even though the series doesn't really depict it in the best light. It became kind of an obsession for me, I suppose. A dream. Something to focus on while...things were not so good in my life."

"What was going on, if you don't mind me asking?"

Warrick let out a deep sigh. "I was in foster care from when I was ten years old. My father died from a work-related accident when I was seven. He worked at a power plant, and a coworker made a mistake, and a high-voltage power line hit my dad. He was dead instantly. My mom couldn't handle doing everything by herself. She'd always been a housewife, a happy homemaker, and in hindsight, she was lost without my dad. She started drinking, and things got bad. My school contacted Child Protective Services, and they took me away from her. The idea was that she'd get herself together, but she never did. She ended up committing suicide, and since she didn't have family and my father's older brothers couldn't give two shits about me, I ended up in foster care."

Kenn's heart went out to him. "W-was it bad?"

"Not as bad as it could have been. I had some good foster families and some mediocre ones. But I was always fed and clothed and taken care of, if rarely loved. It forced me to become self-reliant at a young age. I think West Point became a dream for me, a way out of poverty."

"Isn't it really hard to get accepted?"

Warrick smiled. "You're not accepted into West Point but *appointed*, just like you're not a student but a *candidate*. It's a whole different world with its own rules and lingo. But yes, it's extremely hard. I was lucky with an incredibly supportive high school guidance counselor who was dedicated to seeing me succeed. With her help, I took all the steps and eventually got in. It was my dream come true."

"And then your career ended so soon…" Kenn felt that hurt deep in his soul as if it had happened to himself.

Warrick slowly nodded. "I won't lie. That was the toughest hand I'd been dealt in my life, and I'd already survived a lot."

"How did you get through it?" Losing his mom wasn't the same, but maybe Warrick had some insights that could help Kenn. He'd take any advice at this point, especially from the man who had already proven he had Kenn's best interests at heart.

Warrick's eyes softened. "I wish I could tell you anything better than to talk about it and give it time."

"Is that what you did?"

"Initially, no. I was angry and bitter, and it took time for me to accept the doctor's diagnosis that I'd never return to active duty. The IED caused nerve damage to my back and leg, and I needed a lot of physical therapy to get to where I am. Law school was a diversion, something to focus on, to distract myself. I've always been a disciplined person, so I needed something else to sink my teeth into. But it took me a year to accept my Army career was over and move on, and I only got there after talking to a therapist."

Wasn't it interesting how talking to Warrick made Kenn feel like an adult on one hand, purely because Warrick treated him as an equal, while on the other hand, he felt so wonderfully safe and protected? He could be himself without fearing judgment. Warrick had never uttered a hint of criticism, not even when Kenn had shown his submissive side, his needy traits.

"Thank you for sharing that," he said softly. "It gives me hope that I'll get through this."

Warrick took his hand and squeezed it, but the moment was gone too quickly. "You will, I promise. And I'll be right there if you need me."

Yeah, Kenn was certain now. He wanted something just like this. He wanted someone like Warrick by his side. Or maybe...he wanted Warrick? His cheeks heated up, and his heart fluttered wildly. No, that was a foolish pipe dream. Warrick would never want a needy boy like Kenn. He'd want someone closer to his own age, someone independent and smart and accomplished.

But still, when he went to bed that night, all he could think of was the way Warrick had held his hand, how he had looked at him and talked to him, how he was taking care of Kenn in every way. And when he fell asleep, he dreamed of Warrick.

21

Henley hadn't regretted quitting his job for Time magazine, but he'd be lying if he said he didn't miss being a reporter. The thrill of chasing down a story, of attacking it from every angle until he had answers—nothing could compare. Luckily, Coulson had asked for his input on something that would keep him busy for a while. He needed some background research on President Markinson, and as he'd put it, who better to ask than a reporter who had covered him for years?

Henley had started by composing a brief bio and some highlights from Markinson's term as president, but Coulson had indicated he was looking for something specific: a reason why anyone would want Markinson dead. Now that was a question Henley would like an answer to as well. He'd done his research in what was available online, and he knew quite a bit already, having been on the White House beat, but he still had questions that weren't so easy to find answers to.

The good news was that he knew who to approach, and as always, the man had readily agreed to meet with him. To make up for the trouble, Henley had invited him for lunch in a restaurant in DC that was known for having the best fried chicken north of the Deep South—because that wasn't at all a confusing statement.

"Bryce," he greeted him when he walked up to him outside the restaurant. "It's good to see you."

Bryce chuckled. "I'm glad to see you treating me to a real lunch this time, Platt. You owed me."

"I did. Have you ever been here before?"

"No, but I heard the food's amazing." Bryce rubbed his hands, and Henley laughed. The way to Bryce's affection was definitely through his stomach.

He'd reserved a table in the back, which would afford plenty of privacy. As soon as they'd put their drink orders in, he asked, "How's the job been?"

Bryce had stayed on after Markinson's death and was now polling for President Shafer. Henley was glad he'd been loyal to the new president, since Bryce was so good at what he did.

"Different from before, but I like it. Shafer is addressing many new issues, and it makes my job far more challenging. We've seen real movement of people's opinions on hot topics."

"Like what?"

"The support for gay marriage has gone up, and now that Senator Riggs has been sworn in as vice president, more people support the idea of a female president. Even for me, it was surprising to see the needle move on those issues after Shafer being in power for only seven months."

"That's great news. That proves change is possible."

Bryce nodded as he sipped his Coke. "For sure, but don't forget that at the same time, those who're against it have grown more radical as well. The schism between the two is real."

"How are people seeing President Markinson now that he's been dead for a while?"

"Pretty positive, and I don't think the halo effect of his assassination will wear off anytime soon, just like what happened with JFK. And now that there's such rampant speculation over Annabeth Markinson's fate..."

The implied question was heavy, but Henley ignored it. He wasn't touching that topic with a ten-foot pole. "You were working with Markinson for a long time, way before he ever became president."

Bryce nodded. "I became his poller when he was a senator and considering his first bid for the presidency. He ended up waiting four more years, but I've been with him since."

The server came to take their food order, and Henley waited until he was gone again. "Did you like him?"

"Markinson? Well enough to work for him. I mean, no one's perfect, but generally speaking, I liked his politics."

"What were some big issues he wanted you to poll on before he ran for president?"

Bryce narrowed his eyes for a moment as if he was wondering why Henley was asking. "Mostly smaller issues he didn't have a firm opinion on so he could take the position that had the biggest appeal to voters. But we also polled a few big topics, like health care, immigration, and his personal obsession, the budget."

"He was a staunch supporter of reducing expenditures and balancing the budget, correct?"

"He wanted to cut back on frivolous spending, as he called it, and he supported raising the highest tax bracket to get extra income. Combined, the two would've made it possible to balance the budget."

"How did that poll?"

Bryce reached for his phone. "Let me look up some numbers 'cause that was a while ago."

Henley waited as he flipped through his phone.

Bryce rattled off some numbers. "These measures would've had support from urban women and nonwhite men, but among suburban women and rural white voters, they were unpopular. He needed those groups to win the presidential election, so he backed off on that and came with a compromise."

"Talk to me about his stand on military spending."

Bryce groaned. "God, that topic was the worst... Few things pissed him off more than not getting that fixed."

The server came out with their food, and Bryce licked his lips as he took in the pile of fried chicken on his plate. Henley had opted for a salad with only a few strips of fried chicken. As much as Levar appreciated Henley's rounder body, he wanted to make sure he stayed healthy. Gaining weight had been all too easy at Camp David, what with the constant supply of food and snacks.

"He had a mixed record on everything concerning the military," Henley commented.

"He did. We polled the support for pulling out US troops from Afghanistan and Iraq. I still maintain he could've made it work, but someone leaked we were polling this, and it caused a shitstorm."

Henley vaguely remembered something about that, but he hadn't been on the White House beat yet at the time. "Didn't the Republicans attack him for polarizing the military?"

Bryce, who had stuffed his mouth full of chicken, held

up his finger and chewed furiously. "The timing was bad for them, and they hit hard with their counterlobby."

"What was wrong about the timing?"

"It never got much traction, but there had been a story about a private contractor in Iraq, whose team had raped and killed civilian women. The company buried that story deep with the help of politicians loyal to them, and they managed to make it classified intel after it had already leaked. I wouldn't be surprised if they did it using some questionable tactics and threats. But Markinson knew about it, and so did the senators who served with him on the Senate Armed Services Committee. In fact, that story was one of the reasons why Markinson wanted to poll the issue, but it backfired when others found out."

Henley had to force himself to keep his face neutral. "Do you remember which private contractor that was?"

Bryce sighed. "Kingmakers. They're bad news, I'm telling you. I met one of the owners once, and that dude was cold as ice. Purely in it for the money. Didn't give a shit about any humanitarian aspect."

Kingmakers? Henley smelled blood in the water. "That's a heavy accusation. Was there any proof they committed those atrocities?"

Bryce shrugged. "The powers that be squashed that shit hard, but in my experience, rumors like that are usually at least partially true. Markinson must've believed it because he initiated the bill that sought to reduce military spending and stop using army contractors like Kingmakers. But then his polling into that issue leaked, and he got attacked for politicizing a tragedy and the military, so he withdrew the bill."

Holy shit. For the first time, they had a link between Markinson and Kingmakers. If Markinson had gotten his way back then, Kingmakers would've been out of business, which would've lost them a fortune. "He stopped using them once he became president, though."

"He did, but it was never formalized in a bill. Just his own policy. The next president could have…"

Bryce stopped talking, his eyes growing big. He held Henley's gaze as he swallowed. "Did I just…? Is that why…?" He caught himself, holding up his hands. "On second thought, don't answer that. I don't want to know."

"You don't trust me. Even if I could tell you."

"I'm not asking. But in case you were wondering, as far as I'm aware, Markinson never considered revisiting his position on using private contractors, not even after the Pride Bombing and the hunt for Hamza Bashir and Al Saalihin."

Damn. If Kingmakers was connected to that bombing, their plan hadn't worked. Was that why they'd assassinated Markinson? Henley felt like he'd somehow ended up in a JFK-like conspiracy, only it was all too real.

Bryce cocked his head. "So now you're firmly entrenched in the president's camp?"

"Kinda hard to stay working as a reporter when you share a bed with the press secretary."

"True. You guys do make a cute couple, though. I'm sure it was worth it, no?"

Henley smiled. "It totally was. Haven't regretted it even for a second."

"Good. I'm happy for you, Henley. I'm, like, the least sappy guy on the planet, but even I had actual feelings when I heard the news about you two. Made me genuinely happy…for a minute or two."

Henley laughed. "But not as good as that fried chicken, I bet."

Bryce chuckled. "What can I say? I'm a man of simple pleasures, my friend."

They were quiet for a moment, Bryce devouring his chicken while Henley chewed absentmindedly as his brain was spinning. Kingmakers made most of their money from contracts with the US Government. If that stopped, they'd go bankrupt. Was that why they'd targeted Markinson? When he was still a senator, he'd been clear about his opposition to using private contractors, so they must've seen it coming. If that were true, they must've been scared shitless during the presidential elections when they saw him poll so well.

"Who analyzes the donations during presidential campaigns?" he asked Bryce. If they'd been that opposed, they had to have supported Governor Winkelmann, the Republican presidential candidate who had lost to Markinson.

"Ours or the Republicans?"

"Both, but mostly the Republicans."

"He's retired, but talk to Bill Clampton. No one knows more about campaign finances than he does, and even retired, he still consults for the party. I bet he'd be able to answer a lot of your questions."

They chatted the rest of the lunch, then parted ways. Henley got lucky because when he called, Bill Clampton said he'd be able to see him right away, so Henley drove to his house in Bethesda. He'd heard of Clampton before, but he'd never met him. The man was much older than Henley had expected, probably around seventy-five. He seemed frail, but his sharp eyes showed his mind still functioned well.

"Thanks so much for seeing me, Mr. Clampton," Henley said as the older man led him into a glorious study with floor-to-ceiling built-in bookcases crammed with books. God, he could spend weeks here and never get bored.

"My pleasure, but please call me Bill."

His wife, Doris, brought out some tea and cookies, and then they settled down.

"First of all, who am I talking to?" Bill asked. "I know you left the White House beat, so I need to know in what capacity you're here."

The man was smart, and Henley liked him already, even if he asked a question that was hard to answer without lying or revealing too much. "I'm not here as a reporter. I'm just gathering some background info on President Markinson."

Bill nodded slowly. "I see. And who would that background be reported to?"

Henley hesitated. "I'm not at liberty to say, but I'll say that it's with President Shafer's full knowledge and support."

"Good enough for me. Considering everything that has happened lately, I'd better not ask too many questions. You said you wanted to talk about President Markinson's first campaign."

"Yes. Bryce said no one knew more about campaign finances than you."

Bill laughed. "No need to butter me up, young man. I was willing to talk as soon as you mentioned Bryce's name. If he says you're good people, that's all I need to know. So, what do you want to know?"

"Markinson's first presidential campaign, was there anything that stood out to you about the donations to both his campaign and that of Governor Winkelmann?"

Bill leaned back in his chair as he sipped his tea, a deep frown on his forehead. "I'd say that the thing that most stood out was that Winkelmann set an all-time-high record on donations, out-fundraising Markinson almost two to one...and still lost. We've rarely seen such a disparity in fundraising, and never before did the candidate who had so much more money still lose."

"How did you explain that?"

Another sip of tea. Henley liked that the man weighed his words before he spoke. "I asked that same question, as one is prone to do when facts differ so sharply from historical experiences. In this case, my conclusion was that Winkelmann was a weak candidate and voters recognized that."

"Being governor of North Carolina doesn't exactly prepare you for the White House. His lack of experience and knowledge in foreign matters especially was troubling," Henley agreed.

"Add to that some serious gaffes during the campaign when asked about key issues, and he never got a lead on Markinson. All the money in the world couldn't change that. Plus, they couldn't get dirt on Markinson. He's a moderate Democrat, so any accusations of him being a leftist socialist liberal simply didn't stick."

"What triggered those extra donations?"

"Lots and lots of small donors. That was another fact that baffled me. Winkelmann wasn't known for building a grassroots campaign as a governor, but he must've had an excellent campaign staff who helped him with that. He had the usual donations from companies and action committees, but the big money came in through numerous small-time donations, all under two hundred dollars and half of those under fifty bucks."

Henley immediately recognized the significance of those numbers. Contributions under fifty dollars could be reported to the FEC, the Federal Election Commission, without having to disclose the contributor's name and mailing address if they were done at a fundraising event. That made them anonymous and pretty hard to trace. Contributions under two hundred only required a name and mailing address, not the contributor's occupation and employer, like those above that amount.

"I suppose he did a lot of fundraising events?" he asked.

"More than any other candidate ever."

"Makes it hard to trace that money," Henley said slowly.

"It does, and if one were so inclined, one might find that his campaign reported multiple fundraisers on the same dates...with too far a distance in between for Winkelmann to attend both."

Henley raised an eyebrow. "Campaign fraud?"

"Most likely, yes. But he lost, so no one was interested in prosecuting."

"What about the donations in Markinson's reelection campaign?"

"They were still higher than previous campaigns on the Republican side, but they didn't match the record set by Winkelmann. It's damn near impossible to beat a sitting president, so maybe they were saving their efforts for when Markinson was done?"

Henley had lots to think about and report back. And it might be a wild goose chase, but they definitely should have someone look into those campaign donations. *Follow the money.* The famous catchphrase was still valid. Always follow the money...and sex and power. The trifecta of dirty politics. Which one would prove to be true in this case? Only one way to find out. Dig even deeper.

22

Spending a whole day and evening with Warrick and then seeing him again at breakfast had been an experience that had reminded Kenn of their time together at Camp David—which he wouldn't mind repeating. Even though he'd been with Warrick all day, he'd still been sad when it had been time for Warrick to leave.

Kenn had resisted the urge to offer him to stay another night. Sure, the snowstorm had dumped a good foot of snow, but the roads had been cleared, so technically, there had been no reason for Warrick to stay longer. Sadly. His only consolation had been that Warrick hadn't seemed eager to leave either, staying long after he usually went home.

But eventually, he had left, and since that had been a Friday evening, Kenn wouldn't see him again until Monday. He'd managed to entertain himself Saturday, reading through a reading list Warrick had given him, and now he lay stretched out on the couch, flipping through the channels on the TV. Another perk of living in the White House. They had every TV channel known to man, including all the movie channels. Rogue was with his dad in the Oval, so Kenn was on his own, which he didn't like.

"Hey, kiddo," Uncle Milan said as he walked into the living room.

Kenn perked up at having company. "Hey. What are you doing here?"

Uncle Milan snorted. "It may not seem like it, but I actually do still live here."

Kenn chuckled. "I thought you had moved in with Asher."

Uncle Milan plopped down on the other couch. "I'll admit that his place offers a hell of a lot more privacy than this museum, but since he and Denali are both on shift, I figured I'd come hang out here."

"I'm overjoyed at being third choice," Kenn said dryly.

Uncle Milan just grinned. "Priorities. You'll understand once you've found a partner."

Funny, Kenn had never realized before how strictly gender-neutral Uncle Milan was whenever he referred to a potential partner for Kenn. He'd never said he or she, always leaving the gender unspecified. Was that a coincidence, or had he long suspected Kenn's sexual preferences as well? He might as well tell him, since his father knew already anyway. And now that he had that one out of the way, it didn't seem as scary anymore.

"A boyfriend, you mean."

Uncle Milan shot up straight, his eyes intense as they drilled into Kenn's. "Boyfriend?"

"Yeah. I figured I'd let you know."

"Cool. Does your dad know?"

"He does. And I told Warrick as well."

"Glad you felt confident and safe enough to tell us. You

know I don't give two shits about who you love...or who you fuck."

Kenn wanted to groan but held it back. Maybe he should try to play Uncle Milan's game against him. "Dad said I could come to you for any advice."

Uncle Milan coughed loudly, his eyes wide open. "Excuse me?"

"Yeah, I had a good conversation with Dad, and he said that you would be more than willing to answer all my questions."

"God, that fucker... Sure, I'll answer your questions, but keep in mind you may learn a little more than you bargained for. I'm not exactly an expert on vanilla sex. Or relationships, for that matter, considering I'm still making it up as I go along."

Kenn laughed. "No worries. I wasn't going to take him up on that offer. I have others I can ask if I wanted to in the first place."

Uncle Milan stared at him funny for a moment. "Like Warrick," he then said slowly.

Why was he bringing Warrick into this? "I'm sure he'd be happy to talk to me..."

"Yeah, he sure would."

Kenn frowned. Did Uncle Milan have something against Warrick? Didn't he like him? "He's a good guy, Uncle Milan. He's been a wonderful friend to me in the last few weeks."

His uncle's face softened. "I know, kiddo. And I'm glad he was there for you. It's been one hell of a month for all of us, hasn't it?" He studied Kenn for a few moments more. "I have to say you look better than you did the last time I saw you. I'm happy to see it."

"I feel much better. Warrick helped me by setting up a

schedule for me, and he texts me reminders when he's not here so I don't forget. It's been working for me."

"I bet it has," Uncle Milan said. "And he's a good friend for helping you with this."

Kenn felt like he was still missing something. "I know I should be more mature than I am. I shouldn't need someone to set a schedule for me and help me stick to it. My mom always said I'm a late bloomer."

"It's okay. You do things at your own pace."

Kenn's confusion only grew. Uncle Milan's tone and voice made it clear that he meant what he said, yet at the same time, it still felt like he was saying more, like his words contained a hidden message that Kenn couldn't pick up on. But before he could ask him about it, his phone dinged with the special tone he'd set for Warrick.

Warrick: What did you have for dinner?

Kenn: Grilled asparagus with goat cheese, wild rice, and grilled chicken. Super healthy and yummy.

Warrick: That sounds good. I'm proud of you for sticking to your schedule all week. What are you doing tonight?

Kenn: Not sure. Maybe watch a movie.

Warrick: I can't remember the last time I watched a movie. It's one of those things I love but that I never seem to make the time for.

Kenn didn't even think. His reply came immediately.

Kenn: Wanna come over here and watch a movie with me? We could even use the White House family theater.

Warrick: The White House has a movie theater?

Kenn laughed.

Kenn: It sure does. This house comes with perks, remember?

Warrick: I'll be there in about forty-five minutes.

Kenn: Yay! I'm excited to watch a movie with you.
Warrick: Me too

Kenn was still smiling broadly as he put his phone down, and when he lifted his head, Uncle Milan was studying him. "Who are you texting?" he asked.

"Warrick. He's gonna come over to watch a movie."

"He's coming over on a Saturday night, on a day he's off, to watch a movie with you."

"Yeah. What's the problem?"

"No problem at all, just a little surprised to see you hanging out with him on his days off."

"I told you we're friends. Friends hang out."

Uncle Milan opened his mouth as if he wanted to say something but then closed it again. "You know what? Have a great time, kiddo."

"You're welcome to join us if you want. We're using the White House theater. Warrick didn't even know the White House had its own theater, so I thought it would be fun to show it to him."

"Thanks for the invite, but I have no desire to be a third wheel. You two have fun. I'll go bug your dad and Calix. Last time I checked, they were still at work, so it's high time they relax. Pretty sure I could find a bottle of whiskey somewhere around here."

He threw Kenn one last intense look, then walked out, leaving Kenn behind feeling slightly bewildered at what his uncle had been referring to. But whatever. Warrick was coming over to watch a movie with him, and as far as Kenn was concerned, that was worth far more of his energy than whatever bug had crawled up his uncle's ass this time.

He made a few quick requests with the White House staff, thanking them profusely as they helped him set up the movie and appropriate snacks at such short notice. When

Warrick showed up, everything was ready, and Kenn was practically bouncing with giddiness as he met him in the lobby of the East Wing.

Warrick was thoroughly searched, as always, but he endured it with a smile at Kenn, patiently waiting.

"I've never come in this way before," he told Kenn as soon as the agent had led them through. "After you texted me, I had to look at a map to see where the theater actually was."

"Yeah, the East Wing has mostly offices, but it houses the theater as well."

The buttery smell of fresh popcorn greeted them as they walked into the theater. Warrick let out a gasp. "Oh my gosh, this is gorgeous."

Completely decked out in a classic cinema-red with gold and wooden accents, the long, narrow room had that old-fashioned, luxury feel. Even the carpet was bright red, matching the chairs. It boasted seven rows of five theater chairs, though slightly plusher than the ones in regular movie theaters. But the front row was the best, sporting four super comfortable armchairs with matching footstools.

Kenn pointed them out. "Those are our seats. The best view in the house."

The staff had already rolled out a little cart with the refreshments, including two buckets of fresh popcorn.

"It looks amazing. What movie are we watching?"

Kenn smiled, a happy flutter buzzing in his stomach. "I thought it would be fun to watch *Legally Blonde*."

Warrick laughed. "I love that movie, and it's very appropriate, considering your future career."

They settled in the comfy chairs. Kenn immediately took off his shoes and put his legs up on the footstool, sinking deep into the chair. Next to him, Warrick did the same, and as soon as they were settled, the lights dimmed, and the first notes of "Perfect Day" sounded while on the screen Elle was brushing her hair, getting ready for her big date.

Kenn let the story of the movie draw him in all over again, getting angry when Warner broke up with Elle, mentally cheering her on as she studied for her LSATs, cringing when she showed up on the Harvard campus and was met with rejection from her fellow students.

Warrick touched his hand, and Kenn jumped, spilling some popcorn in his lap. "Sorry," Warrick said with a laugh. "I didn't mean to startle you. I just wanted to say that my favorite line of the whole movie is coming up."

"Oh my god, yes. I love that moment."

He also loved how Warrick's hand felt as it still lay on his. Why hadn't Warrick let go yet? Or was he waiting for a signal from Kenn? The flutter in his stomach intensified. Maybe it was normal for gay men to hold hands? He'd often seen his father be physically affectionate with his friends, including Calix and Uncle Milan. He wasn't too sure about that, though, as holding hands seemed to be on a different level than hugs and brief touches, but who was he to complain?

He refocused his attention on the movie screen, where Elle was pretending not to see Warner as she passed him in the hallway. He held his breath, waiting for her iconic line as Warner expressed his confusion as to what she was doing here. "You got into Harvard Law?"

And then Kenn and Warrick said it out loud at the same time as Elle. "What, like it's hard?"

They burst out laughing, and still Warrick was holding his hand. A thousand butterflies broke free in Kenn's belly at seeing Warrick's big smile, the mirth in his eyes, the warmth in his expression as he regarded Kenn. "Perfect choice for a movie," Warrick said, his voice strangely hoarse. "I love watching this with you."

Kenn could only blink, his thoughts too confusing to verbalize. After a moment or two, he turned back to the screen, but he kept his hand where it was, and during the whole movie, he was aware of every little move Warrick made, every breath he took, every heartbeat that pulsed through his hand into Kenn's. Best movie night ever.

23

Oh, he was treading on dangerous ground. Precarious, perilous ground. Warrick should never have held Kenn's hand during the movie two days before, but he hadn't been able to let go. Something about Kenn drew him in, made him want to hold on to him. He triggered a protectiveness inside Warrick, a deep need to take care of him, to make sure he was not only okay but thriving.

He'd never felt like this. He'd had relationships before. Granted, not many, and they'd all been short-lived, but he'd been in love—or so he'd thought. But never had he faced emotions at this level, so intense and all-consuming to the point where he had trouble not thinking about Kenn, even on his days off or at night, when he was at home.

He missed him. Ridiculous and insane as it sounded, he missed him. They had shared so much time in Camp David that it was hard not to be around him as much, even though they spent all weekdays together. But Warrick was reluctant to go home every time, preferring to stay with Kenn.

He wasn't stupid. He recognized it for what it was: an

infatuation. Or maybe that was too juvenile a word for what he was feeling, but it certainly had the intensity of developing a deep crush on someone. Thirty-six years old and crushing hard on a twenty-two-year-old...who was the president's son. The only thing keeping him from panicking was his conversation with the president back at Camp David. The more he'd thought about it, the more he was convinced that the president had indeed subtly given Warrick permission to become close with his son. All he'd asked was that Warrick was careful with him and didn't break his heart—which he had zero intention to.

It had felt so good to have that slim, soft hand underneath his, Kenn's heartbeat pulsing in tandem with his own. Warrick had been on the lookout for even the smallest signal that Kenn didn't want Warrick to touch him. But he hadn't said anything, hadn't hinted at anything. Hell, he'd barely moved. And the way Kenn's heart had raced, the quick intakes of breath... Warrick had been certain Kenn had liked it as much as he had.

But what was the next step? Did he need to have another talk with the president to make sure he'd understood correctly? God, this whole relationship had disaster written all over it, and yet he couldn't walk away. Every fiber of his being protested at the thought of leaving Kenn behind. He yearned to be with him, and arrogant as it might sound, he knew Kenn pined for him as well when they were apart.

"I'm done," Kenn said, those blue eyes focusing on Warrick with a silent plea for approval. He loved how Kenn always sought his guidance, his opinion. It was intoxicating in a way Warrick could never have imagined.

"Let me see." Warrick held out his hand, and Kenn handed him the test he'd done. Since Kenn wasn't officially enrolled in any kind of program, none of the tests counted for credits, but that hadn't kept Kenn from taking them seriously. The boy's eagerness to learn matched his zeal to please Warrick, and he wasn't sure which of those two he loved more.

He quickly read through Kenn's answers, smiling as Kenn had gotten every single question right. "Great job, Kenn. You're such a fast learner. This isn't easy stuff."

"You're a great teacher." Kenn simply beamed. And how on earth was Warrick supposed to close off his heart from that?

"Maybe, but you're a great student. My favorite one by far."

He'd added that last bit spontaneously, and he hadn't thought it possible for Kenn's smile to grow any bigger, and yet it did. The boy was exuberant, and Warrick had to fight the urge to touch him, to cup his cheek and tell him how proud he was of him, to run his hand through Kenn's hair and praise him some more.

"I am?" Kenn asked.

He shouldn't say anything. In fact, he could think of a million reasons why he should keep his mouth shut. "It's not even a competition," he assured him nonetheless. The air between them crackled, Kenn's blue eyes locking on to Warrick's. He swallowed, unable to look away. Was Kenn feeling it too?

"It's time for our break," Kenn said hoarsely. "Will you work out with me?"

Warrick had avoided it so far, encouraging Kenn to spend half an hour in the exercise room while taking some time to read himself. They were already crossing so many boundaries, and the idea of being that informally dressed in front of Kenn... He'd have to shower somewhere, get changed. It would unleash questions and difficulties and a hell of a lot more intimacy than they were already sharing, which was too much as it stood.

But of course, once again, his heart decided, overruling his brain. "I could use some exercise."

Kenn's face lit up. "Did you bring a change of clothes?"

Warrick nodded. "Yeah. I wasn't sure if I was in the mood, but I brought gym clothes and a pair of sneakers. Is there a place I can change? And shower afterward?"

Kenn nodded immediately. "Of course. You can use one of the guest rooms."

Warrick debated with himself as he grabbed the bag he'd brought, then followed Kenn to the third floor, where the boy led him into a pretty roomy, relatively modern decorated bedroom. "I'll be in the workout room in a few minutes," Kenn said, then hurried off, whistling for Rogue to follow him. A staff member would take care of him, since he wasn't allowed in the exercise room, Warrick knew.

Warrick shook his head at himself. What the hell was he doing? He slowly got changed into a T-shirt and shorts, then put on his sneakers. His running days were over, his legs too uneven to make his gait comfortable while he ran, but he could still do other exercises. He wasn't worried about his weight so much, but exercising regularly did help his muscles stay flexible, which prevented injuries and pain.

Kenn was already waiting for him in the workout room, which was much smaller than he would've expected in the White House. The rectangular room sported bland cream walls, the old-fashioned doors betraying the age of the house. A cramped row of cardio machines lined one long end of the room, with minor equipment, like dumbbells, kettlebells, ropes, and a weight lifting bench, on the other side.

"It's not much, is it?" Kenn said with an apologetic smile.

"Mr. Funnell told me when he gave me a tour that it used to be a sitting room. Apparently, Mrs. Kennedy made it famous, and it was called the Blue Toile Bedroom. The Clintons changed it into a gym, but it's a tad small for that purpose."

Warrick smiled. "I see I have a personal tour guide."

"I'm a bit of a dork like that. After we moved in, I read up on the history of the White House. Seemed kinda fitting, considering how much has happened under this roof."

"Mmm, true. I'll admit I was expecting something bigger and grander. But it'll do the job, right?"

Kenn was dressed in a pair of shorts and a tight T-shirt that stressed his slender physique. He was so stinking cute, so sweet and innocent. On some level, Warrick was grateful Kenn was the president's son. That protected environment would keep him a lot safer than when he had to find his way in the real world. Gay men looking for a pretty boy to fuck would've eaten him alive.

"Thank you for working out with me," Kenn said with a shy smile. God, the boy's genuine gratitude really was Warrick's kryptonite. He'd do anything to see Kenn's eyes so full of affection and admiration, to hear the appreciation in his voice. He'd become addicted to it, and that was not a good thing. Not at all.

"My pleasure. I'm going to start on the rowing machine. Is that okay?"

Kenn nodded. "I'll do ten minutes on the treadmill. I hate running, but Seth said it's a good warm-up before doing anything else."

"It is."

Warrick installed himself on the rowing machine, focusing on getting settled and keeping a good posture until he'd found a rhythm he could maintain for a while. Only then did he look to the side to see what Kenn was doing, and holy shit, that was quite the view he had. The treadmill was facing the other way, so he could only see Kenn's back... and his ass, perfectly outlined in the tight shorts the boy was wearing. And what an ass it was. Round, tight, and firm, not even jiggling a little while he ran. Warrick wanted to bite it, taste it, then bury himself...

He averted his gaze, clenching his teeth. He couldn't give in to this, goddammit. He couldn't. Kenn was his student, fourteen years younger, the president's son. Any of those in itself would be reason enough to walk away, but the combination of those three was like a landmine, no matter what the president had hinted at. If he stepped on it, it would blow up in his face...and his future would go up in flames right with it.

He pulled harder on the rope, increasing his speed until sweat broke out all over his body. But inevitably, his eyes were drawn back to the tantalizing sight in front of him. If it had been a purely physical attraction, he would've been able to resist it. He'd done it before. Hell, hadn't every gay man who wasn't on the ace spectrum? They'd all dealt with physical attraction to someone impossible at one time or another. He could've handled that.

But this, this was different. It wasn't merely Kenn's body that drew him in. Oh, he loved Kenn's slim build, his boyish features, and the innocence he radiated. Knowing that the boy was a virgin only added to that attraction, fueled by some deep instinct to be his first. Also not something he figured he was unique in. Many men had had that primal instinct to claim where no one had gone before. Marking their territory, conquering the innocent, however one wanted to call it.

Still not what attracted him to Kenn primarily. No, it was

his character. The way he watched Warrick's every move with adoration in his eyes. His easy, open affection. His neediness, which might've repelled others but was a total drug to Warrick. His shy smiles, his intelligence, how adorably enthusiastic he could get once he was emotionally invested in a discussion. But above all, how much he *needed* Warrick, how he leaned on him, relied on him, looked at him for guidance.

So what the hell did he do? He couldn't quit his job. He wouldn't do that to Kenn, who had already lost his mom and whose dad couldn't be there for him the way he needed him. That was probably why Kenn had grown so attached to Warrick, his need for another father figure. Though Warrick's thoughts about Kenn weren't exactly fatherly.

Sure, he wanted to make sure the boy was taken care of, that he ate healthy and took good care of himself, but he also wanted much more. He wanted to hold him and kiss him and fuck that bitable ass, and...

Oh, shit.

His arms stopped pulling automatically, the rowing machine slowing down as the implications sank in.

Oh fuck, no.

How was that even possible? He'd never been into that before. Hell, it had never even appealed to him, nor had he considered himself old enough—though in hindsight, that was stupid, since it wasn't an age thing. But how on earth had he become a Daddy, and more importantly, how did he make that desire go away? Because if he thought he was in trouble for wanting to fuck the president's son, wait till the man found out Warrick wanted to be his Daddy...

24

It had taken the FBI weeks to create a comprehensive and exhaustive timeline of the last week of Annabeth Markinson's life, and with every detail that had been added, Coulson had become more and more convinced that someone from the Secret Service had to be involved. When he'd gone through the final result with Seth, they'd both come to the same conclusion...and they knew who it had to be as well: the only agent who'd had the opportunity to take Mrs. Markinson's phone.

That agent was now sitting in an FBI interrogation room, and Coulson and Seth were in the hallway, about to go in. Coulson glanced around him to make sure no one was watching them, then put his hand on Seth's shoulder. "I know this one will hit close to home. Walk out if it gets too much, okay?"

Seth leaned into him for a moment. "I'm dreading this. There's no way she's not involved."

"I know, baby. But you're not doing the interrogation. All you have to do is observe."

"Thank you, boo. I love you."

Would he ever tire of hearing those words? Coulson doubted it. "I love you too. Let's do our job."

He let go of Seth, taking a deep breath as he pushed down all the worries in his head. He and Seth had had little time for each other over the last weeks, nowhere near enough for either of them. Coulson worried about Seth, who looked haggard and exhausted all the time. His man needed something to help him relax, and Coulson was starting to suspect what that was. But not now. He had to do his job first, and the conversation he was about to have wasn't going to be pretty.

He straightened his shoulders, then opened the door of the interrogation room, Seth on his heels. She was dressed in a sharp pantsuit in the style Hillary Clinton had made famous. Her face didn't show anything, but Coulson hadn't expected it to. Seth had warned him that she had a good poker face, which hadn't surprised Coulson, considering how long she'd been on the Secret Service.

"Ms. Russell," he greeted her. "Or can I call you Diane?"

"Diane is fine."

"I'm Special Agent Coulson Padman, one of the assistant special agents in charge of the investigation into the assassination of President Markinson." He pointed toward the other agent already in the room. "That's Special Agent Kathleen Kaufmann, who will be assisting me. And you know Seth, of course. He's the official Secret Service liaison for the investigation. Do you object to his presence?"

She shook her head. "No, Seth can stay."

Coulson and Seth sat down, and Coulson opened his notes, even though he didn't need them. He'd prepared well for this conversation, aided by Seth and his phenomenal memory. And of course his team had done a deep dive into her background. They knew every little detail about her employment history, her personality, the pictures of her cat she posted on her Instagram, and her mother's fragile health.

It had helped him form a picture of a smart, ambitious woman who was well liked and respected but had made the wrong choice when battling her compassion for a woman she'd grown fond of.

"I want to start by reminding you this conversation will be recorded, that you have the right to decline to answer, that you are free to go at any time, and that you're entitled to stop the conversation at any time to obtain legal representation. Are you aware of these rights?"

"I am."

He didn't need to remind her that since she hadn't been arrested, this was technically not an interrogation, but in this case, he wanted to cover his bases. They couldn't afford to have evidence thrown out because of legal inadmissibility. "Diane, for the record, can you state your full name and occupation?"

"Diane Martha Russell, special agent with the United States Secret Service. Up until Mrs. Markinson's death, I was the lead agent on her protective detail."

"Thank you. I'm sure her passing must've hit you hard. From what Seth told me, she was a remarkable woman who endeared many people to her."

"She was. As Seth knows, agents can't become friends with their protectees, but I grew fond of her over the years. As did most of the agents on her detail. It became a coveted spot because of how warm and easygoing she was."

"The president's affair must've angered you on her behalf."

A small nerve near Diane's right eye twitched. "It did. She deserved better."

"Did you ever express this opinion to others?"

"No. I take the confidentiality of my job seriously and don't share anything with others, not even coworkers."

"When was the first time you heard about the affair?"

Diane hesitated for a moment. "I can't recall."

Coulson smiled at her. "I find that hard to believe, Diane. You're a Secret Service agent, and while I'm sure that after some time, the days tend to blend into each other, I can't imagine you'd forget the day you hear about something as shocking as that."

"Let me rephrase that. I don't feel at liberty to say."

"I'd like to remind you that Director James has ordered full cooperation from all Secret Service agents, including revealing information they might otherwise consider confidential. I'm a federal agent, Diane, and this investigation has the full weight of the FBI behind it. Phrases like 'I can't recall' and 'I'm not at liberty to say' won't cut it. If you don't want to answer, you'll have to do it based on your Fifth Amendment right."

He could've kept up a nice front for hours if he wanted to, but he wasn't in the mood. She was hiding something, and if she hadn't come forward so far, she wouldn't do it with friendly pressure either. Maybe the threat of criminal prosecution would be more effective.

"I apologize, Special Agent Padman. It's hard to break a habit I've had for years. I'm not used to freely discussing things I've learned in confidence from my protectees."

"I hate to be blunt, but Mrs. Markinson is dead, and so is her husband. There's not a hell of a lot to protect anymore."

"How about her reputation?" Diane snapped, and damn, Coulson had already scored his first victory. He'd expected her to last longer.

"That's important to you, her reputation?"

Diane's chest rose from a deep intake of breath, and she took her time answering. "The reputation of those we protect should always matter."

"I'm sure it should, but that wasn't what you were referring to. So let me ask again. When did you find out about the president's affair?"

"The same day Mrs. Markinson did," Diane said through gritted teeth. "I was on duty when she found out, and I overheard the conversation they had."

"She must've been upset."

"Of course she was. Upset and deeply hurt. Their marriage might not have been perfect, but I don't think she ever expected him to cheat on her, especially not with someone she knew, someone that much younger."

Diane's loyalties were crystal clear, though Coulson couldn't fault her for those. It was hard to take the side of a cheater, even if he was the president. "Did she threaten him to go public with it?"

"Not in that first conversation. She was too shocked, I think. But later on, yes. I'm sure that by now you've heard about the deal they made. She would stay quiet about the affair if he didn't run for a second term."

"And yet he did."

"He claimed it was because there was no one else, not after his vice president had died."

"Did Mrs. Markinson see the reasonability of that as well?"

"She wasn't happy about it, but they came to another understanding. If he chose Senator Shafer as his running mate, she would agree."

"What did you think of that deal?"

She shrugged. "I didn't have an opinion. Not my place. My main concern was her, but it seemed the president had stopped his affair, so everything returned to normal. Sort of."

"From what I understand, Mrs. Marksinon kept her end of the deal."

"She did. I never heard her talk about his affair with anyone, including her kids."

"Were you there when Professor Dunham, Mrs. Markinson's sister, celebrated her birthday?"

Diane was quiet for a few beats. "Yes."

"Do you know who this is?" Coulson pulled a picture of Basil King from his folder and slid it forward on the table. Diane's eyes fell on it, and she immediately looked back up. She had recognized him, then. Otherwise, it would've taken her longer to study him, trying to place him.

"He looks familiar."

"When we tried to find out who he was, based on pictures from that party, you didn't come forward to identify him."

"I only said he looked familiar. Must've been from that party."

Oh, she was digging a hole for herself now, and Coulson would happily help her make it deeper...then shove her in. "He wasn't on the guest list."

"He wasn't?" She feigned surprise, but she'd never win an Academy Award for her performance. Coulson suspected she was sensing she was in trouble.

"If he had been, you would've known his name. As the head of her detail, you had to sign off on the guest list. So how did he end up at the party? Who let him in?"

Diane let out a long sigh, her professional demeanor cracking. "He's Mrs. Dunham's stepson. He wasn't supposed to be there, as she hadn't invited him for some reason, but he showed up anyway. She didn't want a scene, and she asked me to let him in. Considering he was family, I didn't see any problem. I did search him before he was allowed entrance."

"So you do know him."

Frustration flashed over her face. "Yes. His name is Basil King."

"And the reason you never came forward about him before?"

"Technically, I shouldn't have let him into that party, and I was afraid I'd get into trouble for it."

Coulson leaned back in his chair, crossing his arms in front of his chest. "You know, from anyone else, I might've believed that, but not from you. With your years of service within the Secret Service and you being the head of the First Lady's detail, you couldn't have been afraid to get fired over something so simple, especially since nothing happened at the party, right?"

"I didn't say I feared getting fired, but I was afraid of getting demoted. I wanted to keep my position."

"I'm sure you did, but that's not why you didn't come forward."

"How fascinating that you can read my mind, Special Agent Padman. Please do enlighten me. Why didn't I come forward, in your opinion?"

Coulson ignored the thick irony in her tone. "Because you knew that the reason we asked had to be connected to Mrs. Markinson and the assassination, and you were protecting her. You didn't want her linked to it."

Diane shrugged, but she didn't quite pull off the indifference she was going for. "If you say so. I'm pretty sure I know best what my motivation was."

"Did you tell the agents on your team not to say anything about the uninvited guest?"

Another hesitation. "Just the two who saw me letting him in, but they both quit the Secret Service shortly after."

"How convenient."

"I don't have the power to make others quit, Special Agent Padman. The reasons for their resignation are easy to determine. One agent left because his wife got pregnant with twins, and he needed a job with more regular hours, and the other agent quit because her boyfriend got a promotion and had to move across the country. Personal reasons. Nothing sinister, I promise."

For the first time, her eyes spewed fire. Interesting. Out of everything he'd confronted her with, this was what she got upset about? That was far more telling than she probably realized. It told Coulson that she was telling the truth about the two agents resigning but not about everything he'd thrown at her before.

"Let's talk about Mrs. Markinson's burner phone. Were you aware she had one before Special Agent Wylie pointed it out to you?"

"Yes."

"And you didn't have an issue with her having a phone that wasn't monitored?"

Diane sighed. "I did, and I intended to bring it up with her, but I never got the opportunity."

"What happened to that phone? It was never found."

"I don't know."

Coulson leaned forward, pinning her with a stern gaze. "Time to stop lying, Diane. You do know. What was the last time you saw it?"

"God, you really expect me to remember that?"

She was stalling. Clear as day. "Considering we're talking about something that happened three months ago, yes, I do expect you to remember that. Especially since

Mrs. Markinson was murdered, and I'm sure that ever since you found that out, you've been going over every little detail of the days leading up to her death in your head. So let me ask you again. When was the last time you saw it?"

"The day after Special Agent Wylie reported it."

"And where was it at the time?"

"In her purse, where she always kept it. That thing didn't leave her side."

"Except when she went sailing," Seth spoke up for the first time. "She never took her purse out on the boat. She'd hand it to the lead agent on duty."

"Who was the lead agent on duty when she went sailing that day?"

Coulson knew the answer, of course. They all did. But he needed Diane to feel the net closing around her. "I was," she finally admitted.

"If I ask the other agents on duty, will they confirm that you had her purse?"

"Yes."

"And unlike the others, you knew what was coming. Director James had called you that Friday afternoon, asking you to increase the protection on Mrs. Markinson."

"Yes. We had extra agents coming in that evening."

"As she was out on the water, you were informed she'd be taken into custody as soon as she got back to shore."

Diane's shoulders sagged. "Yes."

"So what happened to her phone, Diane? Because it wasn't in her purse when the FBI searched it."

She dropped her gaze, staring at the table for the longest time. Coulson gave her time to think. She was at a crossroads, faced with the choice of coming clean or maintaining a lie. Both would get her into trouble, but the consequences of the second would be much, much more severe for her in the end. Coulson could only hope she'd realize that as well.

"I took it." Her voice was barely audible. "I took it out of her purse and put it in my pocket."

Next to him, Seth took a sharp intake of breath, and Coulson had to resist the urge to comfort him. What Diane had done went against everything Seth stood for, and he must never have expected this from her.

"What did you do with it?"

"I still have it. It's in a safe at my bank."

A rush of excitement coursed through Coulson. He'd never expected her to hold on to it but had counted on her destroying it, but this meant they'd still have access to whatever data was on the phone.

"Why?" Seth asked, his voice emotional. "Diane, for the love of god, why?"

She broke. "Out of everyone, you should understand, Seth. You know what an amazing woman she was. I wanted to protect her. She deserved to spend her last years with her kids and grandkids."

"Not if she was involved in his assassination. Diane, we have proof she knew about it. Did you know that? Did you know she was involved in all that?"

Diane paled. "What do you mean, involved? She was the source for those articles, the ones Henley Platt wrote about the Secret Service. But that was it."

Oh. My. God. Coulson connected the dots. "It was you," Coulson said. "You were the one who told her to contact Platt."

"The demands he put on the Secret Service were untenable, and she knew it!" Diane burst out, her eyes blazing with fury. "He wanted protection for everyone in his family, and we didn't have the manpower to do it. And the bastard cut our budget and then still expected us to provide protection at the same level. It was insanity. There were weeks where I didn't have a single day off, working nonstop. I had agents on my shift who hadn't gone for training to Beltsville in months, even though they were supposed to go every six weeks. It was irresponsible, insane, and absolutely untenable. And she knew. She saw it, but no matter what she said to him, how she pleaded with him, he wouldn't budge. So finally, I suggested she contact Platt and talk to him about the situation."

And the puzzle pieces came together. "And that was why you were protecting her, why you didn't say anything, and why you took her phone. You were protecting yourself. You were afraid that if we were onto her, we would find out about you as well."

Diane raised her chin in defiance, even as tears streamed down her cheeks. "I don't regret that. I can't. He was killing us, and she knew it. She helped us by exposing our weaknesses so that, finally, someone had to do something about it."

"Except they didn't," Seth said, sounding endlessly sad. "We never got more budget, and we never truly fixed those weaknesses because Markinson wouldn't allow us to. And in revealing our weaknesses, you provided the terrorists with a blueprint that made it possible for them to assassinate the president. That's on you, Diane."

She deflated. "I swear, Seth, that was never my intention. All I wanted was more budget, less pressure on my agents, a more sustainable pace. I never intended him harm."

He had her. With this on tape and the evidence they had so far, they'd be able to formally charge her and get a conviction. Coulson took a deep breath. "Diane Russell, you are under arrest for leaking classified information, obstruction of justice in a federal investigation, willfully hiding evidence, and conspiring to assassinate the president of the United States. More charges may follow. I strongly advise you to contact your attorney."

He signaled to the agents who had watched and recorded their interrogation from behind a window, and then he got up. Seth didn't follow until Coulson gently nudged him, and when they walked out, Seth slouched like he carried the weight of the world on his shoulders.

25

Kenn rushed through the hallway. He and Denali were supposed to hang out, and Kenn was late, not a common occurrence for him. But he'd been texting with Warrick and had lost track of time. Also not something that had ever happened to him before. And then he'd had to run down to the Oval Office to drop off Rogue with his dad, making him even later.

He stormed into the East Sitting Room, then came to a sudden stop. Uncle Milan had Denali pressed against the wall, Denali's legs wrapped around Uncle Milan's waist as they were kissing passionately. Although passionately was too weak a description for the way Kenn's uncle devoured Denali, rubbing himself against him, kissing him with an aggression that had Kenn swallowing. That his uncle was kissing someone shouldn't be as arousing as it was, but he couldn't look away.

"I want you," Uncle Milan growled.

"You had me this morning," Denali said breathlessly. "Twice."

Okay then, Kenn wasn't sure he'd wanted to know that,

but that ship had sailed now.

"Yeah, so? You're addictive, baby boy."

Kenn's stomach fluttered at the sweet nickname. He'd never expected his uncle to use a word like that, but Denali and Asher had changed him in many ways, this being one of them.

"We don't have time. Kenn will be here any moment."

His uncle snapped his hips, driving into Denali with a highly suggestive move. "I'm so fucking hard for you, baby boy. I need to be inside you..." He swiveled his hips again, and Denali let out a low moan.

"Milan..."

"Fuck, you're so sexy...so hot."

"Tonight," Denali whispered. "You and Asher both."

"Mmm, fuck yes. We'll double-team you until you're overflowing with—"

Denali spotted Kenn, his eyes widening. "Kenn is here."

Uncle Milan peeked over his shoulder, letting out a sigh when he saw Kenn. "Your timing needs work."

Kenn swallowed, the idea of Denali being double-stuffed still vivid on his mind. "*My* timing needs work? You're the one who started something you couldn't finish."

Uncle Milan slowly put Denali down, giving him one last, firm kiss. Then he turned around and faced Kenn. "You know, you're getting cheekier by the day. I approve. It was about time you found your voice."

Kenn smiled. "Thank you?"

With a slap on Denali's butt that had Denali squealing, Uncle Milan took off. "Tonight, baby boy. You two have fun hanging out."

Kenn loved that Uncle Milan understood their friendship needed time with the two of them. Kenn had become much more used to seeing Uncle Milan with Denali and even with Asher, but that didn't mean he wanted to witness them lock lips all the time, and those three were rather physically affectionate with each other.

Denali discreetly readjusted himself, and Kenn laughed. "Sorry? Didn't mean to cockblock you."

Denali laughed as well, waving his hands dismissively. "That wasn't cockblocking. That's merely Milan having a high sex drive that happens to match mine. And I'm sorry for sharing too much with you just now. I forget sometimes he's your uncle."

Kenn plopped down on one of the comfortable reading chairs. "It's okay. I'm getting much more used to it. I was thinking that, actually, as you were kissing. That was...hot to watch."

Denali sat down on the chair next to him, folding his legs up and turning sideways so he was facing Kenn. "Yeah? You thought that was hot?"

"Why, is that weird? Because he's my uncle?"

"Nah, that part doesn't bother me. I'm more surprised because so far, you didn't seem that interested in sex."

Kenn's cheeks heated, and he looked away. "I guess I am now?"

"That's okay," Denali said immediately. "Completely normal, in fact. Nothing to worry about. Don't take my response as judgment or any kind of criticism. I was surprised, that's all."

"You did give me quite the show…"

Denali cocked his head. "How long were you standing there?"

"Long enough to hear you express excitement about being…taken by them both."

Denali froze for a moment, then giggled. "Sorry?"

"Do you… You really like that?"

Denali nodded, growing more serious. "I love it. Nothing makes me feel closer to them. It's not always easy making time for us, since we all have different schedules and shifts, but sharing myself with them like that helps me connect on such a deep level..."

Kenn's cheeks grew even warmer at the thought, but he pushed through it. Denali shouldn't think he was judging. "I'm glad that works for you. I assume things are going well, then?"

"They are. We fit, somehow. It's hard to explain, but we're so different, and yet we fit together like puzzle pieces."

"Uncle Milan is different. He's happier, lighter, even when he's grieving my mom."

"He misses her a lot. He talks about her more and more, and Asher and I try to encourage him, as he's not a talker, but you probably know that."

Kenn nodded. "It's good that he's opening up to you. It helps to talk about stuff. I talk a lot about my mom with my dad and Warrick. I still miss her every day, but I feel like I can breathe again, at least."

"I'm glad it's getting a little better."

Kenn let out a long sigh. "You and I always start talking about the heavy stuff immediately. Why can't we ever have a chat where we talk about nothing? Like the weather, the latest movie we watched, and how about the Patriots winning the Super Bowl again and all that?"

Denali laughed. "We can talk about that if you want, though I can guarantee you my answers will be short. The weather is cold, I haven't watched a movie in forever, and I couldn't care less about football if I tried."

That made Kenn laugh as well. "I did watch a movie the other day. *Legally Blonde*."

"Oh my God, I love that one. Every time it's on TV, I have

to watch it, even if it's just parts. It cracks me up. Elle Woods is, like, goals."

"Same. I think I've watched it at least ten times. But this time, I watched it in the White House theater, and it was amazing. The seats there are so comfortable. I love having a private theater."

"I bet." Denali frowned. "Did you watch it alone? It doesn't seem like a movie your father would appreciate."

Kenn giggled at the thought of his father watching *Legally Blonde*. "You know, he might surprise you. He always loves an underdog. But no, I didn't watch it alone or with him. Warrick came over."

"Warrick came over?"

"Yeah. I asked if he wanted to watch the movie with me, and he said yes. Why?"

"On his night off?"

"Why is that so weird? Uncle Milan asked the same thing, and I don't understand. So he came over on his day off to watch a movie with me. We are friends. That's what friends do, right?"

"Sure, if that's what you are..."

"See, there you go again as well, talking in riddles. What the hell is up with everybody and their opinions on why Warrick likes to hang out with me? Am I that boring that no one can imagine anyone would want to spend time with me?"

Ouch, that hurt. When Uncle Milan had said it, it had been one thing, but now that Denali was echoing that same sentiment, it seemed people thought it was ridiculous that Warrick would like to hang out with him.

"No, that's not it, and I'm sorry if I made you feel that way. You're not boring. If you were, you and I wouldn't be friends."

Kenn scoffed. "I hate to break it to you, but our friendship isn't exactly normal, considering you work here. Like, you could've felt obligated to befriend me out of fear of losing your job."

Denali didn't laugh it away as Kenn had expected. "I never had that fear, but I'll admit I was apprehensive about becoming friends with you. It crosses lines, you know, and I thought it would make my job harder. But Mrs. Morelli said Mr. Funnell wouldn't mind, that he would understand."

The thought of Denali having to ask permission to befriend him made Kenn sad. "I hope you didn't feel like you were forced or pressured. Because if that's the case, I don't—"

"I don't. I genuinely like you, and I love hanging out with you." Denali said it so earnestly that Kenn didn't question whether he meant it.

"I'm glad to hear that. But that still doesn't explain why you and others are so surprised about the friendship between Warrick and me. Is that because he's my teacher and teachers and students can't be friends?"

"In the real world, they can't. Outside this special, protective bubble you're in, you wouldn't be able to go to the movies with your professor. It would be highly inappropriate, and his job would be on the line."

Deep down, Kenn had known that, of course, but he had much preferred not to think about it. "Warrick doesn't seem to mind."

"No, which makes me suspect he talked to your dad."

"What? You think he talked to my dad about befriending me?"

"Honestly? Yeah. I can't see him develop a friendship like this with you otherwise. He doesn't seem the type to risk his job. Plus, he's honorable. He'd never do something inappropriate."

Sadness filled Kenn. Why could things never be normal for him? "I'm not sure if I like the idea of Warrick and my father talking about me behind my back. It makes me feel like some kind of charity case, like befriending me was part of his job."

"I can understand why you'd feel that way, but I don't think that's the case at all. He probably wanted to cover his bases, make sure your father was okay with it."

"You think?"

"Kenn, he's not coming over on a Saturday evening to watch a movie with you because he feels sorry for you or because he's scared he'd lose his job. He likes you. He likes spending time with you."

Kenn narrowed his eyes. "There's that *tone* again, the same one Uncle Milan used. What have you guys been saying about me? Because you're in on it, and I don't understand. Why won't you tell me?"

Denali hesitated, only reaffirming Kenn's feeling that he was hiding something. His heart ached as he rose from his chair. "I'm sorry, but if you insist on talking behind my back and not being honest with me, I can't be friends with you. You're making me feel awful, like I'm some kind of stupid child who can't handle the truth."

Denali jumped up, holding up both hands. "That's not how it is at all. We weren't sure if we should tell you. Milan thought you needed to find out for yourself."

So they had talked about him. Kenn's heart ached. What were they hiding from him? "Tell me what?"

Denali straightened his shoulders, then met Kenn's eyes. "That you have a crush on Warrick...and that it looks like he feels the same way about you."

26

When Warrick walked into the White House that morning, Milan Bradbury was waiting for him in the hallway. "Good morning, Professor," he said, and Warrick's Spidey sense tingled. This wasn't an accidental meeting.

"Good morning, Milan. I wasn't aware we'd gone back to using formal titles again."

Milan grinned. "You're sharp, Warrick. It's one of the things I like about you."

"Thank you. But am I correct in assuming you weren't waiting for me to compliment me on my intellect?"

"Yeah, not exactly. Do you have a few minutes?"

Warrick checked his watch. "A few. I don't want to be late. Kenn is waiting for me."

"Yes, and you don't want to keep your precious student waiting."

Ah, that was what this was about. "I despise being late, regardless of who my appointment is with, actually."

"Fair enough. Let's find somewhere a little more private to talk."

Warrick followed Milan into the library, a room Warrick could spend hours in. Milan closed the door behind them, and Warrick had to suppress the urge to ask if he was in trouble. Milan radiated that whole NYPD detective vibe, and it was a little intimidating.

"What's on your mind?" he asked instead.

"Kenn."

He'd been correct, then. Warrick stayed silent, confident that Milan would soon come out with it. The man hadn't struck him as the most patient type.

"I'm just going to come out and say it."

"That would be appreciated."

"I'm concerned about the relationship between you and Kenn."

"Concerned in what way?"

Milan cocked his head, studying him. "You weren't surprised by that."

"Not after you referred to Kenn as my precious student."

"So you don't deny it, then?"

Warrick smiled. "I'm sure that strategy has worked well for you as a cop, but until you tell me what you're concerned about, I can't confirm or deny anything."

"What a highly political answer."

"I have some experience with questions like this. So hit me with it. What's your concern?"

The hardness on Milan's face was replaced with something much softer, showing the man's affection for his nephew. "I'm worried he's growing too attached to you."

Warrick was beyond grateful that Kenn had told him he'd come out to both his uncle and his father. That made this conversation at least somewhat easier, since he didn't have to fear accidentally outing him. "Why would his attachment to me be of concern?"

"Warrick, come on. We both know what we're dealing with here. He's innocent, naïve...and he's rapidly developing a crush on you, if not more. It'll break his heart. Unless..."

Warrick straightened his shoulders. "Unless what?"

Milan took a step closer, his brown eyes drilling into Warrick's. "Unless you reciprocate his feelings."

The moment of truth. What did he say? Did he lie? Deny it? Even if he hadn't hated lying as much as he did, denying the truth still would've felt stupid and dishonest, plus disrespectful to the deep friendship he'd developed with Kenn. "I think it's safe to say I've grown attached to him as well."

"Warrick, can we ditch all the formalities and be straight with each other?"

"That depends on what you're planning on doing with whatever I'm telling you. I hate to point it out, but your brother-in-law is the president of the United States, so pissing off either one of you seems not only a bad career move but also a bad life choice. The man has nuclear launch codes and could order a special forces team to take me out in such a way that no one would ever find out."

Milan blinked a few times, then laughed. "I like you. I really do."

"Then what's the problem? You can't tell me you object to the age difference, considering the gap between you and Denali."

Milan shook his head. "No, I don't care about age as long as all parties are legal and fully consenting. I'm worried about Kenn's inexperience, about the direction the relationship between you two is going."

Warrick frowned. "The direction? I'm not sure I'm following."

"Tell me, Professor, how much experience do you have with kink?"

With kink? Was it possible that Milan had already sensed what Warrick had only realized the day before? It had been so hard to keep acting normal toward Kenn and not show what and who he wanted to be for Kenn. But he couldn't discuss it with Kenn, not until he'd decided what to do about it...and had talked to the president.

"Not much, other than a general awareness."

"You've never played?"

"No. Never had any desire to. Never set foot in any kind of club either. I'm not judging, mind you, but it's never been my scene. Why?"

"Are you asking me to explain or to confirm?"

Warrick shook his head. "At the risk of repeating myself, I can't answer that until you've made it clear what you're referring to. You were the one who wanted to be open and frank."

"And you were the one who wanted to know my intentions first."

"Which, I might point out, you still haven't stated."

Milan chuckled again. "It's becoming clear I'm talking to a lawyer. You could argue someone's socks off, couldn't you?"

Warrick shrugged. "If I wanted to, sure."

"But you're right. I was the one who wanted to be open and frank. So let's try it that way. I have no intention of telling anyone anything, not my brother-in-law, not Kenn, not anyone else. All I want is for you to be honest with me so I can make sure you have Kenn's best interests at heart. I'm by far the worst uncle in the world when it comes to being there for him, but this happens to be an area I have expertise in and can help him with."

"Good enough for me. What do you want to know, Milan?"

"What do you want from Kenn? What and who is he to you?"

Warrick dragged a hand through his hair. "You're asking me the same question I've been asking myself the last few days."

"What happened?"

Could he trust him? Milan hadn't given him any reason to doubt him, to question his sincerity and motives, but it was still a big risk Warrick would be taking. If Milan wanted to fuck him over, he could. More than, in fact. "I had a moment, you could say, a sudden insight. I became aware of something I hadn't realized before about my relationship with Kenn and who and what I want to be in his life."

Milan's face relaxed. "We're on the same page, then. You want to be his Daddy."

If he acknowledged this, it would become real. But how could he deny what he felt so strongly? He held Milan's eyes. "I do. And like I said, I have absolutely no experience with this, which is probably why it took me this long to see it."

"To be able to have this conversation, let's forget for a moment that he's my nephew. Because thinking of him as my nephew makes me think of my sister, and I can't have this kind of talk when I have her in my head. She's never been fully privy to my sex life and my love for kink. I'm sure she knew some of it, but Del and I kept a lot from her to protect her."

"I completely understand."

"If I look at Kenn like I would at any other gay boy, it's hard to deny he's just that... A boy. I'm sure that if he hadn't been my nephew, I would've spotted it much sooner, but this is what he needs. He needs a Daddy."

Sweet relief filled Warrick at the thought he hadn't

imagined it, that Milan agreed Kenn was a Daddy's boy. "Do you think it's something he needs now because of the circumstances? Or will it be something he'd crave in the longer term?"

Milan sighed. "Honestly, that's always a crapshoot. People change, and so do preferences. But Kenn has always been innocent and naïve, and he's always been a person who needed care, who craved touch and both physical and emotional closeness with someone. So it wouldn't surprise me if this is simply how he's wired. The question is, are you truly a Daddy for the long term, or is this something that has been triggered specifically under the circumstances?"

Warrick smiled at that question, which reflected his own words right back at him. "I don't know, and that's the truth. I've never had a desire to be a Daddy before, but when I think about Kenn, I know that's what we're supposed to be, Daddy and boy."

"Fair enough. I guess the only way to find out is by letting it play out."

"Letting it play out, that's easier said than done in this case. I don't know the president that well, but I can't imagine him being excited about the idea of me becoming his son's Daddy. Would any father ever want to know that about his son?"

"Del knows Kenn's gay."

Warrick nodded. "I'm aware. Kenn told me he'd come out to his dad first and then to you. He was elated and grateful you both reacted so well."

"On my end, I know Del had a conversation with you about Kenn, basically telling you that your job wouldn't be in danger, regardless of what happened between you and Kenn."

"How did he know? Did you tell him?"

"Nope, that was all him. Del may be insanely busy, but he is Kenn's father, and the boy hasn't exactly been subtle in his devotion to you."

A rush of warmth spread through Warrick's chest, and Milan chuckled. "You like hearing that, don't you?"

"Wouldn't you?"

"Of course, so I don't blame you. But considering that conversation, I'm not entirely sure why you'd be worried about Del's reaction."

"You don't think it'll be different once the president finds out exactly what kind of relationship I want to have with his son?"

Milan tapped his chin with his index finger. "Honestly? I don't. Del is one of the most open-minded people I've ever met, and it's not like he's unaware of how different Kenn is from him."

"Kenn struggles with being so different from you and his father. I know he wishes he were more dominant and more of a leader," Warrick said softly.

Grief clouded Milan's eyes. "He's Sarah. He has her tender heart, her immense capacity for love, her gentleness and kindness. How could we ever fault him for that when we loved her so much? She lives on in him."

The man's voice broke at the end, and Warrick stayed silent for a few moments, allowing Milan the time to collect himself. Milan was a proud man who wouldn't like to break down in front of someone else, so Warrick would help him keep his dignity.

"Maybe you could bring that up with Kenn sometime," Warrick said when it seemed Milan had gained his composure again. "It would help him embrace who he is, knowing that you and his father accept him exactly the way he is."

Milan quickly wiped his eyes. "If he doubts that, then Del and I have fallen short."

"I wouldn't put it like that, but don't forget that he's been through an awful lot in the last year, and it has rocked his confidence and identity. Hearing confirmed that you love him and accept him, fully embrace him no matter what, would help."

"Spoken like a true Daddy..."

Warrick took a deep breath. "You think I should talk to the president?"

"Yeah. I know you don't want to go behind his back."

"Never," Warrick swore. "I'm not that kind of man. Not in this situation, not with how fragile and vulnerable Kenn is."

"I figured as much, and it speaks to your character."

"But do I talk to the president without even knowing how Kenn feels about me? About being my boy? We haven't discussed it at all, and I don't want to bring it up with his father when Kenn might not even want to."

"Hmm, good point."

"But if I talk to Kenn, he may feel obligated..."

Milan rolled his eyes. "I should've seen this one coming. Fuck, it's like being back in elementary school and having a girl's friend ask me if I like her friend. Only in this case, I'm the go-between."

Warrick chuckled. "Does that mean you'll talk to Kenn for me? I don't want him to feel pressured."

Milan grew serious as he put a hand on Warrick's shoulder. "You're a good man, Warrick. I might never have picked you for Kenn myself, but now that I've seen the two of you together, I think you'd be a perfect fit for him. He needs someone older, someone mature and wise who will help him, guide him, and protect him."

Strangely enough, Milan's words only deepened Warrick's affection for Kenn. Milan was right. He wanted to be that person for Kenn. He wanted to take care of him and cherish him. He wanted to be his Daddy...and he wanted Kenn to be his baby boy.

27

When Henley had reported back about his conversations with Bill Clampton and Bryce, Coulson and Seth had been elated with the information. They'd told him they'd have someone dig deeper into the disparity in campaign contributions and the high level of small donations from supposed fundraisers.

Henley had immediately requested a next assignment, eager to stay involved and do his part. He was all too aware that, as a reporter, he had a vast network of contacts and access that would be much harder for the FBI to realize. Seth had told him he still hadn't figured out why President Markinson had ordered extra Secret Service protection for his family, and anything Henley could find out about that would be greatly appreciated.

He'd asked around but so far had gotten nowhere. None of his contacts knew anything, and a few had informed Henley that the topic had been off-limits in discussions with President Markinson. That indicated only his inner circle would know more, but who could he approach? And who'd be willing to talk to him? He'd tried a few, but none of them had wanted to cooperate. And then he'd had an idea.

Larry. Larry had been a reliable source for Henley back when he'd still covered the White House, often providing him with high-level information. Considering the things Larry had been privy to, he had to have been close to President Markinson, most likely part of that inner circle. Henley knew Larry wasn't his real name but had never attempted to find out his identity. As long as Larry was willing to talk to him, it hadn't mattered much. An anonymous source who shared valuable intel was worth ten times more than the name of a person who wouldn't say another word once Henley knew their identity.

That had changed. Chances were that with the right approach, Henley would be able to make Larry share information once more. But to do that, he needed to know who the man was. He'd always called from a blocked number, so Henley didn't have any contact information for him, but there were other ways to find out his identity.

The first step was easy, and President Shafer was all too happy to talk to him. "Mr. President, back when you were still vice president, at some point, the CIA had credible intel on the location of Hamza Bashir. This was before the Pride Bombing memorial. Do you remember this?"

President Shafer frowned, then slowly nodded. "Yes, I think so. Why?"

"Do you recall who had codeword clearance and the need to know for that information? Within President Markinson's inner circle, I mean?"

"Victor, of course, his chief of staff. The secretary of defense, the national security advisor, the director of national intelligence, the chairman of the joint chiefs of staff..." Shafer checked them off on his fingers. "I'd assume his senior foreign policy advisor, I knew, and so did Calix, but they kept the circle small, considering the sensitivity of that information."

Henley had guessed all those people already and had subsequently crossed them off as a potential Larry. None of them fit the profile in terms of their clearance level. Larry had dropped the snippet about Hamza Bashir by accident, and most of his information had been about the president himself. That ruled out the people the president mentioned. And it definitely hadn't been Victor, since Henley had spoken to him enough times he would've recognized his speech pattern. Larry had used a voice changer, but even if his voice had been modified, his syntax and speech pattern hadn't been.

"I hate to press, Mr. President, but can you think of anyone else?"

Shafer frowned as he dragged a hand through his hair. "Give me a minute."

Henley waited quietly.

"I'm going over the meeting we had about this in my head, trying to remember who was there and who was mentioned. Feels like years ago, considering how much has happened since," the president said with a sigh.

Yeah, no kidding. It had been one hell of a year for President Shafer.

"Some of the deputies may have had access as well, like the deputy director of national intelligence and others at that level."

Henley nodded. "Thank you, Mr. President."

Shafer quirked an eyebrow. "Do I want to know what this is about?"

"I'll let you know when it pans out."

No need to give the president hope when Henley wasn't sure if there was reason to.

Armed with new knowledge, he went back to his computer and, within a few minutes, had come up with a list of names at the deputy level. Like before, he disregarded those within the secretary of defense and the intelligence community. They wouldn't have known about all the other things Larry had told him. That left three names: two senior advisors and Marcus Pizer, who had been Victor Kendall's deputy chief of staff.

Two quick calls to each of the senior advisors—neither man was still working in the White House, but both had found jobs in political consulting—ruled them out. One of them had an accent that Henley surely would've picked up on, even if he'd tried to hide it, and the other one had a distinct speech pattern, speaking quite slowly and clearly enunciated. That left one on his list.

Marcus Pizer had left the White House days after Shafer had become president, presumably having been asked to leave, though Henley hadn't verified that. But it made sense with Calix coming in as chief of staff that he hadn't wanted to work with Markinson's people. Victor Kendall had been let go as well, so it fit the timeline. He finally found a phone number for him at the consultancy firm where Pizer now worked.

"Hello?"

"Hello, Marcus. This is Henley Platt. You may recognize my name from—"

"I have nothing to say to you." Click.

Bingo. With that answer, Henley had all the proof he needed that Marcus was his man. Why else would he have hung up immediately? He'd instantly known who Henley was. If calling didn't work, he'd have to try a personal approach. Sure, he felt like a total stalker, waiting across the street from the building that housed the consultancy firm Marcus worked for, waiting for Marcus to leave, but he'd stand there for days if that was what it took. He'd found a good picture of him, and the man being bald made him relatively easy to recognize.

His patience was rewarded as just after six thirty, Marcus walked out the front door of the office building. He headed for the parking garage across the street, and Henley followed him, catching up with him when he was about to enter the garage. "Marcus," he said, quiet enough not to draw attention from passersby.

Marcus swiveled around, the curiosity on his face quickly replaced by fear. "What do you want?"

"So you know who I am."

"I've been in politics for years. I read the newspapers. You're not exactly a newbie in this world. So let me repeat my question. What do you want?"

Not that Henley had had any doubt, but the way Marcus talked to him confirmed he was Larry. The speech pattern was the same, even if his voice now was different from when he'd been Henley's informant. "The same as always. Information... Larry."

Marcus froze for a second. "I don't know what you're talking about."

"We both know that's a lie."

"I don't want to talk to you."

"Same conditions as always. I won't reveal your identity to anyone."

Marcus looked around them. "I thought you quit your job."

"I have. This isn't for an article."

Marcus narrowed his eyes. "Then who do you work for?"

"President Shafer."

Marcus scoffed. "Why would I want to help him?"

"Because it's not his fault your boss got killed. And because underneath it all, you're loyal to the Democratic Party, even if you don't agree with Shafer as a president."

"He should never have been VP. I still don't understand why President Markinson insisted on recruiting him. He lost us the midterms."

"I understand, though at this point, it seems water under the bridge. The reality is that Shafer is president, and I know you care enough about the future of the Democratic Party that you won't deny a request from the president."

"What, he wants me to come work for him?"

"No. I want to ask you some questions. Off the record, and no one will know it's you. But I need information, and I think you're the only one who can give me the answers."

Yeah, he wasn't playing fair, appealing to Marcus's pride and ego, but what did he care as long as he got his way? That was how the game was played.

"Information? About what? I haven't worked in the White House for eight months now."

"It's from when you were working for President Markinson, in the early days."

Marcus frowned. "What could possibly be still relevant from that time?"

"I don't know if it's relevant, but I haven't asked my question yet."

Marcus finally stepped closer to him, letting go of the door to the parking garage. "Talk fast."

"A few months after the Pride Bombing, President

Markinson demanded Secret Service protection for his extended family. Why?"

Marcus's reaction was immediate, fear clouding his eyes before he looked away. "I don't know anything about that, and even if I did, I can't comment on Secret Service protection details."

"Are you sure you don't know what this is about?"

Marcus's eyes flashed. "That's what I said, isn't it?"

"Yes, I heard you, but that doesn't mean I think you're telling the truth."

"I have no obligation to tell you anything."

"No, you don't, but I'd be happy to give your name to the Secret Service or the FBI and have them ask you questions. Pretty sure they can force you to cooperate. But it doesn't have to go that way if you just answer my question."

"I can't talk to you about this. You don't have clearance."

"Actually, I do, and I'd be happy to give you the name of the FBI agent in charge of the investigation into the assassination of President Markinson, and he'll confirm it for you. Or, you know, you could talk to him directly at FBI headquarters. In an official interrogation."

Marcus swallowed. "The assassination? How the hell is this connected?"

"That's not your problem. The question is, are you going to give me the information, or do I need to call the FBI?"

"I'm not too sure the FBI would approve of you using blackmail."

"It's not blackmail. I'm informing you of the next step if you don't give me the information I need. Blackmail would be forcing you to pay me money or threaten you with bodily harm, and I'm doing neither. All I'm doing is letting you know the consequences. The choice is still yours. If you tell me no, I'll walk away right now, and you'll never see me again."

"And if I answer your questions?"

Henley pinned him with his stare. "You tell me what I need to know, and I'll walk away...and you'll never see me again."

Marcus took a deep breath. "He was scared. Markinson was scared."

"Scared of what? Or of whom?"

"Look, I overheard a conversation I wasn't supposed to. So if this leaks, I could be in trouble."

"You don't even work for the government anymore. How could you possibly get into trouble?"

Marcus scanned around them again, then leaned in toward Henley. "You don't understand. Trust me when I say this isn't something you want to get involved in. I regretted ever overhearing that conversation, and I've never mentioned a word to anyone."

The more Marcus said, the louder Henley's alarm bells were going off. The man knew something. Something that was relevant to the investigation. Henley would bet all his money on it. "I promise you I'll keep you out of this. You know I have never compromised your identity."

"You'll have to forgive me, but I find that hard to believe from a man who, mere minutes ago, threatened to give my name to the FBI."

The man had a point. Maybe Henley had gone about this all wrong. "Fair enough. I believe you when you say this information could endanger you. So I'll retract my earlier statement that if you don't talk to me, I'll contact the FBI. Trust me, and I'll keep your name out of this for as long as I legally can."

"I'm not yanking your chain here, Platt. You have to know I'm not the type to be overly dramatic."

"I know."

He'd have to wait now and trust that Marcus would dare to share what he knew. The man stayed silent for a long time, then let out a deep sigh. "I overheard a conversation between the president and Victor. The president wanted to fire the secretary of defense, but John Doty had cornered him and had warned him not to fire him. He'd hinted to Markinson that he knew more about the Pride Bombing and who was behind it, and that if Markinson fired him, he could be at risk. Doty meant Markinson, not himself."

Henley forced himself to keep the shock off his face. "Doty threatened Markinson if he fired him?"

"That's what it sounded like, as if he was implying another attack could happen, aimed at Markinson. Markinson certainly understood it like that. Victor and the president agreed to let Doty stay on as secretary of defense."

"He's still the secretary. Shafer didn't fire him either."

"I was wondering about that. Maybe he threatened him too."

"I don't know, but I'll find out. Anything else you can tell me?"

Marcus shook his head. "But that was the reason that Markinson ordered extra Secret Service protection. He figured if Doty knew about threats against him, he had to do what he could to protect himself and his family."

"Marcus, why didn't you ever come forward with this information after Markinson was assassinated?"

Marcus scoffed. "And paint a big target on my back? No, thank you. Anyone capable of taking out the president of the United States isn't someone I want to cross, thank you very much. I'm not stupid."

As much as Henley wanted to judge him for being a coward, he couldn't fault him for his reasoning. "I understand. I genuinely do."

"I hope that you guys catch whoever was behind that. Even though I'm not on the inside, as you apparently are now, it seems to me there's a hell of a lot more going on than a terrorist attack by a radical Muslim group."

Henley sighed. "You have no idea."

28

"Hey, kiddo."

Kenn looked up from the book he'd been reading, snuggled on the couch in the living room under a soft blue fleece blanket. "Hey, Uncle Milan. What's up?"

Uncle Milan plopped down on the couch across from him, pulling up his legs and stretching out. Rogue immediately got up from where he'd been chewing on a thick rope knot and nudged Uncle Milan's hand with his snout, begging to be petted. Of course, he got his wish. No one could resist that look, not even Uncle Milan. "Oh, nothing. Just thought I'd come hang out with you for a bit."

Kenn narrowed his eyes. "You thought you'd hang out with me."

"Something wrong with that?"

"In itself, no, but considering you never hang out with me, it raises some questions."

Irritation flashed over his uncle's face, and he picked up Rogue's rope and threw it in the corner, where the German shepherd immediately picked it up, plopped down, and started chewing again. "Oh, for fuck's sake. I'm the worst at this kind of shit."

"What kind of shit? What's going on?" A cold hand curled around Kenn's heart. "Please don't tell me you have more bad news."

"Bad news? No! God, no. Sorry. I should never have volunteered for this."

"Volunteered for what?"

His uncle sat up straight, then leaned forward with his elbows on his knees, studying Kenn. "How are you doing? Let's start with that."

Kenn was sorely tempted to snap at him to skip the bullshit and cut to the chase, but something told him that wouldn't go over well. "I'm okay, I guess. Not, like, great but better than a month ago."

Uncle Milan's face softened. "That's good. I'm glad to hear it."

"And you?"

"We're not here to... Never mind. The same, I suppose. I still think of your mom a lot, but when I do, I don't feel like I'll shatter any moment, so there's that."

"I hate it when clichés turn out to be true. Everybody who kept telling me time would help was right after all."

Uncle Milan chuckled. "There's a reason they're clichés."

Kenn stayed silent, not that inclined to continue the mindless small talk. He'd much rather hear what Uncle Milan had on his mind because it was clear the man had come here with a purpose.

"How are your lessons going?"

Oh, great. More small talk, apparently. "Good. I love learning more about the law, and everything I've heard and discovered so far has only reaffirmed my decision to go to law school."

"That's good. I'm happy you found something you love. I suppose Professor Duvall is a good teacher, no?"

Oh my god, there was that edge again, that deeper layer that Kenn had spotted before. Would his uncle finally come clean about it? "The best I've ever had. I love his lessons."

"I'm glad to see you've become such good friends."

Kenn tilted his head, happy to pretend he'd never had that conversation with Denali and didn't know what this was about. Maybe Denali hadn't told Uncle Milan. "The last time we talked about this, you didn't seem that enthusiastic. In fact, I vividly remember you questioning our friendship."

"I can see the lessons in arguing have borne fruit," Uncle Milan said dryly.

"Am I wrong?"

"No, you're not. I did have some doubts."

"Did... As in the past. Not anymore, then?"

"Let's say I've gotten to know him better, and that helped."

"Oh. I didn't know you two had hung out. He's nice, right?"

"I wouldn't exactly call it hanging out, but we had an enlightening conversation."

"About what?" Kenn was still baffled. What could Warrick and Uncle Milan have possibly talked about?

Uncle Milan stared at him for a few beats. "I've been racking my brain how to bring this up subtly, but we both know subtlety has never been my style. So forgive me for being blunt, but I'm just gonna go ahead and ask."

"Yes, please because I'm at a complete loss here."

"Kiddo, is it possible that you've developed a crush on Warrick?"

Kenn's cheeks heated instantly. No more pretending, apparently. "D-did Denali talk to you?"

Uncle Milan fiercely shook his head. "No. If you told him anything, he hasn't said a word to me. He'd never betray your confidence. But I'm not blind. I can practically see you swoon whenever you're in a room with him. Which is fine, don't get me wrong."

Kenn blew out a breath. "It is?"

"Of course."

"You don't object?"

Uncle Milan shrugged. "Why would I? What, because he's older than you? That would be massively hypocritical, wouldn't it? No, it's fine."

"Okay," Kenn said slowly. "I'm glad to hear that."

"So it's true?"

Kenn lowered his gaze to the floor. "I guess? I don't know. This is all new to me."

"It's okay. We'll figure it out."

"We?" Kenn swallowed.

"Well, your father did sort of push me forward as your source of information, didn't he?" Uncle Milan winked at him, and Kenn laughed. But then the man grew more serious. "That's not all I wanted to talk to you about. You don't have to answer this, but I was wondering what kind of relationship you'd like to have with Warrick."

Kenn's throat tightened. "What do you mean?"

"If you imagine yourself in a relationship with Warrick, what kind of dynamic do you see between you two?"

The moment of truth. He'd known for a long time now, and ever since he'd become friends with Denali, things had become even clearer. Denali had confirmed what Kenn had already suspected about himself, and now it had a name. Who he was and what he wanted had a label. But how would Uncle Milan feel about it? Would he be okay with his nephew being on the other side of things?

"I'm... I'm submissive, Uncle Milan. I'm sorry. I know that must be a disappointment for you, considering you're such an experienced Dom, but—"

"Hang on." Uncle Milan held up his hand. "Why the hell would I be disappointed?"

Kenn bit his lip. "Because you and Dad are so strong, so dominant. You're leaders, and I'm... I'm not. I'm not only submissive but also want someone to take care of me. I know I shouldn't, that I should be more independent and adult, but I just can't. I love that Warrick made a schedule for me, makes me eat healthier, and reminds me to exercise. I need that."

Before he realized it, Uncle Milan had moved off the couch and had relocated next to Kenn, his strong arms wrapped around him. "I owe you the biggest of apologies. If you genuinely feel you're somehow less because you're a submissive, then I have failed you. Granted, you and I have never talked about it, and maybe we should have. But, Kenn, you're perfect the way you are. Being submissive isn't less than being dominant or being a switch. It's who you are, how you're wired. And I'm sorry that you felt differently, that you feared your dad or I would be disappointed in you. I'm not, and I know he won't be either. All we want is for you to be happy, to find how and where you belong. That's it. We don't care about the label you choose to identify with. It's all good."

Kenn hated the tears that once again fell, as they had done too many times over the last weeks. And yet they felt different this time. Instead of tears of sadness and grief, they were full of relief and release. "You're not upset?"

"Not even a little bit. Don't you realize how much I love Denali? And that boy is submissive to his core. He loves serving me and Asher."

"B-but I'm not submissive like him."

Uncle Milan gently cupped his cheek. "I didn't think you were, and that's okay. What you want with Warrick has a name. I've watched the dynamic between you two, and from what you told me, I think you've realized that your needs are a little different."

Kenn nodded. "What if he doesn't want that?" he whispered.

Uncle Milan smiled. "I wouldn't worry about that. That man is besotted, kiddo. He has stars in his eyes when he looks at you."

Hope bloomed in Kenn's heart. "Yeah?"

"Did you think he didn't feel the same about you?"

"H-he held my hand when we watched a movie, and my belly was all fluttery and warm."

"God, I envy you that you get to experience all this for the first time...and under the loving care of a Daddy."

Kenn gasped. "A D-Daddy?"

"Mmm. Are you familiar with the concept of a Daddy-boy relationship?"

It clicked, as if a veil had been lifted from his eyes. "That's what I want, isn't it?"

"I don't know. You tell me."

He nodded slowly. "I'd realized I was submissive and that I wanted a caring Dom who'd do a lot for me, but I hadn't made this connection. That's what I want, a Daddy."

"I'm happy you've found where you fit. From what I've seen from you and Warrick, I think this would work well for both of you."

He spoke in a warm and loving tone Kenn had never heard him use before. "Yeah? You th-think Warrick would want to be my Daddy?"

"He'd be crazy not to want a sweet boy like you."

Kenn put his head on his uncle's shoulder. "Thank you. For everything. I was so scared..."

"Was this why you waited so long with coming out?"

Kenn nodded. "I knew you wouldn't be upset with me being gay, but I thought you'd want me to be more like you."

"Kiddo, I wouldn't want anyone to be like me, and I mean that. I'm not an easy person, and I'm amazed every day that Asher and Denali put up with my stubborn ass. You have Sarah's kind heart and her gentle spirit. That's something to be proud of. Which I told Warrick as well. She lives on in you, and I'd love you if only for that."

"Thank you. It makes me happy you said that."

"Your mom was an amazing woman, and I see so much of her in you. And don't ever think your dad doesn't love you just the way you are. He's not his own father, who insists on a certain path for his son. Your dad doesn't care what you do in life as long as you live it authentically. Your happiness is all that matters."

"You think he'd be okay with Warrick being my Daddy? It's gotta be so strange for him."

"It'll be an adjustment, but he'll adapt. He got used to me and my crazy needs, and in comparison, yours are super sweet and mild."

Kenn smiled through his tears. "I can see why Denali and Asher love you so much. Underneath that bad boy exterior, you've got a soft heart, Uncle Milan."

"Ha! Keep dreaming." But his uncle smiled, and warmth spread through him.

They sat for a while, and Kenn's body and mind found peace.

"Can I bring up one more thing?" Uncle Milan asked.

"Sure."

"Would you be okay with not calling me 'uncle'

anymore? I am and always be your uncle, but I feel it makes things more complicated, what with you being so close with Denali and now Warrick being brought into the mix..."

"If Warrick and I were together, would he become your nephew as well? Like a nephew by marriage? A nephew-in-law? Would he technically have to call you 'uncle' as well?"

Milan groaned. "I swear to god, Kenn, if he ever calls me 'uncle,' I'll knock him out cold."

Kenn laughed until his belly hurt.

29

If Warrick had thought his previous conversation with the president had been nerve-racking, this one topped it by far. He could see himself walk into the Oval Office and plop down on one of those uncomfortable couches and say, "Good morning, Mr. President. I'd like to be your son's Daddy, pretty please and thank you."

Yeah, 'cause that would go over well, regardless of what Milan had said.

He was waiting in Max's office for the president to be done with his current appointment, and then it would be time for Warrick's firing squad. Or the Spanish Inquisition followed by a firing squad.

"Nervous?"

Warrick spun around at Milan's voice. "You here to witness my trial and execution?"

Milan grinned. "Yup. I wanted to observe the carnage firsthand."

Warrick drew a shaky hand through his hair. "Not helping, dude. Not helping."

"It'll be fine. I'm actually here as moral support."

"For me or the president?"

"A little of both, but I'll definitely help you make your case. Though if it comes down to it and Del is upset after all, I'll have to take his side. Our friendship demands that."

Warrick sighed. "Fair enough. Thanks for showing up."

The door opened, and Vice President Riggs walked out, smiling. "Good morning, gentlemen."

Warrick mumbled back an acknowledgment, too nervous to give her more attention.

"You can go in," Max said. "And may God have mercy on your soul."

Warrick rolled his eyes. Weren't the two of them hilarious, poking fun at his expense? Not that he could truly blame them.

"Hey, Warrick," the president greeted Warrick as he walked in. He was sitting behind his desk, his sleeves rolled up as he was making some notes on his Remarkable. After seeing the president with the gadget, Warrick had promptly ordered one for himself. He loved how easily it converted his handwritten notes into text.

"Good morning, Mr. President."

"Grab a seat. I'll be with you in a minute."

True to his word, he put his pencil down a minute later and got up. "What are you doing here?" he asked Milan, who had installed himself on the couch across from Warrick.

"Oh, I'm here for the entertainment," Milan said with a big grin. He was having way too much fun with this.

"Entertainment? What's this about?" The president turned to Warrick again. "Did something happen with Kenn? Are you here to ask me for his hand in marriage?"

Warrick choked on his own breath and broke out in a coughing fit, his lungs desperately sucking in air between coughs. The president looked at him with concern as he lowered himself into his chair. "You okay there?"

Warrick nodded. "Sorry. Something went...wrong."

"Breathing is hard," Milan stated, and never had Warrick wanted to slap a man more.

"What can I do for you?" the president asked, subtly checking his watch.

Right. The man had more to do. Warrick would have to cut to the chase, then, and skip all small talk. But how? "After our last conversation, I followed your advice. Kenn and I developed an even closer friendship."

"Good. That's good, right?"

Warrick glanced at Milan for help, and after a second or two of shooting him silent pleas, the man let out a loud sigh. "Oh, for fuck's sake. Do I have to do everything myself? Del, we discovered that Kenn needs something more than a traditional relationship, even a gay one. He's not merely into older guys. He wants a Daddy. And Warrick is here to apply for the job."

Silence filled the Oval Office as the president's mouth dropped open. He darted his eyes from Milan to Warrick. "Is that... Is he right?"

Warrick took a deep breath. "Yes, Mr. President."

"Kenn wants a Daddy-boy relationship?"

"He does," Milan said. "I talked to him about it, and he's been aware he's submissive for a longer time. The Daddy thing is a more recent development, but it fits him to a T."

The president leaned back in his chair and buried his face in his hands. "I don't... I can't... Fuck!"

Warrick sat frozen. That didn't sound like a man who was okay with it. That sounded like an angry father. But Milan subtly signaled him to wait.

The president jumped up from his seat, then strode to a

door that led outside. The next minute he'd disappeared, leaving Warrick and Milan.

"Where... What's happening?"

Milan sighed. "He needs a moment. He'll be fine, I promise. Give him a few minutes to process."

"Where did he go?"

"He's probably right outside, pacing the colonnade that leads to the West Wing entrance."

"It's snowing."

Milan raised an eyebrow. "So? Dude's from Boston. You don't really think a little snow's gonna bother him, do you?"

Warrick sat in silence, millions of thoughts storming through his head. What if the president didn't approve? What if he fired him after all? This must've been the stupidest thing he'd ever done. What had been thinking? Talking to the president before he'd even approached Kenn himself, and yet he'd seen no other way. He refused to go behind the president's back. The man deserved better, but so did Kenn. If they got together, it would be in the open, not as each other's dirty secret. Though come to think of it, the Daddy-boy aspect of their relationship would probably have to stay between them for now. If the press got wind of that...

The president came back as suddenly as he'd left, only now, his eyes were a bit red. Had he been crying? The idea broke Warrick's heart. The last thing he wanted was to cause the man even more pain than he was already dealing with.

"Mr. President, I apologize if I upset you—"

The president held up his hand, and Warrick stopped talking. "Not your fault. I needed a moment to deal with the hard reality that Sarah won't be here to watch our son find his place, and it's..." His face was tight as he clearly fought for composure. "You've lost friends, Warrick. I don't need to tell you that grieving is a constant process and that every time you hit some kind of milestone, it hurts all over again."

"Yes, Mr. President. I do know. I'm so sorry for your loss."

Empty words, but what else could he offer?

"Milan, you sure this is what he wants? What he needs?"

Milan nodded. "He does. He's known he's submissive for a while now. It's why he was scared to come out to us. He feared we'd be upset that he wasn't more dominant, a stronger leader, or in my case, an actual Dom."

"Fuck," the president said. "He thought that? Dammit, I should've picked up on that. I never realized it."

"Me neither. Though that may not mean much as we both know I have zero experience in any kind of parenting, even from an uncle's perspective."

"Don't sell yourself short. You're doing a pretty damn good job right now, advocating for him."

Milan scoffed. "Sure, but I didn't exactly volunteer for this."

"I didn't see Warrick drag your sorry ass in here, now did I? But we're getting sidetracked." The president refocused on Warrick. "Is that what you want as well? Have you had a relationship like that before?"

"I do, sir, and no, I haven't. Never even considered it. But Kenn is... He triggers my protective instincts, makes me want to take care of him."

The president's face softened. "You've been doing a great job so far. He looks so much better than he did even two weeks ago. He's eating better, working out regularly. That's all you, correct?"

"Yes, sir. We set up a schedule for him together, and we made some rules for him to follow. He's been thriving under that regiment."

"So basically, you've already been a Daddy to him, just without the...other stuff."

The other stuff. If that was what the president wanted to call it, Warrick was fine with it. It wasn't like he'd ever wanted to have a conversation about sex with the president of the United States in the first place. "Yes, Mr. President."

Milan laughed. "It's the other stuff that makes it fun, Del..."

The president groaned. "Please, for the love of all that's sacred and holy, don't say anything more. This is uncomfortable enough as it is."

"Mmm, funny, that's not what you said when you were discussing my sex life in front of Kenn at New Year's. If memory serves me, you said it was about damn time he learned more about—"

"It's different, okay? Trust me. It's not the same thing. He's my son, my little boy... Except somehow, he isn't anymore, and that's not easy, okay?"

Milan grew serious. "I know. And losing Sarah makes it even harder."

The president's shoulders dropped, and for a moment, the signs of the stress he'd been under became more pronounced. "She would've known what to say to him, what to do. Instead, I have to make this call on my own, and it's so hard."

"It's not a difficult call, Del. In fact, it's an easy one. The kid loves him, and this is what he wants. Nothing complicated about it. Technically, Warrick doesn't even need your permission, and the fact that he wants it and didn't go behind your back tells you all you need to know."

"True." The president studied Warrick, who stayed silent under his scrutiny, resisting the urge to squirm. "And I've already seen you take great care of him. I trust you'll continue that."

"I will, sir. He's... I care deeply for him."

"I know, Warrick... And while we're talking about all this, I do insist you start calling me Del when no outsiders are around. I'm finding it difficult enough to navigate without you constantly reminding me of my job."

"I'll try, sir. Del. It's gonna take me some time."

The president smiled at him. "I understand. Just try. I think it'll help Kenn as well."

"I'll do my best."

"I still want you to be his tutor. He needs you in that area."

"I'd be honored to. He's got a sharp mind, and he'll excel in law."

"So let's agree that your job is completely separate from everything and anything else that happens. I know it's muddy, but it can't be helped."

"I understand."

The president sighed. "And as much as I hate to say it, this has to stay out of the press. I don't want you to feel like you have anything to be ashamed or embarrassed about, but we both know the media won't see it that way. It's not fair that this should even be a consideration, but unfortunately, that's the reality right now."

"Understood. I'm more than happy to stay in the bubble for now."

"Maybe you guys can return to Camp David at some point, spend some time together there, away from everyone else."

Oh, Warrick wasn't going to say no to that offer. "I'd be more than open to that, sir. Del, I mean."

Del took a deep inhale. "You have my blessing, Warrick. Just please take good care of my son. I'm trusting you."

Warrick squared his shoulders, warm tingles of joy flowing through him. "Thank you. Thank you so much. It means a lot to me that you trust me with him."

"Well, the thorough background check the FBI did on you before you were hired does help," Del said dryly.

Milan nodded. "Besides, we all know that if you ever hurt him, it's not a special forces team you'd have to worry about. I'll pay you a visit myself you won't forget..."

30

Seth and Coulson had left early that morning, but of course they'd still hit traffic. On the busy I-95 between DC and New York, some kind of delay was unavoidable. Seth was driving while Coulson caught up on some sleep. Seth didn't mind. His man needed it. Things had been busy on a level neither of them had ever experienced before, and with the incredible stress and pressure added to it, Coulson was running on fumes. Seth could appreciate spending some time alone with his thoughts. It helped him destress.

They were making progress in the investigation, but god, it was slow and tedious work. Every little bit of information had to be checked out, every lead followed, and now that they had decided to keep the circle of people in the know as small as possible, a lot of that fell on their plate.

With Director James's permission, Seth had further reduced the shifts he did as a Secret Service agent. As much as he enjoyed being on Kenn's detail, he didn't have the time. Plus, as he'd admitted honestly, he was running on too little sleep to do such an important job. His reflexes weren't what they should be, and luckily, Director James had taken that as seriously as Seth had.

When he'd informed her four days ago about Diane's arrest, she'd been devastated and was determined not to screw up again. Not that any of it, especially Diane's decision to commit crimes in a misplaced sense of loyalty to Mrs. Markinson, had been her fault, but at the end of the day, that didn't matter. The director was technically responsible.

Seth sipped his coffee, his brain slowly calming down, even as around him, cars honked as others refused to let them switch lanes. Driving was one of those things he could do on autopilot while he let his mind wander. And wander it did, processing everything that had happened over the last few weeks.

They were getting close to solving the whole case, he could feel it, and that alone was enough to keep him going. It could take a few more weeks or a few more months, but they'd unravel this whole complicated plot. He'd never been one to put much stock in conspiracy theories, but god, when this one hit the press, everyone would have a field day with it. It would fuel conspiracies for years and years to come.

Next to him, Coulson stirred, blinking. "Where are we?" he asked in that adorably sleepy voice.

"About ten minutes out of Philadelphia."

Coulson yawned, stretching carefully. "God, that felt good. Thank you for letting me sleep."

"Not something you need to thank me for, boo. I'm glad you could catch some extra sleep. You needed it."

"I did." Coulson yawned again, then pulled his phone out of his pocket and quickly flipped through it.

"Anything urgent?"

"No, just a whole lot of small stuff. It seems we're making

some progress on identifying the boat the scuba divers used to get access to Annabeth Markinson's boathouse."

"How?"

"Someone familiar with the Chesapeake Bay studied the map and came up with the most likely spots for the boat to get into the water unseen. Once we had those, it was a process of checking traffic cams, CCTV, interviewing possible witnesses, the usual stuff. It took a while, but it seemed most likely the boat hadn't been registered in any of the marinas. Barry said they have a lead now, some camera footage of a pickup truck pulling a small boat."

And that was how they would solve the case, by following every lead, tracing every step, exploring every possible tangent. "That would be great progress."

Coulson clicked his phone off and put it away. "With every detail that emerges, the total picture becomes more and more clear. We're not there yet, but we're getting closer."

"I feel the same. Hopefully, we can make some headway today as well."

They were on their way to the MCC, the Metropolitan Correctional Center, on Manhattan. Seth was still amazed that a high-security federal detention facility like that could even exist smack dab in the middle of New York, but it had been in Lower Manhattan since the seventies, and no prisoner had ever escaped.

Over the years, it had offered involuntary hospitality to famous criminals, including crime bosses, infamous drug dealers, and even some Ponzi scheme fraudsters. And, of course, several terrorists, including the three students who had been apprehended after the Pride Bombing. But within days, they'd been dead. Their deaths had been ruled suicides based on the suicide notes that had been found, but how those three had gotten their hands on the medications they'd used to kill themselves remained a mystery. Coulson had warned Seth it might be a wild goose chase, but they still wanted to pay the facility a visit and see for themselves if they could find any more clues.

"I know we've said it before, but when this whole thing is over, you and I are going to go on vacation together," Coulson said, putting his hand on Seth's thigh. Seth loved how physically affectionate Coulson was, so often seeking his presence, touching him, checking in.

"I can't wait. Where do you want to go? We could book two weeks on some nice ranch, teach you how to ride a horse..." he teased.

"Fuck no. No horses for me. Besides, all that riding must make your ass hurt, and I have other plans for that piece of your anatomy."

Seth laughed. "Do you now? That's good to know."

"Sure do, baby. I pretty much plan on being inside you that whole vacation."

Seth laughed even harder at that wonderfully over-the-top, smug statement. "Sounds like paradise, boo."

"But honestly, baby, I don't care where we go. Somewhere with nice weather would be good, I suppose, though I doubt we'll be outside much. I want to be with you, that's all. Spend some uninterrupted time together. Sleep, talk, have endless rounds of sex. Maybe watch TV together, but that's it. No other activities, no visitors, no socializing. Just you and me."

"I can't wait, boo. I miss you."

Cliché as it was, their busy lives had made sex a challenge. They still managed, but nowhere near as often as they both wanted to, and Seth missed it.

"I miss you too. I'm glad we get to do this together so we

can at least talk in the car. It's not the same, but it's better than nothing."

It was, and they did spend the rest of the ride catching up, chatting about everything and nothing. They made it to the MCC perfectly on schedule, showing their credentials so they could park in the closest parking garage. The guards at the entrance did a thorough check of their credentials, then made them both check their weapons—not that they'd expected anything else. Not in a high-security facility that was often referred to as the Guantánamo of New York.

Their first meeting was with the warden, Ross Ivory, a lean man in his late fifties with a pair of sharp blue eyes and gray hair in a military-style buzz cut. His handshake was firm, and Seth detected no subtle hostility on his end, which bode well.

"What can I do for you? In your email, you referred to the investigation into the suicide of the three pride bombers," Ivory said.

"Correct," Coulson said. "We wanted to ask some more questions."

"Any particular reason for that? Not that you're not allowed to, but it had me curious, since it's been almost six years."

"I'm sure you're aware that the investigation never resulted in full answers. Some aspects are still unknown, even to this day."

Ivory nodded. "I wasn't the warden here when this incident occurred, but I've read up on all the details, and I'll answer your questions as best I can. Other than that, I've ordered everyone to cooperate with you, and you have full access to all our files. If you run into any trouble, any issues, any lack of cooperation from my staff, please let me know."

Wow, someone who genuinely wanted to help the FBI. They hadn't encountered many of those yet.

"We appreciate that. What happened to the previous warden?"

"As is customary, Warden Hazelton was transferred to another facility after those three deaths. The Federal Bureau of Prisons usually does that to aid the investigation and ensure that the warden can't influence the results."

"And he was transferred to...?"

"Chicago."

"Wouldn't Brooklyn have made more sense if the man lived here?"

Ivory smiled thinly. "You're a federal agent, Special Agent Padman. I'm sure you know from experience that federal agencies don't always make decisions based on what would be logical or makes sense. Or I should say, they rarely do."

Coulson laughed. "Good point. And yes, I'm well familiar with that phenomenon. Do you know if Hazelton still works there?"

"I don't. As you can imagine, I don't keep track of coworkers once they've left my facility."

Seth made a quick note, knowing that this was something Coulson wanted to check out later.

"In your professional opinion, do you see any reason to doubt the official conclusion that these three men committed suicide?" Coulson asked.

Ivory leaned back in his chair, steepling his fingers. "I used to be a cop. Worked for the Philadelphia Police Department for twenty years before I made the switch to the Federal Bureau of Prisons. Twenty years on the force leaves you with sharply honed instincts, especially when you've worked homicide, like I have."

Coulson nodded. "I've worked for the NYPD myself, though not for homicide, but I know what you mean."

Smart, mentioning his own background as a cop. Coulson was good at finding those bonding moments.

"Going purely by evidence, I'd have to say that the official conclusion is correct. There's no evidence whatsoever that suggests their deaths weren't self-inflicted."

Coulson leaned forward. "And if you go by instinct?"

"My instinct is screaming at me that something is fishy about the whole thing."

"Like what?"

Ivory slowly shook his head. "Like them having those tablets. We search prisoners pretty thoroughly here, so how on earth did three men smuggle in meds? According to the file, the drugs they took are small tablets. One of them, I would've believed. But all three?"

"The file says it's most likely that they had them protected with Saran wrap and swallowed them at some point."

"Yes, and again, if it happened to one of them, that would've made sense. But all three? Prisoners don't have privacy here. Not when they eat, not when they sleep, not when they shower. And not even when they take a dump, so if three men had had to poop something out and then take it from their feces and hide it somewhere, no way would we have missed that. Not from all three."

"I'm going to play devil's advocate for a moment," Coulson said. "And please keep in mind that this is no personal attack on you whatsoever, but this particular facility doesn't have the best reputation when it comes to the quality of its guards. The MCC has had multiple incidents over the years with unqualified staffers functioning as guards, even though they lacked the necessary training or experience."

"Yes. We've struggled with shortages and staff for years, and more than once, people have been pulled from other departments to fill in as guards."

"Is it possible that the guards on duty at that time missed this? That they weren't adequately watching the surveillance footage and didn't see the prisoners defecate those drugs?"

"Technically, yes. But I did check, and unless the records have been falsified afterward, all the guards on duty during that time were experienced guards. Or at least, they were trained. But can I ask you a question as well?"

"I can't guarantee that I'm able to answer it, but if I can, I'd be happy to."

"I'm puzzled as to why it matters. I understand that with any other type of prisoners, it would be a scandal, but why with these three? They were radical Muslim terrorists, a group of people known for suicide attacks. Wasn't it to be expected that if they were caught alive, they'd commit suicide?"

"That's a good question, Warden. The truth is that yes, most terrorists like that are suicide terrorists. But the reality is also that most of the time, those who don't die during the attack don't kill themselves afterward. They believe Allah will reward them for dying in the attack, but I'm not sure that covers suicides afterward as well. I think they might fear being cheated out of their martyrdom with the accompanying heavenly reward."

"Huh, interesting. I've never looked at it like that. Anyway, any more questions I can answer for you?"

"Yes, I have one more question. How many of the guards who worked that week are still here?"

"That, I don't know of the top of my head, but give me a moment, and I'll find out."

The warden booted up his computer, then typed rapidly, clicking a few times until he'd found what he was looking for. "In total, twenty people had been in contact with them, most of them guards. Thirteen of those have left. The other seven still work here." He typed again, then clicked. "If I'm correct, three of those who left have retired, and the others quit."

"That's helpful, Warden. Could we have a list of all those names?"

Ivory frowned. "I'd think you already had a list like that in your possession."

Coulson smiled at him. "I'm sure we do, but I always prefer to get the evidence fresh myself. You never know what turns up that way."

"True." Ivory turned his attention back to his screen, then clicked twice. In the corner of his room, a big laser printer came to life, spitting out two sheets of paper. The warden grabbed them from the printer and handed them to Coulson. "Here you go. If you have any more questions, I'm happy to answer them."

"Do you have a place where we could look at this?" Coulson asked.

Ten minutes later, they were sitting in a small conference room and had both set up their laptops. Seth loved how easily they worked together, the distribution of tasks never up for debate. In this case, they had each taken ten names to track, searching through personnel records using a login the warden had provided them with, as well as running every name through the federal databases.

"This is interesting..." Seth narrowed his eyes as he scanned the information on his screen. He opened the full résumé of Laurence Paskewich. He followed the dates of his previous employers, then gasped. There it was. The proverbial smoking gun.

"What did you find?" Coulson asked.

"This guy started working at the MCC three months before the Pride Bombing. He left four weeks after the three bombers had died."

"Okay, that's a somewhat suspicious timing, but—"

"He worked for Kingmakers. One of his previous employers was Kingmakers."

31

Kenn wasn't sure what he'd expected when he walked into the dining room, but he came to a full stop at the sight of a table set for two. A romantic table with a gorgeous tablecloth, pretty china, beautifully folded napkins, and even two candles. What was going on?

Warrick stood next to the table, dressed in a pair of dark blue slacks and a baby blue dress shirt that was unbuttoned at the top. He looked utterly sexy, and Kenn's mouth became dry, and his heartbeat accelerated as his insides flooded with warmth.

Warrick rubbed his hands down his pants. "H-hi." He cleared his throat. "I'm glad you're here."

Kenn looked around the room again. "I'm sorry, but what are we doing? Your text just said to show up here at six."

Warrick took a deep breath, then stepped closer to him, and the look on his face changed to tenderness. Kenn's heart thumped even more wildly. Was this...? He didn't dare hope.

"It's time you and I had a conversation, and I figured we'd do that over a nice dinner together. I would've loved to take you out to a restaurant, but considering the security involved in that, I conspired with Mrs. Morelli, and we came up with this." Warrick gestured at the table. "I hope you like it."

A conversation? The butterflies in Kenn's belly broke out in flight, making him lightheaded. If Warrick had specifically requested this setting, this atmosphere, that meant this would be a good conversation, a happy one. How could he not hope when seeing all this? Besides, Milan had said the same thing, that he thought Warrick liked Kenn back.

"What do you think, baby boy?"

Kenn's heart skipped a beat. "B-baby boy?"

"Is it okay if I call you that?"

Kenn nodded, unable to find words.

Warrick closed the distance between them, his face so close to Kenn's that Warrick's breath danced over his skin. "I promise I'll explain everything, baby boy. But before we do all that and before we start on, I hope, a lovely dinner, could I maybe kiss you?"

Kiss him? Warrick wanted to kiss him? What reality had he stepped into? Because a universe in which Warrick wanted to kiss him, where he called Kenn *baby boy*, had to be a different world. His mind couldn't grasp what was happening, but still he nodded. If this was some kind of dream, he didn't want to wake up.

"I'm sorry, baby boy, but you're gonna need to use words for this. I need to know you really want this..." Warrick's thumb swiped over Kenn's mouth as if encouraging him to use it.

Kenn swallowed. "Yes. I mean, yes, please? To the kiss. And the dinner. Everything."

He was stumbling like an idiot, but Warrick only smiled at him, and then he angled his head and, ever so slowly, moved in. Kenn closed his eyes and held his breath in anticipation, but when Warrick's lips touched his, a little gasp came out. His first kiss. He was being kissed for the first time. By Warrick, the man who had his heart, his devotion. His dreams had come true.

Warrick circled his waist, and without thinking, Kenn looped his arms around Warrick's neck. Warrick's lips were soft against his own, a whisper of a kiss, sweet and delicate, and yet Kenn's body lit up everywhere. The pressure increased, and Warrick opened his mouth, the tip of his tongue coming out, pressing against the seam of Kenn's lips. He let him in, and then Warrick's tongue was in his mouth. Warrick was *kissing* him, and Kenn clung to him, dizzy with all the sensations.

He wasn't sure what to do, but his mouth seemed to have instincts he hadn't been aware of, copying Warrick's movements and kissing him back. Their tongues met, and *oh*, the slick contact had heat pooling in his belly. Warrick slid his tongue alongside Kenn's. How could something so simple feel that good? He tasted mint on Warrick's tongue, with a hint of cocoa—had to be the dark chocolate Warrick loved. The flavor was scrumptious. Mouthwatering. The nerves in his tongue had to be connected to the rest of his body, sending sparks outward, setting them on fire.

Warrick's hand, which had been gently rubbing Kenn's back, slipped lower and now caressed his butt. He loved the casual intimacy of that move, and instinctually, he rubbed himself against Warrick, letting out a happy sigh at how that made him feel. He was hard, and so was Warrick, and it made him both happy and proud. Warrick was hard for him. He wanted Kenn.

When Warrick broke off the kiss, Kenn was panting, and

he finally opened his eyes, looking straight into Warrick's. "How are you doing, baby boy?"

Kenn swallowed, then licked his lips. "G-good. Really good. That was... That was my first kiss."

"I had a feeling it was. I hope it lived up to your expectations."

"It was a hundred times better than I'd expected."

Warrick's smile made his heart trip. "I'm glad to hear that. I loved kissing you."

"I wouldn't mind if we kissed some more."

Warrick chuckled. "Neither would I, but let's take it one step at a time. We have some things we need to talk about. So how about we have dinner?"

Kenn let out a sigh. He wanted to whine and stamp his feet in protest, but how could he when he also wanted to have that conversation? "Can we at least kiss some more after dinner, then?"

"I promise, baby boy. I just need you to know a few things first."

"Good things, right?" Kenn asked, suddenly worried.

Warrick cupped his cheek and pressed a last kiss on his lips. "Really good things."

Denali must have been watching them because as soon as they had sat down—Warrick helping Kenn in his seat like a true gentleman—he showed up, sporting a big grin. "Good evening, gentlemen. Can I start you off with something to drink?"

He winked at Kenn, whose cheeks heated up. Why, he wasn't sure, because it wasn't like Denali was innocent. Far from it.

"I'll have a glass of red wine, please, and Kenn will have a Shirley Temple."

Kenn opened his mouth to protest. Why was Warrick

ordering for him? That was... Actually, he didn't mind at all. He loved that Warrick had known what to order for him. It made him feel seen. Taken care of.

Denali didn't even blink. "I'll bring those right out. The appetizers will be ready in a minute or two."

He walked off with another wink at Kenn.

"Were you okay with me ordering for you?" Warrick asked.

Kenn nodded slowly. "Yes. I liked it."

"Good. I love taking care of you, making sure you have everything you need."

"Denali must've seen us kiss," Kenn blurted out.

"I'm sure he did, considering his perfect timing of showing up. Does that idea bother you?"

"Yes. No. I don't know. What if he... No, he wouldn't tell my dad. I can trust him."

Warrick reached across the table and took Kenn's hand in his own, lacing their fingers together. "Your dad knows about this, baby boy. I'd never go behind his back."

Kenn swallowed. "My dad knows? He's okay with you..."

He had no idea how to finish that sentence. They weren't talking about mere kissing anymore; that much had become clear. But what, exactly, did Warrick want from Kenn? Or with Kenn?

"Let's start at the beginning, baby boy, before you worry yourself into a frenzy."

Kenn shot him a sheepish look. "Sorry. I don't have any experience with this, and I guess I'm prone to seeing problems where there are none."

"In this case, the list of potential problems is long, so you're absolutely right to consider those. But, and this actually brings me to the core of what I want to talk to you about, I don't want those to be your problems. They're my problems. I have to solve them and make sure you have nothing to worry about."

"I'd like that," Kenn whispered. "I'd like that very much."

"Baby boy, over the course of the last few weeks, you and I have grown very close. What started as a professional relationship between a teacher and his student developed into a friendship. But even that friendship has evolved into something much deeper, with you allowing me to take care of you and help you make good choices."

"I...I loved that," Kenn admitted.

"So did I. In fact, the whole reason I planned this dinner with you is to ask you if we can continue doing that, only in a more official way. I want to be your Daddy, baby boy, and I'd love for you to be my sweet boy and let me take care of you."

"Yes." Kenn's answer was immediate. "Yes, I really want that."

Warrick's face broke open in the biggest smile he'd ever seen on him. "Yeah? Are you sure about this?"

"One hundred percent."

"So you know what a Daddy-boy dynamic entails?"

"I did some research when...when I realized this was what I wanted."

Kenn had never seen so much love in Warrick's eyes. He looked at Kenn as if he were a precious diamond. "I asked your father for permission, and he gave me his blessing. This is a strange situation, with us having to build a relationship with no privacy at all, but I want to be with you, Kenn. I don't know when I fell for you, but it happened fast, and now I can't imagine my life without you anymore."

"You're serious about this." Kenn tried to wrap his head around it all. After his conversation with his uncle, he'd hoped that Warrick would return his feelings, but never in a million years had he imagined him making it this official this quickly.

Warrick squeezed Kenn's hand. "Am I going too fast? Because if you need to, we'll slow down and take it easy. I want to be with you, baby boy, in whatever way you'll let me."

He would remember this moment forever. Such a strange thought amid the whirlwind of emotions that swirled through his brain, but the thought was so crystal clear that Kenn gasped. Something had been holding him back inside, invisible chains that had made him suppress a part of himself. And now those chains had been broken. He was free.

For so long, he'd felt like he had to be stronger, more independent, more dominant. And even after he talked about it with Milan, he'd still questioned himself. But not anymore. His visceral reaction to Warrick's words had set him free. This was what he wanted. What Warrick was offering right now was who and what he wanted to be. And if Warrick had talked to his dad, and his dad was on board with all this, that meant that Kenn no longer had to hold back. He could allow himself to be who he truly was.

Before he knew what he was doing, he'd pushed back his chair so quickly it fell backward onto the soft carpet. He didn't care, already taking the few steps around the table to reach Warrick, whose expression changed from worry to joy as soon as Kenn launched himself at him. He jumped onto his lap and wrapped his arms around Warrick's chest, then put his head against his shoulder.

This. This was where he belonged. On his Daddy's lap. In his Daddy's arms.

"I'm ready for all of it... Daddy."

32

The rush that went through Warrick at hearing that word fall from Kenn's lips was unlike anything he'd ever experienced before. Shock, exhilaration, excitement, nerves, all wrapped into one explosion of feelings that left him shaking as he held Kenn close. His baby boy on his lap. How perfect could life be?

"I have no words for how happy this makes me," he whispered, nuzzling Kenn's neck.

Kenn mumbled something unintelligible against his chest, and Warrick smiled. "What was that, baby boy?"

"I'm really happy too, Daddy."

The way he said that word, so casually and naturally. As if he'd said it a hundred million times before when in reality, it was as new to him as it was to Warrick. "I love hearing that word out of your mouth."

Kenn lifted his head from his safe spot against Warrick's shoulder, meeting Warrick's eyes. "Good. Because I intend to say it a lot."

He raised his lips in the most adorable fashion, and how Warrick loved that he already had the confidence to ask for a kiss, even though he'd gotten his first kiss ever only minutes ago. Warrick had been his first, and he intended to be Kenn's first in a lot of other things as well.

The first to take him on a date. His first boyfriend. His first Daddy. The first to make love to him. And if Warrick had his way, he'd be the only and last in each case. Now that he'd found his boy, he would never let him go again.

His sweet, shy boy, almost radiating now. Warrick took him up on his offer, kissing him softly. Someone cleared his throat, and Warrick broke off the kiss. Denali stood next to the table, looking apologetic as he put down a plate in front of Warrick. "Sorry for interrupting, but I didn't want your appetizers to get cold."

"No worries, Denali. Thank you," Warrick said.

"My pleasure. I'll give you your privacy. I'll be back in about fifteen minutes to check in, okay?"

Warrick nodded, smiling when Denali winked at Kenn. "Do you want to go back to your own chair, baby boy?" Warrick asked when Denali had left the room again.

"Do I have to?"

"You want to stay on my lap?" Warrick didn't know why that thought made him so happy, but it did. Kenn's eagerness to be close to him aroused Warrick on both a physical and an emotional level.

"Can I, Daddy?"

"Absolutely."

And so Warrick found himself with his boy snuggled against him as he hand-fed him. Mrs. Morelli had outdone herself with the appetizers, fried ravioli with three different sauces: marinara, a cheese dip, and what had to be homemade pesto. Thank goodness she hadn't made soup because that would've been a hell of a lot more challenging to feed to

Kenn, who showed no intention at all of letting go of Warrick.

"When did you realize you wanted to be my boy?" he asked when they were done with the appetizers.

Kenn let out a happy-sounding sigh as he snuggled closer. "Uncle Milan helped me find the word for it, but I've known for a while now that I'm submissive and wanted a Dom to take care of me. Have you been a Daddy before?"

Warrick shook his head. "No, that's all you, baby boy. You made me feel things I'd never felt before. So we'll figure it out together, hmm? How did you come to the conclusion that you were submissive?"

"I overheard Milan and my dad talking about being dominant and submissive a few years ago. I was curious what that was, and so I did some research. Needless to say, I was shocked by what I discovered."

Warrick chuckled. "That, I believe. I don't know much about it myself, but every now and then, when I come across something, I have to blink a few times. Not that I'm kink-shaming in any way. To each his own. But it's not my thing."

"Yeah, a lot of what I read didn't appeal to me at all, but I did recognize some of the descriptions about what it meant to be submissive. I thought I was different, though, because I wasn't attracted to most of the kinks submissives are supposed to enjoy."

"Like what?"

"Any kind of pain. Maybe I should try it before saying it's not my thing, but I didn't connect with it. And neither with serving, like Denali does with Milan and Asher. I can't see myself in that role at all."

"I can understand that. Again, I'm not judging, but I don't enjoy inflicting pain either."

"And when Denali and I grew closer, it became even

clearer to me that I'm a different submissive than he is. He's... He serves them, but he's strong and independent at the same time, if that makes sense. He doesn't *need* them, not like I..."

Kenn stopped talking, averting his eyes as his posture grew rigid. "Not like you need me?" Warrick asked gently.

"Yeah..."

"It's okay, baby boy. Whatever you feel and need is okay."

"How can you say that when you don't know what that is? I don't even know myself. Not all of it anyway."

"Why don't we start with you being open and honest with me about what you do need, and we'll go from there?"

"But you said you've never been a Daddy before. What if you don't want the same things?"

Warrick smiled as he put his index finger under Kenn's chin. "Does what you need involve you and me together?"

Kenn nodded.

"Then I can tell you right now I'll love it. All I want is to be with you and take care of you, baby boy."

"What if I need a whole lot of care?"

"Then I'll be happy to give it to you, my sweet boy. Are you afraid you'll be too needy for me?"

Kenn nodded again, his cheeks bright red. "It's like I have this pent-up need inside me from years and years, and now that I can let it out, it's so *big*."

Warrick's heart damn near exploded with joy. "Good thing I have years of pent-up need to take care of someone inside me. I'm here, baby boy. I'm here to stay."

The expression on Kenn's face as reality sank in with him was one Warrick would never forget. Such happiness, relief...and love. "Thank you, Daddy."

"I do want to set some rules, though, so we both have a clear understanding of what we're doing." He'd done his own research, wanting to come prepared, and he'd even joined a Daddy group online and had asked questions.

"What kind of rules?"

Kenn sounded a little apprehensive. "Nothing big, baby boy, I promise, but I think it would help us get on the right track with this. The first rule would be that we're completely open with each other. You can't lie to me about what you want, what you don't like, or what you're struggling with, and I won't either. Communication is crucial."

"I can do that, Daddy. I like telling you everything anyway."

Fuck, he was adorable. "I know, baby boy, and that brings me such pleasure."

"What else?"

"Rule two is that I'm in charge. I make the decisions."

That got an immediate nod from his boy and, unless Warrick was mistaken, a sigh of relief.

"Rule three. I get to make the decisions when it comes to your body as well. No jerking off without my permission. You can't come unless I say you can, whether I'm with you or not."

It had come out husky, his voice betraying his excitement over this aspect of their relationship. He held his breath. Was this too fast? They hadn't even talked about sex, and yet Warrick wanted to make things clear from the get-go.

A delicious blush crept up Kenn's cheeks. "Y-yes, Daddy." He swallowed. "Is there anything else?"

"We'll start with this for now. Maybe we'll add more later on."

"And what happens if I b-break the rules?"

Warrick tried to look stern, no easy feat with all the

mushy feelings inside him as he held his baby boy on his lap. "Disobeying will have consequences."

"I'll be good, Daddy."

"I know you will." Kenn wasn't the bratty type, way too sweet for that. Warrick kissed his lips once again. "Why don't you sit down for now, hmm? Denali has been waiting in the hallway long enough, as not to disturb us."

Kenn slid off his lap and got back to his own chair. "Yes, Daddy."

More beautiful words didn't exist in the English language.

Denali smiled when he walked in. "Looks like you enjoyed the appetizers. Mrs. Morelli has made lasagna for the main course, and it's heaven."

"Denali," Warrick said, waiting until Denali met his eyes. "Thank you. For everything. You've been a wonderful friend to Kenn."

Denali beamed. "No need to thank me for that, Sir. He's been just as good a friend to me. But I can't tell you how happy I am to know you'll be taking care of him."

And just like that, Denali had already accepted him. Not that Warrick had expected anything else from a boy who was the sub of a Dom and a switch, but still. "You don't have to call me Sir, Denali. You can use my name."

Denali shook his head. "Nope, can't do that. Not because of my job, but also because... You may be a different kind of Dom, Sir, but you're still a Dominant, and it wouldn't be right. Not for me anyway. I wouldn't feel comfortable."

Strangely enough, Warrick could understand where he was coming from. "I see. Well, to be clear, I don't object, but I didn't want you to feel like you have to."

"Thank you, Sir. I appreciate that. Are you ready for the main course?"

"I think we are."

"Coming right up," Denali said with a sunny smile and hurried off.

The lasagna was indeed as scrumptious as Denali had said, and Warrick ate more than he'd intended to. "I'm full," Kenn announced, pushing his plate back.

"So am I. And no room for dessert either."

Kenn groaned. "God, no. I'd explode."

"Why don't we go for a little stroll?"

"A stroll?"

"Yes. You and me, hand in hand, walking through the White House? It's not as romantic as a walk along the beach, but you'd freeze there right now anyway."

Kenn giggled. "Yes, Daddy."

"Okay. Put some shoes on, then."

Kenn lifted one foot and wiggled his toes. "I can walk on socks."

"I'm sure you can, but I'm not risking you slipping somewhere. Shoes, baby boy." He'd made his voice a little sterner, and Kenn blinked at him.

"It's sexy when you use that tone," he finally said.

Warrick laughed. "That's good to know, but it's gonna be a lot less sexy if you don't do as I asked."

Kenn slid off his chair and ran off, coming back within a minute, now wearing sneakers. "That better, Daddy?"

"Much. Let's have our stroll."

Warrick got up and reached for Kenn's hand, then laced their fingers together. They walked from the dining room into the West Sitting Hall, where they usually had their lessons, into the center hall. Asher was positioned in the hallway, and he smiled at them. "Good evening," he said, totally breaking protocol, but Warrick loved it.

"Hey, Asher," Kenn said. "Mrs. Morelli made lasagna if you haven't eaten yet."

"Denali already snuck me some."

"Of course he did." Kenn rolled his eyes, which made Warrick laugh.

"Wanna check out the view?" Warrick asked, and Kenn nodded.

They strolled into the Yellow Oval Room, right above the Oval Office. The room itself was grand—though not Warrick's personal taste, even if it was less formal than many of the other rooms—but the Truman Balcony was the real draw here.

"Honor and Law on the move," Asher spoke discreetly behind them, updating the Secret Service central command on their whereabouts. He followed them into the room, then stayed at the door as Warrick led Kenn to the balcony.

It was freezing outside, which was the perfect excuse for physical proximity, and Warrick immediately pulled his boy close. "I'll keep you warm, baby boy," he said in what had to be the cheesiest line he'd ever uttered in his life, and yet it felt so wonderfully right.

The lights of DC stretched out in front of them in the best view of the city. The Washington Monument rose majestically against the black, moonless night, like a bright finger pointing at the skies. "Did you know that when President Truman proposed building this balcony, there were fierce protests?" Kenn said, shivering in Warrick's arms.

"Why?"

"People felt it would ruin the architectural integrity of the White House. Of course later, everyone agreed it was the best change anyone has made to this building. I mean, the view is pretty damn spectacular."

"It is..."

"You should see it in the summer, when you can sit here in the shade and look out over the South Lawn. It's one of my favorite spots to read."

"Mmm, we'll have to do that together this summer."

The idea of a future where he saw himself with Kenn made his belly warm and tingly. What a wonderful thought.

"I'd like that, Daddy."

"Me too. Let's go back inside, baby boy. You're getting too cold."

Once inside, they took the stairs down to the first floor, where they roamed the hallway and all the rooms, Asher at a tactful distance. He followed them unobtrusively as they made their way to the ground floor, studying the gorgeous dish settings in the China Room. "This room freaks me out," Kenn said. "I can't help but think what would happen if I tripped and fell, breaking, like, George Washington's plate or something."

Warrick laughed. "Aren't you glad then that I made you wear shoes?"

Kenn stuck out his tongue in a gesture so spontaneous and wonderfully bratty, Warrick laughed out loud. "You getting bratty on me, baby boy?"

Kenn batted his eyelashes at him, the little minx. "Would you mind if I was?"

Warrick tugged on his hand and pulled him into his arms, then kissed him firmly. "Not at all. You experiment and test, baby boy. Daddy's here to set your boundaries. That being said, if you ever stick your tongue out at me again, you're gonna find yourself not watching TV for a week, understood?"

33

Coulson had called them all in as soon as he'd heard. This new development was the best news they'd had in ages, and he was certain the president and everyone else involved would want to learn about it right away. When he'd mentioned the word "breakthrough," a meeting had been scheduled promptly.

And so they gathered in the Oval Office at the end of a long day, the sun long down and the stars twinkling against the backdrop of a cloudless heaven. The temperature outside would be frigid, but Coulson was on fire. After months and months of grinding, they were now reaping the benefits. All their hard work and tenacity were finally paying off.

"What do you have for us, Coulson?" the president asked as soon as they'd all found a seat, and the room grew quiet instantly.

Coulson had no desire to draw out the suspense. "Mr. President, I'm happy to report we've made a substantial breakthrough in the case."

President Shafer leaned forward in his chair. "Please bring it. I'm certain we could all use some good news."

Coulson had already opened his laptop and now turned it so everyone else could see the screen, which showed a picture of a man who Coulson had studied for so long that by now he could've given an accurate description to a sketch artist. "This is Steve Duron. We're confident he is the man who did the money order to Puerto Rico, who was seen around Gulat Babur's apartment, and who picked up the bomb from Mohammed Bhat's car."

The gasps he'd expected echoed in the room. "Holy shit," Milan said. "You weren't kidding when you called it a breakthrough."

"How did you guys find him?" the president asked.

"Remember the shooting club Wesley Quirk, the Baltimore cop, belonged to? We managed to put an undercover agent there. He befriended some of the frequent visitors and, bit by bit, successfully identified every man in the group Quirk hangs out with. We did background checks on all of them. Most have had brushes with the law before, running from charges of sexual assault to DWIs, domestic abuse, and in one case, child pornography."

"Jesus, nice company for a cop," Milan muttered.

"Which, I'm sure, is one of the reasons why that shooting club is impossible to get into," Coulson said. "They do what they can to protect their members."

"How did your guy manage it?" Calix asked.

"Let's just say we created a backstory for him that made him fit in well. A few arrests for assault, a military background, the whole nine yards."

"Respect." Calix took off an imaginary hat. "I'd shit my pants."

Milan patted his leg. "You have other qualities. I'm sure you give really good head."

He said the latter with a wink at Rhett, who leaned against the wall, as always in the background. Rhett acutely choked on his own breath, bursting out into a coughing fit, which made Calix jump up and pat his back until his breathing had returned to normal.

"For fuck's sake, asshole, this is the Oval Office," Calix snapped at Milan. "Can we at least strive for some measure of class?"

Milan held up his hands, the picture of innocence. "Class? I'm the classiest guy in this room."

Even Coulson couldn't keep himself from chuckling at that statement, and it took a while before everyone had calmed down.

"Come sit with us, Rhett," the president said. "We're among friends here."

Calix extended his hand, and Rhett settled on his lap. Those two made such a sweet couple, so clearly besotted with each other. Calix gently kissed the top of Rhett's head, and the gesture made Coulson smile.

"Where were we?" the president asked.

Right. Coulson was nowhere near done yet. "Interestingly enough, the three men in Quirk's circle of friends who didn't have a criminal record caught our attention much more than the others. One of them was Duron. The reason we focused on Duron early on was that our agent took a few pictures of him—without Duron noticing, obviously—and we immediately picked up on the similarities between him and the unknown man from the money order, the apartment, and the airport bomb. It took us a while to confirm it because Duron is highly secretive about his real identity and goes by a different name in the shooting club. But our agent managed to get his fingerprints off a beer bottle, and we were able to make a positive ID." He'd kept the best bit for last. He took a deep breath. "Steve Duron is ex-army...and works for Kingmakers."

"Holy shit," Milan said again, his eyes as wide as those of everyone else in the room. "You just found another link between the assassination and Kingmakers."

Coulson nodded. "We did. Now, as I'm sure I don't need to tell you, this isn't enough for an arrest. Yet. We need more intel. Our agent is certain he's not been made yet, and considering the access he still has, I agree with his assessment. So we're leaving him undercover for now, and he'll try to get even closer access to Quirk and his group."

"Coulson, that's incredible work," the president said. "It leaves me with mixed feelings in terms of having to accept that this was domestic terrorism, but the FBI should be proud of their work in this investigation. And you above all. You've shown the determination of a pit bull, and we're so grateful for your hard work and the sacrifices you and Seth have made over the last months."

Funny how those few words meant ten times more to Coulson than the congratulatory phone call he'd received from the FBI director. Which he'd appreciated, but the president knew the toll the investigation had taken on their personal lives. "Thank you, Mr. President. It's been an honor working on this, and I won't quit until we've unraveled every last thread of it."

"When this is all over and done with, you and Seth need to take a long vacation," Calix said, and Coulson smiled because it so perfectly reflected what he and Seth had said to each other. "Where is Seth, anyway?"

"He's on protective duty. They were short due to a large training exercise most of the agents were required to attend.

So he's covering Kenn. And trust me, a long vacation is already on the schedule. Seth has some destinations shortlisted."

"Good," the president said. "And if either of you gets any trouble from your superiors for taking paid extended leave, give me a call. I don't like to use my position, but I will in this case."

"Thank you, Mr. President. We appreciate it."

"Do we have any information on what Duron's job is at Kingmakers?" Milan asked.

Coulson refocused on the topic. "Yes and no. As Henley already mentioned the first time we talked about Kingmakers, this is a company that thrives on secrecy. Because it's privately owned, the owners aren't under any legal obligations to share details publicly. But we've spoken to multiple former employees, and from what we understand, Duron is pretty high up within Kingmakers. We think he's directly working under the owners in the chain of command."

Calix frowned. "Remind me of the owners' names. Basil King, obviously, but who was the other guy again?"

"Kurt Barrow. We don't know much more about him than we do about Basil, but one thing we found out is that he was in the same Army unit as Jonathan Brooks. And at some point, Brooks was Wesley Quirk's CO. In fact, the former Kingmaker employees we talked to mentioned that many of their coworkers have Army connections. Barrow apparently makes good use of his contacts and actively recruits soldiers, persuading them to switch from the Army to a private contractor."

"So we now have a link between the assassination and Kingmakers through Duron," Milan said slowly. "And we have a link between Duron and Quirk, between Quirk and Brooks, between Brooks and Kurt Barrow, between Brooks and Naomi Beckingham...and between Basil King and Annabeth Markinson."

"Yes, and all those links lead to Kingmakers. They're at the core of this," the president said.

"Correct, Mr. President. But the one thing we haven't been able to establish is a link between Kingmakers and Al Saalihin," Coulson said. "Yes, we know Steve Duron was seen near Babur's Baltimore apartment and picked up the bomb from Bhat's car in the airport lot, and we can tie him to the money order that paid for Donnie Smith's rental on Puerto Rico, but that's not enough. It's all circumstantial, and while it's enough to get a warrant to tap his phone, we don't have enough to nail him yet. We need to be able to tie Kingmakers directly to the assassination...and the Pride Bombing."

"So what's the next step?" Milan asked.

"We still have a lot of small leads to follow, but the main objective is now to prove a link between Hamza Bashir and Kingmakers. We're in complicated legal territory, what with Kingmakers being a US-based company with mostly American employees. The intelligence community has to tread carefully there, as they can't investigate US persons or even collect intel on them, so the FBI will do the legwork here, while the other agencies focus on Hamza Bashir and all international activities and persons."

"Do they have any fresh ideas?" the president asked.

"They're going to use the old, time-proven method of following the money. If Kingmakers hired Hamza Bashir, they had to pay him at some point, and it had to have been a large amount. Money always leaves a trail. The CIA has put a new forensic accountant on the case, a guy who's specialized in tracing money internationally, and he's working closely with the lead analyst and the FBI's forensic accountant."

"I hate to ask, and you know I never have before, but what's the timeline on this? It feels to me we're getting close, or am I too optimistic?" Calix asked.

"No, you're not too optimistic. Seth and I said the same thing when I told him about this. But this case has proven to be complicated beyond anything we've ever seen before. Mentioning any kind of timeline feels premature, even in this stage of the investigation. Tracing those kinds of monetary transactions is laborious and complex, since we're not talking about regular international wires."

Calix nodded. "Gotcha."

"But I'll say this. I feel more hopeful now than I have in a long, long time that we're close to cracking the whole case."

Please let it be so. He was running on fumes, and so was Seth, and he wasn't sure how much longer they could keep doing this. That vacation had better come soon, or something had to give.

34

Having a Daddy was amazing. It had been two weeks since Warrick had become his Daddy, and Kenn was still floating on cloud nine. At first, he'd been unsure if Warrick would make a distinction between personal time and their lessons and would stop being a Daddy while he tutored Kenn, but he hadn't. They'd developed a fluid dynamic, switching from deep legal discussions to Daddy admonishing him to eat his veggies and go to bed on time.

Kenn loved it. Absolutely freaking loved it. How had he never realized this lifestyle fit him exactly? Warrick allowed him to be himself in a way Kenn had never dared to before, showing both his intellectual curiosity and hunger and his need to be taken care of. He could be ambitious academically while still being wonderfully needy with his Daddy.

They'd shared every lunch and dinner, sometimes with his dad or Milan joining in. And yes, Kenn had taught himself to say Milan and not Uncle Milan. He understood what his uncle had been trying to accomplish with that small change, and not surprisingly, it did make a difference.

Kenn felt more like Milan's equal now, which in a way, he was.

What had become crystal clear was that no one, absolutely no one, had an issue with Warrick being his Daddy. Not his father, not Milan, not any of his dad's friends, or even any of the agents or White House staff. They'd closed ranks, and so far, nothing about either his relationship or that of Milan, Asher, and Denali had leaked. Kenn had overheard one of the maids say that they owed it to the Shafer family after everything they had been through, and it had almost made him tear up.

Warrick had gone home, and Kenn missed him already as he stepped into the shower. Daddy had kissed him before he'd left, like he always did, and with every kiss, Kenn's impatience increased. Daddy was taking things slow with him, and Kenn understood why. He was a virgin, and what was more, he had no experience with anything sexual.

The funny thing was that now that he'd found how and where he fit in, he didn't want to go slow anymore. Just like he'd jumped in with both feet once he'd realized he wanted Warrick to be his Daddy, he was ready for the next step in their relationship. Hell, he was ready for all the steps. Everything. But how did he communicate that to Daddy? He'd tried being subtle, but apparently, he sucked at that because Daddy hadn't picked up on his signals.

He was still debating it when he crawled under the covers and switched on the light on his nightstand for a little late-night reading. Not too long, though, or Daddy would get on his case. And he couldn't play with himself anymore either; Daddy had made that clear. Kenn liked that he was no longer in charge of himself, even when it came to orgasms. Everything was much better with Daddy anyway—

though orgasms with Daddy hadn't happened yet. They hadn't even made it to second base.

He'd tried some things with Daddy's permission, and yes, he definitely liked having something up his hole. His finger had already felt good, and when he'd graduated to a small dildo—which he suspected to be a present from Milan, since it had shown up under his pillow one night with a bottle of lube—things had gotten *really* good. The "I'm seeing actual stars" kind of good. And knowing that he'd come with Daddy's permission had made it all the better.

Another downside of living in the White House was that he couldn't do his own laundry, and no way had Mrs. Steinway missed the gigantic spunk stains on his sheets in the last two weeks. He'd better not think about that too much, or he'd never be able to face her again. Good thing she spent most of her time in the sub-basement where she ran the laundry room.

A knock on his door sounded, and his dad stuck his head around the corner. "You still up, kiddo?"

"Hey, Dad!"

His dad sat down next to him on his bed, letting out a long sigh. "How was today? Learn anything good?"

Kenn smiled. His father had asked him that same question almost every school day as he'd come home. No matter how busy he had been, he'd always wanted to know about Kenn's day, about what he had done and what he had learned in school.

"We talked about racism in the judicial system."

His father whistled between his teeth. "That's one hell of a topic. Lots and lots to unpack there. We've made some progress in that area, but Lady Justice is far from colorblind, unfortunately."

"Yeah, D-Warrick said we'll be talking about this for a while."

His father gave him a little nudge with his elbow. "You can call him Daddy, you know."

Kenn looked at his fidgeting hands. "Yeah? It feels weird 'cause I used to call you that."

"You never did. I was always Dad to you. Maybe when you were a toddler, but that was ages ago. Besides, we both know the difference."

"Isn't it weird for you, Dad?"

"Honestly? No. It was a little when I first heard about it, but not anymore."

"I know this will be the stupidest question ever, but why not? I mean, I'm your kid. Shouldn't it be weird to know this about me?"

His father laid his hand on Kenn's. "To know what, that you're having sex? You're way past the age of consent."

"No, not sex. We're not... I haven't... That wasn't what I meant. I was talking about the Daddy stuff."

"Ah. Well, I'm sure you've realized by now that Milan isn't exactly vanilla, so my definition of weird has changed a lot over the years. The man has had actual orgies, so your kink is pretty damn mild and sweet compared to that."

"Dad..." Kenn groaned.

"What? If you're old enough to have a Daddy, you're old enough to know about orgies."

"Orgies is one thing, but Milan is still my uncle."

"True. I sometimes forget that you're actually related to him by blood. He was my friend before he became my brother-in-law, so it's different for me."

"Dad..." Could he even ask this? Did it matter? Not really, and yet he was dying to know. "Is it true that you had sex with Milan before you met Mom?"

Much to his surprise, his father didn't react with shock or anything negative. "Sex? That depends on your definition. We never had anal sex, penetrative sex, if that's what you mean, but we did fool around. I mean, between Calix and me and him, we had a gay man, a bisexual man, and a pansexual one who refused a label, so that gave us a lot of options. But that all ended when I met your mom and Calix fell for Matthew."

"Why did you come out as bi and not as pan?"

"Hmm, good question. When I realized I was attracted to men as well as women, the term bisexual seemed to fit me best. Later on, the term pansexual became more common to include nonbinary, trans, genderfluid, and agender people, to name a few. I stuck to bisexual because it felt more relevant to me, and I had an emotional attachment to it. It was something I'd fought hard for to get accepted."

He'd never known that, and now Kenn was glad he'd asked. He'd learned something new about his dad, which gave him the courage to ask something else. "There was a d-dildo in my room last week...under my pillow. Was that from you?"

His father laughed. "Nope, not me. I think we both know who put it there."

Kenn had guessed correctly then. Milan. Fucked up as it might seem, he was grateful that Milan was looking out for him. "Yeah."

"Kenn, if there's anything you want to ask me about sex... I know we had our sex talk, but that was before you came out, and since you said you and Warrick hadn't had sex yet... I want to make sure you know you can ask me stuff. Or Milan if you feel more comfortable with him."

Kenn was so touched tears prickled in his eyes, even if he was mortified at the same time. "We haven't... I don't..."

He stopped and took a deep breath. The truth was that he did have a question, and since this would be equally embarrassing whether he asked his dad or Milan, he might as well take the opportunity now. "How do I tell him I'm ready?"

To his credit, his father didn't miss a beat. "Ready for what? For anal?"

Kenn could only nod.

"You could try moving things along yourself, but in my experience, it's best to come out and say it. Maybe when you're already kissing or in the right mood so it doesn't come out of the blue?"

"O-okay."

"I'll ask Milan to drop off some condoms and lube here so Warrick won't have to worry about smuggling those in. The Secret Service agents don't blink an eye anymore at the stuff Milan brings in."

Kenn wasn't sure whether to laugh or groan, but in the end, a giggle won. "Thanks, Dad."

"And if Warrick wants to spend the night, that's okay too. In fact, I'll learn to knock and actually wait for your answer before barreling in. How's that?"

"Are you sure, Dad? I mean, we'd be just down the hall from you..."

His father frowned. "Maybe we should move you upstairs to the third floor. With Milan and me on this floor, you'd have much more privacy. And Milan is mostly at Asher's anyway."

Oh, he hadn't even thought of that option. "I like that idea, Dad."

His father nodded. "Let's set that in motion. I think room 303 would work. It's the biggest bedroom on the third, and it has both an en-suite bathroom and an adjoining sitting room, which you two could use as a private living room. It's not perfect, but it's better than you having no privacy at all. I wish I could tell you to go over to Warrick's, but if the press got wind of this... I don't want that for you either."

Kenn's heart was all warm, and he'd never loved his dad more. His reactions had been calm, factual, and without any trace of judgment or mockery. "Dad, thank you for everything. For being the best dad I could wish for."

"Oh, kiddo, it makes me happy to hear you say that. I've been feeling like I've failed you lately, especially after Mom died."

Kenn shook his head. "You didn't. If I'd needed you, you would've dropped everything for me."

"I'm so glad you know that. I love you more than anything, Kenn, and I'm sorry you didn't feel validated enough in who you are to come out to me. That, I do blame myself for. I never told you you're perfect the way you are, and I should have."

Kenn snuggled against his father, just like he'd done when he was little. "It's okay, Dad. Like you said, this was my journey."

"I'm proud of you for embracing who you are. And your mom would be too if she were here."

"You think so?"

"I know it for a fact. Don't ever doubt how big her heart was. You take after her. Warrick is a lucky man to be loved by you."

35

"Hey, what's going on here?" Warrick asked, frowning as he stepped into the center hallway of the second floor. Several White House staff members were carrying furniture and boxes out of Kenn's room in a dizzying tempo, bringing them up the stairs and coming back empty-handed. "What are they doing in your room?"

Kenn smiled at him. "Hi, Daddy."

He raised his face for a kiss, and Warrick's heart melted into something warm and mushy, like it always did when he saw his boy. "Hey, baby boy."

He kissed him thoroughly, forcing himself to let go before things grew too heated. They were in quite the public place after all.

"They're moving my things out of my room to a room on the third," Kenn said.

"Why?" Kenn hadn't mentioned anything about it, which surprised Warrick, since his boy usually shared everything.

"My dad and I were talking yesterday, and he suggested I

relocate one floor up. Things go fast here once the president wants something, so they cleaned that bedroom and are now moving all my things in. I can still pick a fresh color for the walls if I want, but they're a neutral cream now, which I kind of like. And since it's a bit chaotic, Rogue is with my dad in the Oval."

"Okay, but I'm still at a loss as to why he'd want you to switch rooms. I thought you liked your room."

Kenn looked...embarrassed? But why? "I did."

Warrick waited. He'd made it clear he didn't understand, so he saw no reason to repeat himself.

"My dad thought I might want...that we would need... more privacy?"

Kenn's voice had dropped to a whisper, and everything became crystal clear. Warrick's heart filled with gratitude all over again at the generosity and kindness of Del Shafer. What an amazing father he was to Kenn not only encouraging him to be himself but also giving him the literal space to do it.

"That's incredibly thoughtful of him. And you're okay with this?"

Kenn nodded instantly, and the eagerness on his face gave Warrick pause. He'd taken things slow with Kenn, constantly reminding himself the boy was a virgin, but maybe his pace had been too sedate. "Come with me." He pulled Kenn down the hallway, through the East Sitting Room, and into the empty Lincoln Bedroom. If this conversation was going where he thought it was, they'd need more privacy.

"What's wrong, Daddy? Don't you want me to move?"

"That's not it, baby boy. It made me wonder how you feel about taking things a step further..."

"Yes." The word flew from Kenn's lips before Warrick had even finished his sentence, and he laughed.

"Well, if you're so excited you won't even let me finish, I'll take that as a good sign. So, can you tell me what you're ready for?"

Kenn bit his lip, his cheeks growing red again. God, Warrick loved his innocence. "Like what?" Kenn finally asked, cleverly putting the ball back in Warrick's court. Hmm, maybe he was going about this the wrong way. He locked the door, then met Kenn's wide-open eyes.

"Come here, baby boy. Let Daddy kiss you properly."

This time, he was the one who didn't wait but simply pulled Kenn toward him and dug in. His mouth was so sweet, but even more arousing was Kenn's eagerness, his hunger. Whatever Warrick did, he responded to it, opening for him, following his lead. Where before, Warrick would've stopped, he now took it further, walking Kenn backward until he had him pinned against the wall.

His boy wasn't even that much shorter than him—maybe an inch and a half, if even that—but he was a hell of a lot slimmer. Warrick had been muscular and fit in his Army days, but he'd now grown into an otter with a bit of a dad bod, and he was fine with it. He liked that he could use his weight to immobilize Kenn, like he did now, sensually grinding into him as he devoured his mouth.

The boy was hard, undeniably. What was more, he was actively seeking friction, though a little less coordinated than Warrick. Warrick loved that he'd get to give Kenn all his first sexual experiences. He'd be the one to teach him about kissing, about hand jobs and blow jobs, about the glorious art of rimming and the pleasures of frotting.

"Do you want Daddy to take care of that?" he murmured against Kenn's warm lips.

"Care of what?"

Warrick slipped his hand between them and gently cupped Kenn's erection. "This."

"Please, Daddy."

"Good boy. Let Daddy take care of you, okay?"

"Y-yes, Daddy."

"Oh, my sweet boy... You're the most perfect boy ever. Give Daddy another kiss."

The words came so naturally to him now, as if he'd been Kenn's Daddy forever, and maybe he'd been for much longer than he'd realized. All he'd done was label it, but the instincts had been there from the moment he'd met Kenn.

Kenn kissed him eagerly, and Warrick roamed his mouth leisurely, not in any rush. Of course he could hurry up, but why would he? Pleasure was ten times more intense when drawn out and gratification was delayed. The boy deserved the most amazing experience Warrick could provide, and besides, Warrick wanted to cherish every moment with him himself. He increased the pressure of his hand, smiling into Kenn's mouth when the boy rubbed himself against Warrick.

"You like how Daddy's hand feels, baby boy?"

"Mmm..."

"How about this?" He grabbed his ass with his other hand and squeezed.

"Y-yes, Daddy. I like it when you touch me."

"Then Daddy had better touch you some more..."

He kissed him again, massaging his ass while plundering his mouth. Kenn gasped into his mouth, squirming against him. Warrick deftly popped the button of Kenn's pants and unzipped him with one hand. His hand encountered a damp pair of underwear. "Are you hard for Daddy?"

"So hard it hurts," Kenn whispered.

The words fired Warrick up even more. "Daddy's got you."

He cupped him through his underwear, causing Kenn to whimper and moan, so Warrick pulled Kenn's underwear down a little, just enough so the tiniest peek of his ass cheeks showed. Mmm, so sexy. He slipped his hand underneath in the back, caressing the swell of Kenn's ass. The skin was soft, with fuzzy hairs that tickled Warrick's fingers. He stroked his globes, squeezing every now and then. He'd always been an ass man, and Kenn had such a perfect butt.

Kenn moaned again, rutting against Warrick's hand with increased pressure. Kenn's breathy whimpers fired Warrick up, and he brushed between his cheeks ever so lightly.

"Daddy..." Kenn whimpered.

"Does that feel good, baby boy?"

"Mmm."

He would love to explore more, but he'd better not do it standing. Plus, he'd need lube for that. But the way his boy responded to even the lightest touch there showed he was ready for more. They would need that privacy of the third floor, it seemed. For now, Warrick could give him something else. He slowly tugged down Kenn's underwear completely, providing the boy with ample opportunity to stop him. But Kenn said nothing, kept staring at Warrick with his blue eyes wide open and those plump lips glistening and red. As if he wasn't tempting enough already.

Warrick pulled Kenn's briefs past his hips, and the boy's cock sprang free, slapping against his stomach with a wet smack. "Mmm, so pretty," Warrick praised him. "Such a gorgeous cock, baby boy. Daddy's gonna make you feel so good, I promise."

Judging by how hard the boy was, his cock wet and occasionally quivering, it wouldn't take much. That was okay.

There would be a second time and a third and after that, many, many more as far as Warrick was concerned. He wished he had lube. He used to carry small packets in his wallet, but he'd stopped doing that a while ago when he'd had enough of hooking up. The old-fashioned way would have to do, then.

He spit in his hand and brought his hand around Kenn's cock. Kenn's lashes fluttered, and the softest of gasps left his mouth. Warrick swiped his thumb over Kenn's slit, spreading the precum that had pearled there. He couldn't resist lifting his hand for a moment and tasting him. "Mmm, delicious, baby boy. Someday soon, Daddy's gonna feast on you... Milk your pretty cock with my mouth... Dine on your gorgeous ass."

Kenn gasped, and Warrick smiled. "You'll love it, I promise. I'll have you squirming on the bed in no time, begging for me to let you come."

No, he couldn't go too fast, but he could tease him, prepare him for what was to come. Suck him off and drink his boy's release. Eat him out and fuck him with his tongue until Kenn would beg for mercy. Bury himself inside Kenn, feeling him clench around his cock as he made the boy come. Warrick wanted to do everything with him, and his cock twitched at the thought.

He circled Kenn's cock again and worked his shaft with slow strokes, squeezing at each upward move. With his other hand, he kept massaging Kenn's ass, caressing, pinching, occasionally teasing with a finger between his cheeks. Kenn let out a stream of sighs and whimpers, and Warrick caught them against his mouth. "Sshh, baby boy, you gotta be quiet for Daddy. Can you do that? You don't want everyone to hear Daddy's pleasuring you, do you?"

He was a little mean, but he loved how Kenn responded,

all desperate and needy. No way would the White House staff be able to hear them, not from that far and while they were making noise moving Kenn's furniture, but that didn't matter. The idea of someone overhearing was enough for Kenn, and if he were honest, Warrick liked the thrill of it as well.

"Daddy!"

The boy sounded close to coming, his cock throbbing in Warrick's hand.

"Are you gonna come for Daddy, baby boy?"

Kenn merely whimpered, his body going tense. His cock jerked in Warrick's hand, and with one more squeeze, the boy came, shooting his thick load onto Warrick's hand. "Good boy," he purred. "Such a good boy for Daddy…"

He milked him until Kenn had nothing left to give and his body went slack. Warrick held him up with his left hand until Kenn's muscles seemed to work again. "Stay here for a moment. Daddy will clean you up."

Thank fuck he'd pulled them into a bedroom and not some random room because he'd have been hard-pressed to find something to clean him with. In this case, the adjoining bathroom made it easy. He washed the cum off his hands, then wetted a washcloth and returned to Kenn. The boy still stood there with his pants and underwear pooled around his ankles, his eyes glassy. Anyone who saw him would immediately know what they had been up to, but Warrick didn't care.

He cleaned him quickly with the cloth, then patted him dry with a towel. He dropped both on the floor and kneeled to pull up Kenn's pants and underwear, zipping and buttoning him back up. "There, all presentable again."

As he pushed himself to his feet again, his leg ached a

little, but he ignored it. Well worth it. He deposited the washcloth and towel in the bathroom, and when he came back, Kenn still hadn't moved. "Everything okay, baby boy?"

Kenn blinked as if awakening from a daydream. "Yeah. I mean, yes, Daddy. That was..." He shuffled his feet, averting his eyes. "That was my first...you know, hand job."

Warrick smiled. "Was it as good as you had hoped?"

Kenn hugged him, resting his head against Warrick's shoulder. "Better. Everything you make me feel is so good... I love it, Daddy. I love you."

The words sent a shock through Warrick's body, then heated up his chest. He'd known, and Kenn had implied it, but he'd never said it outright. "I love you so much."

They stood for a while, Warrick soaking up the amazing sensation of having his boy in his arms, knowing that they were on the same page. Kenn loved him as much as he loved Kenn, and the boy was ready for more. "We'll need to make an appointment to get tested," he said softly.

Kenn tilted his head back. "Tested?"

"Mmm. If we take this further, you need to know I'm negative for all STDs. I know, it's not sexy." He held up a finger when Kenn wanted to protest. "But it matters. We'll do it together."

"B-but I'm a virgin."

"I know, baby boy, and don't think for even a moment that I suspect you're lying about that. But if all this is new to you, I want to teach you to be responsible, and that means testing. For both of us."

"Okay, Daddy. I guess we could go to Dr. Brophy, the White House physician."

"Sounds good. Let's set that up as soon as possible, okay?"

Kenn nodded, then put his head back against Warrick's shoulder. "You're the best Daddy I could wish for."

Warrick held him close. "And you're the sweetest baby boy."

36

Kenn was still floating from what he and Daddy had shared that morning. When Daddy was teaching him, Kenn's thoughts kept going back to how it had felt to have Daddy's hand around his cock, to feel his finger dip so intimately between his ass cheeks... He shivered. If one finger had felt that good, how heavenly would it be to have Daddy's cock stretch him open? He was so ready for it, and now that his stuff had been moved into a new room, they would have the privacy.

Unfortunately, it didn't look like anything would happen tonight, as he'd already said yes to his father's plan when he'd proposed it the day before. Slightly disappointing, but this would be fun too.

"So what, exactly, are we doing tonight?" Daddy asked as he took Kenn's hand and pressed a soft kiss on it. They'd finished dinner in the family room, just the two of them.

Kenn's stomach tumbled like it still did every time Daddy touched him like that. Would it ever go away? He hoped it wouldn't. "My dad thought it would be fun to have a game night in the game room."

"Who else is coming?"

"Oh, his whole inner circle, as he calls it. Calix and Rhett, Levar and Henley, Seth and Coulson, Milan, Asher, and Denali, and you and me. Rogue is being taken care of. That's too many people for him."

Daddy slowly shook his head, smiling. "I know you had way more time to get used to this over the last few months, but doesn't it baffle you sometimes to be in the same room with all those people? The president of the United States, the Secret Service, FBI... They are all amazing people, but I do have to admit they're a little intimidating."

"Oh, absolutely. I've gotten better at talking to them, but it took me a long time. Calix, not so much, since he's been my dad's friend for as long as I can remember, but the others, yeah. Also because they're..."

Could he say that, or would Daddy be offended? He wasn't sure.

"Because they're hot?" Daddy finished the sentence for him.

Kenn giggled. "Yes. They are."

"Your father has assembled a good-looking inner circle. I don't feel like I quite fit in."

Was Daddy serious? Kenn studied him, his head cocked. Daddy hadn't sounded hurt, more factual, though Kenn wasn't sure if that was necessarily a good thing. "Neither do I."

Daddy smiled. "I disagree because, in my eyes, you're the cutest one of them all, but that's okay. We'll be the odd ones out together. How's that?"

"I'm okay with that. But, Daddy, I..." How did he put this? "I hope this doesn't come out wrong, but I wanted to say it anyway. Those men might be hot, but I still fell in love with you, not with them. I chose you. So don't sell yourself short, I guess is what I'm saying."

A myriad of emotions flashed over Daddy's face. "Thank you, baby boy. Thank you for reminding me of that. I needed to hear that."

Hand in hand, they made their way across the third floor to the game room. When they moved in, his parents had left most of the Residence as it was, except Kenn's bedroom for which he'd picked new colors, and his father had requested some changes to the game room. Nothing major, but he'd had the formal-looking paintings removed, as well as a couple of antique dressers and side tables. In their place, a sturdier table had been chosen, with seats for six, so they could play board games.

They'd also brought their foosball table with them, a game Kenn had played with his dad since he was a little boy. Milan loved it too. With some Patriots and Red Sox posters added to the walls, the room looked less like a museum and much more like the game room they had in the basement of their house in Boston.

"I really like the game room," Daddy said. Kenn had shown it to him earlier that week, when they had played Scrabble together. "It's one of the least formal rooms in this whole building."

"I feel the same way. As grand and historically significant this house and all the furniture is, it's hard to feel at home when you always have to worry about breaking something irreplaceable."

Even before they walked into the room, Milan's voice carried out. "You'd better not cheat this time, asshole."

"That's still President Asshole for you," Kenn's father deadpanned, and laughter rose from the room.

Kenn laughed at the now familiar ribbing between his

dad and his uncle. When he was a little boy, he'd been scared that they'd been actually fighting until his father had explained to him that the constant teasing and bantering was part of their dynamic. Now, Kenn recognized it for what it was—a constant sparring with deep underlying affection and respect.

"Hey, Kenn, Warrick." his father said when he spotted Kenn and Warrick walk in. He immediately came over and kissed Kenn on his head. "You're looking good, kiddo. I take it the eating and workout regimen is working for you?"

The room had grown too quiet for Kenn's comfort, the conversations dropping to much softer whispers, but the squeeze Daddy gave his hand helped him. "It has. I'm feeling better."

"Good. Then your Daddy's doing his job well."

Kenn's breath hitched. He recognized the challenge in his father's tone, and for a second or two, the room grew deadly quiet. Kenn had no doubt they'd all known about the relationship between him and Warrick, but with that simple remark, his father had made it crystal clear he accepted them fully. And by bringing it out in the open, he also communicated that they wouldn't have to hide it.

"He is," Kenn managed, and a rush of pride filled him he'd gotten those words out.

His father put a hand on Warrick's shoulder. "I'm glad to hear you're taking such good care of my son, Warrick. Now, let's move on to the important question. Do you play pool?"

With a last squeeze, Daddy let go of Kenn's hand. "That depends on your definition of playing, Del. I've heard others describe my style as more along the lines of destroying and humiliating them."

His father burst out in a booming laugh, then slapped

Warrick on his back. "Fighting words, huh? I approve. Let's see if you can put your money where your mouth is."

Daddy winked at Kenn, then followed Kenn's father to the pool table. For one second, Kenn was at a loss, unsure of what to do next, but then Denali was by his side. "Okay, I know he's the president and all, but if I didn't like him already, that would've sealed the deal. That was seriously cool and awesome from your dad."

He'd spoken soft enough that no one else could have heard it, and Kenn loved how sensitive Denali always was, so careful to affirm him. "I'm lucky with him as a dad."

"Dude, you've got the best dad and the best Daddy. You are one lucky boy."

Kenn laughed. "I am."

"Come on, kiddo," Milan called out. "Let's see if you can still beat my ass in table foosball. How about you and Denali play against me and Asher?"

In any other situation, that would've been a completely unfair match, but in this case, Kenn wasn't too worried about it. He'd played against Denali before, and they'd been equally fanatic. "I'll gladly accept that challenge."

Denali bumped his shoulder. "Let's destroy those cocky bastards."

Their foosball table was the perfect size, allowing one-on-one or two-versus-two games. Kenn and Denali positioned themselves on the end that controlled the red players, their shoulders touching, with Asher and Milan across from them, playing with black.

"We've got this," Kenn said.

"Hell, yeah. They may be hot and sexy, but that's not going to help them win the game."

Across from them, Milan and Asher grinned. "We're gonna crush those two boys, agreed?" Milan said.

"Damn right," Asher replied, and Kenn had to laugh at the verbal posturing. It was so unlike him, but the situation called for it.

He placed the ball in the middle, and the game started. Black got off to a good start, scoring a goal almost instantly, but Kenn wasn't worried. Neither was Denali, by the looks of it, his face tight with concentration as he defended their goal. Kenn was equally focused, waiting for an opportunity. Seconds later, he got it as Denali managed to kick the ball forward, right in front of one of Kenn's players. He passed to the center forward and, with a sharp flick of his wrist, sent the ball flying into the goal.

The game went back and forth, and by the time they were done, sweat dripped down Kenn's forehead. But he was beaming, high-fiving Denali, celebrating their two-point win over Milan and Asher.

"I demand a rematch," Milan said. "And this time, we'll play with red. I'm sure there's some kind of advantage to that side I haven't discovered yet. Red is more my color anyway, right, Denali?"

Denali giggled. "You do like it when my ass is red, Sir."

Whereas even weeks before, Kenn would've been embarrassed by a remark like that, he now took it in stride. If he wanted people to accept his relationship with Warrick, he had to extend them the same courtesy and allow them to express themselves without holding back.

"Damn right I do," Milan growled.

A red ass. Did that mean Milan liked spanking Denali, or did he do more than that? He was a Dom who liked impact play, that much Kenn knew, so maybe he used certain implements as well? Maybe one day, he'd feel confident enough to ask Denali about it. Kenn didn't doubt Denali would tell him everything he wanted to know, as he had only withheld things out of concern for Kenn, not because he was ashamed of it or didn't want to talk about it.

"Round two. Let's do this," Asher announced, and Kenn refocused on the game.

After defeating Milan and Asher again, they took a break, watching Kenn's father play pool with Warrick, while Levar, Henley, and Rhett had installed themselves at the table for a game of Exploding Kittens.

"Your Daddy is just as good as he said he would be," Seth commented to Kenn. He'd joined Kenn and Denali against the wall.

"He is?" A surge of pride flowed through Kenn.

"He's already beaten your father twice, but true to form, the president isn't giving up."

"You know you can call him by his first name in situations like this, right?"

Seth's face tightened. "It's a bit more complicated for some of us, okay? I know for all of you being that informal is no big deal, but if I accidentally slip up and call him Del in front of the wrong person, it could cost me my job."

Kenn swallowed. Seth had sounded harsher than he'd ever heard him before. Had he somehow touched a nerve?

"Bullshit," Milan said. He let go of Asher after giving him a passionate kiss, with tongue and all, which Kenn had tried hard to ignore. "You're not going to get fired for that."

"That's easy for you to say. Not only are you the president's best friend and his brother-in-law, but your job isn't on the line, unlike mine," Seth snapped.

Kenn saw the shock he felt reflected on everyone else's faces. What was the matter with Seth? No one else spoke, and Coulson walked over to Seth, his brows furrowed. "Let's step outside for a moment, baby."

Seth hung his head, allowing his boyfriend to lead him out of the room.

"What's wrong with him?" Milan asked, and Kenn was glad he sounded more confused and worried than upset, even though he'd been the target of Seth's sharp tongue.

"He's exhausted," Asher said softly. "I don't know how he's still standing. He's making eighty, ninety hours a week between two jobs that both demand his full attention and concentration. The director is getting on his case that he needs to go to Beltsville for a week for training, but he doesn't know how to squeeze it in with everything else that's going on. What he needs is a break, but it doesn't look like he's going to get one anytime soon."

Kenn's father shared a look with Calix. "I'll talk to him," Calix said. "To him and Coulson both. We'll make it possible for them to take a day or two off, and if necessary, Del will call Director James himself and order her to approve it."

They continued playing, but the mood was much more subdued. It took about fifteen minutes for Coulson and Seth to return, and when they did, Seth walked straight over to Milan. "I'm sorry. I was way out of line."

Milan grabbed his shoulder. "All good. No harm done. Just... Take care of yourself, okay? We need you."

"I have to say I'm still not used to Milan two point oh," Calix joked, clearly aiming to relieve the tension. "It's jarring to hear you being so nice."

"I'm worried about it myself," Milan said quasi-somberly. "I'm one step away from joining a support group."

That earned him a round of laughter, and Kenn caught the look of gratitude Seth shot Milan. His uncle winked at Seth, and the tension in Kenn's belly released.

"Come on, guys, let's get back to the game." Kenn's father

clapped his hands. "The law of averages says I should beat Warrick anytime now."

"The *average* part of that saying doesn't refer to someone being an average player, you know that, right?" Kenn teased his father.

"Oh, someone's getting sassy!" Calix called out with approval. "Burn, baby, burn."

Kenn laughed, warmth flooding him as he looked around the room. His mother would have loved this. She'd always been fond of games, of inviting friends and laughter into their house. An evening like this would've made her so happy.

And for the first time since she'd died, thinking of his mom filled Kenn with love and gratitude for all that she'd given him, for the legacy she'd left behind. He wouldn't be who he was today without her. And like Milan had said, she lived on in Kenn. And as he stood there, he vowed that his goal in life would be the same as hers: to spread kindness, build a family, and love with his whole heart, holding nothing back.

37

Levar had stopped groaning every morning at five o'clock, when his alarm went off. Did he like getting up that early? No, and especially not since the game night the evening before had run a little late, but by now, he'd gotten used to it. His job required that he read the newspapers every morning before he faced the press.

He shut off the alarm and flicked on the light on his night table, which was just enough for him to be able to see where he was going and not bump into anything, while not bright enough to wake up Henley, who had the luxury of sleeping a little longer. As always, he checked his phone first, which might not be the healthiest habit, according to some articles he'd read on productivity, but it worked for him. He preferred knowing any pending drama so he could mull it over while taking a shower.

He used the news app to get a first impression, relaxing when he didn't spot anything out of the expected. But when he checked his email, his heart stopped. He'd set up Google alerts for several keywords, automatically receiving a message anytime something containing that keyword had been posted online. One of those keywords was *Milan Bradbury*, since Levar wanted to stay on top of any news about him. And this morning, something new had popped up.

With rising dread, he read the headline. Oh, shit. *President's Brother-in-law Involved in Triad with White House Staff Member and Secret Service Agent*. Fuck, fuck, fuck. He scanned the article, nausea bubbling in his stomach. They had sources and even pictures, though grainy ones, taken near Asher's apartment, from what Levar could tell. And the absolute worst thing was that this wasn't some unknown gossip blog. The news had been reported by DC Dash, a blog with a major readership and a highly active social media presence.

"Shit."

Next to him, Henley stirred. "What's wrong, baby?"

He wanted so badly to tell him to go back to sleep, but his need to have someone to talk to won. "The relationship between Milan, Asher, and Denali leaked."

Henley immediately pushed himself up. "Oh, shit. Who has it?"

"DC Dash."

Henley groaned. "That means everyone else will report on it within the hour."

Levar let out a shaky sigh. "Yeah. I'm gonna have to call them and alert Calix and the president."

"I'm sorry, baby. It's gonna be a rough day for you."

Levar straightened his shoulders. "It will be, but I'll get through this as well. I'm gonna take a quick shower. Any chance you can make me some breakfast to go so I can head in right away?"

"You got it, baby."

Fifteen minutes later, Levar kissed Henley, then walked out the door. He usually took the Metro, but considering the calls he had to make, he needed privacy, so he drove in. Calix swore profusely when Levar called him, and Levar couldn't blame him. A scandal like this was about the last thing they wanted to spend time on, but they would have to.

"I'll inform the president," Calix said.

"My next call is to Asher. At least I know he'll pick up his phone."

"Yeah." Calix sighed. "He'd better."

Asher did pick up his phone, sounding much more awake than Levar had expected. "What's wrong?" Asher asked immediately.

Levar skipped the pleasantries as well. "DC Dash has the scoop on the relationship between you three, including your identities."

"Goddammit. I was afraid this would happen."

"Yeah, same. Where are you guys right now?"

"We actually spent the night at the White House, which in this case, is a good thing. I'm guessing the press will be camped out at my apartment."

"I'm sure they will be. I'm on my way in, and so is Calix. You'd better wake your guys up because we need all of you in the Oval Office as soon as possible."

"Oh, fuck. Milan's a pain in the ass before his morning coffee anyway, and this will only make it worse."

"Tough shit. Maybe you can remind him I'm not looking forward to today either, considering I'll be the one explaining the whole thing to the press."

"Right. Good luck with that, and I mean that in the nonsarcastic sense."

"Thanks. I'm gonna need it."

Forty-five minutes later, they'd all gathered in the Oval Office, coffee cups in hand. Denali's face had grown ashen, and Levar's heart went out to the boy. Out of the three of them, this would be the hardest on him.

"Let's get started." Calix gestured at Levar. "Levar, what can we expect?"

"It's already spreading, so it'll be the story of the day. We're going to have to address it."

"Can we cite that this is personal?" Asher wanted to know.

Levar shook his head. "If it had been you and Denali, yes. And if Milan had lived somewhere else, I could've made that work as well. But with him living in the actual White House, 'no comment' won't fly."

The president leaned forward on his desk. "What's the tone so far?"

Levar winced. "It's not good, Mr. President. There's the age gap, especially between Milan and Denali, plus all their jobs. With all three of them officially working in or for the White House, it's a hot mess, and speculation about possible abuse of power is running rampant."

"What are the odds they'll find out about Milan's past?" Calix asked.

"My past?" So far, Milan had been sitting quietly on the couch, sipping his coffee, but his face looked like a thunderstorm was brewing.

"You being a Dom, being a member of a BDSM club, your record with the NYPD, all of it could come into play. We all know the truth, but with some selective reporting, they can make you look like the bad guy in this relationship."

Milan's face tightened even more. "Would they be wrong? We all know that if it had been just Asher and Denali, no one would have had an issue with it."

"It wouldn't have been news," Levar said kindly. "Asher

and Denali aren't that interesting to the press. You are, however, as the president's brother-in-law and someone who has been living in the White House the last months."

"Let's talk about some possible responses." The president pinched the bridge of his nose. "Do you have any ideas, Levar?"

Levar had thought about nothing else since the news broke, but he still wasn't sure what the wisest course of action would be. "We need to make a decision first on what our end goal is in this."

"What do you mean?" The president looked puzzled.

Levar took a deep breath. Here came the hardest part of his job. "Mr. President, as soon as this news lands with the major news media, congressmen and senators are going to ask for Milan's resignation, if not for you to fire him. It doesn't matter that, technically, he did nothing illegal. It's the perceived immorality, the possibility of an abuse of power situation. The optics are, quite frankly, bad. The question is whether you want to hold firm that Milan did nothing wrong, consequently refusing to fire him, or if you're willing to sacrifice him to appease the fiercest protesters."

He shot an apologetic look in Milan's direction, but the man waved it away. "No need to spare my feelings, Levar. I'm a big boy, and I can handle it." Then he turned to the president. "Del, I'll do whatever you need me to do. I'll resign or allow you to fire me, whatever is necessary. I don't want you to catch flack over this or suffer political consequences. This is on me, and you shouldn't have to pay for it."

"They could fire you from the NYPD as well," Calix said quietly. "I'm not sure if you've realized that. This won't play well in New York either."

Milan's quick intake of breath proved that he hadn't

thought that far, but then his jaw tightened. "I'll fight that one, but not my position here. It was always a means to an end anyway."

"If we immediately announced we fired him, would that help?" the president asked Levar.

"Yes and no. In the short term, no, because firing him is basically an admission of at least some degree of guilt. It means everyone and their mother will be over this story, and you can expect to see it play out on literally every news medium. But in terms of political damage, yes, and I also think it'll die down faster. They'll have little to yak about if the problem has already been fixed."

The president nodded thoughtfully, then turned his attention to Denali. "I'm sorry you got caught up in this, Denali. I want you to know that no matter what the media will report, you did nothing wrong."

"Thank you, Mr. President." Denali's voice trembled, and Asher pulled him close to him.

"Will they ask for my resignation?" the Secret Service agent asked.

Levar hesitated. "Under other circumstances, no, but considering the heat the Secret Service has taken recently, it wouldn't surprise me. I have no doubt someone will write a scathing article about all the problems in the Secret Service, quoting this as an example."

Milan paled. "Del, you can't allow him to get fired," he snapped. "He did nothing illegal."

"Technically, I did," Asher said calmly. "My job prohibits me from having a personal relationship with a protectee, and at several points over the last months, I was assigned to your detail."

"Bullshit!" Milan slammed his hand on his thigh. "You've

never compromised your ability to do your job, and I will say so to anybody who asks me."

Asher's eyes were soft as he looked at Milan. "I'm pretty sure no one will ask you, as you're not exactly objective, but thank you for defending me so passionately, baby."

Levar smiled at that affectionate term. It was so unlike Asher to use it in what was technically a professional situation, and it showed how much Milan's words had meant to him.

Milan threw up his hands. "I feel so powerless. It's unfair that Denali and Asher should have to pay the price for this."

"Why?" Denali said. "Why would that be unfair, Sir?"

Even now, Denali was addressing Milan as Sir, and Levar loved him for it.

Milan frowned. "What do you mean?"

"You act as if you alone were responsible for our relationship, as if you were the one who instigated it. We all know that's not true. Asher and I are as much a part of it, and we are equally guilty or responsible or involved or whatever you want to call it. You don't get to be the martyr here and pretend this is all you. I'm not ashamed of who we are and what we share, and I refuse to pretend otherwise. This isn't some kind of seedy affair. This is a real relationship between consenting adults based on love. Sir."

Levar blinked. Wow. Denali usually didn't say much, but when he did, his words sure packed a punch.

"Perfectly said, Blue." Asher pressed a quick kiss on Denali's lips.

"I agree, Denali. Well said." The president's eyes sparkled. "I never thought I'd see the day that Milan Bradbury would be brought to his knees by an itty-bitty boy, and yet here we are. Isn't it amazing what love can do to you?"

Levar wasn't even surprised when Milan shot the president the bird, and they all laughed. Trying to get Milan Bradbury to behave himself, even in the Oval Office, was clearly a lost cause.

"So, what do we do?" Calix said.

The president turned to Levar. "Levar, I'm not sure how you're going to word it, but I want you to find a way to communicate that this is a legal relationship between adults who are in love with each other, that at no point were any laws broken or was there even a hint of impropriety, that I knew about the relationship from the get-go, and that nothing was done in secret. I agree that firing Milan is the right course of action to prevent this from hanging over our heads for the next few weeks, but at the same time, I want you to make it clear this isn't an admission of guilt. This White House supports poly relationships between consenting adults, and it's about damn time we did."

The rest of Levar's day was utter hell, just as he'd expected, with him taking one hit after the other from the press pointing their pens of hatred and spewing vitriol at the White House. And yet he endured it, fueled by the pride of knowing that he was doing the right thing in proudly supporting all colors of the rainbow. It didn't lessen the attacks, but it did make them slightly easier to bear.

38

Warrick woke up slowly, toasty warm, enveloped by the most comfortable mattress...and a warm body. His eyes flew open. He was in Kenn's bed. In the White House. After their evening of fun and games, he'd been dead on his feet and easily persuaded by Kenn's pleading blue eyes to spend the night. Clearly, Kenn's father had no issue with it, seeing as how he'd provided them with privacy in the first place.

It had been a long time since he'd awoken with someone in his bed, and the last time had been after a half-drunk hookup with an ex he'd run into in a gay bar. They'd both been too tired to do anything and had fallen asleep, and the next morning had been awkward as fuck. Nothing like this, where Warrick's heart went all soft as he inhaled his boy's smell, reveling in the feel of his heartbeat, the sounds of his quiet breaths.

Kenn's body fit so perfectly against his. His boy wasn't so much shorter that the height difference was a challenge but slender enough so he could curl around him, spoon him from the back, and press his cock against Kenn's ass, only their underwear separating them. His hard cock, but he ignored that. What he was feeling right now had nothing to do with sexual needs or lust and everything with his love for Kenn. His baby boy, safe in his arms.

Kenn stirred, letting out a soft moan. Warrick nuzzled his neck. "Good morning, baby boy."

Kenn's body froze for a moment, then relaxed again. "Morning, Daddy."

Fuck, he sounded adorable, his voice still sleepy. "Did you sleep well with Daddy in your bed?"

"Mmm, yes, Daddy. I love waking up with you."

"So do I... Even if we've slept in a little longer than we should have. It's eight thirty already."

Kenn slowly turned around. "I'm pretty sure my teacher will understand."

Warrick smiled. "That's a safe bet. Can I get a good morning kiss?"

Some people didn't want to kiss in the morning, what with morning breath and all, but Warrick wasn't one of them. Besides, they'd both brushed their teeth before going to bed, so how bad could it be? Kenn apparently felt the same way, moving in and pressing his lips to Warrick's. Warrick let him set the pace at first, but when Kenn was bold enough to bring out his tongue, he took over. He pulled Kenn against him, and the boy immediately slipped his leg between Warrick's.

He kissed him deeply, lazily roaming his tongue in Kenn's mouth, sliding it against Kenn's, while he rubbed the boy's back, occasionally dipping lower to cup his ass. People never took enough time for kissing. They always wanted to jump ahead to the next step, but a good kiss could be so erotic and intimate.

After a while, Kenn squirmed against him, his hard cock rubbing against Warrick's. "D-Daddy…"

It sounded like a plea. "What do you want, baby boy?"

"Will you teach me how to…" He swallowed. "How to give you a blow job? I want to learn."

Teach him how to… Good god. If he thought about it too much, a vision of Kenn's lips wrapped around his cock in his brain, he'd come on the spot. "I'd be happy to. You sure you're ready?"

"I want it so bad, Daddy."

Warrick would be lying if he said the age difference had never bothered him, but it sure as fuck didn't at this moment. He reveled in being the older man now, the experienced lover who could initiate Kenn into the amazing world of gay sex.

He shifted on his back, letting go of Kenn. "Then I'd be happy to. Are you gonna undress Daddy, baby boy?"

He could've easily done it himself, but he wanted to give Kenn the time to process, to catch his breath. And the time to hit the brakes if he had to, which would be much harder if they kept going at breakneck speed.

Kenn slipped his thumbs underneath the waistband of Warrick's briefs and caressed his skin there as if he were hesitant to take it further. Warrick could wait. Kenn kept rubbing the waistband, his eyes cast downward.

"It's okay, baby boy. There's no rush."

"No, I want to. I want to take the next step."

Warrick kept watching Kenn as he bit his lip and then finally pulled down Warrick's briefs, going slowly and carefully. Warrick's cock slapped free, and Kenn almost jumped. "Oh!"

Kenn looked at him with his blue eyes wide open, his plump lips still swollen and wet from their kisses. His skin was smooth and pale, his body lean and unblemished. He was simply beautiful. Edible. Warrick couldn't stop staring at him, wanting to memorize every line, every angle, every soft swelling.

His innocence was so obvious, and it gave him something angelic, which made Warrick feel all the dirtier from wanting to do very un-angelic things to him. He swiped a stray lock of hair from his forehead. "You're perfect, baby boy. Absolutely perfect."

Kenn leaned into his touch, like he always did, never content with a brief caress. His deep need for Warrick's proximity and touch was the strongest aphrodisiac Warrick could ever have imagined. He scratched his neck, then pulled back his hand. "This will be easier if I sit down."

For a moment, Warrick hesitated. It had been dark when they had undressed the night before, and the darkness had hidden his scars. In the morning light, they'd be fully visible. Was he ready for Kenn to see them? Then he rolled out of bed, Kenn following him. Kenn loved him. He'd said it the night before: he'd fallen in love with Warrick, not with any of the hot men who worked for his father.

As he walked over to the couch in Kenn's room, he caught his reflection in the full-length mirror and froze for a moment, barely recognizing the man. Gone was the somewhat uptight, closed-off, and hurting man he'd been mere months ago. In its place stood a confident, sexy man with a five-o'clock shadow darkening his jawline, eyes flushed with desire, and a body ready for action, above all his cock. His physique might not be anything special—he'd given up on the idea of a six-pack years ago—but his cock was a thing of beauty. Longer than average and thick, it stood up proud, curving upward. As cocks went, his was damn fine, and stupid as it was, Warrick took pride in it.

"Are you gonna keep admiring yourself in the mirror, Daddy?" Kenn teased, and Warrick laughed.

"Come look at us, baby boy." He pulled Kenn in front of him. Kenn had undressed as well, and the antique mirror reflected the differences between them perfectly. Pale and tanned, slim and stockier, older and younger. Mmm, he loved looking at them. Kenn's cock stood up, and while it wasn't as big as Warrick's, it wasn't small either.

Warrick wrapped his hand around it, smiling when Kenn immediately moaned. The boy was so deliciously responsive. Kenn let his head drop back on Warrick's shoulder. "Do you think presidential guests have ever jacked off here? Spraying the mirror with their loads? How much sex has that mirror seen, you think?" Warrick mused while slowly and tightly fisting Kenn's cock.

Kenn gave the softest sound, a whisper of a breath that danced over Warrick's heated skin. "Is it rude if I say I don't care?"

His need was intoxicating, and Warrick let go of him. "Grab us a towel, will you?"

Kenn dashed over to the bathroom and brought back a towel, which Warrick folded in two and put on the couch before he sat down on it. Then he took a pillow from the couch and dropped it on the floor. "Kneel between my legs."

The boy had already sunk onto his knees. Warrick stroked himself, his fist curled tight around his cock, in a long move from the root to the tip. Precum bubbled up, and he swiped it with his thumb. Would Kenn be that brave yet? Or did Warrick need to go slower?

But Kenn opened his mouth, his eyes wide, and Warrick slowly brought his thumb to his boy's mouth, then wiped it off on his tongue. "Taste Daddy, baby boy..."

His voice was hoarse, as if he'd been at a concert and had screamed the lyrics for hours.

Kenn smacked his lips. "It's salty."

"Good or meh?"

"Different. A little strange. But not bad."

Later, Warrick would have to reflect on the utter absurdity of sitting on what had to be an expensive, antique couch in the White House while the president's son was kneeling between his legs, his mouth open in eager anticipation. But not now. He wanted to be in the moment and memorize everything Kenn did, every feeling, every sensation.

"Stick your tongue out, baby boy," he said, and when Kenn did, he slowly dragged the tip of his cock over Kenn's tongue. "Hold it still for me."

Being the good boy that he was, Kenn did, and Warrick rubbed his cock until Kenn's drool dripped down his chin. "Daddy..." he protested in a garbled voice.

"I know, baby boy... You want to swallow, but not yet. I like seeing you all dirty for me... Open a little wider. Can you do that for Daddy?"

Warrick was pretty sure he could ask for the moon and Kenn would bring it to him, what with how eager the boy was to please him. And indeed, Kenn immediately popped his mouth wide open. Fuck, the urge to sink deep inside that sweet, hot throat was strong, but he pushed it down. Kenn was a fragile flower. If Warrick broke him, he would never bloom the way he was supposed to. "Mmm, such a good boy for Daddy. I'm gonna push in a little, okay? If you need me to stop, tap on my thigh."

He placed Kenn's hand on his thigh and patted it. Kenn's eyes drifted shut as Warrick sank in a little deeper, stretching the plump lips wide. "Like that, baby boy. So good. Now can you suck for Daddy?"

Oh, he could, and a low moan drifted up from Warrick's chest, tumbling from his lips. Kenn slurped and sucked, the wet, dirty sounds filling the room. Fuck, that mouth felt good. And it looked damn perfect as well, wrapped around his cock. He cupped his balls with his left hand, rolling the heavy fullness around to bring himself even more pleasure. "Can you take a little more for Daddy? You're doing so good, baby boy."

Kenn's eyes blinked open, then closed again in a wordless confirmation. Warrick went half an inch deeper. Oh, he wanted to sink in all the way, but he wouldn't. He needed to take it slow, to make the experience good for both of them. He kept his thrusts shallow, fisting himself at his base before he pushed into Kenn's mouth. "Keep sucking, baby boy. Mmm, yes, like that. Your mouth feels like heaven, so hot and wet for Daddy."

Kenn shivered, his cock still hard. His boy was getting aroused from sucking off his Daddy. How perfect was that? Warrick sped up, knowing that Kenn's jaw would start aching soon. When his balls clenched, he pulled back. As much as he wanted to, he couldn't make him swallow his morning load on the first try. The poor boy would choke on it.

"Ungh!" he groaned as his muscles contracted and the first wave pushed out of his cock. He caught most of it with his hand, allowing some drops to land in Kenn's mouth. The second spurt came right after, and he wasn't fast enough, so more dribbled onto Kenn's mouth and face. Damn, his boy looked good with cum on his face, slightly debauched and filthy in the best way.

Kenn blinked as if coming out of a trance and licked his lips. "Thank you, Daddy."

He'd sucked Warrick off and then *thanked* him? Fuck, the boy was killing him. Warrick cleaned Kenn's face with the towel he'd put on the couch, wiping off the drool and cum. When he was done, Kenn tilted his head expectantly. "Did I do good, Daddy?"

Warrick bent in and pressed a kiss on his swollen lips. "Best blow job I've ever had."

He wasn't even lying.

39

Asher stared out the window of the black suburban. A few more days and spring would officially arrive, and it looked like nature was ready for it. The last snowstorm had been weeks before, and it wouldn't be long until the trees started budding. Usually, spring was Asher's favorite season, but this year, he could barely muster any enthusiasm.

He was tired. Absolutely exhausted. The last year had been an utter shitshow, and while he was beyond happy with his two men, their relationship was far from easy. It took time and energy to make any relationship work, and even more when it involved three people and one of them was a stubborn ass.

A stubborn ass Asher was deeply in love with and had been for a long time, but that didn't make it less complicated. Nor did the fact that he, too, had a stubborn streak, as Denali kept pointing out. Without their sweet boy, he and Milan would have butted heads even more. He was their go-between, their anchor. But the news about their relationship leaking earlier that week had shaken them all, Denali especially. It had been a rough week, though Levar had taken the brunt of it.

Earlier that Friday morning, the president had ordered them all to report at Camp David for the weekend. Asher strongly suspected he'd done it to get them away from DC, but he honestly didn't care about the real reason. He appreciated the chance to find some peace and quiet. The three of them still said to each other regularly that their time at Camp David had been wonderful, even if they had known it wouldn't last.

Next to him, Denali sighed, and Asher turned his attention to him. "Hey, Blue. You happy to have the weekend off?"

Denali snuggled as close to him as he could while still keeping his seat belt on. On Denali's other side, Milan had fallen asleep, gently snoring. "Yeah. And you're off as well, I heard?"

Asher did a quick check to make sure Milan was, indeed, still sleeping. "I've been placed on administrative leave for two weeks without pay. It's okay," he said quickly when Denali gasped. "Blue, we both know they couldn't let this go entirely. I'm a Secret Service agent, and I have been on Milan's detail."

"Was the director mad at you?"

Asher winced. "Very displeased, in her words. But I honestly can't blame her, not after the hits she's taken lately. This was the last thing she needed."

"I'm sorry," Denali whispered. "And you don't want Milan to know?"

"I'll tell him. I wouldn't keep this from him. But you know he hasn't been sleeping well this week, so I figured I'd let him catch up on some sleep first."

"Mmm, smart. His fuse is considerably shorter when he's operating on too little sleep. Do you think that's why the president is staying at Camp David for the weekend, to allow us all some downtime?"

"We need it. All of us are running on empty. Levar has had one of the worst weeks in his life, at least professionally, so he definitely deserves a break. Kenn and Warrick could do with a little more privacy than they have in the White House, so I'm sure they jumped at this opportunity. Calix has been working nonstop, and while I haven't heard Rhett complain, I'm sure he'd love to spend some time with him. And then there's Seth..."

More than anyone else, Seth and Coulson needed a break and the chance to be together, though Asher couldn't explain that to others. He was privy to information no one else had save Milan. But as soon as he'd heard Seth and Coulson were coming as well, he'd decided that he'd find a private moment with Coulson and have a conversation with him. Asher wasn't the type to meddle in other people's relationships, but in this case, he had to. Coulson didn't have experience with this, and he might not understand that Seth needed this, that it wasn't something he did for fun or kicks, but that it provided him with a much-needed release like nothing else could.

"Will he be okay?" Denali asked, his voice full of concern.

Asher nodded. "We'll make sure of it."

They sat quietly together, their bodies touching wherever they could, until the car passed the armed gate into Camp David. "I'll wake him," Denali said.

Asher smiled. "You do that, Blue. He won't mind if it's you."

Never had Asher seen Milan as soft and tender as he could be with Denali. Oh, he wasn't always like that. They still did scenes together, and when Milan was dominating them both, he was still the hard-core Dom he'd always been, taking pleasure from torturing them. But in moments like this, when Denali kissed him awake with those sweet, soft lips, Milan never responded with anger or abrasiveness. No, he groaned, then hauled Denali onto his lap, deftly releasing him from his seat belt, and kissed him until he was fully awake.

"That, baby boy, is still my favorite way to wake up," Milan said, his voice a little sleepy.

"That's not what you told me when I woke you up with a blow job two weeks ago," Asher teased him.

"Good point. We'll call it a draw," Milan conceded, then laughed.

They'd been given the same cabin he and Milan had shared the first time, and it almost felt like coming home.

"I'm still tired," Milan said after they had unpacked.

Asher studied him for a few moments. It wasn't like Milan to admit that so easily. "Blue, why don't you snuggle with Milan for a bit and help him fall asleep? I bet you know a few ways to help him relax..."

Denali could use the sleep as well, but Asher didn't say that.

"I can do that, Sir." Denali looked at Milan. "Do you want that, Sir?"

Milan smiled at him. "As if I'd ever say no to being in bed with you, baby boy. I think it's an excellent idea. I'm sure I'd fall asleep instantly after a blow job. Or two."

Denali giggled, then laughed out loud as Milan simply picked him up and slung him over his shoulder. Asher watched them with a happy feeling in his belly. He loved that they weren't the kind of triad where they could only have sex if they were all present. While he completely understood that was the best route for some throuples, it didn't work for them with their conflicting schedules.

Instead, they took the opportunity to connect with whoever was home, and if that happened to be all three of them, even better. Milan had even allowed Asher to fuck him again when Denali had been at work. Twice, in fact, which was even more proof of how the man was changing and that he truly was in love with Asher.

The laughter in the bedroom transformed into moans, and Asher nodded at himself, satisfied his plan had worked. He could've joined them, but he was too restless to nap, even after the promise of quick sex. Besides, Denali had kneeled for Asher in the shower that morning, using that glorious mouth of his until Asher had come, so he wasn't that desperate.

He changed into running gear, put on his running shoes, and headed outside. He'd found the perfect trail for a high-intensity run, and that was exactly what he was in the mood for. After taking the time to warm up, he started slow, then increased his tempo as he climbed the hill, his shoes splashing in the mud. He'd need a shower afterward, but god, this felt good.

He'd run the loop once when footsteps pounded behind him. Coulson was catching up to him quickly. Asher held back long enough for the FBI agent to reach him, then picked up speed again. They ran together without saying a word, their feet hitting the mud in an almost identical rhythm. After he'd completed the third loop, Asher slowed down to a jog.

"I'm done," he said between pants.

Coulson matched his speed. "Same. I know you did one round more than me, but it's been enough. I want to preserve some energy for *other activities*."

The last was said with a wink at Asher, and this was as

good a segue as he'd ever get. "What did you have planned?" he asked.

Coulson shot him a curious look. "You interested in my sex life now?"

Asher chuckled. "Normally speaking, no, but..." His smile faded. How did he bring this in a way Coulson wouldn't feel offended or slighted?

Coulson stopped his jog, frowning, and Asher walked as well. "Asher, if there's something I should know, something about Seth, will you please tell me? I'll listen to anything if it helps me take care of him."

Asher's throat was tight for a moment as the depth of Coulson's love for his man sank in. "Seth is lucky to have you, you know that?"

"I'm the lucky one, no doubt about it." His eyes were pleading as he looked at Asher sideways.

Asher stopped, and Coulson did the same, and they stood face-to-face. "I've been reluctant to bring this up with you because I don't want to offend you or hurt you by reminding you that Seth and I have a past together. A sexual one."

"I know, and I appreciate it. I won't lie and say it's easy for me to forget about that, but seeing you with Milan and Denali helps. I know you're in love with them and that you have no feelings for Seth beyond friendship."

"I don't, and I'm glad you can see that. I'm so happy for the two of you."

"So be honest with me, please. Is it the fisting? Is that what he needs?"

Asher nodded, relieved that Coulson had brought it up himself. "This may sound strange to you, but to him, it's more than something that merely brings him pleasure. Allowing someone to do that to you requires mental trust and surrender, and to get there, Seth can't think about anything else. His whole being will be focused on that, which is what he needs right now. Afterward, he'll sleep and sleep and sleep, but it's the stress relief he needs right now."

Coulson swallowed. "Thank you for telling me this. I suspected he wanted this, but I hadn't realized he needed it this much. It's not that I didn't want to do it, but..." He shook his head, fists clenching at his sides. "It's been impossible for me to find the time to do the proper research."

"Please don't take this the wrong way, but I can help. I promise you I won't touch Seth, but I can show you how to do this, how to give him what he needs."

Coulson straightened his shoulders, his jaw setting. "I gladly accept your help. I'll do whatever it takes, even if it means sucking up my pride or being a bit uncomfortable. If this is what he needs, I'll make it happen."

40

If nothing else, the sleeping arrangements for the weekend made it clear that his dad had not only fully accepted the relationship between Warrick and him but also endorsed it. They'd been assigned the same cabin Warrick had had before, only this time, the staff had brought Kenn's luggage in with Warrick's...in the same room.

Funny how seeing their bags together made Kenn's stomach go soft as putty, as if it reinforced that they were together now. He was part of something bigger, something beautiful and valuable. The only thing lacking was Rogue, but he and his dad had agreed it would be better to leave him in the White House so they'd all have their hands free for the weekend. His father probably suspected Kenn had plans that didn't involve a German shepherd...and he'd be right.

"What are we gonna do first, Daddy?" Kenn asked.

He knew he sounded eager, but he didn't care. They'd gotten their test results back that morning, and of course, they'd both been negative. Kenn had understood why

Warrick had made them wait for those, but now that they were done, all systems were go as far as he was concerned.

Warrick stepped closer and leaned in, catching Kenn's lips in a warm, wet kiss. "Are you ready for Daddy's cock, baby boy? Is that what you want?"

"Yes, Daddy. Please. I'm ready."

"Okay."

"Yeah?"

"I'll make it good for you, I promise," Daddy said hoarsely, and the look in his eyes told Kenn he wanted this as much as Kenn did.

"I know, Daddy."

Warrick let go of him. "Lock the front door of the cabin, would you, baby boy? I don't want anyone to interrupt us."

Kenn raced to the door and locked it, then pulled the curtains closed for good measure. He couldn't make it any clearer that they weren't to be disturbed. And if someone tried to, they simply wouldn't answer. He'd waited long enough for this, and no one was ruining it now.

Warrick stood waiting for him when he rushed back, a little out of breath. "That eager, baby boy?"

Kenn nodded, that strange mix of neediness and embarrassment battling inside him. He wanted this, all of it, and at the same time, he was a little ashamed of how much he needed it. How much he needed Warrick. "Can I undress you, Daddy?"

"Mmm, I'd like that."

Kenn took his time unbuttoning Warrick's shirt, revealing his bare skin one inch at a time. He left his shirt on as he kneeled to take off his socks, liking how sexy it made Warrick look. His belt came off easily, and then Kenn found the buttons and zipper of his slacks, and they slid down, pooling at Daddy's feet. He stepped behind him to take off his shirt, then kneeled again and let Daddy lean on him briefly as he stepped out of his pants.

That left him in his underwear, where a growing bulge was visible. He'd tasted so much better than Kenn had expected. He'd thought he would like the sensation of having Daddy's cock in his mouth but not so much the taste, but he'd been wrong. He'd loved every moment of that blow job, drooling and teary eyes and all. Daddy had taken his pleasure from Kenn, and somehow, that made him feel used but in the best, sexiest way.

He took a deep breath and pulled down Daddy's briefs, this time prepared for his cock to spring free. He neatly folded Daddy's clothes, then undressed in a rush, dropping his clothes on the couch. When he turned around, Daddy stood there, watching him with burning eyes.

Kenn had never been that into porn. It had always seemed so fake to him and had never done much for him. But even looking at Warrick made him hard. He might not have the chiseled abs, the bulging muscles, or the sharp V Kenn had admired on others, like the time he'd caught Seth without a shirt on, but to Kenn, he was mouthwatering.

His heart fluttered as he drank him in. Warrick's body was soft and a little furry, with neatly trimmed chest hairs and an equally well-maintained narrow strip of hair that led from his belly button down to the base of his cock. A few gray hairs sparkled from between the dark hairs on his chest, reminding Kenn of their age difference. He didn't care. He never had.

And Warrick's dad bod, as he'd called it himself, was perfect to Kenn, including the faint scars that crisscrossed his lower back and the burn marks on his ass cheeks. One day, he'd kiss each and every one of them. "You're beautiful, Daddy," he said softly. Daddy's eyes lit up.

"So are you, baby boy."

Kenn stepped into Daddy's arms, leaning into him for a moment. Cuddling felt *so* much better when done naked.

"I know you want this, baby boy, and so do I, but please know that if you change your mind at any time, you can say no."

"I know, Daddy." He did, and yet he loved that Daddy had reminded him of it, making sure Kenn felt no pressure at all to do something he didn't want.

Daddy held his hand as they settled on the bed, where Daddy rolled Kenn onto his back and kissed him again as if he didn't even want to give him the opportunity to feel nervous. Kenn let it happen, submitting and trusting Daddy to lead. They kissed for minutes until Kenn squirmed under Daddy's body. Just when he was ready to start begging, Daddy let go of his mouth, kissing a trail down his neck, his collarbone, and then his chest.

Daddy teased his right nipple with his tongue, then scraped it gently. The heat spread out through Kenn's belly, all the way to his fingertips and toes. A little bite and he arched off the bed as he moaned loudly. When Daddy moved on to his left nipple, he left the right one flushed and hard, still wet from his mouth.

Daddy's hand grazed Kenn's cock as he nibbled his way down, shocking Kenn into a shudder as if he'd been touched by electricity. His body felt so alive, every nerve sending pleasure and desire through his system. His inhales were shaky as Daddy continued his exploration, setting Kenn's body on fire bit by bit.

"You're so gorgeous, baby boy. So perfect."

He'd never heard Daddy's voice so raspy and husky, betraying his own arousal. By the time Daddy briefly rolled away from him and grabbed something, Kenn was half-dazed with need. He vaguely registered Daddy flicking open a bottle, coating his fingers. Oh god, finally.

He'd practiced with the dildo so he'd know what to do when the time came, so when Daddy's finger pressed against his hole, he pushed back before Daddy could even tell him to. "Good boy," Daddy praised him, his voice thick.

The first finger slid in with ease. Kenn squirmed not so much because it hurt—it really didn't—but because of the strange sensation. That wasn't his own finger in there, but Daddy's, and the intimacy of it was in itself arousing.

"How does that feel, baby boy?"

"'S good. I can take it."

"I know you can."

One finger became two, and while it burned a little, Kenn still had no trouble taking it. Daddy took his time stretching him, adding a third finger—and that one did sting. His dildo might've been a little on the thin side compared to Daddy's cock. He breathed in deeply, forcing himself to relax his muscles.

"Baby?" Daddy asked, worry lacing his voice.

"I'm good, Daddy."

Daddy still took his time, and when he pulled out his fingers, Kenn was about to start begging him.

"Stay on your back, sweet boy. I want to see your face as I take you."

A shudder tore through Kenn's body as he watched Daddy slick himself up a little more, then stretch out on top of Kenn. "Pull your legs up... Mmm, like that."

He was seconds away from no longer being a virgin, and all he could think about was how glad he was he'd waited. "I'm happy it's you, Daddy."

Daddy's eyes grew tender. "I'll always treasure this gift, baby boy."

He kissed him, then lined up. Kenn held his breath the second he felt Daddy's head press against him. This was it. He was so ready. Daddy pushed, and he bore down, eager to invite him in. The moment Daddy's cock popped past that first tight ring, he held still, allowing Kenn to catch his breath. It hurt, but in an odd way, unlike any pain he'd ever felt before. Discomfort and something pleasant wrapped into one, inseparable.

"You good, baby boy?"

Daddy sounded out of breath, as if he was fighting to control himself. Was it weird that Kenn liked that he had that effect on him? It made it clear how much Daddy wanted him, that none of this was faked or pretend. "Mmm, yes, Daddy."

He focused on his breathing as Daddy sunk inside him inch by inch, prying Kenn open with gentle doggedness. Slowly but surely, his body gave way, accepting Daddy in, hugging the intruder tightly. He was full, so full, but the pressure felt insanely good, pushing against spots that sent waves of pleasure through his body.

"God, you feel good," Daddy growled. "The way your body squeezes my cock..."

"Daddy... Don't stop, don't stop."

"I have no intention to... Couldn't even if I wanted to. I need to... Are you good, baby boy?"

"Mmm, yes. So good, Daddy, so good."

Finally, Daddy bottomed out. He was so deep inside Kenn. They were one body, and never in his life had Kenn felt closer to someone. His body burned, ached, buzzed, and he never wanted it to end. Daddy's cock filled him, splitting him open like he could never have imagined. Pressure, still with that edge of pain, but so unbelievably good.

"Can I move, baby boy? I need to... Fuck, I'm so close already."

"Please, Daddy. Yes, yes..."

He was babbling, unable to find proper words anymore. And when Daddy moved, sliding in and out of him with increasing speed and strength, his mind went completely blank. All he felt was pleasure.

His balls were drawn up tight, and his blood was thrumming in his ears, his body hurtling toward an orgasm faster than ever before. And the *sounds* he was making... It was a good thing their cabin wasn't close to any other buildings because they were giving one hell of a show. Even if Kenn had wanted to, he couldn't have held back the whimpers and moans every time Daddy sank home, hitting that spot inside him that seemed connected to every single one of his pleasure nerves.

Daddy reached for his cock, circling him with that strong hand. "Are you gonna come for Daddy, baby boy? Hmm? Come on my cock so Daddy can feel your hole squeeze tight around me?"

How could mere words be that arousing? If Daddy kept talking like that, Kenn would come within seconds. He tossed his head from left to right, moaning when Daddy fisted him so tight. And so possessive, as if he had every right to touch Kenn, which he did. Another thing that shouldn't be as hot as it was.

He opened his mouth, but no words would come, his body too far gone. Daddy's hips snapped upward as he almost pushed himself off against the mattress, slamming so deep into Kenn he saw stars. His orgasm smashed into him, pulling him under without mercy or respite. Body-shaking pulses roared through him, making him twitch and jerk, his muscles going completely haywire. His mind went empty, every thought disappearing as all he could feel was pure bliss...and Daddy. He let go, content to let the waves roll over him, drowning in ecstasy.

"Oh, fuck..." Daddy grunted, driving into him one more time. "You're so goddamn tight, baby boy. So perfect for Daddy. Gonna fill you up now... Here it comes."

His body jerked, then stiffened, and Kenn lay still as Daddy's cock spurted hot liquid inside him. It tickled, and it felt dirty and wonderful at the same time. Daddy collapsed with a grunt, pulling Kenn with him as he rolled over. His soft cock slipped out of Kenn, leaving a wet trail in its wake. Another new sensation and Kenn wanted to cry with the perfection of it. He felt sore, tired, and thoroughly used.

Kenn went slack with a shuddery exhale, and then they lay panting, the sweat on their skin cooling as their heart rates came down. "How are you feeling, baby boy?" Daddy finally asked, propping his head up on his arm.

"That was perfect, Daddy."

"Yeah?"

"My first time couldn't have been better."

"I'm so glad, baby boy."

A faint smirk teased Daddy's lips, the look of someone who was feeling very pleased with himself. Well, he should. Kenn had already thought his Daddy had many talents, and now he could add sex god to that list. And if Daddy wanted to feel a little smug about that, then well, Kenn wouldn't hold it against him. As far as he was concerned, Daddy had earned it.

They cuddled for a while, the sweat on their bodies evaporated by now. "Let's shower," Daddy said.

"Together? Yes, please."

Kenn had stayed in hotels with much more luxurious features than their cabin, and yet no bathroom had ever been this amazing as he leaned against Daddy under the hot beams of the shower. They were content to just stand there until finally, Daddy moved. "Let me wash your hair, baby boy."

Daddy took his time massaging the shampoo in, shielding Kenn's eyes when he rinsed it out again, just like his mom had done when he'd been a little boy. His body came next, and Daddy squirted shower gel onto a washcloth and proceeded to clean every inch of his body. Kenn didn't even get hard. This brought satisfaction on a much deeper level than merely physical. He felt taken care of to the deepest part of his soul.

"Your skin is so soft," Daddy mused, rinsing him off.

Kenn had never thought of himself as pretty or beautiful, but the genuine admiration in his Daddy's voice and face was undeniable. How amazing was that? "Can I wash you as well, Daddy?" he asked when he was scrubbed clean.

"I'd like that..."

Kenn did the same to Daddy as Daddy had done for him. He'd never washed someone else's hair, but it felt like the most natural thing in the world. And so did washing Daddy, though some body parts still made him blush, like Daddy's heavy cock, swinging low and soft, even when Kenn handled it.

"You do that so well," Daddy praised him, watching Kenn through half-lidded eyes. "Thank you, baby boy."

He loved sliding his hands over Daddy's soft chest and belly, the hairs tickling him. After he was done with the front, he circled him to do the back. When he stroked the area where the scars started, Warrick tensed up under his fingers, and he didn't need to guess why. And so he listened to his heart and sank to his knees, kissing the scars.

"Baby..." Daddy said in a choked-up voice, slapping a hand against the wet tiles as if he needed to hold himself up.

"You're beautiful too, Daddy. Beautiful and strong."

He rose to his feet again and continued to wash Warrick, touching him everywhere. Joy bloomed inside him at the privilege. He'd never dared to imagine himself with someone like Warrick, someone so mature and so kind, who would take such good care of him. It made him want to worship him, almost literally.

The towels weren't as fluffy as the ones in the White House, but it didn't matter. Daddy lovingly patted Kenn dry, stroking his skin with the slightly raspy cotton. He shivered as he stood on the cold tiles, but his insides were warm. Having sex had been everything he'd imagined it to be. Even better.

"How are you feeling?" Daddy asked softly.

"Tired. But good. Really, really good."

"Any pain or discomfort?"

Kenn did a mental check of his body. The only thing that still stung a bit was his ass. Or rather, inside his ass. His hole. "A little, but it's fine. What do we do now, Daddy?"

Daddy smiled at him. "Now we eat so we can refuel for the next round."

41

Coulson had read and reread the information Asher had sent him, doing his part to be prepared. He still wanted Asher there, if only because it would help Seth relax. If Seth had to worry about Coulson doing something wrong, it would defeat the whole purpose.

They had slept in that morning, and then they'd made out, resulting in a sloppy, mutually satisfactory frotting session. If Seth had been disappointed Coulson hadn't fucked him, he hadn't said anything, though he'd gazed at him intently for a few moments. But Coulson had wanted to spare Seth's ass, knowing what would come later.

They'd gone for a run together, had showered, and then they'd lounged in their cabin, watching a documentary on climbers attempting to conquer Mount Everest, and it had been perfect. Around dinner time, Seth suggested they pick up dinner from the kitchen and eat it in their cabin. Asher had warned him to let Seth know around this time so he could decide to skip dinner or eat less.

Coulson took a deep breath. "Babe, I have something planned for us tonight."

Seth paused the documentary. "A surprise?"

"Mmm, not really, 'cause I have to tell you in advance so you can prepare."

Seth's breath caught, and his eyes widened. "Boo…"

"Asher will be here at eight to help me fist you," Coulson said.

Seth pushed himself off the couch into a sitting position. "You talked to him about this?"

Coulson wanted to be honest. Keeping anything from Seth would come between them. "Asher told me you needed this. I'm so sorry I didn't pick up on it. If I had known, I would've done it weeks ago."

"I didn't want you to feel guilty or forced." Seth's voice was barely audible, and Coulson had rarely seen his man so vulnerable.

"I don't."

"Promise me?"

He tilted Seth's chin and looked him in the eyes. "I swear. I want to do this for you, baby. I just couldn't do this on my own, and it took me a while to accept that. Now that Asher is with Milan and Denali, it makes it easier for me. And he came to me, offering me his help. That means a lot to me. So was he right? Is this what you need?"

Seth nodded, but something still wasn't right, his eyes guarded as if he was holding back. Coulson leaned his forehead against Seth's. "Please, baby, tell me how I can help you. I want to take care of you, but you have to be open with me."

Seth was quiet for a while, but Coulson waited patiently. "I need you to do this for me, but I'm scared," his man finally whispered.

"Scared of what?"

"That you'll see me differently after this. You haven't seen this side of me yet, and it's... I don't know how to explain it. You'll literally be looking inside me, and it's not pretty."

Coulson leaned back. "I think I understand what you're trying to say, but, baby, I love you...and that includes this side of you. I'm honored you'd let me see it and that you'll allow me to take care of you."

Seth's body relaxed. "Thank you. Thank you for swallowing your pride and letting Asher help you."

"You okay with that? I thought it might help you relax fully."

"It will. No dinner for me then, thank you. I'll eat an apple or something...and I'll need some time to prepare myself."

Coulson kissed him. "You do whatever you have to do."

Eight on the dot, a knock sounded on their door, and Coulson let Asher in. Coulson's stomach was fluttering with nerves, but he was determined to do this and make it a good experience. Asher held up a massive tub of lube, grinning. "I come bearing gifts."

"We have lube."

"This is special stuff called J-Lube. It's a powder that you mix with water to get the right consistency, and it's better suited for fisting than regular lube."

God, he was so fucking glad he'd asked Asher for advice. "Thanks. I trimmed my nails like you told me."

"Good."

"He's in our bedroom."

Coulson started walking, but Asher put a hand on his shoulder. "He's *your* man, Coulson, you hear me? You're in charge. If I do something you don't like or want, you tell me."

Coulson nodded, relief flooding him. "Thank you."

"Don't mention it."

Seth sat on their bed, naked, and he straightened when Coulson walked in, Asher on his heels. "Hey, Ash."

"Hey, dude." Asher's tone was light, and Coulson appreciated it.

Coulson looked at Seth. "You ready for this, baby?"

"I've already stretched myself, and I've been wearing a plug for the last hour," he said, but his gaze was on Asher.

Asher immediately shook his head. "You talk to him." He pointed at Coulson. "I'm here to help him, so you'll need to communicate with your man. He's your Dom in this, Seth. Not me."

Seth let his shoulders drop. "Thank you. That'll make it easier."

Coulson extended his hand to Seth, and Seth allowed himself to be pulled to his feet. Coulson kissed him firmly, looking deep into Seth's beautiful eyes. "On the bed on your back, baby."

Seth nodded and got into position, pulling his legs up. The flared end of the plug he was wearing was visible, and Coulson reached for it when Asher cleared his throat. "Don't you need to ditch some clothes?"

Should he? He wasn't fucking him, so what did it matter? Maybe Asher had a reason for it, though, and he'd asked for his help, so he couldn't ignore his first words. "Okay."

He stripped down to his boxer briefs, figuring that would be enough.

Seth chuckled. "You just wanna ogle my sexy boyfriend...and his dick," he teased Asher.

Asher shrugged. "Can you blame me? Dude's hot as fuck."

Coulson laughed sheepishly, even though his belly flared hot with the genuine admiration in Asher's voice. This was probably one of those gay things he wasn't used to.

He pulled out the plug, admiring the way Seth's hole tried to keep it in. It always did that, as if it really wanted something in there all the time. A little lube on his fingers and the first two sank in with ease after the prep Seth had done. Asher didn't need to tell him he could add a third, but how did he proceed after that? Usually, this was when he swapped his fingers for his cock. Did he just shove four in?

"Instead of using your three middle fingers, use your thumb, index, and middle finger," Asher said softly. He stood behind Coulson, close enough so he could see what was happening but not in Coulson's line of vision.

Coulson switched fingers.

"Now use your thumb to stretch him. Because you have more flexibility and strength in those three, it's easier to stretch him wider."

Seth had closed his eyes, and soft puffs of breath were falling from his lips, almost rhythmically. When Coulson spread his fingers, Seth moaned, a low guttural sound that shot straight to Coulson's dick, the same sound Seth made when Coulson impaled him on his cock. Oh, yes, he was on the right track.

After a minute or two, Asher tapped his shoulder, holding up four fingers, and Coulson got the hint. He pulled out, added some more lube, and came back with four. He put pressure on Seth's entrance. Four fingers wasn't easy, and Seth puffed a few times before his body gave way and Coulson could slide inside. He slowly pumped his fingers, the copious amounts of lube creating a slick, squishy sound that had Seth opening his eyes.

"You're doing good, baby," Coulson reassured him that he didn't think any of this was weird or embarrassing. The trust Seth displayed here by allowing Coulson to do this was a massive turn-on.

He watched Seth's face closely for any sign of discomfort, but nothing showed. The worry lines that had been etched onto his face almost permanently over the last months relaxed, and his look was dreamy. His cock had been between hard and half mast the whole time, so he was clearly enjoying it on a sexual level as well. It was working, and the thought sent a thrill of determination through Coulson.

Time to move on to the next step. "How do I do this?" he asked Asher.

Asher stretched out his hand, his thumb and pinkie tucked in. "Start like this. When you're up to the knuckle, hold still. His muscles will pull you in the rest of the way once they relax."

Coulson nodded, fully concentrated. More lube and back he went. Seth had his eyes open, but he was staring into space, his body relaxed. He seemed to be in a different state of mind, so Coulson didn't say anything as he brought five fingers to Seth's hole, which was stretched wide. Five fingers was a lot, and his hand wasn't exactly small either, so he went slow, sliding and pushing until Seth's hole gave way.

Then he held still as Seth moaned, his eyes rolling back. "Ohgodohgodohgod..." he grunted. "I need... Gimme all."

Coulson gave one last push, and his knuckles slid past all resistance. He gasped as Seth's body pulled him in, and then he was up till his wrist inside Seth. His adrenaline spiked, his heart beating fast. "Baby?" he checked in with Seth.

Seth didn't answer. "He's good," Asher said quietly. "But he's high on endorphins, so he's not entirely connected to reality right now."

"Do I keep my hand like this? Should I move?"

"Is he clenching around your hand or relaxed?"

"Relaxed."

"Then start moving, shallow at first until you can feel the lack of resistance."

Coulson did, his face tight with focus as he pulled his hand back to the knuckles, then sank it back in. Seth was puffing and groaning, but his cock grew harder and harder. Coulson felt the moment Seth's body accepted him, and then he was able to push in and out with ease.

"Make sure to keep those fingers tucked in," Asher instructed.

If someone had told Coulson a year before that he'd find himself wrist deep into his boyfriend's ass, he would've called them crazy...and yet here he was. And the crazy thing was that it didn't feel strange or gross or whatever at all. He was proud he was able to give Seth what he needed. And if he were honest, seeing his man take a whole fist was badass and arousing, as Coulson's hard cock could attest to.

"How do I know when he's had enough?" he asked Asher.

"When he comes."

Coulson sharply turned his head. "He's gonna come from this?"

Asher smiled at him. "Hands-free and it'll be the most intense orgasm ever."

Damn, Coulson couldn't wait to see that.

"He'll be exhausted afterward, so take good care of him.

Maybe put some aloe on his hole. My job here is done. You're a class act, Coulson." Asher clapped him on the shoulder.

"Thank you, Asher...for everything. I owe you."

Asher grinned. "Nah, seeing you in your underwear was payment enough."

He winked as he walked out, and Coulson laughed, then refocused on Seth. And Asher had been right. Five minutes later, Seth came without ever saying a word, his orgasm so violent his whole body shook. And when Coulson pulled his hand out carefully, Seth was crying, big tears rolling down his cheeks. Stress release. Thank fuck it had worked.

"I love you, baby," Coulson whispered as he cleaned him up. Seth lay like a puddle on the bed, boneless and exhausted. "I love you so much."

He washed him, then put cream on his hole like Asher had suggested. After washing his hands and getting rid of the dirty laundry, he tucked Seth into bed and snuggled close. Seth immediately clung to him, and Coulson held him, whispering sweet nothings in his ear as Seth cried. Just before he fell asleep, he whispered a few words to Coulson. "Thank you, boo."

42

The weekend away in Camp David had clearly been a resounding success, and not only for him and Rhett, Calix thought. If he had to take a guess, most of the couples had done the same thing he and Rhett had, which was spend most of the weekend in bed, only coming out for meals and the occasional stroll outside.

He'd felt bad for Del, the only one who had been on his own, but his friend had assured Calix he hadn't minded at all. He'd caught up on some sleep and taken advantage of everyone being otherwise occupied to get some uninterrupted work hours in. Thank fuck there had been no crisis that had needed their attention either, so the planets had aligned to truly bring them a relaxed weekend with sex, sleep, and snuggles. Hopefully, everyone had recharged enough to last a while again.

"Okay, Cal. Hit me with it. What's on today's agenda?" Del asked, leaning back in his seat in the Oval.

Calix flipped open his list. "Amzi and I have scheduled a series of talks with leaders in the Muslim community, starting this week. We're talking with imams, scholars, ambassadors of a few countries, UN representatives, and more."

"Good. I'm concerned about how much time this will cost you, though."

"Funny you should mention that. Terrell and I had a long conversation yesterday, and he's ready to take on more responsibilities."

Calix had given his deputy time to get settled, which hadn't been easy with them facing one crisis after the other. But even though the investigation into the assassination was still in full swing and they were still recovering from the scandal surrounding Milan, politically, things finally seemed to be calming down. They had a vice president, a full cabinet, and all crucial governmental positions had been filled. The time had come to do some serious governing, and the only way to achieve that was to hand over more responsibilities to Terrell.

"I'm glad to hear it."

"You don't object?"

Del shook his head. "He's smart, he's a fast learner, and he has a lot of energy. It's going to be productive to get a few projects off your plate and make him responsible for them."

"That's the idea." Calix was relieved Del had seen the wisdom of this step. He hadn't expected him to have a problem with it, but he'd definitely counted on a longer conversation than this, so that was a win.

"What else?"

Calix didn't need to check his notes for this one. "John Doty."

Ever since Henley had reported back on his conversation with one of Markinson's staffers—Calix respected the hell out of him for not naming him, though Henley had promised to share the name with the FBI if Coulson needed him to—they'd been going back and forth on what to do. Firing Doty seemed like a dangerous move, considering what they knew, but so did allowing him to have access to highly classified intel on Hamza Bashir and Al Saalihin. What if he warned them they were onto them?

Del rubbed his temples. "I don't know what to do here. I hate the idea of having a traitor in that position, but if we do fire him, what's to say he won't somehow take revenge? If he was involved in it, he could cause a lot of trouble for us."

"I did some discreet asking around. He's not popular in his department. I doubt a lot of people will protest his departure, so that's something at least."

"The Republican leadership likes him..."

Calix lifted an eyebrow. "And since when do we let them decide for us? How about we start with the Democratic leadership? They already have candidates lined up to replace him. They've never been a fan."

"I know, I know. I'm scared, okay? I'm plain scared. If Markinson was intimidated enough to keep him on as a secretary, Doty must've threatened with something real. To ignore that feels stupid."

"Things have changed, Del. Markinson is dead, and we're closing in on those behind it. Doty may not be read into the investigation, but he knows enough to realize we're on Hamza Bashir's trail. It would be stupid of him to even try anything right now. His name has been kept out of it so far, and my guess is he'd like to keep it that way."

"Good point. So what excuse do I use?"

"Fresh blood. He's been the secretary of defense for six years. It's time for a change. Praise him into high heavens in public. Problem solved. If it turns out he's involved, we'll nail the bastard afterward."

"Okay. I'm convinced. Put it in motion. But I want witnesses when I meet with him."

"I'll make sure of it."

"What's next?"

He'd kept the best for last, and Calix mentally braced himself. "It's time you hired a body man."

Del sighed. "That's become a priority?"

"It is. You need someone on a day-to-day basis to help you with all the small stuff."

Del had resisted the idea of a body man from the get-go. The president's body man was a combination of a valet, a personal assistant, and a secretary all in one. A position traditionally fulfilled by young college graduates, the job required having constant access to the president and assisting him in every possible need.

In the beginning, Calix had understood why Del hadn't wanted anyone. Markinson had just been assassinated, throwing Del into the presidency, and the young guy who had been Markinson's body man had quit right after the assassination, too shaken up to continue. Not that Calix could blame him for that. The kid had been present at that fundraiser and had watched his president get blown up. And with the heightened security after the assassination, no new hires had gotten access to the president.

"Let's say for argument's sake that you're right and that I do need someone. Is it wise to hire when we still haven't wrapped up the investigation? What if we employ the wrong person?"

Calix leaned back in his chair, tapping his pen against his fingers. "There are two ways to look at this. The first is what you just pointed out. The masterminds behind the Pride Bombing and the assassination are still out there, and what if this only affords them another opportunity to get someone close to you? It's not an unreasonable concern."

"Glad to hear you don't think I'm being hysterical. What's the other way?"

"We can't stop living. I know we don't have all the answers yet, though we're getting closer and closer now that we know where to look. But regardless, you have a job to do, Del, and little time left to do it. Your reelection is far from guaranteed, so we need to stop surviving and start governing."

Del averted his gaze. "I'm going to say this as kindly as I can, but that's a little easier for you to say than for me to do. My grief for Sarah is still fresh."

"I know, and no one understands that better than I do. But you're still the president, and that's not the kind of job where you can get by with an average performance. You have a unique chance to make a difference, and the time is now. If you can't motivate yourself for that, if you find that, without Sarah, you can't do it, then that's a legitimate viewpoint, but it has consequences."

Del met his eyes again, and understanding dawned. "You're talking about resigning."

"Those are the only two choices you have. You either get yourself back in the saddle and be the best president you can be...or you step back and let someone else take over. I won't blame you for the second choice. How could I? But you have to make the decision."

Del walked over to the window, where he stared outside, shoving his hands into his pockets. "What does hiring a body man have to do with this?"

"Del, you were wearing two different socks last week, and if Rhett hadn't spotted it and subtly handed you a new pair of socks, it could've gotten embarrassing for you. You keep losing your reading glasses, Max is working more overtime than ever, and stuff is falling through the cracks."

Del's shoulders dropped. "Sarah did a lot of those things for me."

"I know. We can't replace her, and I'd never suggest that, but she was already picking up the slack from a position that should've been filled. We'll have to start the reelection campaign soon, and you'll be on the road a lot. You'll need a body man. Someone has to travel with you and take care of all the stupid small stuff, and it's not going to be me."

Del slowly turned around. "You know, people said I was crazy to appoint my best friend as my chief of staff. Multiple senators warned me against it, even when I was still a vice president. I even had former chiefs of staff reach out to me and tell me the same. Everyone used the same argument that you would be too close to me to see my weaknesses and point them out to me, too close to tell me the truth."

Calix smiled. "Little did they know..."

"No one else could've done this job the way you have, and in case I've never told you before, I'm grateful you're always honest with me."

"Always. Professional or personal, I'd never lie to you, Del. And now that I've got you in a grateful mood, let me present you with a shortlist of candidates."

Calix pulled the folder he'd prepared and held it out to Del, who took it with visible reluctance. The president flipped through the five résumé summaries, then let out a deep sigh. "How will I know if I have a click with any of them? I can't have someone around me the whole time who annoys the fuck out of me."

"By meeting with them and see who you like?"

Del looked through them again, then closed the folder and handed it back to Calix. "You choose. I don't have the right state of mind to do this or the time, and you know me better anyway."

Okay, then. Calix opened the folder again. He didn't need to reread the résumés to know who his favorite was. "Him." He handed Del the résumé.

Del frowned. "You met with all of them already?"

Calix raised his eyebrows. "Did you really think I'd give you a shortlist and not interview them myself first?"

"True, sorry. So why this"—Del glanced at the paper he was holding—"Issa?"

Calix smiled at the memory of the most entertaining job interview he'd ever done in his life. Issa was a riot...and exactly what Del needed. Not that Calix would tell him that in those words because the man was stubborn enough to pick someone else on principle. He'd never liked being told what to do. "He's wicked smart, as you would say, and so organized it made my eyes twitch—and that's saying something. He's got a good sense of humor, he's athletic, and he's a problem solver."

With a sigh, Del read the résumé. "He just finished a degree in...hospitality management?"

"Correct. He's done internships at The Beekman in New York City and the Ritz in Boston."

"Hmm."

Calix bit his tongue. If he pushed too hard, Del would know something was up. He didn't even know why he was convinced Issa was the right man for the job, but he did. The guy had been a ray of sunshine, filled with energy and positivity, and Del might not realize it, but he needed someone like that in his life. His friends had all suffered the same losses he had, so none of them was able to be that person for him. Issa could, and he might be able to help Del refocus on the future.

Another long sigh. "Oh, whatever. Hire him. If it doesn't work out, we can reassign him somewhere else, right?"

"With his résumé, I can think of a lot of positions he'd be great in."

Del handed him the paper back. "When can he start?"

"As soon as he has clearance. Shouldn't be more than a week."

"Cal, you need to go over things with him, okay? I don't want someone watching my every move. I need privacy."

"He knows."

"And he'd better not start changing things. I like my routine the way it is now. Unlike my son, I don't need someone telling me what to do."

"No Daddy for you. Duly noted."

Del's mouth pulled up at the corners. "You're getting cheeky."

"I learned from the best." He leaned forward. "Trust me on this, Del. I promise you won't regret it."

43

The difference in Seth was so remarkable Coulson wouldn't have believed it if he didn't witness it with his own eyes. Seth was sleeping better, the spring in his step was back, and he radiated energy. Coulson would never make the mistake again to think that fisting was something Seth wanted rather than needed. He'd take care of him.

"Hey, boo, where are you with your thoughts?" Seth asked softly. He was driving, and they were on the George Washington Parkway, on their way to Langley.

"I was thinking about you, actually." Coulson squeezed Seth's thigh. He loved touching him in general, but especially in situations like this. It might be such a small thing, but the intimacy of it still made his belly weak. How had he gotten so lucky that this gorgeous man was his?

"Mmm, good things, I hope?"

"Sexy things, baby. Very sexy things."

Seth shot him a quick look sideways. "Glad to hear it."

"I don't think it would be possible for me to think unsexy thoughts about you."

"Ha! Look at you, being all flirty and romantic. You got game, boo."

Coulson puffed up his chest. "Damn right I do. I work hard to keep my man, I'll have you know."

"You sure do, boo. I love you."

"Love you too."

One day, Coulson hoped they'd have more time for personal conversations on the short car rides they shared, but alas, today wasn't that day. When they walked into the CIA building, Branson was waiting for him in the central hallway.

"Hey, guys." Branson smiled broadly.

Coulson always had to push down the wave of irritation he felt at seeing Branson. Funny how being near Asher or Milan didn't bother him much, even though both of them had fucked Seth as well. For some reason, Branson felt different. Maybe because he was single and had previously made it clear he'd wanted to continue meeting Seth.

"Hey," he and Seth said at the same time, then looked at each other and laughed.

Branson rolled his eyes. "Oh my god, you guys have reached the twinning stage of your relationship. Nauseating."

Coulson shrugged. "I can't help it if we're so tuned in to each other."

Branson made a gagging sound. "Dial back the sweetness, man. You're killing me here."

Coulson raised an eyebrow. "Are we gonna stand here debating the sugar level of my relationship, or can we get down to business?"

Branson grew serious. "We have a lot to discuss."

Branson brought them to a small conference room

without windows, where a guy with dark-rimmed glasses was furiously tapping away on a computer. "Ry," Branson said, and the guy snapped his head up.

"Ryder. My name is Ryder, as I have reminded you at least twenty times by now."

"What can I say? I'm bad with names," Branson said with a wink at Seth and Coulson.

"Actually, you're exceptionally good with names, as you are with all details, which is why it's so remarkable you can't seem to remember mine. One would almost think you did it on purpose."

"I'm hurt that you would think so low of me." Branson's pretending-to-be-innocent look needed work.

"Do we need to be here for this?" Seth asked, clearly losing patience.

Branson straightened. "This is Ryder Treese. He's our new forensic accountant, and he's specialized in tracing international payments of the shady variety. Ryder, meet Special Agent Coulson Padman and Special Agent Seth Rodecker, FBI and Secret Service respectively."

Ryder got up, and Coulson gave him the once-over. Brown hair with a touch of red in it, slender build, remarkably light green eyes, and a pair of full lips framed by a five-o'clock shadow. His handshake was firm. "Pleased to meet you," Coulson said.

"Likewise."

They sat down around the table. "Coffee?" Branson offered.

Seth shuddered. "No thanks. I'd rather not get poisoned."

"We have some new information we thought we'd best share with you in person," Branson said.

Coulson frowned. "Why?"

"Because we don't want the wrong people to get their hands on this info. We think we've found the first images of Hamza Bashir."

Coulson's heart skipped a beat. "You have our attention."

"We sent some assets to Qatar to see if we could trace Muhammed Bhat's steps. We know he spent a whole day in Qatar when he flew from Dulles to Islamabad, and the hypothesis was that he could've met up with someone. Since 2011, Qatar has had a law that mandates that surveillance cameras be installed in residential compounds, hospitals, malls, banks, hotels, warehouses, and other public locations, and they're strict about enforcing it. That meant that once we had ensured the full cooperation of the Qatari government, we had access to a ton of data. All we needed was to sift through it, and that took some time, as you can imagine. After we found Bhat arriving at the airport in Doha, we tracked him, using all the footage we could get our hands on."

Branson tapped on his laptop, then turned the screen to Coulson and Seth. The grainy picture was clearly pulled from CCTV footage. "This is Bhat after arriving in Qatar. He applied for a visa waiver at the airport and was granted one."

The next image showed the same man outside, getting into a cab.

"He took a taxi to the Golden Ocean hotel, which is an affordable hotel at the airport. He spent the night there, then took a taxi the next morning to the Mall of Qatar, outside of Doha and Ar-Rayyan."

He clicked, and now the screen showed the inside of a luxurious mall with Bhat walking. The next picture portrayed him sitting in a restaurant across from another man. Coulson squinted, but the image was too grainy to make out much.

"This was lifted from the security footage from the mall, which isn't the best quality, as you can see. But using other security feeds, we've tracked both of them while in the mall. The other man is a Middle Eastern-looking man dressed in an Emirati-style kandura, that long white dress men wear."

"They have different styles?" Seth asked.

Branson nodded. "They have different names and styles, depending on the country or region. Kuwaiti ones, called dishdashas, have a one-button collar, for example, while the Omani style has no collar at all but a short tassel. Qatari ones have a small collar as well, but they have a breast pocket, whereas the Bahraini style has an open soft collar, like on a shirt. Emirati kanduras, like this man is wearing, have no collar at all, but theirs sport one long tassel and have embroidery on the sleeves."

"Does that mean he's Emirati?" Coulson asked.

"He might be. Men in that region tend to be tribal about their clothing as it communicates a lot about them. Everything this guy was wearing fits with someone from the UAE."

"Not from Yemen, then," Seth commented.

"He could travel there easily from the Emirates... through Qatar."

"So this guy had a meeting with Bhat?" Coulson asked.

"Yes. They shared tea and food, and according to the timestamps, they spent at least an hour together. What's interesting is that they didn't behave suspiciously in any way. No increased situational awareness, no looking around. All very relaxed. But wait."

The picture on the screen changed again, this time two side-by-side screenshots from security footage. Coulson snapped his fingers. "The unknown guy had a bag when he came in, but not when he walked out."

Branson nodded. "Exactly. He didn't, but Bhat did."

"Money?" Seth suggested.

"Could very well be. It would be risky, considering Bhat still had to fly to Islamabad, but it's not impossible to get it through customs there. After their meeting, Bhat returned to the airport, where he waited for hours for his 8:15 p.m. flight to Islamabad."

"You think this man Bhat met with is Hamza Bashir," Coulson said.

"Yes."

"Based on what?"

"He fits the profile, and who else would Bhat meet with at that time? It has to be Bashir or someone working directly for him, and since we haven't encountered any evidence for other leaders within Al Saalihin, we're reasonably confident this is Bashir. But obviously, we're gonna find out everything we can about this guy, which is where Ryder comes in."

Ryder took a deep breath. "My specialty is tracing money in any kind of transaction, especially international transactions. The forensic accountant from the FBI and I are working together on this, and we've created a list of all suspected payments over the last seven years. These include transactions between Hamza Bashir and Kingmakers and between Hamza Bashir and the Pride Bombers, but also between all the domestic suspects, like Richard Quirk and Jon Brooks. We're now going over all their finances with a fine-tooth comb to flag anything suspicious."

"How are you going to investigate Kingmaker's finances? They're not a public company," Coulson said.

"My suggestion is to have the IRS audit them so we can get access to their financial data without alerting them we're onto them. Corey, the FBI accountant, said he'd take it up with you."

Oh, that was brilliant. Coulson's biggest worry was that Kingmakers would find out they were hot on their trail and cover their tracks even more. Which they were too good at. "I'll double-check with the agent in charge, but I like that idea."

Ryder nodded. "Good. I want to fly under the radar as long as I can so we have time to build our case."

"Have you found anything yet?" Seth asked.

"Corey's been digging into the campaign donations, since that's outside my purview, and there's definitely something illegal going on there. He's been in touch with Bill Clampton, and based on what Clampton told him, Corey knew where to start looking. Clampton was right that according to the reported donations, multiple campaign events were on the same day, but they couldn't possibly have taken place with the candidate attending. Not unless they invented time travel or teleporting. A second issue is that the donations above five hundred dollars that need to be reported with all data from the donor included some suspicious ones as well. Lots of empty LLCs and unknown PACs, so he's tracing all those down. It's slow going, but we'll get there."

People often made jokes about accounting being boring, but Coulson could totally see the appeal of it, especially forensic accounting. Wasn't it like a puzzle that needed to be solved, much like the whole investigation, only on a smaller scale? "Great work, Ryder. And, Branson," he added when he caught a quirked eyebrow from the CIA analyst.

"Dare I ask about a timeline?" Seth asked.

Ryder and Branson shared a look. "Two months," Branson said. "That's our goal. We want to have all the data analyzed within the next two months, and if we find what we're hoping for, we'll have the evidence to catch these bastards."

44

Their weekend at Camp David had been perfect, but the return to reality hadn't been bad either. In the week since they'd been back, Warrick had spent only one night in his own home, and that had been to pick up his mail, water his dying plants, and pack more clothes. He'd all but moved in with Kenn into the boy's room, but no one seemed to mind, least of all Kenn. And Warrick loved being with his boy, even if the White House wouldn't have been his first choice.

The only change they'd made was to permanently move Rogue out of Kenn's room so they'd have a bit more privacy. Even having a dog around could be too much, they had discovered. Luckily, the president had been all too happy to relocate Rogue to his room.

Kenn was open to exploring, and Warrick reveled in being his first in everything. He'd noticed Kenn loved using his mouth to discover and taste, whether it was to suck on Warrick's cock or other parts of his body. And obviously, Warrick didn't mind being the "victim" of that oral fixation. On the contrary.

He had another idea of how Kenn could use his mouth, something he would probably have to demonstrate. But before he'd do that, he needed to teach him something else first. Something that had the potential of being a bit embarrassing, but that had to be addressed, regardless.

"Listen, baby boy, I want to do something with you that may make you a little embarrassed, but it's important, okay?"

Kenn glanced up from the book he'd been reading, his face adorably serious. "What is it, Daddy?"

"We're gonna take a shower together, and I'm gonna show you how to clean yourself...inside."

As expected, Kenn's cheeks flushed a bright red. "Daddy!"

"No, baby boy, we're not gonna avoid this topic. This should become part of your routine, okay? There's nothing weird or shameful about it. It'll make sex a lot easier for us, and that's what you want, isn't it? For Daddy to be able to take you whenever he wants?"

Oh, the *look* in Kenn's eyes... The way his irises darkened, his pupils dilated, the gasp that rushed from his lips. He wanted this. Hell, Warrick would put money on him needing it.

"Y-yes, Daddy. I'll be good."

"You always are, sweetheart. Come, give Daddy a kiss."

He undressed both of them while kissing him in between, and Kenn followed his every cue until he stood naked in front of Warrick, shivering. Warrick tugged on his hand. "Let's go, baby boy."

He grabbed the supplies he'd gotten with help from Milan and laid them out on the bathroom counter. Kenn's cheeks were fiery red. "Listen, baby boy. This is the part that no one wants to talk about, but it's important." He held up the douche bulb. "We'll use this with lukewarm water in it and a bit of salt. Never use hot water. Your insides are much more sensitive to temperature than your skin. Use this every other day. If you do it too often, it'll mess up your intestinal flora, and we don't want that."

He'd hoped adopting a more clinical tone would help, and it seemed to work, as Kenn was listening attentively.

"If you ever need to buy one on your own, don't buy the ones labeled anal douche bulb. This is actually a baby mucous sucker." Kenn's eyes widened, and Warrick laughed. "I'm not kidding. Parents use it to clean the noses of kids who can't blow their noses yet. The difference is that they have a much softer tip, which makes it more comfortable."

"Talk about a multifunctional object."

"Never say that gays aren't creative. Put a little lube on the tip after you've filled it with saline water." He demonstrated it. "Then it's time to use it. Just insert and squeeze. Because this one is small, you'll have enough in one go."

"W-will it come out right away?"

"Most of it, yes, so you'll want to either be on the toilet or run the shower while you do it. I prefer the latter."

Kenn frowned. "What do you mean? This is for me, not for you, isn't it?"

Warrick smiled. "Maybe in the future, you'd like to top me some time as well, baby boy."

Kenn's mouth dropped open. "You'd want that?"

"I'm vers, baby boy. I may prefer to top, but I'd love to bottom for you and share that with you." Kenn's face made it clear he hadn't considered that possibility. "Something to think about, not for right now."

"Okay, Daddy."

"So we'll do it together this time, okay? We turn on the

shower, and the water will flush it all away instantly. And, baby boy, this isn't something to be ashamed of."

He prepared both bulbs, then ran the shower. Kenn's face was red again as Warrick demonstrated how to use the bulb, but once he'd done it, Kenn seemed more at ease to use it on himself. "Good job, baby boy. It's a good practice to do this at least an hour before sex, so the last bit can come out, okay? That way, you'll feel fresh and clean for Daddy."

"I like that, Daddy."

"So do I. Because do you know what good boys who do what their Daddy tells them get?"

Kenn's face lit up. "A reward?"

"Yes, baby boy, a reward. A very pleasurable reward." He winked.

He toweled his boy off, then told him to read for a little bit so his system could settle.

"It's been an hour, Daddy," Kenn said after a while.

Warrick looked up from his laptop. "Someone is keeping time, I see..."

"I'm excited for my reward, Daddy."

Warrick closed his laptop. "Mmm, what do you think it is?"

Kenn's smile was sweet and sexy. "I don't know, but if it involved that demonstration as foreplay, I'm gonna go ahead and guess it's something sexual, so I'm in."

Warrick threw his head back and laughed. His boy was getting saucy, and he loved it. "You're not wrong, baby boy. Why don't you undress and get on the bed, present yourself to Daddy?"

Kenn didn't need to be told twice, though he neatly hung his clothes over the clothes rack like Warrick had asked him to. Then he dove onto the bed and turned on his side, looking at Warrick with eager eyes. "Like this, Daddy?"

"Mmm, so pretty, baby boy. Turn onto your stomach for Daddy. Show me that pretty hole of yours."

Cheeks red, Kenn obeyed, pulling up his knees. He lay spread out for Warrick, his back arched and his ass pushed upward as if he was presenting himself to be ravished. His ass looked even plumper like this, his star on full display, and the sight made Warrick's mouth water.

He whipped off his shirt and dragged down his pants, underwear, and socks in a few quick tugs. For once, he didn't care if they got crinkled on the floor. Priorities.

He couldn't hold back a growl, the sound originating deep inside him. "Time for your reward, baby boy."

He crawled onto the bed, dropped down on the bed between Kenn's spread legs, and found his target. He lapped the pretty pink hole with his tongue.

"Daddy!"

Kenn's voice was high-pitched, full of shock, and Warrick laughed. "I'll show you how good rimming can feel, baby boy. Drive you crazy with my tongue."

Rimming had always been okay-ish for him. Not something he particularly enjoyed, but he didn't hate it either. With Kenn, everything was different. He wanted to savor him everywhere. He licked him again, smiling at Kenn's squeal. "Hush now, baby boy. You don't want the Secret Service to come storming in because they think you're being attacked, do you?"

God, the idea... Although if he were completely honest, it did provide him with a bit of a thrill as well.

He nibbled on Kenn's ass cheeks, licked a hot stripe down his crack, then feasted on that little star until it became all soft and pliant. Mmm, yes, that was how he wanted it. His tongue speared inside without an issue, and then he made love to Kenn's ass. Straight up dug in until he ran out of breath. After taking a big gulp of oxygen, he dove back in.

Kenn lay squirming on the bed, whimpering and pleading, though for what, he didn't even seem to know himself. Warrick caught "more" amid the garbled words. When Warrick took another breather, Kenn uttered a more understandable phrase. "I need you, Daddy."

"Daddy's got you, baby boy. Daddy needs you too. Turn onto your back for me."

Kenn scrambled up to do as he was told, and Warrick placed a pillow under his ass to make the angle better for both of them. With how pliant Kenn's hole was from the rimming, he only needed a little prep before he was good. Warrick held his slicked-up cock and slapped Kenn's hole with the underside of his cock, making Kenn whimper. "Daddy..."

Mmm, he loved that sound of wet flesh against wet flesh. "Patience, baby boy. Daddy will fuck you when he's ready."

He didn't make him wait long, if only because his own patience and self-control were wearing thin. The head of his cock slipped between those round cheeks, pressing against Kenn's glistening pucker. He went slowly, not even because of Kenn but because he wanted to see himself breach that hole, watch himself sink inside his boy. He penetrated him inch by inch, deeper and deeper, until he could go no farther. Even then, he pulled Kenn's hips backward, impaling him on his cock as far as he could—and then he stayed there.

"Daddy..." Kenn begged, his restless fingers searching for something to hold on to.

"I wish you could see this," Warrick said, his voice raw. "The way your ass is clenching around me, my cock buried inside you. You're so sexy, baby boy, and so fucking tight around my dick. You make Daddy feel so good."

He thrust inside him, his strokes slow and gentle but filling up his boy as deep as he could. The movements were almost mesmerizing, and he couldn't tear his eyes away as he fucked him, claiming every inch of his ass. Kenn pushed back on his cock and rubbed himself against the sheets, whimpering as he sought more every time Warrick sank into him. His needy baby boy. They were such a perfect match. He couldn't hold this pace up for long, his back and legs burning.

"Daddy, can I come?"

The whine in Kenn's voice was strangely satisfying, as was the fact that he was already on the brink. "A little longer, baby boy. Can you do that for Daddy? Can you be Daddy's good boy?"

"Yes, D-Daddy..."

Waves of bliss hummed through his body with the promise of more around the corner. A few more strokes, a few more thrusts, and he'd be right there as well, ready to fly. He rolled them onto their sides, his back protesting too much to continue in this position, but Kenn immediately opened himself up, and Warrick sank back in. He couldn't go as deep like this, but he did have more access, and he snapped his hips as he rocked into him.

His right hand found Kenn's cock, so wet and ready to erupt. He gave a long stroke as he nuzzled his neck, pressing kisses everywhere. "Let's slow down, baby boy. Daddy wants to enjoy every second with you."

His body crawled back from the edge as he decreased his pace, and yet it felt even better, if possible. So close to his boy, their bodies melding, as closely connected as their hearts. "I love you so much, Kenn..."

"I love you too, Daddy."

It came out on a half sob, but Warrick understood. They weren't fucking, weren't having sex. He was making love to him, and everything felt different. He slid into him again, sighing with pleasure.

He tightened his grip on Kenn's cock, squeezing it as he moved his hand upward, then down again. "Come for Daddy, my beautiful boy."

Kenn arched his back, his body going taut as his cock spurted out his cum, coating Warrick's hand and the sheets. Warrick followed suit, his hips surging as he drove into Kenn as deep as he could, his muscles flexing to the point of burning. Once more. He unloaded, the orgasm as unhurried as his lovemaking had been, rippling through him in gentle waves that lasted forever.

They stayed like that, not saying anything, just cuddling, until Warrick's soft cock slipped out. He rolled onto his back and held out his arms. Kenn put his head on his shoulder, wriggling one leg over Warrick's. He clung to Warrick like they were magnets, and what should've been annoying and clingy instead felt perfect and right.

"One day, when your dad is no longer president, I'll get on one knee for you and ask you to be mine officially. I won't do it now because it would cause too many political problems for him, but know that I'm dead serious about this, about us, baby boy. You're mine."

"I'm yours, Daddy."

He'd wait forever if he had to. Now that he'd found his baby boy, he would never let him go again. Ever.

∼

To be continued...

FREEBIES

If you love FREE novellas and bonus chapters, head on over to my website where I offer bonus scenes for several of my books, as well as as two free novellas. Grab them here: **https://www.noraphoenix.com/free-stuff/**

BOOKS BY NORA PHOENIX

🎧 indicates book is also available as audio book

White House Men
A romantic suspense series set in the White House that combines romance with suspense, a dash of kink, and all the feels.

- **Press** (rivals fall in love in an impossible love) 🎧
- **Friends** (friends to lovers between an FBI and a Secret Service agent)
- **Click** (a sexy first-time romance with an age gap and an awkward virgin)
- **Serve** (a high heat MMM romance with age gap and D/s play)
- **Care** (the president's son falls for his tutor; age gap and daddy kink)

No Regrets Series
Sexy, kinky, emotional, with a touch of suspense, the No

Regrets series is a spin off from the No Shame series that can be read on its own.

- **No Surrender** (bisexual awakening, first time gay, D/s play)

Perfect Hands Series

Raw, emotional, both sweet and sexy, with a solid dash of kink, that's the Perfect Hands series. All books can be read as standalones.

- **Firm Hand** (daddy care with a younger daddy and an older boy) 🎧
- **Gentle Hand** (sweet daddy care with age play) 🎧
- **Naughty Hand** (a holiday novella to read after Firm Hand and Gentle Hand) 🎧
- **Slow Hand** (a Dom who never wanted to be a Daddy takes in two abused boys) 🎧
- **Healing Hand** (a broken boy finds the perfect Daddy) 🎧

No Shame Series

If you love steamy MM romance with a little twist, you'll love the No Shame series. Sexy, emotional, with a bit of suspense and all the feels. Make sure to read in order, as this is a series with a continuing storyline.

- **No Filter** 🎧
- **No Limits** 🎧
- **No Fear** 🎧
- **No Shame** 🎧
- **No Angel** 🎧

And for all the fun, grab the **No Shame box set** 🎧 which includes all five books plus exclusive bonus chapters and deleted scenes.

Irresistible Omegas Series

An mpreg series with all the heat, epic world building, poly romances (the first two books are MMMM and the rest of the series is MMM), a bit of suspense, and characters that will stay with you for a long time. This is a continuing series, so read in order.

- **Alpha's Sacrifice** 🎧
- **Alpha's Submission** 🎧
- **Beta's Surrender** 🎧
- **Alpha's Pride** 🎧
- **Beta's Strength** 🎧
- **Omega's Protector** 🎧
- **Alpha's Obedience** 🎧
- **Omega's Power** 🎧
- **Beta's Love** 🎧
- **Omega's Truth** 🎧

Or grab *the first box set*, which contains books 1-3 plus exclusive bonus material and *the second box set*, which has books 4-6 and exclusive extras.

Ballsy Boys Series

Sexy porn stars looking for real love! Expect plenty of steam, but all the feels as well. They can be read as stand-alones, but are more fun when read in order.

- **Ballsy** (free prequel)
- **Rebel** 🎧

- Tank 🎧
- Heart 🎧
- Campy 🎧
- Pixie 🎧

Or grab *the box set*, which contains all five books plus an exclusive bonus novella!

Kinky Boys Series

Super sexy, slightly kinky, with all the feels.

- Daddy 🎧
- Ziggy 🎧

Ignite Series

An epic dystopian sci-fi trilogy (one book out, two more to follow) where three men have to not only escape a government that wants to jail them for being gay but aliens as well. Slow burn MMM romance.

- Ignite 🎧
- Smolder 🎧
- Burn 🎧

Now also available in a *box set* 🎧, which includes all three books, bonus chapters, and a bonus novella.

Stand Alones

I also have a few stand alones, so check these out!

- **Professor Daddy** (sexy daddy kink between a college prof and his student. Age gap, no ABDL) 🎧

- **Out to Win** (two men meet at a TV singing contest) 🎧
- **Captain Silver Fox** (falling for the boss on a cruise ship) 🎧
- **Coming Out on Top** (snowed in, age gap, size difference, and a bossy twink) 🎧
- **Ranger** (struggling Army vet meets a sunshiney animal trainer - cowritten with K.M. Neuhold) 🎧

Books in German

Quite a few of my books have been translated into German, with more to come!

Indys Männer

- **Indys Flucht** No Filter)
- **Josh Wunsch** (No Limits)
- **Aarons Handler** (No Fear)
- **Brads Bedürfnisse** (No Shame)
- **Indys Weihnachten** (No Angel)

Mein Daddy Dom

- **Daddy Rhys** (Firm Hand)
- **Daddy Brendan** (Gentle Hand)
- **Weihnachten mit den Daddys** (Naughty Hand)
- **Daddy Ford** (Slow Hand)
- **Daddy Gale** (Healing Hand)

Das Hayes Rudel

- **Lidons Angebot** (Alpha's Sacrifice)
- **Enars Unterordnung** (Alpha's Submission)
- **Lars' Hingabe** (Beta's Surrender)

- **Brays Stolz** (Alpha's Pride)
- **Keans Stärke** (Beta's Strength)
- **Gias Beschützer** (Omega's Protector)

Standalones

- **Mein Professor Daddy** (Professor Daddy)
- **Eingeschneit mit dem Bären** (Coming Out on Top)
- **Eine Nacht mit dem Kapitän** (Captain Silver Fox)
- **Ranger** (Ranger, cowritten with K.M. Neuhold)

Books in Other Languages

- **L'Occasione Della Vita** - (Italian - The Time of my Life / Out to Win)

MORE ABOUT NORA PHOENIX

Would you like the long or the short version of my bio?

The short? You got it.

I write steamy gay romance books and I love it. I also love reading books. Books are everything.

How was that?

A little more detail? Gotcha.

I started writing my first stories when I was a teen...on a freaking typewriter. I still have these, and they're adorably romantic. And bad, haha. Fear of failing kept me from following my dream to become a romance author, so you can imagine how proud and ecstatic I am that I finally overcame my fears and self doubt and did it. I adore my genre because I love writing and reading about flawed, strong men who are just a tad broken..but find their happy ever after anyway.

My favorite books to read are pretty much all MM/gay romances as long as it has a happy end. Kink is a plus... Aside from that, I also read a lot of nonfiction and not just books on writing. Popular psychology is a favorite topic of mine and so are self help and sociology.

Hobbies? Ain't nobody got time for that. Just kidding. I love traveling, spending time near the ocean, and hiking. But I love books more.

Come hang out with me in my Facebook Group Nora's Nook where I share previews, sneak peeks, freebies, fun stuff, and much more: https://www.facebook.com/groups/norasnook/

My weekly newsletter not only gives you updates, exclusive content, and all the inside news on what I'm working on, but also lists the best new releases, 99c deals, and freebies in gay romance for that weekend. Load up your Kindle for less money! Sign up here: http://www.noraphoenix.com/newsletter/

You can also stalk me on Twitter: @NoraFromBHR

On Instagram:

https://www.instagram.com/nora.phoenix/

On Bookbub:

https://www.bookbub.com/profile/nora-phoenix

Or become my patron on Patreon: https://www.patreon.com/noraphoenix